DEEPBLACK

ALSO BY SEAN McFATE AND BRET WITTER
SHADOWWAR

DEEPBLACK

SEAN McFATE
& BRET WITTER

WM

WILLIAM MORROW
An Imprint of HarperCollinsPublishers

This is a work of fiction. Names, characters, places, and incidents are products of the author's imagination or are used fictitiously and are not to be construed as real. Any resemblance to actual events, locales, organizations, or persons, living or dead, is entirely coincidental.

HarperCollins books may be purchased for educational, business, or sales promotional use. For information, please email the Special Markets Department at SPsales@harpercollins.com.

FIRST EDITION

Designed by William Ruoto

Photo credit: John Greim/REX/Shutterstock

Library of Congress Cataloging-in-Publication Data

McFate, Sean, author. | Witter, Bret, author.
Deep black : a Tom Locke novel / Sean McFate and Bret Witter.
First edition. | New York, NY : William Morrow, an imprint of
    HarperCollins Publishers, [2017]
LCCN 2016053387 (print) | LCCN 2017000659 (ebook) | ISBN
    9780062403735 (hardcover) | ISBN 0062403737 (hardcover) | ISBN
    9780062403759 (eBook) | ISBN 0062403753 (eBook)
LCSH: Missing persons--Investigation--Fiction. | Tracking and
    trailing--Fiction. | BISAC: FICTION / War & Military. | GSAFD: Suspense
    fiction. | War stories.
LCC PS3613.C43965 D44 2017 (print) | LCC PS3613.C43965
    (ebook) | DDC 813/.6--dc23
LC record available at https://lccn.loc.gov/2016053387

17 18 19 20 21   RS/LSC   10 9 8 7 6 5 4 3 2 1

FOR JESSICA

— S M

FOR ELIZABETH

— B W

Behind the ostensible government sits enthroned an invisible government, owing no allegiance and acknowledging no responsibility to the people.

—THEODORE ROOSEVELT

DEEPBLACK

PROLOGUE

The Saudi prince wiped his coke-coated nostrils and squinted as he strolled out of the Four Seasons Hotel George V in Paris, surrounded by his entourage. The sunlight was a shock, even though he was wearing a head scarf and black sunglasses. He'd been holed up in his cluster of eight suites on the seventh floor—an insult. He deserved the entire floor. Especially considering he was related to the owner, and he was here (partially) on business.

Earlier in the day, he had visited the Saudi Embassy but otherwise kept to the night, frequenting the clubs of the Eighth Arrondissement. Now it was what, 5:00 P.M. on a Monday? Not that weekends meant anything, they were just days to Prince Mishaal bin Abdulaziz al Saud, distant relative of kings but not too distant to matter. Mishaal was a middle-aged, plump playboy who considered himself an aficionado of blow, thirty-year-old Scotch, and $15,000-a-night prostitutes.

Your decadence is a perfect cover for action, his father had said. His father was always saying things like that, trying to turn Mishaal's lifestyle into an asset.

His father, Prince Abdulaziz, was an ambitious man, the seventh son of the second wife of a minor prince who refused to enjoy the advantages life had afforded him. Mishaal could never understand it. His father had a hundred million dollars and three beautiful wives (in addition to the two ugly ones he'd married for their connections), and yet he worried—about his position, his influence, his legacy.

His younger brother, Farhan, was worse. He cared only about the Koran, wasting his life on prayer rugs in madrassas filled with the desperate poor. Both men could have had anything they wanted, and both chose illusions. His father craved power and his brother piety.

Better to enjoy life before you die, Mishaal thought. But instead he was popping antacid tablets, worrying about his father's lack of respect for him.

Maybe respect wasn't such a bad thing, though, especially when you could get it so cheap. Mishaal had smuggled thousands of kilos on his private jet in his life, usually cocaine or Captagon pills. For the first time, his father entrusted him with something important: picking up this briefcase.

Guard it with your life, his father had instructed. *And do not open it.*

Mishaal had no idea what was inside, nor did he care. His father finally treated him seriously, that was what mattered most. Young men enjoy being an embarrassment to the older generation, but there comes a time when it's no longer a badge of honor but instead a mark of shame. Mishaal was forty-two.

"Drive fast," he demanded, as his bodyguard opened the door of his rented all-black Mercedes Viano minivan. He slid into the back and laid the metal briefcase beside him on the seat. Ten minutes ago, a group of well-attired men had come to his suites. A trade was made. Five billion in big blocks of cash, €500 notes, for this aluminum briefcase and whatever it contained. It was only twenty kilometers to Bourget Airport, where his Hawker jet was waiting to take him home to Riyadh.

Already, the ten-car convoy was on the Champs-Élysées, pushing aggressively through the rush-hour traffic. The prince watched absently from the fourth car as the tourists swept past, then the convoy was rounding the Arc de Triomphe and accelerating as it turned toward the Périphérique ring road. All these white buildings, all these stones. The prince thought of blonde girls, and champagne, and his fire-breathing father, who had never availed himself of either. He reached for his cocaine. He could hear the pressure thumping behind his eyes as he snorted, so he closed them and leaned back, feeling the world speed up beneath him, letting himself drift.

He didn't come out of his trance until the Mercedes jerked sideways, causing his head to bump the window. He opened his eyes. They were speeding 120 kilometers per hour, passing cars as if they were standing still. He watched as the driver swerved onto the shoulder following the lead car. It was mesmerizing, almost peaceful, as if the other cars were being pulled backward, allowing them to pass.

And then he saw the black BMW. It had tinted windows with no plates, and it was racing up the left side of the convoy, pausing at each vehicle before punching forward to the next one. It pulled alongside the minivan, artfully dodging traffic, and hovered. Mishaal leaned forward, but all he could see was his own reflection in the BMW's dark windows. He looked like hell, clean-shaven and swollen from self-abuse, until the minivan jerked suddenly and his image disappeared. The convoy was on a local road now. It blew by a traffic light and sped through a working-class neighborhood, nearly clipping a pedestrian.

"Shortcut," his bodyguard said, but his gun was out.

"Who was—" the prince started, but before he could finish the BMW reappeared, screeching around a corner and blocking the road. The convoy's lead vehicle slammed its brakes, skidding out of control. The next two cars swerved to avoid hitting each other, and the prince's Mercedes skidded clockwise as the driver frantically pumped the brakes.

The prince clutched the briefcase as the centrifugal force seemed to lift him in slow motion from his seat. He thought of his father, with his hand raised in anger. He thought of his mother eating oranges and laughing. He thought of the fountain in their courtyard in Riyadh and the taste of beautiful girls. Then his seat belt caught him and snapped him backward, slamming his head into the hard leather seat.

The driver threw the Mercedes into reverse as another BMW swooped in behind them, blocking their exit route. Glass shattered and metal crumpled as the Mercedes smashed into the BMW's left side. The prince's head whiplashed, shooting pain through his neck. People were shouting in Arabic and French. The air smelled of burned rubber.

He heard gunfire. He saw his bodyguard turning to fire. He saw the handcuff attached to the briefcase and knew it should have been around his arm, but before he could reach it his bodyguard lunged on top of him, pinning him to the floor. He heard an explosion. He felt his window shatter.

And then the Mercedes was moving, tearing away from the ambush site. The prince could feel the car careening on two wheels as it barreled back onto the highway. They were free. They had escaped. But he couldn't get up, his bodyguard still on top of him.

Then the minivan swerved sharply, and the bodyguard's weight lifted. The engine revved as the vehicle jumped a curve and accelerated down a side street. The gunfire faded behind them. A hand grabbed his shoulder, pulling him up. The prince felt it: lightness. Relief. They had escaped.

The bodyguard slumped forward, dead. The man sitting next to him wore a black balaclava, and Mishaal saw the driver wearing a black ski mask, too. The attackers must have slipped into the car during the firefight, when he was facedown. He had been kidnapped.

No, the prince thought. *We're in the middle of Paris in daylight!*

He clutched the briefcase. He saw the handcuff dangling from it like his father's disapproval and snapped it around his wrist.

"Mauvaise idée," the kidnapper said calmly. Bad idea. "We'll have to saw it off. And the steel is stronger than your wrist."

The man in the balaclava smiled. All the prince could see were eyes and teeth. "Don't worry. We need your bio-coded fingerprint to open the case, so the hand won't go to waste."

Instinctively, the prince rubbed his wrist. His head was pounding. He tried not to think of his father.

"Je suis désolé," the kidnapper said. "Your men flinched . . . once they saw these." He waved his Heckler & Koch MP7 submachine gun with silencer. "I'm afraid you're on your own, Prince Mishaal Abdulaziz. Perhaps it's time to talk? Or will I be needing this?"

It was a bone saw.

A thousand miles away, Prince Farhan's mobile phone was ringing. Not the one in his hand, but the satellite phone. The specially encrypted one given to him by his father, Prince Abdulaziz, head of Saudi intelligence. Only three of its kind existed. His father and brother, Mishaal, held the other two.

He didn't bother to answer it. He knew it was the signal. Two rings. The caller hung up.

This is it, he thought, rising from the couch in the lobby of the Four Seasons Sultanahmet Hotel in Istanbul, Turkey. Farhan stood six feet tall, a muscular build with dark beard and eyes. He smoothed his thawb, a long white tunic common to Arabia, and walked toward the stairs. He held out his hand to stop his guards—please, some privacy—and started down.

I have only minutes, he thought as he vaulted down the stairs, three at a time. One floor below was a conference room complex. He rushed to the staff door at the far end and darted down a long, tunnel-like hallway. The Four Seasons Sultanahmet was a former prison, surrounded by a dry moat on two sides and perched on a hillside next to the Hagia Sophia and the Blue Mosque. It had several courtyards, but only one entrance for guests. This staff tunnel would exit him a hundred meters from the main entrance.

The satellite phone started ringing as he ripped off his red-and-white-checkered keffiyeh, the head scarf common to Saudi Arabia. The ring seemed louder this time, maybe because of the concrete passageway. Or maybe because he knew it was his father calling, displeased. Farhan powered the phone off; it was too late to turn back. He tossed his keffiyeh in a trash can, followed by his thawb, and pushed open the metal door.

The two janitors smoking outside the employee entrance startled as he banged onto the sidewalk. He ignored them and looked back at the main entrance, scanning the situation. Two doormen were arguing with an Asian woman lugging an impossibly large pile of pastel luggage, especially for the taxi with its trunk open in the middle of the street. A perfect distraction.

He walked the other way. It was one block to the Hagia Sophia. Halfway there, he glanced back. One of his bodyguards was in the road, trying to help with the luggage. He walked faster. On his second glance back, he noticed the black Land Cruiser pulling away from the curb, lights off. It came toward him, slowly, like a lion stalking prey. When he saw it accelerate past the taxi, Farhan knew they were coming for him. He turned and ran.

He didn't see the crash. He heard the impact, like a car bomb. He smelled smoke. He looked back. The Land Cruiser had been crushed on one side by a small green Renault. His contact was in the Renault driver's seat, body slumped over the steering wheel. The man's courage had bought him time, but he'd also crashed the getaway car.

Gunshots. The prince didn't look back to see who was shooting. He turned and sprinted full speed past a barricade into a small parking lot full of taxis and minibuses. The drivers stared as he passed, cigarettes dangling from their lips. A few shouted, but he didn't slow down as he hit the edge of Sultanahmet Park, where the ancient hippodrome once stood. The Blue Mosque was at one end of the park, the Hagia Sophia at the other, but ahead was a central pedestrian path, wide enough for cars, and two acres of flat ground filled with tourists, roasted corn vendors, and women with their heads covered on their way to prayer.

He heard shots being fired behind him. Tourists scattered in panic; policemen rushed past toward the shooting. He used the shadows and ducked into the nearby building, the pink-and-white-striped Ayasofya Hurrem Hamami, a Turkish bathhouse built hundreds of years ago by the favorite wife of Sultan Suleiman the Magnificent.

He hurtled through the entryway and into the central domed sitting area, with its vibrant white ceiling and multistory wooden staircases and inlaid ceramic tiles. Men stood up from the heated marble benches, clearly shocked by a man in clothes.

Farhan heard shoed footsteps chasing him, and he bolted into the steam room, the heart of the bathhouse. Women lay facedown on white marble slabs, some being scrubbed with soapy foam by attendants, some being splashed with water from a shallow wooden bowl. A woman sat at the far end, washing herself. She stared at the prince, letting the water run over her shoulders and down her bare torso, far less ashamed of her nakedness than he was.

He looked away like a good, observant Muslim, and his feet slid out from under him. He slammed into the floor hard, as the men entered, pistols in hand. In an instant, Farhan was on his feet. The first man leveled his pistol at Farhan, but the prince stepped behind a pillar, breaking the gunman's line of sight. Another man lunged for him. Farhan's training kicked in as he sidestepped, grabbed the assailant's arm in a joint lock, pivoted his hips, and threw his attacker into the wall, leaving a red stain on the marble. The first man charged, but this time Farhan was ready, delivering a powerful kick to the man's thigh. The man went down and Farhan pounced, landing a solid punch to the bridge of his nose, shattering it.

The man screamed, holding his bloody nose as Farhan grabbed the man's 9 mm pistol, extra clip, and radio.

Two more men burst through the doorway. Farhan sprinted out the far end of the room, past a row of showers. He emerged into the courtyard at the back of the hammam, with its reflecting pool and snack tables and decadently half-robed people on recliners, taking in the late afternoon sun. There was a wall. He didn't slow down. He bounded up the fountain and vaulted the wall in a smooth leap, but he fell harder than he expected on the other side.

Farhan lay in a heap, expecting a baton to the head, or a gun in the back, but nothing came. He looked around, cautiously, expecting to see three or four men bearing down on him. There was nobody. Or rather, there were hundreds of people snapping photographs of their loved ones with the Blue Mosque lit up in the evening background, but nobody seemed to notice him. He was just another Arab lying prone on the street.

He hobbled off, his right ankle throbbing. He must have twisted it when he fell. But he had to move. The police would be here . . . or the men trying to kill him, or, worse, his father's men.

He limped into a narrow alley, away from the crowds, and put on the radio's earpiece. They were his father's men, shouting in Arabic. They were on his trail, so he picked up the pace.

He kept going, into a copse of Dumpsters behind a restaurant, hobbling faster. He thought he heard shouting from a nearby alley, but couldn't be sure.

He staggered past a few sleeping dogs and into the old Jewish Quarter. There were shops and crowds, and men urging him to sample their merchandise.

"You walk like a man who intends to buy a rug," someone laughed, grabbing him by the elbow. He ignored the pain and turned the next corner, almost running into two policemen. Over the radio, he heard his father's men searching this bazaar. He ducked into a store.

"A hookah for you? Perhaps a set of decorative plates? Rugs? We have many rugs," the owner said, beckoning to the shop's interior. Neither of them were native English speakers, but it was the modern lingua franca. "We are a family business. We make our own rugs. See." The man pointed at a loom.

Farhan knew that wasn't true. They couldn't make a rug a month on that ancient relic, even if this man knew how to use it. He pushed past the shopkeeper into the pestemal section; the traditional Turkish blankets were stocked all the way to the ceiling.

"Best quality," the man said, fingering a blue patterned pestemal. "Everything here made in Middle East. All authentic goods."

Farhan squeezed all the way to the rear of the shop and looked back. He couldn't see the front. He waited. Silence. No one else came into the shop. He pulled a cash roll from his pocket and undid the rubber band. "Do you have a car?" he asked in Arabic, then switched to English.

The man looked at the roll. It was €100 bills. Crisp.

"I am not a criminal," Farhan whispered.

The man sized up Farhan with a salesman's acumen and nodded. He led Farhan through a curtain that concealed the back portion of the shop. It was stacked with boxes stamped in Mandarin. The man snapped something in Turkish to an old woman dozing in a chair, and then the two men went out the back door and into a closed courtyard full of cats. The man took the prince through another door, apparently a small apartment, also full of cats, and out onto a narrow street. He pointed to a small van.

Farhan handed him half the money. He could hear the drone of the *adhan*, the Muslim call to prayer, starting in the distance. It was joined by a second call from farther away, and finally a mellifluous chanting from the Blue Mosque. Reflexively, Farhan faced Mecca and almost got down on his hands and knees to pray. He had an *urge* to do it, but now was not the time. He had broken his father's trust; he had forsaken his birthright. If he left now, he would be dead to his family. He could never return, not even for his mother's funeral. But he had a more important calling.

"Drive for ten minutes," Farhan said, as he climbed into the passenger's seat. "Get as far away from here as you can. Then I will tell you where to go."

The man nodded. "I am not a criminal," he said, echoing Farhan's earlier words.

"I know."

"I am a Muslim. We are duty-bound to help those in need."

"I know," Farhan said, as the man shoved the money into his robe. "So am I."

In the port city of Gwadar, Pakistan, a rusty scupper sat unmoored and waiting. The captain, a Methuselah of a man, tossed his cigarette into the water as his satellite phone rang. He looked at his watch. Exactly on time. He answered, but said nothing. The deal was on. He hung up and nodded to the first mate, a man he'd known since they were both children on the docks of their small hometown in the Azores Islands, a thousand miles in the sea. The mate nodded back. The stack billowed smoke and, quietly and efficiently, they headed out to sea.

CHAPTER 1

We'd been operating deep in ISIS territory north of Mosul, Iraq, for two weeks, living off the kindness of the locals we saved and the fanatics we pillaged, when the call came in from Nassib, our friend in Mosul. Search and rescue, a young girl in peril, thirty minutes to plan an operation. My kind of job.

I was a former U.S. Army paratrooper in the Eighty-Second Airborne Division, recruited to the "dark side" by Apollo Outcomes, a high-end private military company. Their recruiting pool was the world's most elite military units: U.S. Navy SEALs, Army Delta and Rangers, British SAS, German GSG 9, French GIGN, Australian SASR, Israeli Shayetet 13, Central American anti-Communist hunter-killer patrols, and Southeast Asian commandos. Apollo did the jobs that were too dangerous for the CIA and too politically sensitive for the Pentagon. When you wanted plausible deniability, you called Apollo Outcomes. To be honest, I liked Apollo because rules didn't apply; the only thing that mattered was mission success. And I was always successful.

That was before Ukraine. Three months earlier my boss and mentor, Brad Winters, sent me there to defeat Russia's shadow war in that country, a CIA black-ops contract. It turned out I wasn't working for the CIA; Winters had gone into business for himself and sold out my team to the Russians. Only three of us survived—Boon, Wildman, and me. I had to mercy-kill my best friend, Miles, with my bare hands in a shitty Eastern Ukrainian forest to save him from the pain of bleeding out. I've killed a hundred men in my time, and a few women, too. All for a good cause, of course. I still feel the silence in my bones, the moment when Miles stopped breathing.

Now we were on the run, working as slum mercs in Kurdistan fighting ISIS. It was a big fall from being in the world's most elite and secretive military unit. I figured Winters thought I was dead, or dead enough to not come after me, as long as we kept off the grid. That is, until I was ready to go after Winters.

Until then, I was biding my time, playing Robin Hood to reclaim my soul. There was no money in it, but I didn't care. I was past that. We infiltrated ISIS's Caliphate to rescue the innocent from the terrorist group's ghoulish version of Islam. Even al Qaeda found ISIS's brutality extreme.

"This is the spot," I said, signaling to stop.

We were on the ridgeline above the main highway in two up-armored Humvees, each with a fifty-caliber machine gun on the turret. This was twenty kilometers, or "klicks," outside Mosul, ISIS's capital in Iraq, and the country was mountainous, full of steep rock gullies and evergreen trees. A few weeks earlier, ISIS had blitzkrieged through here in pickup trucks, sending the much superior Iraqi army fleeing for the hills, throwing down their weapons and ripping off their uniforms in the process. That's what you get for a few billion dollars of U.S. taxpayer money.

I stepped out of the Humvee. Perfect vantage point above a perfect ambush point. Sometimes, that's all it takes to feel alive.

"Anything?" I asked Boonchu "Boon" Tripnet, who was already on his knee with the binoculars to his eyes. Boon was Thai, and we joked he was our Buddhist mercenary. Short with ropy muscles, he was born poor among the poppy fields and heroin smugglers, who terrorized villagers and kidnapped their girls, selling them to Bangkok brothels. After his brother, a Buddhist monk, was gunned down, he walked out of the mountains and joined Thai Special Forces. It was a three-week walk. He was fourteen.

"Nothing," Boon replied calmly. He was always calm.

I turned to Wildman, our ex-SAS commando, who was sitting in the gun turret. Wildman was huge, with a shaved head, a thick neck, and two teeth short of a smile. He was whittling a block of C-4 with a bowie knife. It looked like a hunchback squirrel. He held it up for me to see with a grin.

"Not bad, eh?" he said in a Welsh-infused British accent. "Not Ogun," he said, giving me shit, like he always did, "but not bad."

Ogun was an African god of iron and war. He was sort of my spirit guide, the orisha who had looked out for me when I was a newbie in the jungle. He once came to me in a dream, after I built a small army in Liberia, a huge black man with scars on his face, wearing blue coveralls. He thanked me as we sat on an I-beam at a construction site, having a beer. I honored Ogun with a carving of him on my bar back in Washington, DC. Whenever I was home, I gave him a traditional gift: a shot of gin, a bottle of palm wine, chalk dust, and African money. I would never see Ogun or that apartment again. Not after what happened in Ukraine.

"It sucks," I said, eyeing the hideous creature. "The sooner you blow it up the better."

"You should talk," Wildman said, glancing at my black robes. It looked like I'd gone native. Looks can be deceiving.

"Johnny Jihad," Boon said. "One klick out."

I felt the excitement jumping under my skin. Combat is like heroin. Even after it's worn you out and thrown you away, you need more.

"Single vehicle," Boon said. "A bus."

Good, they were alone. Just like Nassib promised.

"Lock and load," I told what was left of my team. I didn't even need to say that much. We'd done this countless times. The men knew what to do. Wildman grabbed his SA-80 assault rifle and smiled wide enough for me to see his missing teeth. Boon scrambled up a rocky overhang with his Dragunov sniper rifle. The Kurds we'd hired manned the turrets, as I scrambled down the steep hillside onto the road.

The white bus appeared at the bend, grinding up the hill. The windows were curtained. My SCAR assault rifle was concealed beneath my black Bedouin robe, as were my twin Berettas on thigh holsters. My face was totally concealed behind a black turban and sunglasses, the standard ISIS uniform. It wouldn't fool them for long, but it didn't have to. It only had to fool them long enough for the driver to slow when he saw us. He did.

Wait for it, Locke, I thought, as the bus coasted to a stop. *Wait for it.*

A man appeared in the windshield. He was armed and bearded. The driver pointed at me. They were twenty meters away.

I walked toward the bus, my hands raised in supplication. The brakes began to squeal. At ten meters, Boon fired—I saw the crack of the windshield before I heard the shot—killing the driver. The militant beside him froze in horror as Wildman took him out, three-round bursts through the windshield.

Within seconds, I had smashed through the bus door and was up the steps, a Beretta pistol in each hand, ready for close-quarter combat. There was a militant a few rows back, fumbling to aim his Kalashnikov in the tight space. Someone hit his arm. Bullets sprayed the ceiling, hitting Allah in the ass. A woman screamed, and I put a bullet in the militant's forehead.

A man lunged from my peripheral vision. I pivoted to aim but he plowed me off my feet, sending both pistols flying as I hit the floor. I hit hard, my assailant falling on top of me. He bit my face. I head-butted him. My right hand pulled my double-edged Gerber blade and sunk it into his side, twice in rapid succession. He rolled backward; I leapt to my feet. Berserking, he charged with his Kalashnikov. I wrenched it from his hands, flipped it, and pounded him in the face with the stock.

I looked around, as warm blood trickled into my mouth—mine or his, I wasn't sure. The bus was twenty rows long, and every row was filled with girls and women in veils. At the back was one last ISIS militant. He was holding a girl as a human shield, a knife at her throat. She was eleven or twelve. He couldn't have been much older.

He watched. I watched. His hands were steady, but his eyes flashed from one person to another, a sign of weakness. What did his god want him to do? Slowly he lowered the knife, his hand shaking.

A woman jumped him. First one, tearing at his face. Then two, three, and the kid went down shrieking, crying for mercy until his screams were muffled.

I collected my weapons. "Du'a," I yelled, holstering my Berettas. "Du'a Aswad."

A woman stood up. She was middle-aged. Blood covered the left side of her face, where she had fought the militant. She spoke English.

"What do you want with her?" she asked.

"Her uncle has paid for her rescue."

"Take us all," the bloody woman said.

"We only have two vehicles. We don't have room. You can take this bus."

"None of us know how to drive."

Women in this part of the world were denied the opportunity to drive, seek an education, have a profession. . . .

A preteen girl spoke, barely audible. The older woman translated. "She says she won't leave us to be *sabaya*."

"What's *sabaya*?"

"Sex slaves," the woman said without flinching. "We are Christian and Yazidi prisoners. We are to be sold to ISIS fighters. They say it is *ibadah*, religious worship, to rape unbelievers."

I could feel anger, uncontrollable anger. There was a time when I would have felt nothing. It was good to feel again.

"New plan," I said over my headset. "Wildman, you and Boon take the Humvees. I'll drive the bus and meet you in Kalak." The bus would draw less attention without a Humvee escort.

"Rock and roll," Wildman replied. Nothing fazed him. If I'd said we were loading the bus with explosives and driving it into Tehran, he'd have reacted the same way.

I pulled the driver's body out and slid behind the steering wheel, adjusting my head scarf to conceal my face. I had a month's worth of growth, but my thin beard was nothing compared with the facial output of these religious professionals.

"Curtains closed," I yelled, knowing the woman would translate. "When the shooting starts, get down."

It was twelve kilometers to the bridge over the Great Zab River, the border between the ISIS Caliphate and the free "country" of Kurdistan.

"They know this bus," the bloody woman said, as we were waved through an ISIS checkpoint. "We are the *sabaya* bus on its weekly delivery of sex slaves."

We crested the last hill. Below us lay the dusty border town of Kalak, straddling the Great Zab River. It was smoldering, as if a battle were just fought. The road ahead led to a blown river bridge. Trucks and a 155-millimeter cannon sat mangled in its steel carcass.

"There's another bridge, to the north," the woman said. "I will guide you. I know this town."

Women shouted "left" and "right" in Arabic as we navigated the street maze. We emerged on a road that led to another bridge over the Zab River, its entrance heavily guarded. I floored the accelerator.

"Everyone down!" I shouted. Ahead, I counted two ISIS Humvees and half a dozen militants. Two men grabbed their guns and walked into the road, holding up their hands for me to stop.

I pushed the gas pedal to the floor. The bus was sluggish, but once it was at top speed it would be hard to stop—unless they were smart enough to aim for the driver.

Protect me, Ogun, I thought, as the men leveled their AK-47s.

The moment slowed, as it always does right before the shit hits the fan, and then it exploded. The road opened up in a tower of dirt, and two bodies blew toward me as an RPG hit behind them, blowing the turret off the left Humvee. Wildman. Just in time. Fifty-caliber machine-gun fire tore through the militants, keeping their heads down as we crashed through their checkpoint and onto the two-lane bridge.

Bullets ripped into the bus. I could hear the *plink-plink* of bullets on metal, the crash of windows cracking, screaming. Tracers streamed across the bridge, going both directions. I rammed a small car, sending it over the bridge.

Ahead of me at the far end of the bridge our two up-armored Humvees sat idling, their turrets working the ISIS outpost. The

Hummers were covered with metal armor salvaged from scrap and welded on one piece at a time over the last two months. They looked more like science fiction than tanks. Wildman called them "hajified." His was the one with the homemade Jolly Roger flying from its whip antenna: a crude white skull on a tattered, bloodstained black cloth. He'd ripped the head scarf from the head of a still-breathing ISIS militant and drawn the skull himself.

"Fuck yeah!" he yelled into the wind, as we passed.

And then Boon fired the second RPG, and the last ISIS militants disappeared in a cloud of red mist.

CHAPTER 2

It was dark by the time we entered Erbil, the capital of Kurdistan, a country in name only. Erbil was like El Paso, Texas, circa 1880: a dusty and lawless frontier town, and the last stop before pandemonium. In the mid-2000s, the newly liberated Kurds of north Iraq had poured money into building projects, thinking that thanks to the U.S. occupation, their capital city would float on oil revenue forever. But most of the money flowed out with the oil, the world economy collapsed, then ISIS invaded Iraq. Now Erbil was a half-built ghost town.

Our Kurdish partners took their Humvee and went home, while we drove to the Christian district where we'd been flopping for the last two months. We approached the World Trade Center Apartments, the inappropriately named megacomplex. It was a hulking monolith, half completed and a tenth occupied, the owner having abandoned construction long before the ISIS advance.

We slowed half a block away and Wildman jumped out, as always falling instinctively into a security mind-set. I nodded to Boon, who put his hand on his sidearm as we approached the arched doorway to the parking area. We backed into our garage and chained the barnlike steel doors. It would take a block of C-4 to break it.

Good thing, too, since the back half of our garage was full of rugs, silk floor cushions, jewelry, wedding garb, silverware, brass candlesticks, and all the other worthless shit we'd been "paid" over the last three months to rescue innocent refugees trapped behind ISIS lines.

We were lousy mercenaries. But we were damn fine humanitarians, for whatever that was worth.

"Eyes front," Boon said, as we entered the courtyard.

It was dark, but at the far end I could see a man sitting casually on a folding chair with his legs crossed in the dim light falling from an upper-story window. He was wearing a white linen suit, neatly pressed, and smoking a cigarette. He looked like a banana plantation owner from the 1920s, except for the red-and-white-checkered keffiyah on his head. He wasn't trying to hide. In fact, he was sitting in the most conspicuous spot. He wanted to be seen.

"Good evening, Dr. Locke," he said, as we approached. Years ago I finished my doctorate at the London School of Economics, a fact few knew. I approached with caution.

"Who are you?"

"I have a proposition." His English was ridiculously precise.

"From the Saudis?" The Saudi upper class always wore the keffiyah.

"No." He dropped his cigarette and smothered it with an Italian loafer. "Not quite."

I could see a bulge on the left side of his suit, easily accessible to a right-handed man. He was no fool, but also no assassin.

"Inside," I said.

Boon prepared the chai, a sweet concoction of mint and black tea. I would have preferred the bottle of Woodford Reserve I kept stashed in my go bag, but I needed to stay frosty for this conversation. I offered him a seat by the window and sat cross-legged on a Bedouin pillow we'd been given for saving a six-year-old boy.

"I hear you're good at finding people in ISIS territory," the man said. "And you're even better at getting them out."

We sipped our tea. Silence was the best policy in these situations. It never gave anything away.

"I work for a Saudi prince, a man whose name is unimportant, but you can assume the man himself is not." Obviously. "Yesterday, his son disappeared in Istanbul. We have reason to believe he may now be in Iraq."

"Why?"

"He has contacts here."

I sipped my tea. "What kind of contacts?"

The Saudi sipped his tea. "That is something his father would like to know."

Fanatics, in other words. It wasn't unheard of for wealthy Saudis to support or even join ISIS. In fact, it was common. Religious Saudis, including members of the royal family, were the primary financiers of Sunni terrorist groups like al Qaeda and ISIS. But even the most Wahhabi of princes preferred their sons to stay clear of the battlefield. Osama bin Laden's flamboyant fanaticism had almost brought down his billionaire wing of the royal family, after all, and martyrdom was for the poor.

"So he went of his own free will?"

"That is my assumption." I noticed the *my*, not our. Maybe the father didn't know?

"And you know he is in Iraq?"

"No."

"But you know he ran away?"

"Not exactly."

The man reached into his jacket—at this point a novice might reach for his gun, but Boon didn't blink—and pulled out a stack of greenbacks. American money. Unusual. Most connected people in the black-ops world dealt in Euros. He placed the cash on the floor, since we didn't have a table, or any furniture, for that matter.

"That's a $100,000 retainer. It's yours, whether you find the boy or not. If you find him, and return him safely, and with the utmost discretion—and I can't stress that last part enough—my employer will pay you one million dollars. Cash."

I was going to tell him we weren't in that line of business. We worked with people in need. We didn't risk our lives for spoiled brats gone jihad. But I had a responsibility to Boon and Wildman, and being Robin Hood was an impecunious trade. A million dollars would pay our way out of this dust pit in style.

"It's only three days," the man said, sensing my hesitancy.

"Why?"

"Because that is my employer's deadline."

I didn't like the setup. Too much secrecy. Too little time. Too many unknowns. On the other hand, three days on a wild goose chase wasn't much of a loss. If I was bending my newfound principles, at least this contortion was small and lucrative.

The man pulled a photograph from another inside suit pocket. Clearly bespoke tailoring, Italian like the loafers, if I had to guess. He handed the photo to Boon.

"Prince Farhan Abdulaziz," he said.

Boon studied the face. "Handsome," he said. He handed me the photo. A young man, late twenties in a white thawb and keffiyeh, stared back at me. He had angular features and a thick neck. I didn't like the looks of his beard.

"Why us?" Boon asked.

"Because you are the best."

"Says who?"

The man sipped his tea.

"We're not the only mercs in Kurdistan who can get in and out of ISIS territory," Boon pressed.

"But we're the only ones with solid contacts in Mosul," I guessed.

The man nodded. "It might be wise to start your search there."

"Why would he be in Mosul?"

I knew the answer: Mosul was the primary sign-in for ISIS wannabes following the terrorist pipeline from Europe through Turkey, and the prince had disappeared from Istanbul. But would this man tell me that much?

"I don't know if he's in Mosul," the man said. "I don't know if he's in Iraq. But I have $100,000 worth of incentive for you to check."

It wasn't a bad bargain. And if it involved getting some rich fool out of ISIS, then it was good for the world, and therefore not against my moral code. Not that I had a moral code, but I was working on it.

"Who recommended us?"

The Saudi laughed. "If you were well-known enough to be recommended by anyone who mattered, you wouldn't be right for this job."

"You don't want anyone to know he is missing," I guessed. *And we're expendable.*

The Saudi nodded.

"Is anyone else looking for him?"

"Of course."

I looked at Boon. He nodded. I accepted with misgivings, but I always had misgivings. The Saudi gave me a phone number. I was to call him with any news. He would be my only contact.

He stood up to leave. "One last thing," he said on the doorstep. "Farhan won't come willingly. But I want him alive."

I again, not *we,* or *my boss.* Who was this Saudi?

The man disappeared. I went to the window and, a minute later, watched him walk casually down the deserted street, as if he was out for a paseo in Madrid. A dog slunk past, its ears cut down to nubs. The Saudi never looked back.

I waved out the window once he was out of sight.

Our apartment was on the second floor. Harder to break into, but low enough to jump, if it came to that. The building across from us was half-built and abandoned. Wildman had been perched on its third floor for the past twenty minutes, the night sight on his customized M24 Win Mag sniper rifle with silencer fixed on the Saudi's head. Now he stood up, folded up the bipod, and slung the rifle over his shoulder.

Being too far away to hear the conversation, he gestured: *Good meeting?*

You'll like it, I gestured back.

Wildman did a dance with his M24 that said, *Let's celebrate.*

Wildman always wanted to celebrate.

CHAPTER 3

I cased the T-Top American Night Club & Hamburger Bar as we entered: twenty-four patrons, almost all men, all drinkers, none too suspicious. It was the only bar in Erbil for guys like us. It was a cheap American sports bar meets Western saloon, complete with warm beer, cigarette smoke, and armed patrons. Like Erbil itself, the place was filled with those too stupid or too poor to leave.

"To mercs and refugees," Boon toasted and we downed our drinks.

I hated it here. If I was still in my old job, as a mission commander for Apollo Outcomes, I would be wearing a blue Harvie and Hudson suit and sipping my favorite bourbon, Woodford Reserve, in the Sky Bar of the Noble Hotel across town. I'd be sleeping on five-hundred-thread-count pillows and eating on an expense account. But I couldn't go to a place like the Noble now. I couldn't afford it, and I couldn't afford to be seen. Not with Brad Winters looking for me. The only things I had left from my old life were my SCAR special forces combat assault rifle, my twin Beretta pistols, and two Nicaraguan cigars I was saving for a special occasion. Those and my wounds.

"Another Jack Daniel's," I said to the bartender. Jack wasn't my favorite, but it was a reliable American friend in places like this.

"Another Bud," Boon said, crushing his empty Budweiser can

in his fist. There was something about the King of Beers. It always tasted better overseas.

Wildman grunted in disgust.

I couldn't blame him. We had saved two hundred women, but we'd been forced to deliver them to the only place that would take them: the decrepit parking garage where more than a thousand Iraqi refugees were living without water or bathrooms. Better than sex slavery, but nothing even the worst-off American would tolerate.

Our reward, meanwhile, was two rolled rugs and a copper lantern. The uncle was a refugee himself; it was all he had. I'd tried to talk him out of the exchange, since the heirlooms weren't worth twenty dollars, but he refused. We split the loot with our Kurdish partners, as per our agreement, so in the end all we got for risking our necks was a rug. That and the satisfaction of knowing we'd saved more than fifty women from a fate worse than death. That was worth something . . . wasn't it?

"Wankers," Wildman said.

I followed his gaze. In a corner sat a burly set of guys in action slacks and Glocks, laughing a bit too loud and slamming red Stoli shooters, a T-Top special.

War tourists.

For weeks now, these amateurs had been showing up in ones and twos, weapons in hand and ready to fight. I'd seen their kind before: vets who couldn't adjust to life back home, adventure-seeking yahoos, life's castaways. Some were good, but most were dangerous. The worst were the idealists. I met a guy in June from a Baptist church in middle America. He said he was going to make a Christian legion of mercenaries to fight ISIS with funding from Internet donations. Wildman had punched him in the face. The guy was probably bones in the desert by now.

"Hey boys," a woman's voice greeted us in a heavy Irish accent.

"Hi, Kylah," I said, signaling the bartender for two Jameson whiskies. Kylah was in her midtwenties, had a slender frame, green eyes, long flame-red hair, and pale skin. Wildman joked she needed SPF-million to live in Iraq, but around here, she was the wild Irish Rose, a drink of cool water, everybody's dream. Outside she donned a black chador, but tonight she wore her usual: tank top, cargo pants, and bloused combat boots, all black.

"*Tiocfaidh ár lá*," we toasted, when the Jamesons arrived. Our day will come, the motto of the Irish Republican Army. Her father was a martyr, South Armagh Brigade.

"I heard you boys were back in town," she said, turning to Boon with a smile.

"How did you hear that?" Boon asked. He was always worried about operational security, or "OpSec."

"The old woman you saved on the bride bus," Kylah replied, signaling for another shot. "The one with the 762 bullet in her arm and bits of bus in her arse. The one you left on my doorstep, remember? I patched her up pretty and put her on a morphine drip. Then she told me everything." Kylah ran a medical clinic. She patched us up, along with most of the strays that showed up at her door.

"Speaking of which . . ." She slipped off her barstool to take a closer look at the jihadi bite on my face. I batted her mothering away.

"That's going to leave a scar," she said.

"Just add it to the others."

"Ugly dog," Boon said. I wasn't sure if he was referring to me or the man who bit me.

"What happened to the bridge at Kalak?" I asked. "No way

the Peshmerga could blow that bridge." The Peshmerga was
Kurdistan's militia, and the last line of defense against ISIS.

"The U.S. finally entered the war," she said. "Two American
fighter jets bombed the bridge last week."

I laughed. "Really? Why now?"

She shrugged. "ISIS took over the city of Sinjar near the Syrian
border and did one of their 'forced conversion' campaigns with
the Yazidis there. They slaughtered five thousand. The rest fled to
Mount Sinjar, where they're stuck now, either starving to death or
facing the scimitar. The U.S. declared it a genocide, and they've
been bombing ISIS ever since."

Five thousand killed and the U.S. declares it genocide? Put a few
zeroes after that number and it's just another day in Africa. Hell,
250,000 were massacred in the Congo; 500,000 in Darfur; and
more than 800,000 in Rwanda, and the Pentagon still couldn't
find those places on a map.

"Let me see what I can do about this music," Kylah said,
as vintage Metallica screeched from the jukebox. War tourists
loved Metallica. Her hips and hair mesmerized as she moved.

I felt a presence behind me, swiveled, and pulled my Beretta
pistol.

"I could have blasted your face off," I said.

"Good to see you, too, Captain."

"Goddamn Bear," I said with a laugh, as we clasped forearms.
"Once a dumb-ass, always a dumb-ass."

He shrugged and sat next to me. "Some things don't change."

Bear had been one of my Airborne grunts during our Balkans
tour in the '90s. He was huge, and he looked like he could still
bench four hundred pounds, but otherwise things definitely had
changed. He used to be a nice young man; now he had a shaved
head, bushy brown beard, and tattoo sleeves, featuring skulls
and sickles. I couldn't for the life of me remember the name his

mother had given him, but that didn't matter. Most of us in this life lost our names, one way or the other.

"Buy you a drink?" he offered.

"Hell no," I said, signaling the bartender for another round. "I'm buying. It's on credit, and I have no intention of paying my tab."

Two Jack Daniel's slid down the bar and we tapped shot glasses and drank, my fifth straight whiskey in fifteen minutes. I'd been working up a tolerance for Irish and Tennessee firewater along with my bar tab.

"What are you doing here?" Bear asked.

Laying low. Staying off the grid. Trying not to get assassinated by Apollo Outcomes and my ex-boss, Brad Winters, who didn't like loose ends.

"Odd jobs," I said, hoping Bear would take the hint and change the subject. He didn't, so I kept talking. "In the underground railroad business, out of Mosul."

"For Apollo?"

No, not for Apollo. But I didn't need to tell Bear that. In fact, it was a good sign he didn't know. It meant Winters probably hadn't put a contract out on me.

"Working for myself," I said, nodding at Wildman and Boon. "Three-man team."

"Figured," Bear said. "Not enough money out here for the big boys."

"What about you?"

Bear downed a second Jack. The T-Top always kept them coming. "I've got my own company now," he said.

That surprised me. The kid had his own team? But then again, he also had gray hair in his beard, now that I looked. Jesus. Bear wasn't a kid anymore. How long had it been since Bosnia? Twenty years?

"Small operation. Sixteen-man team and some local talent. We're down near Baiji, working the oil fields. Infrastructure protection. We're a subcontractor to a subcontractor for an unnamed oil company."

"Gulf Keystone?"

"Can't say."

Probably Chevron or Talisman, I thought.

Baiji was the biggest oil refinery in north Iraq, at the edge of the Makhmour oil field and just beyond the Kurdish boundary. It was also the frontline between ISIS, Shia militia, the Iraqi army, and Iranian Quds special forces, not to mention the criminal gangs and tribal strongmen bunkering oil for profit. They came in from the Jazira, the lawless desert in the middle of Iraq. Bear must have been busy.

"So what brings you to the T-Top?"

"Personal security detail," Bear said, nodding toward two older men who were half in the bag and flirting shamelessly with Kylah. "Erbil is the last free airport in northern Iraq. The oil men have no intention of being cut off."

One of the executives got up to dance and "accidentally" grabbed Kylah's ass.

"They seem to be enjoying your girlfriend's company," Bear said.

Boon laughed.

"Just a friend," I said, hoping to hell Kylah was staying away from mercs like me. I didn't begrudge a young woman her fun, but I knew that by the time she was my age, Dr. Kylah Murphy would be back in Europe with two redheaded kids, a terrier, and a minivan. "But for their own safety, you might think about getting those assholes on their airplane."

Bear laughed. "I hear you," he said. He downed his third Jack, then stared at the empty tumbler.

"You should join us," he said. "In Baiji, I mean. As a partner. The bunkhouse is no-frills—we're laid up at the U.S. Army's old Camp Speicher—but the pay is top-notch, Tom, and always on time. And you can operate as you please, I promise you that."

I couldn't help but feel annoyed. This was the second time I'd been propositioned in one night. And this was no casual offer. Bear wanted me. He was probably desperate for good men. But I could hear it in his voice; it was more than that.

It hit me then, what I must look like. Scruffy, boozing, and desperate in a shithole like the T-Top. Bear thought I was a squaddie, washed up here like the other losers, and he . . . goddammit, he *pitied* me. A soldier I once commanded pitied *me*.

But Bear didn't know me. I'd spent ten years working for a multi-billion-dollar mercenary corporation that did things the CIA wished it could do, with the firepower of a SEAL team: manipulating foreign presidential elections, staging "color revolutions" to overthrow governments, undermining terrorist plots, assassinating anyone, and "shaping the environment"— basically making shit happen for the client, no questions asked. I did questionable things, and I was the best.

Until three months ago in Ukraine.

"I don't do that kind of work anymore," I said.

"What kind?"

Warfare, twenty-first-century style. "We're okay with our current employment situation," I said.

I heard Wildman grunt disapproval and walk off. I didn't even look at Boon.

Bear wrote his sat phone number on a beer coaster and slid it to me. "If you change your mind."

"I won't. But thanks." I took it anyway and we did a bro hug: only our chests made contact and we loudly slapped each other on the back. "It was good seeing you, Bear."

I watched him walk out the door with the executives at his heel.

"Am I doing the right thing?" I said, to myself as much as to Boon.

"The thing I like about this job," Boon said, beer in hand, "is that I don't have to answer those questions."

"What about Wildman?"

Boon took a long drink. "He'll be back."

"You don't need to stay with me," I said.

"No, I don't. But I will."

"Why?"

"I believe in you."

We clinked drinks, but Boon didn't catch my eye. He was still watching Kylah dance.

"We're leaving," I said.

Boon nodded. He knew I didn't mean the bar. Bear would put the word out, in casual conversation over beers, and pretty soon others would find me, too. Including Brad Winters or someone who wanted to curry favor with him. Winters was a powerful man and Apollo Outcomes had incredible reach. It wasn't safe here anymore. It never really was.

"Where to?"

I shrugged. "Anywhere, once this last job is done."

CHAPTER 4

General Suleimani sat in a back room of the Al-Askari shrine in Samarra, Iraq, listening quietly while his aides-de-camp argued about the best way to defeat ISIS. He was not an Iraqi general, but an Iranian one operating in the shadows. Behind him was a map showing the ISIS presence oozing east across Iraq, and beheading, raping, torturing, enslaving, and crucifying as they went, all in the name of Islam.

Not my Islam, Suleimani thought. A handsome man in his late fifties, with a well-trimmed salt-and-pepper beard going to full gray, Suleimani was one of the most powerful yet least known men in the Middle East. To many, he was simply the "Shadow Commander," the man who commanded Iran's elite Quds special forces. The man who had shaped Hezbollah into a potent fighting force, instead of a collection of hotheads, and defeated Israel in 2006. The man who organized the Shia insurgency that helped drive the United States out of Iraq and install Iran's puppet, Nouri al-Maliki, as prime minister. In the last few years, he had spent his time propping up Syrian President Bashar al-Assad. Suleimani was one of the most powerful and wanted men in the Middle East.

"Tactical update," Suleimani ordered.

"Sir, ISIS is thirty kilometers from Baghdad, from here to here." The aide swept his hands from the seven o'clock to the one o'clock position. "They could break through Baghdad's last ring of defense in days."

"Start with their reserve, then tell me about their flanking maneuvers."

"The Zab River Triangle in the north is an ISIS stronghold, with Mosul their capital. They continue to push east, into Kurdistan, but the Peshmerga have stopped their advance at the Great Zab River. For now."

"How long will the Kurds hold?" Kurdistan was a narrow buffer zone between ISIS and Iran, and the general didn't like assuming strategic risk, especially when it hinged on the amateur Peshmerga forces.

"Unknown. The United States is secretly arming the Kurds, but Turkey is secretly undermining them."

Suleimani chuckled. That was not so secret. "Continue."

"Our eastern flank is in crisis." The aide pointed to a wedge of land south of Kurdistan and north of Baghdad, an open avenue for ISIS to the Iranian border. That threat was why General Suleimani had been rushed here from the Syrian quagmire. "Only one Shia town is left," the aide said. "Amerli. It has been under siege for three months."

And the feckless Iraqi Army is cowering in its barracks, Suleimani thought, rubbing his beard. It was a nervous habit; his only outward tell.

"What are we doing to relieve them?"

"We are massing our Shia militia to break the siege."

"What units?"

"Mostly the Badr Corps."

"When do we initiate the attack?"

"Ten days. The Americans may even support us with air strikes. Not on purpose, of course."

The enemy of my enemy, the general thought. It had been the calculus of war in the region for the last fifteen years. A multi-sided conflict—Iran, Iraq, the Great Satan, the corrupt Saudis, the Kurds, the rebels, the Israelis, the Turks—produced strange alignments, to say the least.

"Sir, we have multiple reports of U.S. Special Operations Forces in Kurdistan," said another aide.

Suleimani nodded. Quds commandos battling ISIS in the same grid square as American special forces. He wondered what his American counterpart, Gen. John Allen, thought of all the possibilities in this secret, perennial shadow war.

Allen would kill me, Suleimani thought, *if he had the chance. And I him.*

That was why Suleimani had set up living quarters in the Al-Askari mosque in Samarra, one of the most sacred Shia shrines. The Americans wanted him dead. So did the Israelis and the Sunnis. But only ISIS would dare bomb the Al-Askari shrine to kill him. Al Qaeda blew the ancient gold dome off the mosque in 2006. It sparked a Sunni-Shia civil war right under the Americans' noses, a struggle that Suleimani helped the Shia to win.

That's what the West didn't understand about the Middle East, Suleimani thought. War wasn't about countries; it was about faith. Since the death of the Prophet, the Sunni and Shia Muslims had locked in a 1,400-year-old civil war over the soul of Islam. Today they battled as "deep states"—states within states—with a front line that stretched from the Mediterranean to the Arabian Sea. The Shia deep state, led by the Ayatollahs of Iran, included Hezbollah in Lebanon, the Alawite regime in Syria, the Shia in Iraq, and the Houthis in Yemen—the "Shia Crescent." The Sunni deep state was led by the royal house of Saud under the watchful eye of the Wahhabi clerics of Saudi Arabia. Their allies included the Gulf States, Jordan, Egypt, Pakistan, North Africa, and Sunni strongholds in Asia. ISIS was a monster of their making. And then there was the third, unwelcome deep state: America and Israel. They were the most profane trespassers, just like the Crusaders a millennium before.

"It's confirmed, sir," an aide interrupted, pushing a report in front of him.

"What now?"

"Six hundred seventy Shia prisoners executed," the aide read. "ISIS militants entered Badoush Prison in Mosul. They took out the prisoners and sorted them into two groups, Sunnis and Shias. The Shiites were lined up in four rows and told to kneel. The Sunnis were told to shoot them in the head, or be shot themselves."

Someone mumbled a prayer for the dead, but Suleimani preferred not to picture the scene. He'd seen enough over the years.

"We're getting additional reports," the aide continued. "More of the same. Do you want to read them?"

"No. I want to stop them."

He stood up and strode to the front of the room, where he could examine the map board. Outside, the new dome of the Al-Askari shrine glittered in the morning sun.

"We must break the siege of Amerli," he said. "Muster all available Quds and militia. I will personally lead the assault."

The aides nodded. Suleimani was known to lead from the front.

"But we need to secure our flank. Send word to Colonel Hosseini," he said, choosing out his favorite Quds commander. "I need him to scout northwest, looking for a soft spot where we can cut off ISIS reinforcements. I need all Quds with me. What militia force can accompany him?"

Silence, as the aides checked their rolls.

"Badr Corps is sending a contingent to Amerli," someone said, "and also defending the shrine in Karbala."

"That's fine. We need them there."

"The Sadrists won't leave Baghdad, and answer only to Muqtada al-Sadr. Kataib Hezbollah has battalions in Baghdad and Samarra, but they aren't strong."

"Who else?"

"Asaib Ahl al-Haq"—the League of the Righteous—"has just redeployed from Damascus. Right now, they are refitting in Baghdad."

The League of the Righteous, the general thought, rubbing his beard. They were one of his fiercest Iraqi militia, which was why he had sent them to fight in Syria, and why he had recalled them to Iraq when Mosul fell. He sat back, nodding.

"Sir?" one of the aides asked.

Suleimani stared at the map board. He was never hasty, but he never wasted time, either, especially when there was no time to waste.

"Sir, what are your orders? When do we move?"

"Tonight."

CHAPTER 5

Prince Abdulaziz frowned at his son Mishaal, who was sitting across the aisle from him in a plush red leather seat. Around them, the curved walls of the private airplane were gold-plated, polished, and etched with an intricate, interlocking pattern. The red and gold were echoed in the prayer rug on the floor, which quivered like a compass needle on a rotating platform. To a Western eye, the jet was gaudy, like red lipstick had exploded inside its gold tube, but in Saudi Arabia, the look was only slightly out of date. The prince's primary plane was more stylish, but he had brought his smaller jet, since this trip was only for father and son, not his important contacts. Still, even in the smaller space, it felt like the two men were miles apart. Or more accurately, Abdulaziz was cruising at thirty thousand feet, while Mishaal was sinking into the ground.

"It was simple," the father said.

Mishaal shook his head. "So you keep saying, but that doesn't make it true."

"All you had to do was pick up a briefcase."

"I picked up the briefcase."

"I paid five billion dollars on your promise that all was in order."

"All was in order."

"And less than one hour later, you bury our family in shame."

"It's only money . . ." The younger prince sighed, although he knew money wasn't the point.

"There's no such thing as only money," the older prince said, glaring at his son. When Abdulaziz was a boy in the 1960s, $5 billion would have been his family's entire net worth. He'd worked hard all his life to turn that pittance into a fortune, and it seemed his eldest son had been working his whole life to squander everything he'd accomplished.

"I understand."

"You don't understand," Abdulaziz snapped. "There are fifteen thousand members of the royal family. Ten thousand are like you: fools. I have outmaneuvered, outstrategized, and outmuscled most of the others to give our family this opportunity. I worked for a year to put this deal in place. I have spent considerable capital, Mishaal, the personal kind, the kind you have never bothered to accumulate, calling in favors. I have been to Bangladesh. Do you understand that sacrifice? You should have seen the squalor. The streets were crawling with vermin."

Abdulaziz paused, remembering the grubby beggars and the neediness of the middlemen. It was preposterous that they called themselves patriots.

"I trusted you with one task," he continued. "One. To bring a briefcase from Paris to Riyadh. Our future rests on the contents of that briefcase, and I could trust only a member of our family to make the pickup. That person was you. And what do you do? What do you decide to do? You decide to fail."

"They had guns."

"So did you."

"They were going to cut off my hand. With a saw."

"It would have shown your faith."

"It would have killed me!"

"Better to be a martyr than a fool!"

Mishaal turned away, appalled but not surprised. His father was always ruthless, never kind, forever ambitious. Certainly not a father.

"I'm not going to die," Mishaal muttered, staring out the window like a teenager, even though he was forty-two, "simply because I'm your son."

Abdulaziz felt the plane shifting, banking toward home. He watched the prayer rug rotate, finding its true direction facing Mecca. Why did they keep having this conversation? Why did it have to be so hard? He had given so much for his children, his whole life, and yet he had received nothing in return.

Why had Allah cursed him? How could a man with five wives have only two worthless sons?

"The older generation is dying," he said, trying to control his anger. "When King Abdullah dies there will be no more sons of al-Saud to take the throne. And his health is failing. For the first time in my life, there will be meaningful change in the Kingdom. Generational change. And our family will be part of it, Mishaal. We have been given this opportunity, through my hard work, to set the Kingdom on a new course. And we will succeed. Salman will become King of Saudi Arabia, Custodian of the Two Holy Mosques and Head of the House of Saud. This is not a debate. We are Sudairi blood, just like Salman, and we will help him outmaneuver his rivals for the throne. In return, he will grant the Abdulaziz family a place on his Foreign Council."

"You mean Farhan."

"I mean the family, Mishaal."

"Farhan is your chosen," Mishaal said, slumping in his seat. "No matter what he does, you forgive. With me . . ."

Abdulaziz turned away, a gesture both symbolic and disrespectful. He didn't have to listen to Mishaal and his petty grievances against his younger brother. He never had. Farhan was superior in every way, even if Farhan *had* let him down. But fanaticism in the young was far better than degeneracy in the old. He could turn Farhan's passion; he could do nothing with Mishaal.

"None of this is your concern anymore," he said, allowing the anger in his voice to kill the rising regret. "You are going to Ha'il, to the desert, to be cleansed."

Mishaal shot out of his slouch. Ha'il meant drug rehabilitation in one of the notorious Wahhabi religious institutions, and the thought of living without his medicine was unbearable. The Wahhabis were unkind to men like him; his time in Ha'il would be torture. But he knew the sentence was worse than that. This was exile. From the family. From his father's influence. And maybe, because Abdulaziz was a cruel man, from his wealth.

"You can't—" he stammered, but Abdulaziz raised his hand.

"Prince . . . Father."

Abdulaziz bowed his head. The midmorning call to prayer had started over the jet's sound system. The elder prince lifted his considerable bulk and knelt on the prayer rug. He touched his forehead to the golden silk, in a pose of supplication. The plane banked, and Abdulaziz's rotund figure rotated on the rug, his head bowed toward Mecca in humility before the vast numinousness of Allah.

Mishaal watched, his lip curling in disgust. He hated this false piety. But more than that, he hated this man.

The man curled his torso to the ground as the midmorning prayer call rose toward its conclusion. As a Wahhabi Muslim, he was more pious than most, some might have said extreme. But the judgments of man did not concern him; only submission to God mattered.

He held his hands in front of him, his forehead nearly touching the carpet in supplication. The exact position had taken him more than a year to perfect, but now it was a part of him. That was the nature of ritual. It became automatic to the body, something that existed beyond the need to think or consider. Then you could free your mind to understand *tawhid*, the oneness of God. Or to size up your fellow worshippers.

The Wahhabi sat up, his eyes calmly scanning the eight other men in the mosque. The women had their own worship corner behind the cubbyholes for shoes, but he never concerned himself with them. In fact, for all his practiced watchfulness, he didn't know if there were women present at all.

The Rüstem Pasha Mosque of Istanbul was small but old, accessed by one nondescript door and a dark flight of stairs. Thousands walked past without realizing it was there, because the mosque was in the middle of the downtown spice market, and merchants' stalls covered the ground floor, while pigeons and their filth obscured the windows. Many who found the mosque considered its blue-tiled dome the most beautiful in Istanbul, especially in the softer morning light, but as the Wahhabi raised his head from prayer, he didn't even glance at the artistry above. He studied the men instead, searching their lack of piety. They were small and poor, from the underclass of Turkish society, but that was no excuse. The Wahhabi had once been small and poor himself.

Prayers ended. The Wahhabi bowed one last time. *Allahu Akbar.* Dear Father. Raise up your son.

He rose. Another man rose with him. Neither looked at the other. They walked to the back of the room to retrieve their shoes. The Wahhabi put his on slowly, with deliberate care, as he did everything now. He was a tall man, long and angular in every way, from his skeletal fingers to his thin face. He wasn't young or old but of indeterminate age. It was a number that didn't matter to him anyway, and was in fact something he'd begun to forget. He preferred not to think of his childhood or young adulthood, but only of his rebirth, after he'd found his purpose and awoken into the joys of submission to God.

The small man bumped him, fumbling with his shoes. The Wahhabi stared down his nose at him. The man was inefficient, full of unnecessary movement. He was unworthy. Or worse, an apostate.

The Wahhabi reached over and, in one smooth motion, snatched the purse and a piece of paper from the other man's hands. The paper was a photograph, but the Wahhabi didn't bother to look at it. There was no escape. If the man in the photograph had been given to the Wahhabi, the man was dead already.

"*Allahu akbar*," the informant said, lowering his eyes. God is the greatest.

True, little man, the Wahhabi thought. *And I am his instrument.*

CHAPTER 6

Half a world away, Brad Winters was being escorted into the appalling CIA cafeteria in the basement at Langley. He was a member of both the Cosmos Club and the Metropolitan Club, the most prestigious social clubs in town; he kept a cigar locker with a bronze nameplate at Morton's steakhouse on Connecticut Avenue; and the Palm had his caricature over his favorite booth. After all, a man will not be defined by the food he eats, but he will be defined by the places where he eats it.

The CIA cafeteria was not prestigious, despite its exclusivity. Unlike the Pentagon or White House, there were no tours. Visitors had to be invited. They had to be on the right list at the main gate, ride a bus to the New Building, go through a second security check, get an escort, and walk through those ridiculous white "wave tunnels"—security passages in the shape of an "S." On the other end was a multistory atrium with half-size models of U-2 and A-12 spy planes suspended from the ceiling.

Then you had to descend. At the bottom of the escalator sat the world's most pointless gift shop. Next to it was the world's most pointless museum, just one hallway long. On exhibit was bin Laden's AK-47, snatched during the Abbottabad raid. Other war trophies included trinkets taken from Saddam Hussein, Pablo Escobar, Fidel Castro, the KGB, and other villains of freedom. At least it was better than the ridiculous modern art that adorned the atrium. Brad Winters hated modern art.

The subterranean cafeteria had a wall of glass facing the

sunken atrium garden. *Depressing,* Winters thought. *All of it is depressing.* Still, the atrium was the only sky most of these cave dwellers ever saw, since analyst offices were windowless vaults. Who said the CIA wasn't glamorous?

Winters's escort, a young Mormon fresh out of Brigham Young University, smiled and motioned toward the entrance to the cafeteria. The Agency loved Mormons. They had foreign-language skills, lived abroad on their two-year proselytization mission, and, most important of all, could pass a CIA poly-graph. But they sucked at infiltrating terrorist organizations. Obviously.

"Thanks," Winters said, with a Dick Cheney–ish smile-scowl. No use wasting charm on the young.

Disgusting, he thought, as he eyed the food stations. He did a circuit twice before finally settling on a "jazz salad." *Christ,* he thought, *who names this stuff?* He would have to stop at the Metropolitan Grill for real food on his return to the city.

Winters strode aggressively across the cafeteria to his friend Larry Fitzhugh. Larry was a "Washington friend," meaning a friend of convenience. Winters knew no other kind. As the CEO of Apollo Outcomes, a multi-billion-dollar private mili-tary company in deep with the national security establishment, he could have lunched with the director of the CIA, but it would have been useless. Larry was a better source, because Larry ac-tually knew things.

Plus, the CIA director would wonder what a mover and shaker like Winters was after with all these questions. Larry never thought that way, which was why Larry was still eating tuna salad in the CIA basement.

"Mr. Fitzhugh," Winters said with barely feigned enthusiasm. "It's been too long."

Larry smiled but didn't get up. There was tuna salad on the

corner of his mouth. Larry was a bit of a legend, too, within the Agency's MENA division (Middle East and North Africa, the Muslim beat). The other analysts called him Yoda, because he knew everything and had a sixth sense about what was important. Also, he was old, squat, and had big ears, with wisps of white hair protruding from the holes.

"How's the Middle East?" Winters joked as he sat down.

"I assume you're wondering about Paris," Larry said.

"What have you heard?" Winters asked. As usual, Larry was right. Winters was wondering about Paris.

"I doubt it was a robbery for $350,000, as has been reported in the media. Frankly, I doubt any money was stolen at all."

"Cocaine?"

"Mishaal certainly has a history. I still don't know how he managed to evade arrest when his party boat was boarded on the Nile. A hundred pounds of pure cocaine and thousands of Captagon and Adderall pills." Larry shook his head. "His father doesn't have that kind of *wasta*," an Arab word for power.

You only say that, Larry, because you don't know where true power lies, Winters thought. Abdulaziz didn't have an impressive title, but he knew how to work the system. He was a crocodile you pass every day, sleeping quietly on the bank. Just because you've never seen him eat doesn't mean he goes hungry.

"My sources tell me it was a professional hit," Winters said.

"It took place in Paris during rush hour, against an armed convoy. Of course it was a professional hit. The question is what they were after."

"Not drugs."

"It would have gotten bloody."

"Not money."

"There are easier ways to steal $350,000. The ransom alone—"

"What then?" Winters asked, feeding Larry's ego. *Help me, Larry, you're my only hope.* When Larry flexed his Jedi muscles, Larry got chatty.

"Mishaal met with someone in his hotel room the afternoon of the robbery. Don't ask, because I don't know. The Four Seasons Hotel George V is Saudi owned. The Saudis are playing this close to the vest. No security footage from the hotel or parking garage. No interviews. The Paris police only had the prince for ten minutes before a Saudi diplomat showed up and claimed Mishaal had diplomatic protections. Very odd."

"Very Saudi."

Larry nodded. The Kingdom was notoriously secretive. Even tourism was illegal. "They took him to the embassy and kept him behind closed doors. His father flew in immediately to retrieve him. Poor guy. Abdulaziz is a beast."

"And an associate of mine."

"Of course," Larry said without contrition. Larry was clearly on the spectrum; he couldn't figure out social graces to save his life. "I forgot about your Yemen contract." And also apparently that the Yemen operation was black, not to be discussed openly, even in the CIA cafeteria. "It's just that . . . when you're a billionaire like Abdulaziz, why bother, you know? Why take so many risks?"

That was Larry's other problem. He was one of most knowledgeable Arabists in the business, but he thought small. He never risked. He was happy with his windowless cubicle at age sixty and his middle-class life in McLean, Virginia. Happiness, Brad Winters knew, was the first step to starvation. It didn't matter how much you had. When you lose the hunger, you die.

"So what was it, Larry? An inside job? Royal politics?"

Larry nodded. "Three factors point that way. First, the knowledge needed to hit Mishaal at that precise time and place. Second, the cover-up, because you know the Saudis planted that drug-and-money rumor. Abdulaziz wouldn't have agreed to the embarrassment if the real story wasn't worse. Third, Mishaal picked up a package from the Saudi Embassy an hour before the robbery."

"And?"

"It wasn't with him two hours later," Larry said. Clearly, this wasn't widely known, and probably TS/SCI classified. *That's why I'm here,* Brad thought, as he forced a waxy tomato into his mouth. Personal contact springs leaks.

"Diplomatic papers?"

Larry shook his head. "It was a private package, not official government."

"Business arrangement, perhaps?"

"Likely a secret pact between princes jockeying for the crown. You know how factional they are, with the Sudairi, Yamaniyah, and other clans. And the Wahhabi clerics are a force, too. The king is sick, and we're getting lots of chatter. Powerful people in the Kingdom are ready to dispense with tradition and break with the Council of Princes. You got the liberals, emboldened by the Arab Spring. You have the conservatives, who think the king took reforms too far. There's even talk of a palace coup."

"Liberals or conservatives?"

"Both."

Winters waited, hoping Larry would fill the awkward silence with more information. But Larry took a bite of his tuna sandwich, and then changed the subject.

"Prince Farhan," Larry said. "Your friend Abdulaziz's other son. The former ISIS commando. He disappeared in Istanbul."

"Five minutes after Mishaal's hit," Winters said, "there was a brief shoot-out in front of the Four Seasons Hotel. Nobody hurt except a bodyguard, clipped in the thigh. A woman loading her luggage chipped a tooth when she fainted. A bellboy crapped his pants—and I mean that literally, Larry, he shit his uniform. The assailants got away. So did Farhan. That seemed to be his plan all along, to the chagrin of his father."

Larry's face fell. "Oh, so you know."

"Of course I know, Larry. It's my business to know."

"Then you know why we're worried."

Winters sighed. He knew, and it was bad for business. "You don't want a guy like Farhan in play again."

"Farhan is a member of the Emni, ISIS's assassination unit. One of the few to survive the training. He killed in Syria, until his father had Saudi intelligence kidnap and return him to Riyadh. I'm guessing the deradicalization program failed."

"What do you make of it? Are the two events connected? Mishaal's capture and Farhan's escape?"

"Unlikely," Larry said. "Farhan went jihad. Istanbul is the main junction in the ISIS recruitment pipeline, and it's the first time his father let him out of the Kingdom in six months. He's probably in Syria or Iraq by now. His skill set, contacts, knowledge of English, and access to wealth makes him dangerous, so we put a bounty on him last night. A hundred thousand dollars. Seems like the kind of wet work your company does."

"I'll check into it," Winters said, although the bounty was a pittance, not even a rounding error for a typical Apollo contract. Still, it was good politics to take small jobs sometimes.

"Nothing wrong with doing the right thing and making a little money on the side," Winters said. "It's the American way."

Larry sighed. He was a public servant who despised contractors of all stripes, especially private military ones. Some things were inherently governmental, Larry believed, like national security. Larry was living in 1979.

"It was blackmail," Winters said, leaning back and straightening the monogrammed cuffs of his shirt. His watch cost more than Larry would make in a year.

"What was?"

"Paris. Someone wanted leverage on Abdulaziz."

"Is that what he told you?"

"That's what I'm telling you, Larry. As payment."

"Who?" Larry said, staring at Winters. He had forgotten he was holding his half-eaten sandwich.

"I think you know."

"Prince Khalid," Larry said, and Winters could see the lightbulb flickering to life in his head. The lightbulb Winters had switched on.

"It makes sense," Larry said, thinking it through. "Abdulaziz is a Sudairi and Khalid a Wahhabi fanatic, so they're natural rivals. Khalid was Crown Prince Nayef's protégé in the Ministry of Interior, before Nayef died in 2012, causing Abdulaziz's faction to rise in power. Khalid has taken his mentor's position and commands the respect of the clerics. He's perfectly placed for a palace coup."

"He also directs the Mabahith," Winters said. The Mabahith were the Kingdom's powerful secret police, notoriously religious. Some of their leaders quietly advocated the overthrow of the royal family and a return to the stern Islam of the seventh century, but not too quietly for everyone not to know. A prince with the Mabahith behind him would be formidable indeed.

"You're here on Abdulaziz's behalf," Larry said.

"I'm here on your behalf, Larry," Winters said. "Our interests are aligned. Nobody wants to see a religious fanatic take the Saudi throne."

Both men knew Abdulaziz and Khalid themselves would never ascend the throne. They were small powers behind a big throne. But having a king in your debt was no small thing, especially when he controlled most of the world's oil supply.

"I'll take a closer look into Khalid," Larry agreed.

"Any information you discover would be helpful."

Larry nodded as Winters stood to leave. "When do you need it?"

"Yesterday," Winters kidded, sort of. "Before Paris."

"No really." Larry didn't understand jokes.

"I leave for Riyadh in three hours."

Larry took off his smudgy glasses and cleaned them with his tie. "Okay. I'll see what I can do."

"You know I would do the same for you," Winters said, as he walked away, leaving his "jazz salad" mostly untouched on the table. Larry waddled after him as they passed the ridiculous gift shop, huffing to keep up.

"Do you mind giving me an escort to the Yemen team?" Winters said over his shoulder. It chafed that the government trusted him with $4 billion worth of secret contracts every year, but not to walk the halls at Langley without an escort. He couldn't even take a piss in this rathole without a chaperone. Not that he'd want to. The sanitary conditions were appalling.

"Sure," Larry said as they took the up escalator. "Routine consultations?"

"We got some hot intel I need to deliver in person."

"Off your Yemen contract?"

Winters didn't answer. He knew nothing tormented an intel analyst more than being left out of the loop.

Larry broke down. "Care to share?"

"You'll owe me," Winters said. Larry nodded, and Winters leaned in close and whispered. "It has to do with the Kingdom's nuclear option."

Larry turned pale.

Decades ago the Americans persuaded the Saudis to give up their nuclear program in exchange for a U.S. promise to defend the Kingdom if threatened by a hostile power, like their great traditional enemy Iran. But the nuclear program wasn't dismantled. The Saudis secretly transferred it to Pakistan and bankrolled the program, with an understanding that if the Kingdom ever needed a nuke, Pakistan would oblige.

"Saudi Arabia is going to buy a nuke from Pakistan?" Larry whispered, and Winters could see his Yoda ears twitching. Larry would be on this tip within minutes and, pretty soon, so would everyone else in MENA.

Like giving candy to a baby, Winters thought.

A twenty-minute bus ride later, Brad Winters called his associate in London, Sir Kabir Basrami-Heatherington, from the backseat of his chauffeured Town Car. Winters assumed the NSA was monitoring his calls; they were monitoring everyone's calls, especially the CEOs of companies like Apollo Outcomes, which did the government's dirty work. That was why he and Kabir only used encrypted phones with proprietary tech.

"Yes," Kabir said. He sounded annoyed. Winters could hear him breathing heavily. He was probably on his treadmill.

"They don't believe the cocaine story," Winters said.

"And Farhan?"

"They don't know anything more than we do."

Kabir grunted. Winters wasn't sure how to take that. He imagined the man at his Mayfair gym, running himself into the ground surrounded by chilled Evian waters. He could picture it, because he'd seen the surveillance photos. Know your enemy; surveil your friends.

"I want this contained," Kabir said, huffing.

"It has to be Khalid. I've just put the CIA on his scent." Kabir didn't respond. "And we've got the green light to action Farhan." *Action* was military lingo for "eliminate." "That will keep Abdulaziz in check. His arrogance created this problem."

"It wasn't *his* arrogance."

Winters knew whose arrogance Kabir was referring to, but he chose to ignore the insult. "It was using his sons. The man placed too much faith in his sons."

Kabir breathed deep. He was definitely on his treadmill. "Men always place too much faith in their sons."

Kabir Basrami-Heatherington was a seventh-generation banker who could trace his lineage back to the early days of the British Empire, when his Indian forebears had been among the first to embrace their new masters. Winters, a self-made man, always liked to stick it to the inheritors of the world.

"I don't want your philosophy," Kabir said. "I want a Sudairi on the throne. I want *our* Sudairi on the throne, someone who will open the Kingdom for business."

"Don't worry. That's why I'm working through Abdulaziz."

"I want my man at the future king's right hand."

"Understood."

"And I want my name left out of it."

"Your name won't come up. Hardly anyone even knows your name."

Kabir took a deep breath. It sounded like a sigh. "Good. Don't call me again until it's done."

CHAPTER 7

Boon, Wildman, and I spent most of the day obtaining supplies and rigging our vehicles for the mission ahead. We'd split
the $100,000 with our Kurd partners, as always, but there was
plenty left over. Wildman had wanted to ditch them, but Boon
and I disagreed. The Kurds had been helping us for eight weeks,
with almost no pay. They were good fighters, dedicated to their
people's cause. They deserved to be cut in on the retainer.

The million if we succeeded? That was still to be determined.

"Where do you want to go?" Boon asked, as he strapped on
our extra water.

"Morocco," I said. "Nicest police state I've ever seen."

"Beaches, booze, and naked bodies," Wildman said, loading
his C-4. Wildman was our explosives expert, the best in the
world, in my humble opinion. It was a good thing when you
enjoyed your work.

"I guess that rules out the Muslim world," Boon said.

"*Inshallah*," Wildman replied. *Inshallah* was Arabic for "God
willing." The only other Arabic word Wildman knew was *mush-
kila*, problem.

"What about you, Boon?"

Boon shrugged. "I'm comforted by the wisdom of Wildman."

Wildman grunted approval.

I returned to our near-empty flat to pack my rucksack with
combat essentials, then threw in whatever personal effects I had

left: a pair of chopsticks, the *I Ching*, my ballistic humidor, the bottle of Woodford Reserve bourbon I'd been nursing since Ankara.

I looked at the bottle, wrapped in the blue bespoke sport coat I hadn't worn since arriving in Kiev to save a Ukrainian oligarch's family from murderous thugs. I drank, hung the coat on the shower rod—we didn't have a curtain—and showered under a pathetic dribble of water. The rough shave took twenty minutes, but it turns out I was still there, under the beard. I donned my coat and sunglasses, and wheeled out a motorbike from our garage. Boon had traded loot for it, then fixed it up.

I got to the clinic around 1800, just after it officially closed. Outside a bearded man lay on a stretcher, clutching his bloodstained side. I leaned the motorcycle against the wall, stepped over the moaning man, and peeked inside the front door.

Kylah's clinic was no-frills. She treated the indigent, the criminal, those with no other recourse. These days, that described half the people in Erbil. God knew who she swindled to get the medicine and pay her staff of three. Usually she worked after hours, and I thought she might still be there tonight. I was right. She sat in her back office, the glow of a laptop's screen illuminating her face.

I banged on the door. She jumped, then smiled, then walked over and unlocked the door. I had to hand it to her. Kylah knew how to walk.

"What are you doing here?"

"Couldn't sleep."

"You clean up nice," she said, eyeing my linen blazer and clean shave.

"You know there's a guy dying outside," I said as we walked through the tiny waiting room. On a table sat Arab magazines, three years old.

"He's a jihadist," she said, tossing her white lab coat over a chair. "He'll just kill more people if I patch him up."

"Isn't that violating the Hippocratic oath or something?"

"If he's alive tomorrow, I'll save him."

She bent over her desk (nice) and pulled out a bottle of whiskey, but I waved it away and put down the Woodford. "Get some ice," I said.

"What's the occasion?" she said, reaching into the medical fridge.

"I'm leaving."

I poured two fingers of Kentucky's finest into two plastic medical cups, the kind you pee in for a sample. The ice crackled when the warm liquor hit, the aroma of buttery bourbon perfuming the air. "That should pay our tab, with a generous tip," I said, sliding an envelope across her desk.

Kylah peeked at the pile of dollars, but didn't count them, so she didn't know how very generous the tip was. "You're a mystery, Tom Locke."

"Just a drifter."

She took a drink and nodded her satisfaction. "There's more to you than that."

I thought about the twenty years I'd spent in the line of fire, first U.S. Army Airborne, then Apollo. I thought about all the lives I'd taken: hundreds of men, and a few women and children, too. I balanced them against the lives I'd saved: hundreds of thousands when I stopped a genocide in Burundi, hundreds in Mosul, an entire village in northern Mali, and a busload of women on their way to a life of slavery and rape. Then I thought of the girl who didn't make it off that *sabaya* bus and my best friend, Jimmy Miles, bleeding out in my arms. I still didn't know what to do with that last one, so I buried it before it could grow on me. It's what mercenaries do.

"Just a drifter with a gun," I said.

"These young guys," Kylah said, fingering the edge of the cup. "They come in once, usually after a knife fight outside the T-Top, they want to tell me everything they've done. Most of them haven't done anything more than graduate from high school. Some of them haven't even done that. You come in for months, you don't say anything."

Not much to say.

"The strong, silent type," she laughed, when she saw I wasn't going to answer. "A man with a past."

"I'm tired, that's all. It's what happens when you get old."

She chuckled. "I don't really care about your story. I just like a man who has one."

"The more you know about mine, the less impressed you'll be."

"Let me guess: deaths you can't forget, mistakes you can't let go, a career you walked away from for . . ." She was winding me up, so I waited. She had it right so far. "A woman."

I thought about Alie MacFarlane, the woman I'd reconnected with in Ukraine after a decade apart. I'd fallen for her in Burundi, when she was a twenty-four-year-old ex-nun with legs that wouldn't quit. I'd met her again in Ukraine, and a whole lot of trouble had gone down. Still, I couldn't let her go. She was the love of my life. Maybe. She had made me realize what I'd given up—a family, a house, a normal life—but she hadn't been the cause. I'd given those things up years ago, when I dropped out of graduate school at Harvard to put my boots on the ground for Apollo Outcomes and Brad Winters.

"I don't think so," I said.

Kylah wasn't convinced. She leaned on the desk and smiled. Her tank top fell open, and it was an effort to keep my eyes from drifting down. The effort failed. She wasn't wearing a bra.

"Then what broke you?" she asked.

Failure, I wanted to tell her. *The deeply personal kind. The kind that gets your best friend killed and makes you question everything you've ever done, and all the things you've ever believed, both about yourself and the world.*

But I wasn't sure that was the right answer, and I didn't know how to tell her that anyway. So instead I touched her hand.

"I don't think so, cowboy," she said. "I'm not a one-night kind of girl."

Good, it's probably better that way, I thought, even though I didn't believe it.

"And this isn't what you want."

She was wrong. Right now, it was the only thing I wanted.

"We've a good friendship going, Tommy, and that's not easy to find. Why ruin it for a roll? Especially when I'm not what you're looking for."

"You're wrong, Kylah."

"You didn't shave that mangy beard for me, Tommy, and we both know it."

Alie? I thought, and the memory came to me: her creamy skin in the hot bed in Amsterdam, and the surprising darkness of her nipples, and the way she screamed. The way she forgave me for what I'd done.

"You're looking for yourself under all that shit," Kylah said. "Believe me, I've seen it, and you're not going to find it here." *It's only sex,* I almost said, but she wasn't finished. "Besides," she continued as a sly smile started to touch her pretty face, "I've had a man for a while now, and I don't think it would be right to sleep with his boss."

My jaw dropped. "Wildman!? You've been fucking Wildman?"

"Hell no," she said. "Do you even know your friends?"

"Boon?"

She shrugged, and I could tell she was enjoying my surprise. "I like a man with a story," she said. "And he's got one. Besides, he's sexy as hell."

"He's a Buddhist!"

"Well then, he's the dirtiest damn Buddhist I've ever met," she said. I didn't know if she was being serious or pulling my leg with that last sentence, but I knew the image was going to haunt me.

We arrived at the T-Top as the sun disappeared behind the edge of the world, Kylah clinging to me on the back of the motorcycle. I loved Erbil at dusk; it had a desert swank to it. We zoomed through its empty streets, me still in sunglasses as I had no goggles or helmet, and Kylah with her fiery hair in the wind. I wanted to be happy, and mostly I was. She was a good friend; we understood each other. But I couldn't get the image of her with that dirty little Buddhist I called my running partner out of my head.

I pulled up next to a row of technicals: modified pickup trucks, each with a heavy-caliber machine gun mounted on the bed. They were modern warfare's ubiquitous cavalry, and a tool of the trade in my line of work.

The bar was crowded, but I spotted Wildman right away. His outsize laugh and burly frame were hard to miss. He was playing darts with throwing knives, his version of a drinking game. He smiled when he saw me with Kylah, then laughed when she put her arm around Boon.

"He's a killer," Wildman said, slapping me on the back and ordering me a double Jack straight up.

I thought of replying, but I didn't have anything to say. I finished my drink and told him I was hitting the head. On the way back, I passed the empty stage. There was a cheap Yamaha keyboard in the corner. I plugged it in, set the program to concert piano, and started playing Chopin's third Étude, called "The Farewell." Of all his music, Chopin thought this piece his most poignant. It begins simple enough but ends in a maelstrom of emotion, which suited my mood.

The piano wasn't my instrument. I'd been a violin virtuoso until I gave it up at fourteen, after I realized I'd never be the best in the world. I had the work ethic, but not the innate talent. I could never play Carnegie Hall, but I had the talent to impress someone like Kylah, and that was what I wanted tonight. I wanted to show her I was more than a drifter with a gun.

I guess I wanted to lose myself, too. Music can do that, just like a slug of high-end bourbon or a two-week walkabout in the ISIS-infested mountains. Running my fingers along that keyboard could take me to any moment in my life, or anywhere else I wanted to go. But at the T-Top, all it took me to was my regret.

I lifted my fingers, letting the music crescendo around me. The Yamaha was tinny and the T-Top a bunker, but the chords lingered, buzzing around me, until my revelry was interrupted by yelling from the bar. It was the war tourists. I thought for sure they were barking at me to play Lynyrd Skynyrd.

I turned, but nobody was even looking my way. Everyone was focused on the television above the bar. An American was on his knees in front of a masked man, who was reading a prepared message. He was wearing an orange jumpsuit, like the ones at Guantanamo Bay. The executioner was in black. The desert was empty behind them. I looked away, but I knew it was done when the squaddies exploded with anger, smashing their glasses on the bar. Someone's beer hit the television set and shattered. I walked out without another word, my heart in my shoes.

Wildman caught up to me two blocks later. "I'll cut their cocks off and feed them to the dogs," he said. "They'll fucking pay."

"We're leaving," I said. "Tell the Kurds. And where the hell is Boon?"

"He had already left," Wildman said. He didn't need to stay with Kylah. "Give him an hour."

I didn't want to. I really didn't want to. But I did.

CHAPTER 8

"Where have you been?"

Brad Winters dismissed the menace in the question. It had been only twenty-three hours since the robbery. He had traveled halfway around the world. What did the prince expect? "It's important not to seem impatient," he said casually.

"Why?"

"Because I'm here, officially, to fight Iranian-backed Houthi rebels in Yemen on your behalf, a battle that is timely but not urgent. And you're being tracked."

"By whom?"

"The CIA. I have it directly from government sources."

"It's not a matter of international politics for a man to avenge his sons. And it's not suspicious."

"Not yet," Winters agreed.

Abdulaziz sighed. "Ten billion dollars," he said absently, "and a lifetime's work."

"Ten billion is nothing. You'll lose your head for this."

"I'm not going to lose my head. I'm going to be a national hero."

"If you let me do my job."

Winters raised the leg rest in Abdulaziz's Rolls-Royce Phantom and stared out the window at the sunset over Riyadh. Lovely Riyadh. Sleek and curved like an unveiled woman, and hot as hell.

"If Farhan has gone back to ISIS . . ." Winters said smoothly, knowing the words were knives.

"Farhan escaped assassination by my enemies. Farhan is smart. He's laying low."

"Don't be proud. He was running. If he rejoins ISIS . . ."

"Then I'll find him again."

"I hear Baghdadi is headed to northern Iraq."

"That's only rumor."

"They say he'll be in Mosul tomorrow."

Abdulaziz laughed harshly. "If a man like you or me knew where the leader of ISIS was going to be tomorrow, he'd be dead already."

"This is serious, Abdulaziz. There is more at stake than just your son. Much more. Let me help you."

"I'll find my son," the man barked. "You focus on Yemen. That's all I should have ever hired you for."

You hired me, Winters thought, *you don't own me.* But he kept his mouth shut and his eyes on Riyadh, all the way to his hotel. After all, this was the hard part, and it was only beginning.

CHAPTER 9

It was well past midnight by the time our two Humvees forded the Zab River and entered ISIS territory. We'd been using this series of smuggler trails for months, driving up through the mountains to the north of the highway, where the terrain was rough and people scarce. It was only eighty-five kilometers from Mosul to Erbil on the main road, about an hour's drive, but this route would take us all night. We let the Kurds lead in their Humvee, out of tradition more than anything. By now I knew the way, but the Kurds had shown it to us way back when we arrived, and it was good to keep them on as guides.

It was our last time through here, I realized, as we topped a ridge and spotted St. Matthew's Monastery atop Mount Alfaf, one of the oldest Christian monasteries in existence and only thirty klicks from Mosul. It was a miracle it remained Christian.

We followed the switchbacks up Mount Bashiqa. At the top was a craterlike depression, and in it was a secret military air-base, now abandoned. Our Kurdish guides had told us ISIS booby-trapped it, burying hundred-pound bombs in its single-strip runway and surrounding area, so we skirted the lip of the bowl as always. On the other side, we dismounted and walked the last few meters to the top of the ridgeline.

"Ain't it beautiful," I said.

Before us spread a vast plain with Mosul in the distance, the second largest city in Iraq. It was a hard twenty klicks: down this mountain, across the desert, through ISIS perimeter defenses, and into a city crawling with ISIS spies—all without being detected. But from up here, it was beautiful.

"The moon's killing us," Wildman said. The gibbous moon lit up the desert in ways inconceivable to those raised among wooded hills.

"We're going to have to take it slow and easy," Boon said.

"Yeah. But we need to make our meet before dawn prayers." That was when the city woke.

"Activity to the south." Wildman pointed. We held up our binos in unison. A convoy was traveling fast on the highway toward the city.

"ISIS," Boon said. "Six trucks. Humvees."

Most of ISIS's military equipment was made in America and captured from the Iraqi army. We'd procured our two up-armored Humvees by ambushing an ISIS patrol on a scouting run a few days after our arrival in Erbil. Usually Boon, Wildman, and I would have split up between the two vehicles, but I'd given one to the Kurds as a show of respect. That had bought a few extra weeks of loyalty.

"Looks like they're towing artillery," I said. "Probably heading to the Syrian front by night to avoid air strikes."

I traced the road ahead of the convoy into Mosul. An ISIS checkpoint guarded a roadblock with an artillery piece pointed straight down the highway. Just beyond, a huge black ISIS flag was draped over a WELCOME TO MOSUL road sign. Twelve to fifteen crucified bodies lined the road.

"Let's move out," I said. "Switch to blackout drive."

The Hummers hobbled down the mountainside at a nearly vertical angle, the Kurds in the lead. This part of the trek always made me nervous. This "mountain" was little more than a hunk of rock covered with loose dirt, and our path a goat trail. Every windstorm shifted the dirt and disguised the cliff edges, making our guides' work treacherous. Worse, night vision came at the expense of depth perception and peripheral vision. One wrong move and a Humvee would tumble off the edge. That was why ISIS never came this way. They never even bothered to watch it.

"Easy does it," I said to Boon, as the path narrowed and the drop-off grew to a few hundred meters.

Buddha calm, I thought, focusing on my breathing. I hated this part, because it was out of my control. But I trusted Boon. Not as much as I trusted myself, but about as much as I could trust anyone, even if he'd stolen my girl.

Funny how it seemed like that now, I thought, as we skidded on the edge, even though Kylah was never more than a friend with an AK-47 and a hell of a set of legs.

"Not gonna miss that," Wildman said, when the cliff's edge finally gave way to the desert plain.

The ride was bumpy, but we made good time. When we got close to the city, we found a narrow, ten-foot-deep dry river bed, known as a *wadi,* our usual highway into Mosul. We followed the muddy oxbows for four kilometers, past orchards and farm buildings. We were one klick out when I saw the artillery.

"Halt!" I yelled to the Kurds through the headset.

Two hundred meters in front of us sat a 155-millimeter cannon, pointed over our heads at a major road junction. There was no movement through my night-vision goggles. Maybe the crew was asleep. Maybe they were aiming.

"Back up," I whispered. The Humvees reversed around the last oxbow and out of the cannon's line of sight. We hadn't seen this gun emplacement before. It was new. I stepped out of the Humvee to caucus with the Kurds, who had lived all their lives within a hundred kilometers of Mosul and knew this land. A vigorous debate ensued in Kurdish, hands gesticulating wildly as they whispered, arguing about the best way around.

"Ah, guys." Boon's voice. "Guys. Silence!"

He nodded behind him. Above us, on the edge of the wadi, stood a young boy. He was backlit against the moonlit night, so his expression was unreadable. We froze, as if posing for a portrait, staring at each other in mortified disbelief. I put my hand to my SCAR assault rifle as another face appeared, staring down at us with slanted, devilish eyes. A goat. The boy must have been a herder. We must have woken him, meaning his family was nearby.

If he gives our position away, we're dead.

Boon held out a chocolate bar, flashing his Thai smile. My index finger moved to the trigger well of my SCAR. The kid didn't move, but the goat sniffed the air.

The older Kurd spoke. I don't know what he said, but the child relaxed, shoulders slumping. He disappeared and I lifted my SCAR, but the old man put his hand over my barrel.

"No," he said. "He will help us."

I lowered my weapon, and the boy returned with his older brother. They skidded down the wadi bank on their butts.

"The gun isn't manned tonight," the Kurd translated, "but there are bombs ahead, buried in the ground."

Improvised explosive devices, or IEDs, were a trademark of al Qaeda and now ISIS. Some were triggered remotely; others, like those ahead, would blow under the pressure of a Humvee tire. In a wadi this narrow, there wasn't much hope of getting past them, and culvert IEDs were hard to spot, especially at night.

"Holy hell," Wildman said, as the boy spoke to the older Kurd.

"For us," the Kurd translated, "for enemies of ISIS, he knows a way through."

CHAPTER 10

The two militants were surprised to see the gaunt figure walking toward them out of the dry grasslands just south of al Hasaka, Syria. It was three in the morning, after all, and only lizards were walking this deep in the desert at this time of night. Sometimes they would see people flee the city by night, dragging their children with one arm and holding their pathetic bundles in the other. They were headed to Turkey via border crossings like Qamishli and maybe to Europe, if they didn't die along the way. But walking? Into the city? From the south?

An opportunity, the first militant thought. Three weeks ago, their Chechen Muslim commander, Omar al Shishani, had seized a Syrian artillery base nearby, decimating Syrian Regiment 121. Since then, it had been quiet, and the militant kept boredom at bay by harassing passersby. The smugglers' trucks paid well to travel through the Caliphate, and even some of the desperate refugees had valuables they would trade for safe passage. If they didn't comply, and his mood was righteous, the militant wasn't above beating them and destroying the few things they owned. The walkers were fair game, in his opinion, because they had chosen to flee the Caliphate. This gaunt stranger was fair game because he was entering the land born of martyrs, and an entry tax was a small price to pay for an eternity of bliss.

The second guard wasn't as sure. He was almost sixteen, from the slums of Damascus, and he had joined ISIS primarily for food. And the promise of *tawhid,* mystical union with Allah. He wanted to be moved by faith. He wanted to believe there was a divine purpose to his life of crushing injustice. But for weeks, he had experienced only the daily grind of desperate people stumbling toward Turkey, just as his family had walked out of Damascus last winter when the rebels opened a gap. They were dead now, all but him.

So he watched the elongated figure emerge out of the grasslands, where no one had ever come from before, with a certain hopefulness. He countenanced the white robes against the dark night, and the corona of hair and beard. The stranger was bareheaded, save a white skullcap, and he carried no bags, but he had a *jambiya*—a curved dagger—tucked in his belt and a leather strap across his chest. He looked neither Syrian army nor Kurdish fighter nor fellow mujahideen.

"Madman," the first guard said.

Prophet, thought Ish, the younger guard. He had been waiting for wisdom to emerge from this emptiness. He believed the teachings of his former imam: that the desert could drive men mad with the knowledge of Allah.

"*As-salamu alaykum,*" the older guard yelled when the stranger was less than fifty meters away.

The stranger kept walking toward them, slow and steady, holding their gaze until Ish looked away. When he looked back, the stranger was uncomfortably close. He had an empty look in his eyes, as if he didn't know they were there. His hands were outstretched, palms up and cupped in supplication. He glanced up at the black ISIS flag above the former Syrian Army outpost, then stared straight into the younger man. Ish felt his heart explode with longing. Surely this was a holy man.

"*As-salamu alaykum*," the older guard repeated, bringing his Kalashnikov across his chest as a threat, his finger on the trigger. The stranger stopped in front of him.

"*Wa-Alaikum Salaam*," the stranger said calmly, his black eyes glittering like beetles but the rest of his face impassive. "I'm looking for a man," he said in Gulf Arabic. "I believe he passed through here earlier today."

"We were not here earlier today," the guard replied.

The stranger reached behind his back with his left arm, pulled out a scimitar, and sliced the guard's neck in one motion. The head fell one way; the body the other. Ish fell to his knees and began to pray, his forehead to the bloody ground, his body wracked with sobs.

"Then you cannot help me," the stranger said, walking toward the city.

If Ish had looked up, he would have seen the smile of satisfaction on the formerly stoic face, the electricity of delight. Allah willed his arm to discipline and punish, but also to inspire. The Wahhabi had sensed the fear and longing in the second guard's eyes, and he knew that he could give the young man what he desired: revelation.

The American white-knuckled his night-vision binoculars and watched the gaunt figure walk undisturbed into the Syrian night. He looked back at the outpost. The headless body lay crumpled on the ground and the second jihadi lay crumpled beside it, rocking back and forth in prostration.

"What was that?" he whispered, lowering the night-vision binoculars.

"Fuck if I know," said his partner, lowering his, too.

"The guard didn't even provoke him. He didn't even have time to be an asshole. He just . . ."

"I know. I saw it."

The second operative put the binoculars back to his eyes and watched the assassin walk along the road. The man wasn't hurrying, and he never looked back. He was . . . Jesus Christ, the guy was strutting.

"You think that was our guy?" He was referring to the new intelligence requirements on the whereabouts of a missing Saudi princeling.

His partner, a former U.S. Navy SEAL turned CIA Ground Division, laughed. "No chance. We're looking for a Saudi prince leading an ISIS death squad, not a lone sociopath with a sword. Not that one can't be the other, but no sane person is going to just walk out of the desert alone."

They set up the satcom array and called in the incident. Reporting bizarre murders wasn't the assignment; the job was to keep eyes on the tactical situation and take out leadership, if the opportunity presented itself. But this was the first interesting thing they'd seen in days.

"I don't get it," the second commando said, still staring through his binos. "Three combat tours in Iraq. Two in Afghanistan, one in the Sahel. I've seen some fucked-up shit in my time, but I ain't seen nothin' like that."

"FIDO," his partner said. Fuck It Drive On.

CHAPTER 11

Two hundred fifty kilometers away, Jase Campbell stepped onto the tarmac, the props of the Airbus military transport plane lashing his desert fatigues. The land was flat and dusty, but he could see the black outline of distant mountains against the deep purple of the midmorning sky. Iraq. It had been four years. God, he'd missed it.

"Get those Sand Vipers off the bird," he shouted over the prop wash to the three mercs standing on the rear loading ramp. "Square that shit away," he yelled to Black Jack Burns, his lead sniper, who was fiddling with a tie-down. "Get a move on!"

The Erbil airport terminal was a few hundred meters away, bright white against the black sky. It was sleek and modern, one of the nicest buildings he'd seen in Iraq, but he wasn't going there. He was headed in the other direction. Into the Jazira.

"Let's go, go, go!" he shouted, because if he didn't shout over the sound of the plane, no one would hear him. "I want to be in those mountains before first light."

Campbell had a nine-man team, all Tier One, all outfitted to destroy. Their equipment was next-generation, beyond anything U.S. Special Operations Command possessed. The three strike vehicles, currently being unchained by the plane's loadmaster, were kitted out with a mini Gatling gun turret, reactive armor, Stinger missiles, antitank rockets, and enough demolitions to carve a new face on Mount Rushmore. They even had a recon drone. The vehicles would never pass unnoticed on the open road, but Jase Campbell had no interest in staying low profile. And he had no interest in shooting through his supplies. If this job took a week, he would consider himself a failure. And Jase Campbell never failed.

He had been in this region before, starting in 2004 in Tal Afar, when he had taken part in Operation Black Typhoon as part of a U.S. Army Stryker Brigade. He returned to Tal Afar in 2005 for Operation Restoring Rights, sweeping out al Qaeda as a para-trooper in the Eighty-Second Airborne Division. After that, he "hopped the fence" and joined the Combat Applications Group, also known as Delta Force. His next tour in Iraq was at Balad Air Base, seventy-five kilometers northeast of Baghdad, where he was assigned to the Joint Special Operations Command, or JSOC, or simply "the Task Force." It was America's hunter-killer machine, and he was at the pointy edge of its spear. When the war ended, JSOC changed. Campbell went home, got a job, hated it, missed the action. One of his buddies from the Task Force recruited him to "the dark side," as the old soldiers called it—private contract work. The pay was good. Very good. So were the missions.

God damn, it's good to be back, Campbell thought.

"Ready," Luke Murphy yelled over the prop blast, sliding up beside him. Murphy had also served in the Task Force, one of three he'd recruited to work with him when he went private sector. Murphy knew this country like the back of his ass: by feel, if not necessarily by sight.

"Then get a move on," Campbell yelled. The Vipers' honey-comb wheels spun and vehicles leapt out of the plane and onto the tarmac, lined up and ready to prowl. If a Humvee, a Porsche, and a tank had an orgy, it would produce a Sand Viper. They were quicker than a Hummer, more maneuverable than a tank, and could take a hit in battle. They were the opposite of the armed dune buggies U.S. SpecOps favored, which had zero armor protection. Campbell always felt like he was riding around in an eggshell in those things; they were only good for running the wrong way rather than closing with the enemy. The Vipers could eat a dune buggy and shit it into the dirt.

God damn, it's good to be back, Campbell thought again, as the Vipers lined up. The aircraft's rear ramp retracted, and he returned the crew chief's thumbs-up. The pilots throttled the engines, and Campbell saluted as the bird rolled down the runway and into the sky.

"Adios, dipshits," he said, swapping his salute for the middle finger. In Vietnam, the soldiers loved their combat pilots, because combat pilots landed in enemy fire to save their asses. For mercs, the pilots were nothing more than bus drivers. They took the men close to where they needed to go, then got the hell out.

Campbell watched the plane disappear, its silhouette fading into the dawn sky as he removed his ear plugs. The air felt heavy after standing inside a sonic event, but damn if it didn't feel good. This place, Iraq, had forged a generation of warriors, for good and for bad. It was their place: the professional members of the gladiatorial class, millennial generation. Whether that was a moral thing or not, Jase Campbell didn't much care. He wasn't a politician or a philosopher. He just came to kick ass until there was no more ass to kick.

He took out his satellite phone as he hopped into the lead vehicle and dialed the Apollo Outcomes tactical operations center outside Washington, DC. His mission officer, Rodriguez, picked up.

"We're here," Campbell confirmed. He waited. He nodded. "Got it."

"Move out," he called to his team, drawing circles in the air with his right hand, and then pointing forward like he was chopping air.

Twelve minutes after hitting the ground in Erbil, they were gone.

CHAPTER 12

We left the kid on the edge of the wadi in the last dry field before Mosul. He had guided us, slowly, for nearly an hour, around a series of half-completed minefields and abandoned trenches. At one point, we passed a bulldozer sitting idle in a field and a pile of plastic pipe and wood. Someone in ISIS had planned on building defensives, but the energy of the men gave out. The fanatics weren't an army; they had come to cleanse with fire, not dig holes.

Boon gave the boy an energy bar, and then a sniper bullet as a memento. Wildman promised to kill some ISIS for him, and I gave him a thumbs-up. I'd taken a chance on the kid, and he'd done right by us, but the horizon was turning purple, and that meant it was time to go.

One oxbow later, the farmland turned into neighborhoods. We were inside Mosul now, but still hidden ten feet deep. During rainy season, this river would swell to the width of a four-lane highway, but right now it was less than half that.

"Cross the water here," the old Kurd said.

Everyone except the drivers clambered atop the Humvees and held on as the vehicle inched into the water and snorkeled across. The passenger compartment flooded, and I could hear Boon inhale as cold water engulfed him up to his chest. The engine was breathing through an extended air intake and exhaust system that rose to the cab's rooftop, above the water. Still, our Humvee slowed at the center of the small river, its tires clawing the mud.

For a moment, I thought we would have to use the bumper winch, but then the Hummer staggered free and came up on the other side. Humvees were beasts.

"Everyone back inside."

We drove up the bank and onto a hilly plain in the middle of Mosul. Six square kilometers of darkness right in the heart of the city, and a perfect shortcut. These were the ancient ruins of Nineveh, seat of the Assyrian empire from the Bible. Now it was just dust and a few marble edifices, reminding me of Ozymandias's hubris, the pathetic Pharaoh of Shelley's poem. ISIS had blown up what was left, including the ancient tomb of Jonah, who escaped a whale but not the fanatics.

"Drive west through the ruins," the old Kurd said, as we continued in blackout drive.

It was nearly dawn, and the *adhan*, or Muslim call to prayer, would soon sound. Our time was limited. Mosul had the ubiquitous Arab city feel: two-story cinder-block buildings, tangles of electrical wires, parched ground, litter. Thank goodness the Kurds knew the way; it all looked the same to me.

"Here we are," the old man said. I recognized the automotive garage, owned by a friend of the Mosul resistance, from previous trips into the city. The Kurds got out, opened the garage doors, and swung them shut behind the Humvees.

"Stay here," I said. "We'll be back."

"When?" the old man asked.

"I don't know."

We'd come to trust each other, the old Kurd and me. Battle does that.

"Time to put on the man-jammies," Wildman said, taking off his night-vision goggles. We each put black tunics over our fatigues and wrapped a black turban around our heads, a jihadi disguise that could be ripped off if we got into a firefight. We set out on foot, just Wildman, Boon, and me.

This was the most dangerous part of the journey. We were at the epicenter of ISIS in Iraq, without the firepower or speed of our Humvees. If we were discovered, we would be captured, tortured, and publicly beheaded. There would be no rescue or ransom for men like us.

We walked as casually as we could muster. The morning call to prayer was imminent, and we had to find our contact, Nassib, before the city awoke. I had called in Farhan's details yesterday, after the Saudi left but before heading to the T-Top. If he was in Mosul, Nassib would know.

"Where should I leave the mark?" Nassib had asked.

"Same place as last time," I said, hanging up. That was eighteen hours ago. *The mark better be up.*

I started, alerted by the sound of movement. Twenty meters in front of us, a dog walked out of an alley. It was a stray, the feral kind that crowded cities across Africa and the Middle East. He stopped and studied us. I reached for a Powerbar, hoping to bribe our way out of this, but my cargo pockets were empty. The dog's curiosity roused, he approached, hair up. My right hand slowly found my knife's handle under the tunic, but Wildman stepped in front, leaned forward, and stared. The dog stopped, ears flattened backward. Wildman moved forward, and the dog trotted off.

"Allahu akbar, allahu akbar, allahu akbar, allahu akbar." The drone of the morning prayers whispered over a loudspeaker. All at once, the call erupted from every corner of the city. One by one, lights turned on. The city was awake.

Keep it together, I told myself.

"Hayya'alas-ṣalāh, hayya'alas-ṣalāh!"

We flipped our weapons' safeties off.

Two more blocks. We double-timed it, running in the shadows.

"There it is," Boon whispered. The small number *42* was chalked on the side of the building. A normal person would take no notice, and it would soon fade in the sun or wash away in the rain. But to us, it was clear.

"That's only a few blocks," I said. Each number corresponded to a prearranged meeting place in the city. Nassib was a member of Mosul's underground resistance, and he was paranoid of the *hisbah*, ISIS's secret police, who were cruel, vicious, and everywhere. Let the CIA have its fancy gadgets. Old-school spy tradecraft, like dead drops and code, never went obsolete.

Using backstreets, we cut our way to our 42: a shuttered Internet café. The first things ISIS did when they took over Mosul, besides convert everyone to Sunni fundamentalism on pain of death, was take over all the bakeries (social control) and cut off access to the Internet.

I gave two knocks. Pause. Three knocks.

A bolt slid open and the door cracked ajar. A bearded face greeted us with a blank smile. Nassib. Before the war, he had been a professor of English. Mosul was a university town, one of the most important in the Muslim world. Now Nassib, like Mosul, was a shell of his former self.

"*As-salamu alaykum*," he said. Peace be unto you.

"*Wa-Alaikum Salaam*," I replied. And unto you peace.

We followed him inside the abandoned café, which smelled of food. I hadn't realized how hungry I was. The room was bare, as our meeting places always were, except for a large platter of rice and lamb on a nice carpet.

"Welcome, friends. Eat!" Nassib said, spreading his hands generously, although he could not hide his nervousness.

We sat cross-legged on the floor and ate, out of both respect and hunger. Next to Nassib were two resistance fighters and a slight, uneasy man. The stranger was young, probably mid-twenties, with the golden complexion of the Arabian Peninsula, an unscarred face, and good teeth. He was dressed in the local style, but he was clearly from the Gulf.

"The prince is not in Mosul," Nassib said. "But this is . . . I'm sorry. No names. This man knew Prince Farhan."

"I am honored," the young man said in English, although his primary emotion was clearly nervousness. "You are well-known here. They fear you as *Zill Almaharib*, Shadow Warrior." I nodded to acknowledge the compliment. "But I know you are kind. You helped a friend of mine last month. Her father was sick, too weak, and . . . notorious to go to the hospital. You carried him out."

The phrases weren't metaphors. We had killed a lot of jihadis in our two months, and I had carried an old man half a klick to our waiting Humvee. He was a scholar, I was told, a world-renowned expert in seventeenth-century Persian poetry. That seemed like something ISIS had no reason to hate, but of course, they hated everything.

"I remember," I said. "How is he?"

"Dead."

"And your friend?"

The man looked at the floor.

"Let no good deed go unrewarded," Nassib said sadly. He had no doubt dragged this young man in to settle his debt to me, even though my efforts had been futile. Maybe Nassib was hoping to settle his own accounts as well. He didn't need to worry. I wasn't keeping a tab.

"Why are you looking for Farhan?" the man asked.

"I'm being paid."

"To bring him home?"

"Probably."

The young man waited. "Do you know his father?"

"No."

"He is a leader in the Kingdom's spy agency, the General Intelligence Directorate. He runs the terrorist capture and interrogation program for the Saudi and American governments."

Secret renditions, I thought. Helping America in its war on terror, one black site at a time. "This isn't about politics," I said. "I'm here to make sure Farhan is safe."

"Oh, I'm sure Farhan is safe. He's a hard man to kill."

"What do you mean?" Wildman asked, piqued by the challenge. I shot him a look that said: *We're not here to kill the prince.*

"Farhan is part of the Emni, ISIS's special forces unit. He saved me."

"Where?"

"In Aleppo, the mother of all battles. I was a foot soldier for ISIS. The Syrian army had us surrounded while helicopters dropped barrel bombs on us. Hundreds were killed, ISIS and civilians alike."

He paused, the memory still painful. Aleppo was Syria's Stalingrad.

"On the third day, the Syrian army charged our position. We had run out of ammunition. We resorted to hand-to-hand combat. Two of my friends were killed. I was shot in the leg. Three Syrian soldiers approached me, one pulled a knife and smiled. Farhan appeared from nowhere, like a ghost. He killed them all. He is not a monster, as some people say. He is a hero. Like you."

I didn't like that comparison. Not at all.

"Where is he now?" Wildman asked.

"I don't know. After the battle, they sent me here, where I . . . saw the error of my ways. I never saw Farhan again. That was a year ago."

I waited. That wasn't enough. Nassib wouldn't risk bringing this spy here for nothing. He knew more.

"Where is he now?"

"They say he was kidnapped by his family and returned to Riyadh," the young man said, "but now he is back in the Caliphate. I heard the military council discussing it yesterday. They offered a reward to all mujahideen fighters."

"A reward? For what?"

"Farhan's head."

Nassib sucked in air between his teeth, and the resistance fighters shifted uncomfortably. Nobody liked to think about beheadings.

"Why is ISIS hunting him?"

"I don't know. Only that he did something *haram*, forbidden, before he was kidnapped. The Shura Council declared him apostate."

A death sentence. "Then why would he come back?"

The stranger looked up at me. "Farhan wasn't alone. He traveled with companions. Rumor has it they were deserting the Caliphate, that they were on the road to Turkey when he was taken. Rumor also has it that his companions are still there, in hiding."

"Where?"

"Sinjar."

Sinjar. I should have known. Sinjar was the final stop on the road to Syria, and a complete shit show. As Kylah had told me, ISIS controlled the town and was waging genocide against the Yazidis who had fled to a mountain nearby, while the Americans pounded the fanatics from the air. Those still in the city were no doubt under siege, starving and desperate.

"I know the city," the older Kurd offered, speaking for the first time. "I have friends there."

This is a bad idea, I thought.

I turned to the stranger. "You know more," I said. "You were one of them."

He nodded. "Yes. For a short while."

"But enough to get you killed if your ISIS contacts knew."

He nodded again. "But also enough to know a place. If Farhan is in Sinjar, you will probably find them there."

I glanced at Boon, who nodded subtly. This was a long chain of trust, but Boon felt confident in it, and Boon had a sixth sense about these things. He had been a Buddhist monk, briefly, plus he had twenty years of battlefield experience. Nothing got past a man like that. Not even, apparently, Kylah.

"Sinjar is dangerous," Nassib said. "It is surrounded by ISIS, and the countryside is crawling with jihadis."

"Good," Wildman muttered, reaching for a piece of goat.

That was it. The three of us had agreed. We were going to Sinjar.

CHAPTER 13

Security at the United States Embassy in Riyadh was tight, but inside, the imposing sandstone building was an oasis. The ceiling beams in the entry plaza cut the sunlight into strips of shadow, and a large central fountain and palm trees provided a soothing counterpoint to the emptiness of the rest of the space. In design, it was a cathedral and a courtyard, with the enormous black metal seal of the United States hanging above the door like a crucifix, adding the right amount of gravitas to what was, after all, one of the most important diplomatic posts in the world.

Brad Winters didn't notice any of it as he strolled past the security checkpoint and fountain to the far door. He rarely took stock of his aesthetic surroundings, and he couldn't have cared less about architecture, except for the architectural underpinnings of power known as the deep state, those subterranean networks of elites that drove world politics. They knew no national borders or allegiances, other than self-service, and were invisible to the casual eye. The deep state was the structural load-bearing points of the international system, and they weren't where most people thought they were.

This building was just such a point. While embassies in general were worthless showpieces, the United States Embassy in Saudi Arabia was an exception. Much of that had to do with the ambassador. Henry Ensher was not a career diplomat but a political appointee and personal friend of the president. The Saudis threw out the last career diplomat, Ambassador Hume

Horan, in the late 1980s, after he delivered some official bad news. They made sure the State Department remembered the lesson and held firm on the moratorium against career ambassadors ever since.

This suited Ensher just fine. He was an American business legend in the Middle East, and he didn't suffer gladly the bureaucratic dithering of Washington. After studying Arabic literature as a hobby in college (his official degree was in Russian), he received a masters at the American University in Beirut and then worked for Saudi Aramco, the huge Saudi state-owned oil company, before becoming an independent deal maker in the region. The Ensher Group had offices in Houston, Washington, DC, and Dubai. When a big oil company needed political leverage in the Gulf, they called him first. When Gulf states wanted to push their agendas through Washington, they retained his firm.

This had made Mr. Ensher a rich and powerful man, with more clout in the region than the secretary of state. He was the most connected player in the Middle East deep state, although he would never use the term "deep state." No one like Ensher ever would. It sounded like a conspiracy. Ensher would merely have said that he had friends and acquaintances, without deigning to name them. That was why the president appointed him ambassador, the Saudis accepted him, and Brad Winters waited in his lobby like a plebeian.

"Winters," a marine barked after a clearly symbolic thirty-minute wait. "Mr. Brad Winters."

Winters stood up and flashed his brown American passport, marked "Official" on the cover. He passed through an additional set of metal detectors, then the marine escorted him to the ambassador's waiting room, where he sat for another ten minutes. Winters and Ensher were professional friends, but Ensher had a thousand professional friends. Winters couldn't pretend to be important. Not to this man. It was an uncomfortable bit of reversal from Winters's normal position in a room, but it was also inspiration. It was good to be reminded there were more rungs to climb.

"Mr. Winters," Ensher said, standing up as Winters entered the large office. "So nice to see you again."

It was a formality, from a legendary formal man. Ensher was the University of Missouri–educated son of a scrap metal dealer from St. Louis, but he had the bearing of British aristocracy, circa 1937. He was svelte and dressed impeccably in a three-piece suit with pocket watch and fob. The outfit looked spectacularly out of place in Saudi Arabia, but then again, he'd dressed that way his entire career, so it wasn't as if Ensher was trying to make a statement. His personal style exuded late British Empire.

They chatted briefly over a finger of Scotch on the rocks—the embassy offering an unofficial reprieve from the strict alcohol policies of the Kingdom—until Ensher apologized and asked why, exactly, Winters had come. The ambassador could cut to the chase with the same imposing grace as the cut of his three-piece suits.

"Yemen," Winters said. "Just giving you a courtesy update."

"And how goes Yemen?" asked the ambassador.

Apollo was two years into a $500 million annual contract, with three more option years, to fight the Shiite Houthi rebels in Yemen. After the debacles in Iraq and Afghanistan, the United States preferred to outsource inconvenient wars of choice, like Yemen, rather than get bogged down. Companies like Apollo offered politicians a new way to wage war without risking political capital or American blood, and business was booming. Military contractors didn't count as "boots on the ground," nor

did the American public care about dead mercenaries. Lawless
cesspools like Yemen courted catastrophe, and mercenary firms
offered clients "plausible deniability" if things went badly. They
often did.

"We have white SOF on the ground, plus eight hunter-killer
teams," Winters said, trying to drown the ambassador in military jargon. "That's in addition to our standard security package
for critical persons and infrastructure protection. But it's a messy
conflict, Henry."

Ensher grunted. Maybe it was the use of his first name? Winters enjoyed these little power plays.

"And what of your other client," Ensher asked with a tang of
disdain. "Prince Abdulaziz? Do you find it difficult to serve two
masters?"

Ensher's reverse power play was not lost on Winters. Apollo
had secretly accepted a contract from Abdulaziz to do the same
work in Yemen as the U.S. contract. By the time the U.S. found
out that Winters was double-dipping, it was too late to cancel
the operation.

His best move was to change the subject. "You don't like him."

"I don't like Yemen. Saudi Arabia's first war of choice since
'sixty-two and a strategic blunder, made worse by our—and
your—complicity." Winters knew Yemen was a rare fight Ensher
had lost in Washington. "We risk being sucked into another war,
and war empowers creatures like Abdulaziz."

And enriches men like me, Winters thought. "He is a bit Ma-
chiavellian, I agree, with an instinct toward overstatement. But
that's one of the reasons you brought me in."

"Indeed," Ensher sighed. The "you" in that sentence referred
to the Department of Defense. Ensher, and most of the diplomatic corps, hadn't agreed to Apollo's involvement. The man
was an icon, but *icon* also means "old." He'd come up in a

time before private military companies were fixtures of modern war.

"Another reason, unofficial of course, was for me to keep an eye on him and the General Intelligence Directorate."

"I don't think so, Mr. Winters. We have spooks for that."

"Then you know about the Paris heist."

"Of course."

"And Istanbul."

"Yes, we know of the incident." Ensher was playing it close to his tailored vest, as any cagey diplomat would.

"What does the CIA think?"

Ensher smiled. "I'm not at liberty."

"I have top secret clearance, level TS/SCI-poly with multiple caveats."

"Not with me."

Time to try a different tact, Winters thought. "I hear the younger son, Farhan, may be back in northern Iraq."

"It is probable," the ambassador said languidly, "and if so, then he's having a time of it. I assume you saw the beheading of the American reporter?"

"I did."

"Ghastly. To turn such violence into public spectacle."

Ensher shook his head, as if spectacle was new, but what about Roman crucifixions in the Colosseum? The guillotine during the French Revolution's Reign of Terror? The black men left swinging from trees by the KKK? Public beheadings in Saudi Arabia, still taking place as they spoke? The only thing new was the video camera and the Internet.

"The boys are giving them hell for it," Ensher continued, sipping Scotch. "Operation Inherent Resolve, $11 million a day of American fury. We're taking it personally." The ambassador's words were fervent but reserved.

"Good. Show some American steel," Winters responded, equally rote.

"We put a $100,000 bounty on the younger son," Ensher added, glancing at Winters, "as I'm sure you know." Winters kept his face blank, although being thought of as a bounty hunter by such a man was tough to take. "He has money, passports, and English. He could prove a great embarrassment for a father with . . . ambition."

"His father insists that he's changed."

"They always do." Ensher meant fathers. Not wayward sons.

"And the other boy? The older brother, Mishaal?"

"A wasted life," Ensher murmured, pulling an antique watch out of a vest pocket by its fob and glancing at the time. It reminded Winters of the white rabbit in *Alice in Wonderland*, right down to the long gold chain and worried expression. It was not meant to be subtle. Ensher didn't care about Abdulaziz and his reverse Oedipal complex.

Time to push, Winters thought. He took a deep breath. That wasn't meant to be subtle, either.

"What if I told you," Winters said, "that Paris and Istanbul were not a coincidence, but are linked? That they were black-ops hits? The Paris abduction was a success, but Istanbul failed. Farhan was meant to be killed, but escaped."

Ensher gave no reaction.

Good, Winters thought. The ambassador would have probably denied such an accusation as preposterous, had the CIA not already briefed him. It confirmed the intel Winters had planted with Larry the day before had made its way here.

"You know what they were after, right?" Winters said.

Ensher didn't fall for the bait. No good diplomat would.

"My sources tell me Mishaal went to the Saudi embassy that

day to pick up a suitcase of cash. But he'd given it to his contact, *before* the heist."

Ensher played along. "What do you think he bought?"

"A metal briefcase," Winters said, knowing this was the point of no return.

Ensher frowned at the joke.

Winters made his face look serious. "It was the control device for a nuclear bomb."

Ensher frowned for real this time. "And Istanbul?"

"Same thing," Winters said. "I think Farhan delivered the cash and received a controller for another nuclear weapon."

"Two nukes?"

"Or two parts, both needed to arm one device."

Ensher sat back. He pursed his lips and tented his fingers in front of his face. He'd clearly heard the theory, no doubt from Larry Fitzhugh and MENA. Now he was having it confirmed by a second source—who just so happened to be the source for the first rumor, too. Operation Curveball.

"What makes you so sure," Ensher asked, "that Paris and Istanbul were about procuring nuclear weapons?"

"I'm not sure. But ten billion in secret funds went somewhere."

Ensher remained motionless, waiting for more. It was one of Winters's favorite tricks, too.

"Diplomacy is a game of leverage, Mr. Ensher. I don't need to tell you that." Ensher nodded, in clear agreement that he didn't need to be told. "Saudi Arabia has never been more isolated. Shia militants threaten them from the north in Iraq and from the south in Yemen. Israel has nukes and Iran is developing them. Many in the Kingdom think the U.S. no longer has their back. So the smart Saudis are focused on leveraging up. It was only a matter of time before they tapped their friends in Pakistan."

Ensher knew the reference, since it was an open secret among the foreign policy illuminati. Decades ago the Saudis gave up their nuclear weapons program in exchange for American security guarantees. However, Saudi Arabia secretly transferred the program to Pakistan on the condition that the Kingdom could buy a nuclear weapon when it wanted one.

"But why buy Pakistani nukes now?" Ensher asked. "We are still honoring our security agreements."

Bingo, Winters thought. Ensher wanted a story. Winters was happy to give him one. "Internal politics," he said.

Ensher blinked. It was as much of a reaction as Winters had ever seen from him. "Are you implying this action was *not* sanctioned by the Saudi government?"

Winters sat back, allowing his silence to convey the gravity of the situation.

Ensher rubbed his thumb on his watch fob, clearly vexed. The secret Saudi-Pakistan nuclear deal was a curse and always had been. Pakistan's lead nuclear physicist, A. Q. Khan, had sold the technology to Libya, North Korea, Iran, and China. Now they all bullied their neighbors. But the world was built on the screwups of the past. That was why he was posted to Riyadh, and that was what made men like Brad Winters, no matter how much he detested them, valuable commodities.

"A private transaction would explain why we haven't heard anything from our sources," Ensher muttered.

Except for me, your best source in Riyadh. Remember that.

"Abdulaziz played this close," Winters agreed, "but not close enough. Someone knew."

Ensher nodded. "Clearly. But who?"

"Prince Khalid." Winters hoped Larry had mentioned that name.

"Khalid? The head of the Kingdom's internal security? Why

not just kill Abdulaziz, if that was the case? Or arrest him, since the end result would be the same?"

"Because Khalid wants the nuclear weapons."

"For himself?"

"For the Wahhabis. For the fanatics. And because if things get messy—and they will when the old king dies—a man with nuclear weapons is the only man that matters."

"Let me get this straight," Ensher said. "You're telling me this is all about secession politics? That Abdulaziz used his intelligence assets to secretly buy nukes from Pakistan for the Sudairi faction of the royal family? And then Khalid used his secret police to steal the weapon controllers for the Wahhabi conservatives? Just so they could blackmail the Kingdom for the throne after the king's death?"

"It's the only thing that makes sense."

Ensher didn't like it. "I don't think Abdulaziz or Khalid would take such risks."

"Now is exactly the moment to take a risk, Ambassador, especially if you are a minor player with major ambitions."

"Something you are familiar with, Mr. Winters," Ensher said.

Winters didn't know if that was a specific or a general observation, but Ensher disabused him of any doubt.

"I know of your misadventure in Ukraine. I know that you went, shall we say, beyond the mission mandate. Threatening the natural gas supply of Europe and the European economy. Tempting war with Putin. Bargaining with senior Russian officials beyond the purview of sanctioned channels."

Winters was irritated by this hypocrisy, given what the Ensher Group did on a daily basis, but he couldn't let it show. "I did what I thought was best to contain Putin," Winters said. "It's certainly more than what the White House has done. I'm still doing it in the gas fields of Azerbaijan and . . . other places."

Those last words were a slip; he should never have divulged Apollo's operations in Eurasia. He was letting Ensher get the best of him, and judging by his smug grin, the ambassador knew it.

"I'm a patriot," Winters said.

Ensher smiled even more. "Is that why you are telling me this?"

"Yes. And because I assume you've been looking into Abdulaziz in light of recent events, and you know about his travels to Islamabad and Gwadar last year."

"So you've suspected for quite some time?"

Yikes, Ensher was good. He was walking him into traps.

"Paris and Istanbul confirmed a few things, yes," Winters admitted, with a show of reluctance. "But Abdulaziz kept the operation tight. Family tight. That's why he sent his sons to do the exchange. You know how much the Saudis value their sons."

"Not that much, apparently," Ensher said. "I hear Mishaal is buried in the south."

"Dead?" Winters couldn't contain his surprise.

"Rehabilitation," Ensher replied.

The ambassador's level of knowledge was high. Larry must have taken yesterday's tip about Abdulaziz and run with it.

"Assuming your theory is correct, Mr. Winters, it leaves one essential question."

"Where are the nukes now?"

"Exactly."

"Probably in transit from Pakistan. By sea. It's easier to smuggle by sea than by air."

"You would know," Ensher said, but Winters refused to be distracted.

"Abdulaziz would not arrange to bring them directly into the Kingdom. Too many eyes and ears on the Saudi coast, especially if Khalid is watching. But there's no border control in the Arabian desert. Hell, Henry, there's no border in the desert. Which brings us back to—"

"Yemen," Ensher said sternly.

"It's not just lawless. It's not just a war zone. *It's Abdulaziz's war.*"

"And you are prosecuting it for him."

Winters smiled. "For *us*, Mr. Ambassador. I'm prosecuting it for us."

Henry Ensher studied the man across from him, a man he realized he had underestimated for most of this conversation. "Do you have proof of any of this?"

"If I had proof, Ambassador, Abdulaziz would be dead already."

The two men stared each other down, one trying to read the other, the other confident he was completely unreadable.

"We'll check it out," the ambassador said finally, rising to signal the meeting was over.

"You know where to reach me," Winters said, extending his hand for a shake. Ensher didn't take it.

"Wonderful to see you again, Henry," Winters grinned. *You smug bastard.*

"Truly, the pleasure is mine," *you pompous bottom feeder,* Ensher beamed back.

CHAPTER 14

"Turn off the Navtex," Goncalves said.

"But Captain . . ." the radio operator began, before remembering that no one argued with the captain, especially on this ship. Even if turning the Navtex off meant they would be incommunicado with the world.

"And the AIS, too," the captain said.

The radio operator complied. It was illegal to turn off the Automatic Identification System transponder, the device that let the authorities track every ship at sea, but the radio operator wasn't surprised by the order. Captain Goncalves was a smuggler. He often ran dark, knowing the ocean was too big and the jurisdiction too dispersed for anyone to notice him.

"Good man," the captain said sarcastically, as he left the compartment.

Capt. Emanuel Goncalves stood on the deck of his freighter and looked out at the Indian Ocean. The *Eleutheria* was an old bulker by today's standards, with rust oozing from its every orifice, but Goncalves loved her like the child his long-dead wife had never been able to conceive. At three hundred feet, she was small enough to navigate almost any port, travel up rivers, and even drop cargo at shorelines, all very handy in his line of work.

It was their second day at sea, and so far the weather had been perfect. For a man like Goncalves, there was nothing better. He was fifty-eight but looked older, with deep wrinkles etched into his face, and he had been on the water since he was eight. Such was life in the Azores, the Portuguese Islands that lie a thousand miles from the nearest landmass. Everyone was a sailor, and sailors craved the open sea.

Freedom, Goncalves thought. Blue horizon in every direction.

Besides, the second day meant they were far enough away that nobody would see them. He had charted a course outside normal shipping lanes, past where the tankers and other ships were visible but not so far to attract unwanted attention. Not that there was anything untoward about this voyage or his ship, of course; they were just one more rust bucket steaming the Arabian Sea.

Goncalves worked his way aft.

"Morning, Captain," said the first mate, a burly Macedonian smoking along the stern railing and watching the white foam of the wake below.

"No one must ever find the *Dona Iluire*," the captain said. The alerts had been coming in all morning over the Navtex before he turned it off. Someone was searching for a cargo vessel, approximately 1,500 gross tons, sailing from Gwadar, Pakistan, heading west by southwest. Their size. Their route.

"We're working on it," the mate said.

"Work faster." They had three days to their next port of call, and a lot of open ocean to cover.

"There's something big going on," the mate said, with a tinge of unease.

"I know," the captain said. Forty years in the smuggling business and he'd never seen anything like this. A full-scale search across thousands of square miles of ocean for a cargo ship that had left port forty-eight hours earlier. Every coast guard cutter and naval frigate had a description on their bridge by now. But why? Who would go to such lengths to find a small freighter?

I've weathered worse storms, the captain thought. Heavy machinery filled his hold, nothing exotic. Inside the hidden compartments were crates of high-end electronic gear, or at least that was what it looked like to him. Nothing unusual, but surprisingly heavy. They took the contraband on in Gwadar and were well paid for their extra discretion, including taking on the name of a sister ship the smuggling company had secretly lost at sea four months ago. Goncalves made a habit of never being inquisitive, but he was worried now. What was he carrying?

A crew member trundled past, dragging a piece of cloth. He lowered the Panamanian flag and hoisted a Malaysian one.

"Just make sure we're clean by sundown," the captain said. The mate nodded and flicked his cigarette into the ocean. The burning butt twisted in the air, falling ten feet a second past two men dangling over the side of the boat on ropes, paint brushes in hand. Only the *e* of the old name, *Dona Iluire,* remained, soon to be obliterated by black paint; only the final *a* was missing from the new name, *Eleutheria.*

Dona Iluire meant "free woman" in Spanish. The new name meant "freedom" in Greek. It was more than a jab at those who wished to haul smugglers to the brig; it was a life's creed for Capt. Emanuel Goncalves and all of those like him. If you couldn't be free of the system in the middle of the open ocean, where could you be free?

CHAPTER 15

"What's our time hack?" Boon asked.

"Thirty minutes to city limits," I said. "*Inshallah.*" It's in God's hands.

We were on the road to Sinjar, driving fast in blackout drive using only the moon and night-vision goggles. It was dangerous, but we made better time that way.

"How long do we stay on the hardball?" Boon asked, meaning the paved highway.

"As long as we can," I answered. "We don't want Farhan to slip by while we're dicking around in the back country."

"Curious, no patrols," Boon said.

"Count your good karma," Wildman answered.

"I don't like it," Boon replied.

I checked his profile as he drove in silence: stiff jaw, high cheekbones, nothing squirrely in the shape of his head. Kylah was right, Boon was a good-looking guy.

"How'd you do it?" I asked. "With Kylah, I mean."

He smiled. "I figured you'd get around to asking."

But he didn't answer. Maybe that was part of his secret. He'd never let on that he was sleeping with Kylah, but it must have been going on for a while. Why had I never noticed? I guess I could have asked for more info. I guess I could have been asking him about his life all these years. But I didn't. Instead, I leaned my head back and watched the moonlit landscape fly by. My mind wandered to Dvořák's "Song to the Moon" from his opera *Rusalka*. A hundred years before Disney's *The Little Mermaid*, Dvořák's mermaid sings a song to the moon, asking it to tell the prince of her love. Things go badly from there. But the aria is like the mermaid herself: beautiful, poignant, and vulnerable. The music makes you want to reach out and grab her, hug her and tell her he's not worth it. Princes can be found everywhere. Your hero is right here, Kylah, staring at the same moon in the same silver-black sky.

The moon winked. Or at least that's what it looked like. I sat up and looked out the bulletproof glass, but all I could see was the distant hills to the north. No lights, no human settlements. Then a shadow blinked across the moon.

"Eyes right," I said.

A minute passed. Nothing.

"Uh, boss, what are we looking for?" It was Wildman.

Good question, I thought. "Stand down. My bad."

Three minutes later, we heard the unmistakable whine of a drone overhead.

"Bogie, ten o'clock!" Wildman yelled.

"Two o'clock!" he yelled seconds later. It was circling us.

"Should I get off the road?" Boon asked, calm as always.

"Too late," I said, cursing my overconfidence. By now, it would have locked its Hellfire missiles on us. If it fired, we'd never know what hit us. There was no way to signal that we weren't ISIS militants, cruising along in stolen American vehicles. Wildman's Jolly Roger on the whip antenna didn't help; it looked like a black ISIS flag, even close up.

"Let's hope we aren't worth it," I said.

"Explains the lack of ISIS on the road," Boon replied.

We held our breaths for a solid minute, keeping our pace while the drone whined overhead. It would be just our luck to be taken out by our own guys, but of course the drone operators wouldn't see it that way. We were off the grid. They'd never figure out who we were, if they even bothered to check.

Eventually the drone whined off to the west, toward Sinjar.

"That's your Buddhist karma," I said to Boon, when it was out of range. "You must have been a hero in a past life."

"I'm not a Buddhist," Boon said.

I looked at him. "What are you talking about?"

"My brother was a Buddhist. A monk. He was burned alive by heroin smugglers. I gave up on Buddha that day."

"But you were a monk, right?"

"I was twelve. An apprentice."

He was serious. I could tell it by the set of his jaw. Buddhism meant something to Boon, and whatever it was, he wasn't a part of it. "So what are you?" I asked.

"I'm a merc," he said.

Twenty minutes of silence later, Boon pointed toward a crag rising against the horizon on our right. It would have good overwatch of the city.

"Roger, let's head there."

We stayed on the highway until the hillock was at one o'clock, then we turned off road. Sinjar's edge was only a kilometer ahead; to the north sat a mountain, long and flat on top, with steep sides. It was by far the largest thing around, so it had to be Mount Sinjar, where the Yazidis were trapped by ISIS. There were seven gray smoke columns near the mountain, barely visible in the purpling morning sky.

Air strikes, I thought. The United States effort was focused in this quadrant.

"Stick to the low ground," I said.

Twenty minutes of creeping later, the morning sun was peeking across the horizon, turning the desert dirt Martian red and throwing long shadows off the rocks. We found a good place to conceal the vehicles, a small but deep saddle with a couple of boulders. The younger Kurds quietly ate their breakfast while

Boon, Wildman, the older Kurd, and I reconned the area on foot.

Good thing. When we topped the rise, we saw Sinjar on the other side of a low, flat plain at the same moment we saw the militants. There were six, sitting below us in a natural shelter in the windward ridge, looking back toward the city. They had rugs spread around them, and they were talking casually as they ate breakfast with their fingers. The way they moved suggested familiarity with the land and each other, as did their peasant garb. If it hadn't been for their AK-47s, they could have been Bedouin.

For a second I thought about sniping them out. We could take all six in two quick rounds, but it would attract attention—and who knew how many other jihadis were hidden among the boulders?

I signaled Boon, Wildman, and the older Kurd to move away from the edge, so that we wouldn't be seen or heard. The jihadis should have posted a guard here. They hadn't. I looked back to make sure the Humvees and Kurds were hidden. They were. I couldn't see any dust tracks leading to this spot from the city side, but I could see other tracks leading to other locations along the rise. No truck in sight. These jihadis hadn't driven up to this lookout. They must have walked. They might have been local shepherds, conscripted into lookout duty. Their AK-47s looked older than me; I wasn't even sure they would fire.

"Not too bad in town," Boon said. He was lying on his stomach and peering through his field glasses.

I flattened myself beside him and peered through my glasses at our objective. Sinjar was just another dingy, impoverished desert town: two-story buildings, brown on brown, no natural or artificial charm. It looked like every other settlement for a thousand klicks around.

Boon was right, there wasn't much movement. ISIS checkpoints sat at main intersections around the city, but many appeared unmanned. Three were smoldering ruins. I looked up and saw two drones circling high above. Boon saw them, too.

"Death from above," he said.

One drone banked sharply and took an attack profile. A Hellfire smoked off its rails and streaked toward the ground. A fireball, black smoke, and then, a few milliseconds later, a loud thunderclap. One less checkpoint.

"I want one of those," Wildman whispered.

Allah's vengeance, I thought. Or, as Boon put it, death from above. The militants below us must have seen it, too. They were jabbering loudly to themselves. When I peeked over the edge, they were packing up their meal. It looked like they were in a hurry.

Above us, the drones veered north and disappeared. Low on fuel, or maybe they hunted at night and always went home at first light.

"Three technicals, moving along the ring road around the city," Boon said, staring through his binos.

"I'm seeing two more checkpoints being set up, nine o'clock position," Wildman said.

"The mice come out when the hawk's away," Boon said, and I had to agree. If we'd been here at night, I might have chanced a dash across the plain. But with no drones, the ISIS lines became active, and I couldn't see a clean way in. In any event, this ridge-line was probably crawling with ISIS.

"We'll have to find another avenue of approach," I whispered. "We'll never get across this plain in daylight without being seen."

"Not our worst problem," the Kurd said.

He pointed south across the desert, and now I understood why the drones and jihadis had left in such a hurry. The morning sky was clear and blue, but a brown smudge was developing in the lower quadrant. I watched it grow, swirling upward and outward an inch at a time. It was a dust storm, headed our way. Fast.

CHAPTER 16

I ran halfway down the ridge toward our Humvees, calculating what needed to be done before the sandstorm hit. The Kurds must have seen the storm coming, too, because they had already dismounted the fifty-cals and removed the whip antennae, sparing them from what was to come.

"Can you lead us in?" I said to the older Kurd, when I was sure we were far enough down for the jihadis not to hear us.

"What?"

"Through the dust storm. Can you lead us?"

"You can't see," he protested. "You can't breathe. It will—"

"We're going. That's not the question. Do you know Sinjar well enough to lead us to your friend once we get there?"

He stared at me for a moment, and I could feel the dust starting to whip up against my skin. He nodded.

"I'm going to calculate the course. Winch the Humvees together," I yelled to Boon over the rising wind, "with the Kurds in front."

I ran to the low point in the ridgeline where the Humvees would crest. The whipped sand was already abrasive, but I pulled out my compass and took a reading on the exact line we'd need to take to hit Sinjar. As I turned to leave, I heard shouting, and I saw one of the jihadis pointing toward me. His comrades looked right at me, then signaled to their friend. He turned and ran the other way, following them toward what must have been shelter.

I turned and ran back to the Humvees. The sky was turning dark with sand as I yanked open the bulletproof door and leapt in beside Wildman, who had taken the wheel. We had half a minute, maybe less, before we'd be blind. I radioed the compass reading to the Kurds, and they started up the slope. They weren't pulling us; Wildman was steering and giving our Humvee gas, but the winch line was short, and it was a lurching ride as the two vehicles fought each other.

"Keep her steady, cowboy," I said.

The storm hit us ten meters from the top of the ridge, turning the air to sandpaper. We had to make it past the boulders while we could still see where they were. After that, it was open country. As long as we stayed relatively on line, and the sandstorm wasn't too strong, we'd make it into Sinjar. We pushed forward as the world collapsed. The light was brightest in front of us, but the light was getting smaller as we drove toward it, the sand rising like the mouth of a million-toothed monster closing from all directions, trying to trap us inside.

"Hell yeah!" I yelled as we hit the top of the hill in a brownout, a hundred decibels of abrasion on the vehicle's skin. If it had been a regular car we would have been airborne, but the Humvee lumbered over the crest like a beast, crushing rocks beneath it, and barreled down into the storm, the sand lashing our windows with a vicious scraping sound.

The Humvee wasn't airtight. There was flying sand inside, and it hurt. I popped my desert goggles over my eyes, then rewrapped my black turban around the rest of my head. The other Humvee was no more than three meters in front of us, but we couldn't see it at all. The biggest danger was ramming them from behind, and we almost did that three or four times, but without the tether, there was no way we'd stay together in the storm.

"You're cut," Boon yelled into my ear above the screaming wind. "Give me your arm." He turned on the Humvee's interior compartment light.

I looked down. I had a slice in my desert camo. Something in the storm, like a sharp rock, must have sliced me as I ran. Boon reached across the Hummer's cramped interior and tore off the sleeve for access, then slathered a disinfectant inside. I could see the gash now, and I felt the pain.

"It's going to need suturing," Boon said.

"Now? You must be joking."

"Afraid not," he said, as he reached for his med kit. Boon had been a surgical medic in the Thai Special Forces, and he'd even graduated the U.S. Army Special Forces 18 Delta course at Fort Bragg. They took a few foreign soldiers each year from partner countries.

He placed a gauze pad over my gash. "Hold that," he shouted as he pulled out a roll of hundred-mile-per-hour tape, known to civilians as duct tape.

"What are you doing?"

"Patching you up," he said, winding the duct tape around my wound, hands oscillating with every bump we hit.

"Bugger!" Wildman yelled, skidding right as a structure reared up suddenly at our six. I didn't remember any structures.

"What is going on, driver?"

"I believe we are in Sinjar, *sir*!" Wildman said in a mock British officer's accent.

The storm had engulfed us so completely. Our headlights were on, but they weren't helping. I couldn't even gauge our speed, except that structures seemed to be rising from the brownout and whipping past us, far too close.

"Bugger," Wildman yelled again, as he clipped a building and sent the Humvee lurching onto two wheels. He hit the ground with a thud, the winch jerking us forward like a water skier at the end of the line, almost smashing me into the windshield.

The storm was clearing. I could see the rear lights of the Kurd's Humvee, weaving in front of us at the end of the tether. They were speeding up and starting to whip us from side to side.

"Take it slow," I yelled into the headset, but they were already rounding a corner too fast, flinging us into a building as Wildman battled for control. We scraped concrete, and the whole vehicle shuddered against the centrifugal force, but Wildman managed to straighten her out.

"Slow down," I yelled into the headset again.

Two blocks on, blue patches started to emerge in the sky, and the wind began to die. I looked at my taped-together arm in the morning light, gave Boon a thumbs-up, and looked back just in time to see a one-story building with an open rolled metal door looming in front of us. We slammed inside at fifty kilometers an hour, Wildman and the Kurds pounding the brakes and fishtailing to a stop a meter from the back wall. Behind us, the barn doors slammed shut, plunging us into darkness.

It was suddenly quiet, except for the sawing of the wind outside. Then I heard the scurrying.

"What is this place?" Boon said. I heard a bullet being chambered and knew it was Wildman.

"Stay calm," I said. I took off my goggles and licked the sand from my teeth. I flexed my arm. The tape was tight, but I could move it in a firefight.

The lights came up. We were in a small warehouse full of bedrolls, water, and other detritus of despair. About thirty people lined the walls, silently staring at us. I counted. Eight of the men were armed.

The older Kurd stepped out of his Humvee. For a moment,

everyone waited, and then a man rushed him. They embraced. The old Kurd began to speak rapidly. Finally, he turned to us.

"It wasn't safe in the Humvees outside," he explained. "They would have marked us immediately, and it would have given this place away. There are . . . religious police. Spies and thugs. They are checking everywhere. I don't know how much longer . . ." He stopped, looked at the man beside him, and gave him a hug.

"Who are they?" I asked.

"Refugees," the Kurd replied. "Kurds and Yazidis. They will be killed if ISIS finds them."

"We have to help them," Boon said.

My first thought was, *No, we don't. That isn't our job.*

But then I thought of something Boon had said to me, back in the African jungle. I couldn't remember where or why, but I remembered his words. We'd been talking about Buddhism, I realized, but why?

Monks are judgment without action, Boon had said. *Soldiers are action without judgment. A mercenary has the privilege and the burden of both.*

As an army officer, I was trained to never question orders, no matter how questionable. A soldier's ethics were never marked by the wars he fought in, only the way he fought them. But now I could pick and choose my missions. Mercenaries have to own their ethics, unlike soldiers. Many didn't give a shit, but I did. Or was trying.

"We'll see what happens," I said, turning to Boon. "We'll make this right, if we can. But right now, I have to take a shit, and then we have a job to do."

It was my old standby. *The job. I'm just doing a job.* Instead of turning away from it, I turned to the old man. "Please tell me they have plumbing in here," I said, but I already knew the answer from the way he was shaking his head.

We followed a Yazidi child through the streets of Sinjar. Our weapons clinked under our Bedouin disguises as we climbed a wall, crawled through a hole, snuck through the ruins of a building, walked a rooftop. It was a child's route to mischief, in more peaceful times. But these weren't peaceful times.

ISIS had swept in, killing the men they encountered, without even the pretense of false conversions. Mass graves marked the center of the city. That was two weeks ago. The killings had moved to the smaller Yazidi villages around Mount Sinjar, leaving the city postapocalyptic. Garbage lined the streets and there was no power, since social services were dead. A burned-out car squatted in an alley; an old woman carried a bucket of water to whatever squalid corner she made home. We avoided her. We avoided the orphans huddled in filth, staring at us with a mixture of hope and disease. I'd been here before: Monrovia, Goma, Bangui, Juba, Gao, and a hundred other places whose names I had forgotten.

"You sure about this?" Wildman asked.

No, I wasn't sure, but what choice did we have?

"The boy knows where to go," our Kurdish guide said, wheezing as he rolled over a wall.

"Be ready," I whispered to Wildman, although I knew it wasn't necessary. In territory like this, we were always ready.

"So, what did you trade for such a little guide?" I asked the Kurd, extending him a hand as we climbed through the remnants of a wrecked market.

He grunted, either from the physical exertion or my question. "I said you will help them escape," he said.

Is that all? I thought, keeping my eyes on the lookout for the ISIS religious police.

We stopped at an intersection, where a homeless man staggered in an advanced state of disrepair, a target of opportunity for the self-righteous. A block farther, a mother was wrapped around two small children in a doorway, but after that it was eight blocks of shuttered buildings and rutting dogs.

The boy stopped and pointed to a local business; it had no sign out front, but the light blue ceramic tile around the door was unmistakable in a town of earth tones. This was the meeting spot given to us by the man in Mosul. A Saudi. An ISIS informant. The Yazidi boy was a safe bet, by comparison.

"Wildman, stay out of sight and guard our six. Keep an eye on the kid. Boon and the old man, with me," I said.

"Foocking 'ell, babysitting?" Wildman groaned. Children were like Wildman repellent, but I needed someone watching our backs, and Boon had a good instinct for people. Also, I'd learned the hard way never to trust children in war zones, because they are creatures of supreme survival. I knew Wildman would never be taken in by this boy's charm.

"Flex-cuff the kid if you have to," I semi-joked, and Wildman's expression perked up. Boon shook his head.

"Ready?"

The old man nodded. We slipped around the corner, opened the door, and entered.

The business was a room, lit only by the sunlight through the door. There was a broken cooler for drinks on one wall, and an empty bin for bread. Four men sat on chairs to the right. I suspected they were armed, but no guns were visible. On the left was a counter and a display of cigarettes, also empty. Cigarettes were illegal in the Caliphate.

"Abu Nadel?" the old Kurd asked the man behind the counter, who looked up in shock. He had been talking rapidly on a mobile phone, but stopped when we entered. Now he looked us over, his eyes stopping at the rifle barrels peeking out from beneath our Bedouin robes. He said a few more words before hanging up.

"Abu Nadel?" I asked this time. It was clearly a code name. The man behind the counter clearly knew the code.

"You are from Mosul?" he asked in English.

"That's me."

His mouth dropped open. "How?"

He obviously knew we were coming—the ISIS informant, no doubt—but hadn't expected us to get here so quickly, or maybe not at all. Good. I wanted him to understand the kind of men he was dealing with.

"You have an answer?" I said. If he'd talked with the man in Mosul, I had to assume he knew what I wanted.

Someone shifted behind me. Abu Nadel—or whatever his name was—glanced over my shoulder at his friends.

"Not yet," he said. "Come back in an hour."

"No."

"What do you mean?"

Instead of answering, I opened my black robe and put my hands on my hips, a few inches from the handles of my Berettas. If the men resisted, a two-hand draw with pistols would be faster in close quarters than swinging an assault rifle. Not that I wanted it that way. I didn't come here to kill anyone. Did I?

Boon followed my lead, as the old man stepped back, out of the direct line of fire.

Abu Nadel didn't flinch, but he didn't bother to stare me down, either. He wrote on a piece of paper and handed it to me. It was an address. "Two o'clock. Lunch. It's the best I can do."

It was. I was sure of it.

"Now you must go," he urged, coming around the counter. "It isn't safe with you here. Naboo," he said (I might have missed the name), "take him to . . . wherever he needs to go."

The old man looked at me, and I nodded. I'd gotten as much as I could expect. I let "Naboo" escort us a few blocks, knowing he was there to make sure we didn't double back and scout the joint. Fine. That was Wildman's job.

Five minutes later, the Welsh merc showed up at the appointed rendezvous without the kid. "Did you track them?" I asked.

Wildman shook his head. "Four men came out as soon as you left. They scattered like cockroaches. I picked the wrong one to follow."

Damn. They were smart. They had to be, I suppose, to have survived this long.

"The kid?"

Wildman shrugged. "He was slowing me down."

"No worries," I said, feeling worried. "We have an address."

Wildman spit into the dust. "Sounds like a stakeout."

It was 0900, and already scalding. Iraq in August was an oven. "Let's head back to the hideout and get some rack," I said. "It's five hours until our meet at 1400."

A lot could happen in five hours. A lot could happen in a lot less time than that.

CHAPTER 18

Jase Campbell leaned back on the hood of his Viper and drank water from his canteen. Murphy, his second, was dipping Copenhagen and spitting over the side, looking for a varmint to hit. Campbell had been straight-edge since the age of seventeen. He didn't drink alcohol or smoke, avoided over-the-counter drugs, and didn't touch coffee. If he needed a quick pick-me-up, he chugged a Red Bull or a Rip It energy drink. But he preferred action to sugar, caffeine, and artificial color.

"I don't like it," he said.

"I agree," Murphy replied.

They had been watching the road into Mosul since first light, with both their binos and their unarmed spy drone. Campbell thought of the drone along the same lines as energy drinks: nice enhancement, but no substitute for the real thing. Technology would never replace human judgment or instinct.

An hour ago, the traffic was light. Now the road was jammed with cars, and security was heavy. Vehicles were being stopped and searched at a checkpoint. Sizable groups of militants were congregating near a large mosque, where they figured the United States wouldn't bomb. His instincts said something was happening; ISIS was paying attention. Campbell hadn't fought ISIS, but he'd fought plenty of other Arab militias. They never paid attention. He'd have to rethink his strategy.

"Something's coming from the west," Campbell said. "ISIS is watching. If our boy made it this far, we could be fuzucked."

"You think he's the reason for the roundup?"

"Doubt it. I think something's going on. I think if the SOB is coming this way, it's because of this shitstorm, not the reason for it."

"Probably," Murphy said. Jase Campbell had strong opinions. The kind that gave a man the confidence to lead eleven human beings into the line of fire, or to get a python tattooed around his neck like a tourniquet. But he had good instincts, and he never risked a life unnecessarily. Murphy knew it was best to keep his opinions to himself and trust his leader. Unless it was important.

Campbell was playing with his knife, tossing it in the air and catching it different ways, always a bad sign. The boss didn't like waiting on intel from the boys back at Apollo HQ in Falls Church, Virginia. Murphy knew exactly what his CO was thinking: *We're the hammer, goddammit, find a nail.*

The knife began to pick up velocity, until Campbell caught it with finality. "I say we head down the road, raise some ruckus, see what we can stir up. That way, we'll meet the SOB on our terms."

Murphy spat. He figured he knew what was coming.

"I'm done standing around here with our dicks in our hands," Campbell said. "We're wasting daylight."

Murphy spat one more time, then rolled off the Viper to his feet. He knew Jase Campbell. He knew how much the man loved this region. Not like one of the residents, whose families had been here for centuries, but like someone who had given the best years of his life to this patch of sand, and who died a little inside when he watched it go to shit after he was gone. That was why Jase was here, because Apollo Outcomes was his ticket back to the fight. And he was itching to get wet.

But he was no butter bar hothead. And no fool. Jase Campbell knew what he was doing, and Luke Murphy was going to follow him, no matter how inconvenient the man's moods, or how unnerving his neck tattoo.

"Mount up," he yelled to the team. "We're moving out."

CHAPTER 19

"Nothing," I said, taking the binoculars from my eyes.

We were on the roof of a building down the block from the address Abu Nadel had given me for the lunch meeting. It had only one entrance and one window, covered by a closed wooden shutter. Nobody had gone into or out of the building in the past half hour, and we had only fifteen minutes to go before the meeting.

"Agreed," Boon said. "It's quiet."

"Too quiet?"

He smiled. "That's what they say in the movies."

Boon and I had been making small talk since we got on this roof. It wasn't mission protocol, perhaps, but it distracted us from the baking sun. Like all men in our business, we never talked about combat or childhood or anything personal like that. Those topics were dangerous. We only had two safe topics: the future and the opposite sex. I'd been avoiding the second, but it was eating at me and, eventually, curiosity kills cats.

"So how'd it happen?" I asked, without taking my eyes from the door down the block. He knew what I meant, but I knew he'd make me spell it out. "How did you and Kylah get together?"

Boon took a long time to answer. "Remember that night you passed out at the T-Top?"

Not particularly, but I guess that was the nature of my affliction. I'd been on a steady skid in those early weeks in Erbil, beating myself up over everything I had and hadn't done. I guess that's what happens when a man like me stops running and takes the time to think. That night, falling apart like that in public, had snapped me out of my slide.

"Wildman had disappeared, so Kylah and I took you home. Put you to bed. We talked." He wasn't looking at me. He was eyeing the meeting point. "It was pretty inevitable after that."

I didn't say anything. I was starting to see how I must have looked to Kylah in those first few weeks. And to Boon.

"She was just killing time, Locke, until the right thing comes along." He paused. "Just like the rest of us."

I thought of what Kylah had said, about Boon being a damn dirty Buddhist in bed. I couldn't help myself.

"What was she like?"

Boon smiled and shook his head, and for a while I thought he wasn't going to answer. Finally, he said, "A long time ago, I knew a woman in Chiang Mai. I was just out of jump school. She was older, rich, maybe married. She called me *chawna*—peasant. She was always laughing, especially when I ran my tongue up and down the back of her neck, and afterward, she would lie back and tell me to do whatever I wanted, as long as I did it very slowly, and it pleased her. I still remember the smell of her *khao soi Mae Sai*. And the taste. Salty and spicy and slick."

"And that's what it was like with Kylah?"

"No," Boon said. "It wasn't exactly the opposite of that."

I stared at Abu Nadel's meeting place across the street, not sure what to say. Boon was a weird dude.

Finally, he broke the silence. "Do you remember that brothel in Sudan?"

I knew the one he meant. It had been a hard week, one of the hardest of my life. We'd gotten into a firefight with a separatist army and another outfit hired by an oil company. Some of the fighters were no more than boys, barefoot, carrying knives and rocks. We'd done what we had to do and Jimmy Miles, ever vigilant to our moods, thought we needed some R&R.

"I remember the woman you chose," I said. She was dark, black, and huge. Not fat, but tall. She towered over Boon. It seemed like an odd choice at the time, and still did.

Boon nodded. His eye was to his riflescope. "A woman stepped out of the enemy position," he said. "She was almost naked, just beads . . . necklaces . . . but she seemed important. She didn't come toward us. She just stared at me. Into me. You understand."

"You shot her," I said. "Was she the first woman you ever killed?"

"No."

I wasn't surprised. Americans thought of Thailand as an exotic beach, but it had a violent side. Boon did two tours in the special forces as part of Narathiwat Task Force 32, fighting the Runda Kumpulan Kecil, known as the RKK, a ruthless Islamic terrorist group that murdered Buddhist monks collecting alms and villagers going about their work. They killed schoolteachers, politicians, and civil servants. They torched schools simply because they flew a Thai flag. Boon was no sheltered innocent. I knew the world.

"She was the one," he said. "After all the others, she was the one who got to me. And that woman, at the brothel . . ." Reminded him of her. I knew that feeling. Of course I did. It was natural, but dangerous. It needed to be killed away.

"I cried the whole hour I was in the room."

I didn't know what to say. It was the most open Boon had ever been with me. I suspected it was the most open he'd ever been with anyone. Why me? Why now, on a scalding-hot rooftop in northern Iraq?

"Do you remember your choice?" he asked.

That surprised me. "I do," I said tentatively.

"Me too. That's why I stay with you," he said.

I hadn't slept with a woman that night. I had bought something far more profound and dangerous: a solo concert from an older woman, sung in the Dinka style. The music had been outlawed in 1989, when Islamists took over the country. I had paid far more for the song than Boon had paid for his hour, but maybe the music had been redemption for us both. Until that moment, I didn't even realize he had heard it.

"Chiang Mai, huh?" I said, thinking back to his earlier story. "I spent time there."

Boon put down his binos. I guess he wanted to see me clearly, or maybe I'd finally surprised him. "No shit. When?"

"Between high school and college. I took a year off, to do a solo walkabout around the world. I spent a summer as a novice at the Buddhist monastery there, teaching English and seeking enlightenment."

"What happened?"

"My visa expired."

"*Farang*"—white foreigner—Boon chuckled. My enlightenment had been lost to paperwork, what could be more *farang* than that?

"I tasted my share of *khao soi Mae Sai* while I was there, though. It's quite spicy, if I remember correctly."

Boon nodded. "It's my favorite soup. But only if you get it in Chiang Mai. They don't know how to make it right down south."

I took a drink of water and wiped sweat with my head scarf. The roof was a sweatbox, no shade.

"I don't think this is the place," I said. "I think Abu Nadel gave us the first address he could think of. He isn't coming back, or if he is, he's taking us somewhere else."

"Odds are better it's a trap," Boon said.

"Why do you say that?" I asked, watching the empty building.

Boon shrugged. "Because if I think that and I'm wrong, it won't kill me. If I think the other way . . ."

Wildman's head popped up above the edge of the meeting site. He looked around, then back toward us. I gave a thumbs-up: coast is clear. He worked quickly, taping loops of detonation cord and blocks of C-4 to key points of the building. We didn't have as many supplies since leaving Apollo, but we had plenty of C-4 and det cord. Wildman made sure of that.

Boon was right: better safe than sorry. That was why I'd sent Wildman down with the explosives and remote detonators. If I was going to be walking into an ambush, and I very well might be, I wanted to make sure someone was ready to blast me out.

Or blast us all.

CHAPTER 20

Nothing, Mishaal thought as he watched the attendant in his heavy thawb approach down the long hallway. *I want nothing. I am nothing.*

He was an inmate at the al Ha'ir prison south of Riyadh. It was the Kingdom's primary detention facility and recovery center for addictions, whether to drugs or terrorism. The conjugal-visit wing felt like a boutique hotel, if you ignored the narrow windows and high walls. Most rooms each had an en suite bathroom and a big-screen TV, a king-size bed and shiny wallpaper. Only the Saudis deradicalize vicious terrorists with opulence, as if hedonism was a cure-all.

Opulence for everyone, that is, except Mishaal. Abdulaziz wanted his son punished and broken—the "old way," he had said. Mishaal's universe consisted of a cot, a lavatory, the Koran, and a prayer rug.

In the beginning he had lain on the floor, screaming from withdrawal. He had shat himself and drooled. His attendant had come. The prince had seen the man's sandals from his prostrate position on the floor. He had reached for the man, anticipating relief, but the attendant had beaten him and left him lying in a pool of blood-streaked retch.

It had gone on like that for two days, alternating between sickness and beatings, until he had begun to forget who he was and where he was. Eventually, the room had gone dark, and he had slept. Later, he had hauled himself to a sitting position. He drank water straight from the sink, only to vomit it back. Then they beat him again.

Now he cowered, recoiling as he listened to the footsteps coming down the corridor.

"Get up," said the attendant.

The prince didn't rise. He stayed on his prayer rug, his head bowed to the west, toward Mecca. He tried not to look at the man's feet, only a few inches away. He had the impression, somehow, that the prayer rug was a safe zone, that they wouldn't beat him here.

"Get up," the attendant said again. But the prince didn't rise.

"You are a disgrace."

The prince didn't argue. He could feel disgrace leaking out of every pore of his body. He could no longer defy his father. He could not be anyone but who the old man wanted him to be. The other path was too painful, and he feared pain most of all.

"You shame our world." The man stepped forward, and Mishaal expected to be kicked again. He flinched, as he had flinched from his father when he was a boy.

Instead Mishaal felt the prick of the needle in his neck, then the relief as the heroin flooded his body.

"*Shukraan*," he whispered. Thank you. "*Shukraan. Allahu Akbar. Allahu Akbar.*" God is good.

He heard the attendant—the cleric—scoff. He felt the man's hot breath an inch from his ear. "The first one is free."

The feet started to retreat, and Mishaal knew this was not an attendant but a messenger. *Allahu Akbar. Allahu Akbar.* Thank God.

At 1355, to my surprise, Abu Nadel arrived. He came quickly up the street with four bodyguards, all dressed in local fashion, sandals and Kalashnikovs. Two hustled inside without hesitating. The other two remained outside, standing casually, holding their AK-47s. It was a sorry display.

"I have a bead on the front door," Boon said, aiming through his Dragunov sniper rifle. "These two . . . they won't know what hit them."

I waited, watching the entrance. No one else came. At 1405, I made my way down to the street. There was no need to give Boon and Wildman instructions; they were used to covering me during arms negotiations and strategy talks. My headset was in clear view, letting Abu Nadel know I was in contact with my team. If he tried to take the headset, I wouldn't let him. Boon and Wildman needed to hear the conversation. Long ago we had worked out code words that I would slip into the conversation: *naturally* meant "yes"; *okay* meant "no"; *perhaps* meant "everything is fine"; *interesting* meant "I need help."

"Good luck," Wildman said over the headset, as I did a functions check on my SCAR. I made sure my holsters were loose, for a quick draw. Walking into a blind meeting with armed men in a small space with no backup was foolish, but our options were limited. I could have taken Boon or Wildman with me, but being ambushed outside was a bigger threat. For all we knew, Abu Nadel, or whatever his name was, had sold us out to ISIS.

"You sure he's worth it?" Boon asked over my earpiece.

"It's okay," I responded, meaning *no*. It was a question that had been on my mind, too. "But what's life without risks?"

I walked across the street and entered the building. Two guards were inside the door, where passersby wouldn't notice them. They walked me to the second floor, one ahead and the other behind, weapons drawn. Abu Nadel was waiting cross-legged on the floor with guards standing on either side of him. They were wearing black robes and turbans that covered their faces, like ISIS, and holding AK-47s.

I hesitated, an involuntary tell. Where had the additional men come from? There was no other door. They must have been here all along. But why hadn't Wildman seen them when he was setting the explosives?

Abu smiled, then motioned me forward. A rifle in the back convinced me it was a good idea.

"It is a good thing to be underestimated," he said in English. He was right, but the line was rehearsed. It was meant to show his confidence, but unfortunately for him, everything else gave him away. The nervous energy in the room. The way the guards kept glancing at each other, instead of watching me. Terrorists thrived on overconfidence; it was the best way to bend sacrificial lambs to a twisted worldview. Abu Nadel couldn't pull it off. He was sweating like a horse. The room was hot, but not that hot. The man was out of his depth. I didn't know yet if that was a good or a dangerous thing.

"You surprised me this morning," he said, when I had settled across from him with my legs crossed. It was the local custom, and it provided access to my boot knife. Sometimes you bowed in wonder to the god of small things. Sometimes you planned them.

"Yes," I said. "Now you know who you are dealing with."

"A small team," he replied. "Two Humvees, seven men. Good for stealth and speed, but lacking firepower. I know you have explosives on the roof and a sniper on the door. They are listening now. But you cannot kill your way out of this situation. You have no hope of leaving this city without my permission."

Impressive. He must have had eyes everywhere. Wildman hummed Darth Vader's Imperial Death March over the headset. Not helping.

"Perhaps," I said, signaling to Boon and Wildman that everything was okay. "But you are fearful."

He didn't deny it. "And yet we both came. Why?"

I shrugged. "Because we each have something the other wants."

Abu Nadel flicked his right index finger. A woman appeared in the doorway carrying a tea tray. She was covered in a head-to-toe burka with only a narrow slit for the eyes, the type favored by ultrareligious Muslims so that no visible skin would tempt men to corruption. A second woman, dressed the same way but quite overweight, followed with two platters of sweets. A man followed in black ISIS robes, no doubt the guard that pressed these locals into service.

So many people, and they hadn't entered from the outside. Boon and Wildman would have seen them and alerted me through the earpiece.

"Decadent," I said, as the first woman poured the tea, arcing it high into each glass, then pouring each glass back into the kettle. She repeated this cycle several times with mesmerizing skill. The cookies were fancy and fresh, made in a bakery. People were starving on the streets yet here were confections of indulgence. Abu Nadel was messaging me: This was his turf. Sinjar was in a desperate situation, he was not.

"I have heard of your reputation. They call you *Zill Almaharib*, but we both know you are just a paid assassin. That you can be hired to do almost anything."

When I was at Apollo Outcomes, I would have barely registered the insult, but now the truth hurt. Was I still that man?

"Are you okay?" Boon whispered, inaudible to those in the room. He sensed my hesitancy.

"Naturally I stand by my reputation," I said to Nadel. *Yes, I'm fine.*

"I have heard you kill the servants of the Caliphate."

No use lying. "When I have to. I don't believe in unnecessary violence."

One of the guards shifted uneasily. Did he understand our conversation, or was he reacting to Abu Nadel's surprise? "But you are an assassin."

"Assassin, soldier, terrorist . . . humanitarian. They are different names for the same thing, depending on your point of view."

Abu Nadel licked his lips. He was nervous. "You would have me believe that you fight for a better world?"

I wasn't sure, but I gave him what he wanted. "Yes."

"You are lying. You are a soldier for hire."

"I choose my own jobs and my own causes."

"Then why are you looking for the prince?"

I hesitated. There was only one answer: He was my ticket out. I wanted a new life, and that required money.

Abu Nadel must have read it on my face. "How much are you being paid?"

"One million dollars on delivery."

"Alive or dead?"

"Alive. Do you think a father would pay a million dollars for his son's corpse?"

"Yes," Abu Nadel said.

I let the comment slide. There were too many possible motivations for such a statement. "Do you know where the prince is?"

Silence.

"Where is your master?"

"I am asking the questions," Nadel said harshly.

I laughed. Harshness wasn't his natural disposition. It was a robe he put on to survive in ISIS territory, or a habit he learned from his fellow holy warriors. The rough fit only made him more dangerous. He could shoot me in the face out of weakness, just to prove he was strong. One of the guards stiffened at my laughter, finger on trigger. I needed to cool the situation's temperature.

"Fine," I said, picking up my tea. I had no intention of drinking it until I saw Abu Nadel take a good sip. "But you don't have to be so serious. I am trying to help him, not kill him. Assassins don't negotiate."

Nadel took his tea without looking at the server. It was as if the woman wasn't even there. "You don't think ours is a worthy cause?"

"No," I said flatly.

"Uh, Locke." Boon's voice in my ear. "Don't pick a fight."

"You don't think this town is worth anything?"

"It's worth a great deal," I said, "to the people who live here. But Farhan doesn't live here."

"This is our home. These are our people. We take care of them."

"Saudi Arabia is your home," I said. Abu Nadel, or whatever his real name, blinked but said nothing. I didn't need him to confirm that, like the young man in Mosul, he had come to Iraq from the Gulf States. It was obvious.

"The world is our home," he said slowly. "All people need saving."

"This thing with ISIS or Daesh or the Caliphate or whatever you call yourselves . . . it's not going to end well for you. A better world built on blood? Conversion by the sword? Piety through crucifixion? Surely you see the folly of your crusade."

He slammed his fist down, catching the edge of the cookie platter and sending a squadron of sweets through the air. The trigger-happy guard shouted, lunging for me. Before I could dodge, he jammed his AK-47 barrel into the side of my head, tilting me over. Reflexively, my hand pulled my Beretta and shoved it up to his balls, thumb cocking the weapon's hammer. The other guard shouted at him in Arabic, telling him to stand down.

Abu Nadel held up his hand for silence. The gunman and I froze: his AK-47 barrel against my temple and my Beretta in his crotch. Tea poured out of the overturned glass, a dark stain on the carpet, spreading toward me. The gunman spit on my face but backed off, his rifle still trained on my head. I lowered my Beretta and sat upright, wiping the saliva off my cheek.

"You okay?" It was Boon over my earpiece.

"Give us the word and we'll send those buggers straight to Allah," Wildman said. I knew his finger was on the detonator trigger. I closed my eyes and considered my next words carefully, since they might be my last.

"Perhaps," I began (*I'm fine. I'm in control.*), "you could tell the prince I come in peace, but that I need to see him at once. His life is in danger. Other men will come who are less . . . deferential."

"I will pass along the message."

"No," I said, reaching for a cookie in a show of exaggerated calm, "you will tell him now, since he is here."

CHAPTER 22

Silence, except for the sharp intake of Boon's breath in my ear. Then Wildman whispered, "You're fucking me."

I waited, watching the room. Everyone looked so tense that I couldn't help but smile. Chords played in my head, Gottschalk's "A Night in the Tropics," an orchestra tangoing with itself. I'd guessed right, that much was clear, and the infectious swooping rhythm of the notes were the sound of my happiness, but also my caution. Gottschalk, a nineteenth-century Cajun pianist who took Europe by storm, died at forty in the Empire of Brazil, at the height of his powers.

I popped a cookie into my mouth, to show that I was at ease. It was truly delicious, surprisingly so. It tasted like marzipan, with a soft center, baked within the last few hours. If I closed my eyes, I could taste belle époque Paris on a balmy midsummer's evening. But I wasn't about to close my eyes. Not even to blink.

"Good, right?" It was the guard on Abu Nadel's right.

"Absolutely," I said, tossing another one in my mouth, as the prince removed his turban and black robes and sat cross-legged across from me, as if this were merely a casual business meeting. I wasn't fooled by his ease. The tension hadn't left the room.

"Abu Nadel, as you call him, was once a baker in Aleppo. He has laid in quite a stash of supplies."

"My compliments to the chef," I said. "But surely he didn't bake these for me? He didn't have time."

"No," Farhan said. "You're right. He didn't bake them for you."

Farhan did not look like a Saudi princeling but rather an Army Ranger. He was over six feet tall and stacked. His beard had the dark black of a man in his twenties, yet his eyes watched me like a man double that age.

"I hope you know what you're doing," Wildman said over my earpiece. He didn't need to see the prince to know he was part of our world. He could hear it in his voice.

I started to respond in code that I was fine. Then I noticed. Farhan wasn't eating. I put down my third cookie, hoping the food wasn't poisoned.

The prince chuckled. "The sweets are fine, but I won't eat while others go hungry, even though this extravagance was prepared to celebrate my return."

Poor Abu Nadel, I thought, *to have his great gift spoiled.* "You recently arrived?"

"In the night, hours before you. The road was more dangerous than I anticipated."

And it was only getting worse.

"Why?" I said, shoveling in another sweet. I hadn't realized how hungry I was.

"Why return?"

"No. Why grow that hideous beard?"

Farhan smiled with ease. "I came to Syria nearly two years ago. There were twenty of us then, old friends, mostly sons of the men who worked for my father. We would gather at our madrassa in Riyadh. One Friday after prayers we met a man our age, a boy, really. He had grown up in Homs, Syria, but fled the Shiites. The situation, he said, was very bad. Civilians being gunned down in the street, children starving. People burned alive."

"Assad is ruthless."

"That night, all twenty of us declared jihad to save our brothers.

It was easy to find sponsorship in the Kingdom. A week later, we were fighting in the Farouq Brigades." He paused, but he didn't look away. "A month later, only three of us remained.

"That's when Abu Muhammad al-Adnani found me. He commanded the Emni, the ISIS special forces. He told me I was God's chosen."

I had heard of the Emni, but thought it was battlefield legend.

"The next day I was driven to Adnani's camp in the desert outside Raqqa. There were a dozen recruits: Moroccans, Egyptians, a Tunisian, an Indonesian, two Germans, a Canadian, a Belgian, and a man from Virginia. They dropped us off in the middle of nowhere and told us, 'We are here.' We thought to ourselves, 'What's going on?' When I looked more closely, I realized there were cave dwellings around us. Everything aboveground was painted with mud and invisible to drones. Each dwelling received two cups of water a day. The purpose was to test us."

He reached for a glass of water.

"Then the training began: hours of running, jumping, push-ups, parallel bars, crawling. By the second week, we were each given an AK-47 and told to sleep with it between our legs until it became like a third arm. One day during training, the Tunisian collapsed from exhaustion. They beat him, but he could not stand. So they tied him to a pole in the desert and left him there. We never returned."

Savages, I thought.

"We were sent to Aleppo, where I killed many enemies of the Caliphate. But I came to realize that the jihad was a farce, and I a murderer."

A guard put a hand on his shoulder in sympathy. Farhan didn't flinch. He hadn't looked away. He was testing me, like the desert had tested him.

"I fled, knowing the punishment was death. Outside of Aleppo, I ran into a group of refugees. They cried and begged me to spare their lives, as if I were a monster. I helped them."

I nodded. I knew that transition. I had made it myself. But I'd never been a monster. Right?

"We moved northeast, sprinting and crawling toward Turkey and freedom. We were ambushed. I tried to fight our attackers off, but they were too many. Most of the refugees were slaughtered. When I awoke three days later, I was chained to a bed in a Riyadh cell, my father standing over me. Six months, I played the dutiful son, but I thought only of the friends I had abandoned here."

I nodded again. I knew that feeling, too, that you'd abandoned the only things that mattered in your life. "You came to fight?"

"I came to rescue them."

"Then call your father." I handed him my sat phone.

"You don't know my father."

"It's the only way."

"My father is head of Saudi intelligence, black-ops division," Farhan said. He was watching for my reaction. I didn't have one. "He is a killer."

"He wouldn't offer a million dollars to have you back, alive, if he didn't care."

The prince scoffed. "A million dollars is nothing to my father. I had a second cousin who went on a $20 million Paris shopping spree and skipped out on the bill. Her second uncle paid her debts to preserve the family name. The year before I left, my father spent $100,000 in bribes to get our family slaves travel visas into the EU. Yes, I said slaves. Are you surprised? Rafik"—he motioned toward the baker—"was born a slave. His family has served us for generations. It is the Saudi way."

"Call your father."

"He will kill her."

"Who?"

Silence. For the first time, Farhan glanced away.

"Who will your father kill?"

"His wife," a voice said from behind me, and I turned to see a beautiful young woman with feline eyes, a delicately hooked nose, and a cascade of black hair.

"You're Iranian," I said, before I could stop myself. Iranians were Persian, not Arabic, and like all ethnicities, they had distinctive features, if you knew what to look for.

"I'm American," she said. "From Los Angeles."

She had a modern woman's attitude about her social place. But even more important, she had a very swollen belly.

"How long?" I asked.

"One week, if I make it full term."

Farhan was staring at me again. He seemed to think this was a superpower. It was growing tiresome. "Will you help us?" he asked.

"Your father won't kill her. Not if she's carrying your child."

"That's why he'll kill her," Farhan said.

"How can you say such a thing?"

"Because he's already tried. The men who ambushed us on the road to Turkey weren't ISIS. They were working for my father."

I didn't believe it. "Are you sure?"

Farhan nodded. "My father's majordomo was with them. He was directing them. I saw him on the battlefield, and I recognized his white suit. Even in the dirt, he always wears a white suit." My heart sank. Farhan must have seen it falling down my chest. "You know him?"

I nodded.

"He hired you?"

"Worse," I said. "I called him two hours ago. He's on his way."

CHAPTER 23

The ISIS militant's torso exploded, flinging viscera at the Iraqi army prisoners lined up against the wall. Milliseconds later, a loud *thunderclap* echoed in the valley. The prisoners flinched and waited, their eyes still closed. They thought the executions had begun.

The next shot hit the second jihadist's center mass, pulping his insides. The carcass thumped to the ground.

The other militants spun around, looking for the source of the gunfire. Some of the prisoners opened their eyes, wondering why they were alive. Others waited, holding their breath. The lead jihadist started barking instructions, but his head exploded, followed by another *thunderclap*.

The militants ran for their Humvees, forgetting they had guns. Forgetting they could have gone ahead and shot all the prisoners, since it would have taken only a few seconds more. They were hardened fighters, but the explosion of their commander's head had terrified them as nothing else had in the last two years.

The ISIS trucks kicked up stone as they accelerated away from the execution area and down the mountainside. The lead truck blew up first. A second later, the next two blew up, not from a single-source explosion, like a tank round, but simultaneous multiple explosions. The last two Humvees were shredded, their armor plating perforated like tin foil. The trail vehicle rolled off the ridge ledge on fire, tumbling end over end until it hit the valley floor and exploded.

"Hoo-AH!" Jase Campbell yelled, assessing the battle damage through his binoculars. "Good snipering, Black Jack. Way to move them down off that ridgeline into range of our heavy weapons."

"Roger that," Black Jack said flatly, as he heaved his fifty-cal sniper rifle off its bipod. He didn't look toward the men he had killed. They were gone. On to the next job.

"Fucktards," Campbell said, as he watched the prisoners scamper off, some looking to the sky in thanks. "They think Allah saved their sorry asses."

"When it was the mighty hand of God," Murphy said.

"Don't I know it."

Campbell watched the prisoners scatter. He had mixed feelings. He wasn't sure they wouldn't be trying to kill him and his fellow Americans six weeks, six months, six years from now. But at this moment, they were allies. Sort of.

"Let's move out!" he bellowed. The three Vipers peeled off the landscape as if they were a part of it, their camouflage so effective, and made their way down the ridge to the kill site. As they approached, Campbell saw a militant injured and struggling.

"Halt," he said. He stepped out and shot the man in the chest, then head. That's what he liked about being private sector: sensible rules of engagement. That terrorist could have been wearing a suicide vest, to be detonated as a final act of religious nihilism. Campbell doubted it. Most of these militants were armed with old rusty Kalashnikovs. But you could never be too sure.

"All clear?" he asked the team, as he stared down at the dead man.

"All clear," they confirmed, one after another.

He checked the sun. It was high. His watch read 1500.

A ring tone sounded in his earpiece. The timing of those office jockeys was always exquisite. It was like they were watching, Campbell thought, although he knew they weren't. That was another reason he liked this job.

"Falcon Six, over." Ten seconds later he nodded. "Wilco," he replied and hung up.

"Command?" Murphy asked, striding through the carnage.

"Fun's over," Campbell said. "Duty calls."

"Operation Urgent Vigilance," Colonel Brooks said in his briefing voice. Forty officers and a handful of NCOs crammed into the briefing room in the Tampa, Florida, headquarters of the U.S. military's Central Command (CENTCOM). Large monitors hung on the walls, streaming in more briefing rooms from U.S. embassies and bases around the Middle East, making the total audience closer to 120.

"This is a flash mission," Brooks continued, "and a top NSC priority."

Pressed against a back wall was Andrea Lewis. She was the only woman in the room, and the youngest person, at thirty, by far. Dressed in tailored navy blue pants and a lavender blouse, she looked like a business executive. No one would have guessed she was a West Pointer with two combat tours in Iraq with U.S. Army Intelligence. Now she was a contractor with Booz Allen Hamilton, doing intel work at CENTCOM. Her husband was Special Forces, and they decided both couldn't be in the military with two small kids. They knew too many army couples who had to leave their children with grandparents for fifteen-month tours, again and again. It was no way to raise a family, she thought, and she resigned her commission. Jack, her husband, was currently in Afghanistan for six months.

"Defense Intelligence Agency," Brooks continued, "has un-confirmed intel that a freighter left Pakistan a little over forty-eight hours ago. It may be carrying nuclear weapons. Destination is believed to be Yemen, possibly al Qaeda in the Arabian Peninsula, or an affiliate."

The officer next to Lewis let out a small gasp. This was a nightmare scenario they had war-gamed but hoped would never happen. Not all the planning exercises had happy endings.

"We're looking for a group-three freighter, aft pilothouse, somewhere between Karachi and Yemen."

Hell, Lewis thought. That's like looking for one specific pickup truck in Texas. She hoped they had a license plate number.

"We don't know the ship's name or flag, and can assume the crew already changed them at sea since leaving their last port of call."

Damn.

"Also, we can assume they switched off their AIS tracking device. In other words, they've gone dark."

Double damn.

She eyeballed the map. Yemen had about 1,200 miles of coastline, almost as much as the United States eastern seaboard.

"CENTCOM is scrambling every available asset. Our job is to corroborate the intelligence so we don't end up on a wild goose chase. We're retasking satellites to cover the AOR. CIA operatives are on the ground in Pakistani ports, searching for details."

Hoping to get lucky, more like it, Lewis thought. An operation like this was no doubt locked down. But not watertight. She wondered how it had sprung the leak that brought them all here. Somebody out there was in for a life-changing reward . . . if this whole story wasn't bullshit. Which it probably was.

"Yemen is the problem," the colonel continued. "It's in a

nasty civil war, so we have few assets there. We are reassigning all available HUMINT to this mission. If anyone is talking about this in the Middle East, I want to know. SIGINT, work up an emitter profile for this ship ASAP, and get it out to the fleet. Locate every ship that matches the profile, and we'll whittle down from there."

We're looking for an ordinary ship in 1.5 million square miles of ocean, Lewis thought. *We're going to have to do a lot of whittling.*

"Everyone else, I need you to search the databases for corroborating intel reporting. We have twenty-four hours, assuming a standard sailing speed. We'll regroup in six."

Not enough time, Lewis thought. *Not even close. Better call the babysitter.*

The Wahhabi stood on a small rise outside Sinjar, watching the convoy pass the ISIS blockade around the small city. He had watched for twenty minutes as they negotiated passage. He watched money being exchanged and fingers being pointed. He recognized the convoy's leader, a human smuggler, and he knew Allah had provided him with an opportunity. It would be a failure of faith not to seize it.

He turned, and a fighter jet screeched overhead, coming up on him suddenly from behind. The jets were active, but they were more sound than substance, a sign of weakness and fear. He couldn't see the bombs, but he could feel them exploding around the mountain. He could see the death clouds rising below its narrow spine.

There was talk among the mujahideen of Jordanian fighters bombing Muslims.

Haram! Forbidden! Most unclean! Jordan was the puppet of infidels, an Islamic nation joining the Americans and Israelis in killing fellow Muslims. *Haram!* The pilots should be burned alive for their sins.

He knelt, cupped his hands in supplication, and offered a prayer:

Allah is the greatest, who has guided me to this place. You created me and I am Your slave-servant. Let me be Your sword! Let me be Your Prophet! Continue to guide me to the man I seek. Bestow upon me the courage these unholy pilots lack. The courage to smite Your enemies face-to-face so that they may know Your judgment, and know themselves lacking. I seek refuge in You from my greatest evil deeds. So forgive me for what I am about to do.

The Wahhabi stood up and walked into Sinjar.

CHAPTER 24

The majordomo was clearly in a bad mood as he wiped the dust from his white linen suit. It was the same one he'd been wearing two days ago, but he'd had it pressed. He must have been staying at a five-star hotel in Erbil, sipping single malt Scotch in the sky bar, while I'd been crawling in a ditch. Still, the road from Erbil to Sinjar was rough and dangerous, even for a pampered majordomo with a guard of twelve black-ops operatives, which was why the man snapped his fashionable red handkerchief out of his pocket and wiped his hands of the metaphorical road.

What I wouldn't give for a shave, a pressed Jermyn Street suit, a ticket to La Scala in Milan, or even a decent cup of coffee. What I wouldn't give to be able to wash my hands of it all. Instead, I was encased in two days of sweat, blood, and combat gear. I was feeling itchy, and I suspected it was more than my neck stubble.

"I've bent for you, Dr. Locke," the majordomo said, meaning he'd come down to my low level. "I am no longer a man who shits in the dirt."

Meaning he probably had been such a man, before Abdulaziz brought him into higher service. It wasn't a surprise. According to Farhan's briefing an hour ago, Abdulaziz had made his name in Saudi intelligence. Most of his men had probably come up that way, too. They made for loyal operatives.

"Leave your guards," I said.

The majordomo glared. His eyes were hooded, more vicious than I remembered them being in Erbil. Of course, it had been dark, and I had been drinking, and he had been on the charm. *Don't underestimate this coyote,* I thought.

"I don't do that," he said.

"It's a condition. Your second is me."

He paused, considering. "I'm keeping my weapons."

"So am I."

He turned to his men and said something in Arabic.

"Checks out," our Kurdish guide said over my earpiece. He could hear everything I could, and would let me know if the majordomo said something threatening in Arabic.

I nodded to Boon and Wildman. "We're walking," I said.

The meeting spot was a few blocks away, but we took a zigzag route, overwatched by the Kurds with night-vision goggles at regular intervals. It was night, and the streets were empty. The building I'd chosen loomed before us, darkened and burned.

"You're taking me there?" the majordomo sighed. He was right; it was a proper shithole.

"It's the only thing we could afford," I said, hand outstretched toward the front door. "You haven't paid us our finder's fee yet."

Farhan's men had enacted their tough-guy imitation, just as before, with the baker, Abu Nadel, as tough-guy-in-chief. The guards were wrapped in black robes and standing motionless with AK-47s, looking like they had just smelled something vile. It was an excellent approximation of nasty jihadis.

"You're no militant," the majordomo said to Abu Nadel, as we took seats on the floor side by side. The majordomo snarled something in Arabic. Abu Nadel's face fell.

"English," I snapped.

Abu Nadel thought he was keeping his face blank but it betrayed fear, and I knew the majordomo saw it, too. It was nearly midnight and chilly, as deserts get at night, but the young man was sweating under his thawb.

"Infidel . . ." the baker began, but he fumbled.

The majordomo laughed, like a man who found torture amusing. "You may call me Sayyid."

Sayyid, I thought. Winters had taught me using people's first names disarms them, and that might prove an advantage.

"Where is Farhan?" the majordomo demanded. His voice was cruel, accustomed to getting his way.

The man was strong, though. He didn't fold. Instead, he sat up straighter, and I saw his fear turn to determination. The majordomo saw it, too, and knew what it meant. The baker had grown during his time as a hapless refugee. It would take enhanced interrogation, at least, for the man to give up his friend.

"He is not here, Sayyid. He has gone to a place where you cannot touch him."

"I have terms," I said, as planned. "From the prince. You must provide safe passage to one of his companions, and promise to let the others go."

"Oath breaker," the majordomo scoffed. "Why did I even bother?"

"He has a wife," I said.

"He does not," the majordomo snapped. It was true. Technically.

"She's pregnant."

"It isn't his. He's been under my protection for six months."

And you let him get away, I thought, realizing the majordomo was probably as desperate as we were. If he didn't find the prince, Sayyid might spend six months in Farhan's old jail cell. Or he might not make it that long, depending on how cruel this Abdulaziz really was.

"Pregnancies are nine months long," Abu Nadel said.

"I'm surprised you know that much."

A serving girl entered, covered in a burka. She was carrying a large platter with only a meager portion of bulgur wheat mixed with leftover rice. Once again, the food was a message: *Nothing special here. We are refugees.* Sayyid didn't even look up.

"I will spare her," he said slowly, as if biting every word. "If she renounces her claim to Farhan. She can have the child. I am sure Farhan will support it. But he must not acknowledge it . . ."

"It is a girl."

"A relief," the majordomo said. "A son would complicate things. A girl I can give you."

"She's eight and a half months pregnant," Abu Nadel said, as instructed. "She cannot have the baby here, and she cannot be driven out. She needs an airplane—"

"No," Sayyid said firmly, as the serving woman reached to put the platter between us. I could see the arm hair on her large wrist, but like a well-conditioned sexist, the majordomo didn't even glance. "Impossible. We cannot attract attention. Abdulaziz can never know. I am doing you a favor. Accidents happen in places like Sinjar. An accident is the easiest solution by far."

He lashed out, suddenly, grabbing the serving woman by the arm and pulling her down. Before I could move, he stuck a small pistol into her ribs. "You understand that, don't you, Farhan?" he hissed in the serving woman's ear. "You understand that your precious Marhaz will die, if you don't come with me?"

The majordomo twisted the serving girl's arm behind her back, as if he were trying to break it. *I wouldn't do that,* I thought at the very instant Wildman said the exact same thing.

The majordomo flinched.

"You don't want to do that, mate," Wildman said again from beneath the burka.

The majordomo didn't move.

"Go on," Wildman said, with violence and amusement in his

voice. He had more fun being held at gunpoint than anyone I'd ever met. "Check my dress. Don't be shy. Pull it up. I'm packing more heat between my legs than you can handle. And oh yeah, two blocks of wired C-4, too."

The majordomo pushed Wildman away in disgust. Wildman lounged where he had fallen, his burka obscenely lifted around his thighs. The majordomo looked away, clearly repulsed, and Wildman laughed. He was loving this. I couldn't blame him. I was loving it, too.

But the bodyguard wasn't laughing. He was pointing his AK-47 at the majordomo's face. "You ambushed us in Tell Abyad! You killed Ahmed, Omar, Faizah, Awadi, Sana, Bayan Mohammad, Abdullah!"

The majordomo looked up. He held up his Kahr PM9 pistol in a sign of surrender and placed it beside him, on the far side from where I was sitting. "Is that what you think, Prince Farhan?"

"I saw you. You were doing my father's dirty work, as always."

"I was saving your life, *fata 'ahmaq*. I am always saving your life. Even now."

"Those were your men."

"Those were militants. They had been tracking you for a week, and I had been protecting you. Seven days of watching you walk around as if you were untouchable. Seven days of watching you fuck that *waqihhat al'amrikia*, when I knew how pure you always were. I should have killed her then, but—"

Farhan slammed the rifle butt into the majordomo's face, knocking him backward.

The majordomo sat back up, slowly, making a show. He touched his bloody nose and laughed. Blood had splattered his white suit. He calmly removed his pocket square and dabbed his broken nose.

"Nonviolence is a virtue, right, my prince?"

The prince wasn't taking the bait. He kept the AK-47 steady, half a foot from the majordomo's face. "You executed Nasser," he said. "Personally. I saw you."

The majordomo was steadier than Farhan, whose anger had festered. "I don't know Nasser," he said calmly.

"You're a murderer."

"When your father gives the order," the majordomo replied, grimacing as he reset his nose.

"Did he order you to kill Marhaz?"

"Not in so many words."

"But you've been talking with him about her."

The majordomo laughed. "Your father, Prince Abdulaziz, talks *to* me. He does not talk *with* me. I certainly don't talk to him. You know that."

"You're unfit for my sister, Umm Abiha," Farhan said. "You always will be. That's why she rejected your marriage proposal."

The majordomo's anger flared. I could see it in his face. He hated this kid. Or feared him. Even the most trusted aide fears a son. A second later, though, he had regained control. "We share a favorite," he said. "That should bring us together."

"I will protect my sister from you."

"That is her misfortune. If only you ignored her like the rest of your sisters."

"You'll never marry into my family," the prince sneered. "You are unfit. A street urchin turned assassin. I don't care what she thinks she feels. She's a princess. You're a . . . slave. My father would never allow it. Love doesn't matter."

"But when a prince falls in love—"

"You are beneath her!"

"Funny," the majordomo said smoothly, "because most of the time, when we meet, she is beneath me."

Farhan lunged at the majordomo, and I leapt to block him.

"I will cut off your head at Deera Square myself!" Farhan shouted at the majordomo, while I wrestled him into a headlock. Hot-headed allies are almost as bad as cold-blooded enemies.

"Let him go!" I said. "Let him go, Farhan. Think of your wife and unborn child."

The world hung, suspended, as Farhan considered his next move. Then he relaxed, but it wouldn't take much to set him off again. The situation was deteriorating, and I needed to regroup fast before I lost control.

"What now?" the majordomo said, sensing the same thing. He might have hated Farhan, but he was a professional. He knew a losing situation when he saw one.

"You walk out," I said. "You take your men. You wait."

"For what?"

"For the sun to rise. I need to talk to Farhan."

The majordomo sneered. "How do I know he won't run?"

"You trust me."

"I trusted you already, *algharbi*. It was a mistake. You've gone over to the other side."

"I'm not on anyone's side. I'm negotiating."

"I didn't pay you to negotiate."

"That's negotiable," I said. I waved my gun. "And right now, you don't have a choice. Wildman!"

"Oy."

"Take the majordomo back to his men. Let's agree to meet again, Sayyid, right here, at 0600."

The majordomo snarled. He was getting animal on me. Good. I wanted to see his true nature. "Don't try this again, *algharbi*. I won't be fooled twice."

"You lost the prince when he went to Syria. You lost him again in Istanbul, from what he tells me. We're here, Sayyid, because you're easily fooled."

Wildman poked a gun in his back before the majordomo could respond and ushered him to the door.

"You're a dead man if you betray me again," he called over his shoulder. Wildman shoved him hard into the wall, then continued escorting him out.

"Exiting," I told Boon over the radio.

I watched them disappear, waited one breath, then turned to Farhan and the baker. "Okay, let's go," I said, pushing them toward the back door. "This is the most dangerous part. You never know what a man like that is going to do, after a humiliation like this."

"But you have some ideas."

"Let's see if I'm right," I said, as we headed out the back into an alley. I could see Farhan's men on the roof with their AK-47s covering our departure. The majordomo hadn't tried to double-cross us. So far so good.

"I'm glad you're on our side," Farhan said.

"I'm not. I'm on my own side."

We stayed quiet as we ran, taking our preplanned route. I tried to clear my mind and focus on the journey, on the danger of being wide open, surrounded by enemies, in a city like Sinjar, but something was nagging me, and after a few quiet blocks, I let down my guard.

"What's Al Garbage?" I asked, as we jogged along another empty alley.

"What?" Farhan said. He sounded confused.

"That's what Sayyid kept calling me. Al Garbage."

"*Algharbi*," he said. "It means *Westerner*." He laughed. "And that man's name isn't Sayyid, you stupid *algharbi*. *Sayyid* means *sir*."

CHAPTER 25

"NAV, when do we hit the CHOP line?"

"We out-CHOP in seventy-three hours," the voice came back. Lieutenant Commander Lopez let out a sigh. Three days until a new unit from 7th Fleet took over patrolling these waters, and the USS *Ernest E. Evans* could go home. The Arleigh Burke class destroyer had been in Condition III, wartime steaming, for months, and the crew was exhausted. Now they were heading to Jebel Ali, just south of Dubai, to resupply before the long journey home to Mayport, Florida.

"Scuttlebutt is once we get into Jebel Ali we're on restricted liberty," one of the sailors carped. "Probably some hyped-up terrorist threat again."

"Beer on the pier?" his buddy replied. "You're shitting me. We've been confined to the ship for weeks, and now our only shore leave is the sandbox." The *sandbox* was the derogatory term for the U.S. Navy's recreation area in Jebel Ali. It was a parking lot converted into the food court from hell: white plastic chairs and tables on asphalt, blaring rock music, warm beer, and chewy steaks, all under the Arabian sun.

"Another fine navy day!" another said sardonically. "Beer, boom box, and kebab."

Lopez had had enough, even though they were right. "Stop your bellyaching, or I'll administer some fan-room counseling sessions," he said.

That shut them up. Lopez was the Tactical Action Officer

and the senior man on deck. It was 0126, and they were pulling watch in the Combat Information Center, or CIC, the ship's brain center. Large color monitors with charts lined the bulk-heads, while smaller screens glowed green with text. The crew worked electronic consoles, monitoring everything above, below, and on the sea.

Silence again, Lopez thought. *Alleluia.* A cruise in the Persian Gulf was like being a goalie: boredom interspersed with brief moments of terror. Tonight was boredom. That was good, from Lopez's point of view.

A sailor stepped through the hatch carrying a folder marked TOP SECRET in large red letters.

"Sir, radio just received a flash message from fleet."

"What is it?" Lopez asked, taking the folder.

"They're looking for a ship traveling through these waters, highest priority."

"Details?"

"It's a small group-three freighter. Out of Pakistan, heading to Yemen. Flag and name unknown, probably a flag of convenience. Intel thinks the crew changed both flag and vessel name after they hit international waters."

"Cargo?"

"Possibly nuclear contraband, sir. That's all we're being told."

"Nukes in Yemen?" one of the sailors said. "Oh shit. Sounds like the Big Bang Theory."

"Sounds like Operation Haystack Needle," another added.

Lopez turned in his chair and shot them a glance. "No one said nukes," he snapped. "They said nuclear contraband: proba-bly rods or cylinders for centrifuges, something like that."

Nobody responded. Good men.

"What was the last POSIT and heading?" he asked, meaning the last known position, identification, and time.

"Unknown, sir. The message is fleet wide."

"Shit." Lopez knew their shore leave would be canceled and their return home delayed until the fleet found the mystery freighter, but he dared not tell his watch team. "I'll take it to the captain myself."

Lopez took one last sip of navy coffee and winced. It was as cold as the devil's dick. *How would you know, Chief?* came the imagined reply from his ensign. *You been getting friendly with Bee-el-ze-bub?*

He stepped through the hatch, leaving the red-light dim of the CIC, and entered the harsh fluorescence of the passageway. He climbed a ladderwell and entered the bridge. The skipper was slumped in the captain's chair, boots on a console, staring at the night horizon.

"Captain," Lopez said. "We just received this flash traffic from fleet."

The captain snapped out of his daze. He had spent most of the last few weeks in this chair, missing meals and his bunk, chasing Iranian warships in the Strait of Hormuz.

"What is it, Lopez?"

"You better read it for yourself, sir," Lopez said, handing him the folder containing the top secret message.

Turner scanned it, then shoved it back in the folder with disdain. Lopez could see the captain's displeasure.

"The men are calling it Operation Haystack Needle, sir."

"They're not wrong." The captain leaned forward, right hand rubbing his forehead in sleep-deprived thought. Small freighters of this description were ubiquitous in the Indian Ocean. "Where are the gaps in my satellite and SIGINT coverage?"

"Here, here, and here," the chief said, pointing to the map on the NAV console. "And here, too."

The captain rubbed his forehead again. "Come to 165 at

thirty knots. Have the slick-32 look for J-band emitters. Request a shift in our operational box to compensate for those gaps. We need better coverage."

Lopez nodded and turned to leave.

"And Lopez."

"Yes sir."

"Better cancel shore leave."

"Yes sir," Lopez said, as he started to walk back to the CIC.

"And Lopez, get the Fire Scout ready. We'll need to see in the dark."

And shoot in the dark, Lopez thought. Fire Scout would hunt and kill anything they told it to.

Ten minutes later, three crew members rolled the large rotary-wing Fire Scout drone onto the destroyer's flight deck. The rotors began to turn and the machine took off, zooming toward the dark horizon.

CHAPTER 26

The majordomo, right-hand man and enforcer for Abdulaziz, middling-tier prince of the Sudairi lineage of the House of Saud, chewed on a handful of nuts as he watched the two American mercenaries move away from the burned-out building in the northern part of the town of Sinjar. Farhan had escaped with the double-crossing mercenary and that ridiculous cook, but the majordomo wasn't worried. They wouldn't get far. If he followed these two, he'd find where the prince was holed up. A good thing, too. He needed the prince, and he needed him badly.

The majordomo had worked in the Saudi intelligence forces for thirty years, since he was sixteen, and his uncle, a tailor for Abdulaziz's father's chauffeur, had used that connection to secure him a junior assistant position in the General Intelligence Directorate, the Saudi CIA. Within five years, he had come to General Abdulaziz's attention. The prince sent him to England for an education in languages, international relations, and business. On his return, he discovered that royal connections exempted him from the Kingdom's harsh rules. Forbidden fruits such as alcohol, drugs, and whores were all on tap. If only he could have had Princess Umm Abiha, too. The old man had suffered an unlucky draw, twelve daughters and two sons. He despised his daughters for that, but despised even more any man who tried to take them from under his thumb. The old man craved power, and there is nothing more powerful than a father's hold over a pliant daughter.

Funny that the old man was having a granddaughter now, even if he did not know it. If Marhaz had been pregnant with a son, Abdulaziz might have relented to the marriage. But then again, probably not. The girl was an Iranian Christian, born and raised in the United States. It was *haram*, forbidden, and, even more important, unwise. A Westerner marrying into the royal family would never work in the Kingdom, especially for an ambitious prince still several rungs down from the Saudi throne.

As Abdulaziz had barked at him two days ago, when Farhan escaped again: *You should have killed the whore last year. That was your chance.* He still didn't know if the old man had meant it sincerely.

What he shouldn't have done, the majordomo knew, was approve Abdulaziz's decision to send Farhan to Istanbul. Abdulaziz should have entrusted that sensitive mission to him, his most trusted servant. Instead the old man indulged a soft spot for his youngest son, and soft spots, after all, were signs of rot. It was the grave personal insult of being passed over for the most important task of Abdulaziz's life that, more than anything else, had led him here.

He chewed on a medjool date and watched the two mercs slinking up the road, checking their six o'clock every half block. The man from the house was still in the burka, but the disguise wouldn't fool anyone, since women weren't six feet three inches tall. These guys weren't trying for disguise, though. The majordomo was sure they would gun down any patrol that stopped them.

They disappeared around a corner. The majordomo waited a full minute. No one else followed. It was time to go.

He split his twelve men, following at a safe distance. The mercenary was good. He had found the baker in less than two days, when Abdulaziz's men had forgotten the man existed.

But the majordomo was good, too. His men were an elite Saudi counterterrorism unit, trained in the volatile Middle East. Together, they had busted dozens of terror plots and Shia subterfuge, sending hundreds of men and a few women to their deaths. No more than five or six had been political enemies of Abdulaziz and his allies, and even with those few, the majordomo had always found a compelling reason. Drugs, homosexuality, treasonous ambition: there were plenty of offenses that would allow a problematic man to lose his head in the Kingdom.

Not the least of which was letting your patron prince's favorite son disappear into a civil war. Or falling in love with that patron prince's daughter.

He moved into the shadows at the edge of the dark streets. No windows were lit, but even the waning moon threw bright light in the dry desert. He couldn't see the prince, but he kept an eye on the Asian merc covering his back. Farhan was four blocks ahead at least, but there was no need to get closer. As he had learned with Umm Abiha, there was never any good in getting too close to the Abdulaziz family.

His heart hurt when he thought of her, isolated and held house captive. He hadn't seen her for two years. No one had. And all because she had spoken to her father's majordomo in private. If the prince knew how close they had really become . . .

What he'd said to Farhan, in his anger, about her being under him. What he'd stupidly said. If that ever got back to Abdulaziz, it would get her killed.

Thankfully, Farhan knew that, too. He would never cause the death of his favorite sister.

But her lover? Farhan would kill him, the majordomo knew, if he ever got the chance. Farhan could never get back to Riyadh to speak to his father.

The merc slowed, then stopped, settling in a doorway. The majordomo faded into the side street, the darkness swallowing even his bloodstained white suit. He followed the merc's gaze to a plain two-story building a half block farther on. Wooden shutters, unusual for this area, were being pulled securely over the one door and one window. A light flicked on, leaking past the edge of the shutter. Two minutes later, it went out. Five minutes after that, the mercenary looked both ways, walked across the street, pulled open the front door shutters, and disappeared inside.

This is the place, the majordomo thought.

He took out his radio and beeped once, signaling his position. Two beeps responded. He checked up and down the street. There was nothing. It was another nondescript block, in a world full of them. He always found it ironic, the boring places such stories ended. But end it would. Tonight. Within the hour, the majordomo would kill Farhan and the girl. When Abdulaziz confronted him, the majordomo would find someone to blame. There was always someone else to blame. The American, probably. Then he would be free of this royal brat and never have to spend another day in the hellhole of northern Iraq.

He looked at his watch, an oyster-banded stainless steel Rolex submariner he'd picked up during his first year at King's College London. Two minutes to midnight. It was time.

CHAPTER 27

Prince Mishaal heard the footsteps approaching as if they were underwater. The sound seemed distant and soggy. He lay on his cot and listened, hoping they belonged to his friend, his benefactor, his savior. He thought it might be the middle of the night, since it had been quiet for as long as he could remember, or perhaps it was early morning, the light just beginning to brighten . . .

He heard the footsteps getting louder, and he stopped thinking to listen. It felt as if his body's cells were calling out for drugs, as if they were crawling toward the door, but he knew he was lying motionless on the bed. He closed his eyes so he wouldn't vomit. The idea of moving made him sick.

The lock turned. He was afraid to open his eyes, afraid it wouldn't be true. He heard the door creak and smelled . . . almonds. He could taste almond paste on his tongue. He thought it would gag him.

The man's robes swept. His feet shuffled. The lock clicked shut again. The prince could hear the stranger breathing. He could feel his own breath. Something touched his neck. It was cool and damp. The man was swabbing a spot on his neck. Mishaal could hardly breathe.

"What did you have with you in Paris?" the man whispered.

Mishaal's brain flashed, searching for the right answer. He felt sick. "Pride," he offered.

The man was silent.

"Indulgence," the prince said hurriedly, before the opportunity got away. "Appe . . . appe, appetites. I had appetites. Sins." *What did this cleric want to hear?*

The prince heard the chink of a needle being removed from a metal box. His body shivered in anticipation.

"What did you have with you when you were apprehended?" the man whispered. The prince could feel his breath.

"Cocaine," he said, shutting his eyes tighter, and listened. He heard a plunger being drawn back. "Dilaudid." He heard liquid being sucked into a needle. He stopped breathing, waiting. "Captagon," he said. "Synthetic amphetamines. One thousand pills. In an overnight bag. For my personal use."

"The briefcase," the man said. "What was in the briefcase?"

"Nothing," he said automatically, feeling his brain recoil.

"Nothing," he said again, as he felt the man drawing away, like a shadow retreating from the light.

"Nothing," he said through his tears. "Believe me, it was nothing. It was for my father. It was a favor. It was . . ." He felt relief pulling away, and fear flooding in, flooding every cell in his body.

"It was electronic," he whimpered, "a detonator. It controls a weapon. Please! I don't know any more. I don't know anything."

"That's what I thought," the man whispered, as he plunged in the needle.

CHAPTER 28

Midnight. Sinjar was quiet, as the world always is before the hammer comes down. There might have been an American drone high overhead, invisible in the night, but the bombs were gone until morning, when the targets would be crawling, and the snakes were tucked up in their corners with their rifles and their murderous certainty. Mount Sinjar was burning, but the smoke was gray on black and the fires too small to be seen from several kilometers away, where the empty desert fed into empty streets.

The majordomo waited, it wasn't clear what for. Nothing was moving in the building. No lights were on.

His radio beeped. He beeped twice in return. A figure started forward twenty meters away, gaining momentum as he ran. The majordomo watched. When the figure neared the shuttered door, the majordomo dropped his arm to signal his men. The night exploded with gunfire. The front of the building began to chip and scatter. The running man kicked open the shutters, which didn't seem to be locked—or maybe it was his adrenaline that smashed them so easily—and disappeared inside.

Another man followed, sprinting beneath the automatic covering fire, and another followed him. The majordomo watched, his Kahr PM9 in his hand, as his men poured into the building. For a long moment it was bedlam, as assault rifles blasted away in the shadows. He could hear his men yelling to each other in Arabic as they cleared each room. There was no one in the window on the second floor. There was no one trying to escape through the door. He waited, his pistol raised, but nothing happened. The shooting and shouting died away. He dropped his arm to his side.

It's done, he thought, as he walked toward the building.

Then something exploded, shaking the street, and before he had thought through his next actions, he rushed toward the building.

Smoke was pouring out the door. Behind it, the sound of heavy fire had doubled, and he knew two sides were fighting. He could hear his men shouting. The orderly assault had devolved into a firefight, bullets ripping crosswise against each other. The majordomo held his breath and plunged into the smoke. He slammed into a wall and stood with his back against it, catching his breath, until he saw one of his men dead at its base, saw the holes in the plaster, and realized the wall wouldn't stop the enemy's rounds.

He hit the floor. He wasn't wearing a vest. He had assumed the mercenaries would surrender. There was no reason for the prince to fight, and even less for the mercs. Negotiating was one thing. But why were they willing to die here, in this nothing place? He wasn't willing, and this job was his life.

He glanced around the wall into the main room. Visibility was near zero, save for the red laser sites skipping through the smoke. He aimed at one and fired six quick shots. Immediately, automatic fire sprayed the wall around him and he dove for cover.

A small canister arced through the air, bounced off a wall, and landed two meters in front of him. It exploded, a white light and boom that left him blind and deaf. A flashbang grenade.

A hand reached out and tapped him. A man was signaling to him from behind an upturned wooden trestle table. It was one of his men . . . but who? He was wearing a gas mask, making him unrecognizable, and besides, the majordomo had never bothered to learn most of their names.

The man lifted his mask. The majordomo knew him by sight. He scrambled behind the trestle table. "False targets," the man said in Arabic, meaning the laser sites.

The majordomo nodded. The man lowered the mask, making him look once again like an alien in the smoke. The mercenary had set up laser sights to draw their fire. Had they anticipated the attack? Had they planned a counterambush all along?

But why?

"*Aistaslam*," he yelled. "*Aistaslam!*" Surrender.

But the prince didn't surrender. Instead, the majordomo's call was greeted with a fresh barrage of gunfire. If that was the way he wanted it . . .

"Aim low," the majordomo said, pointing toward the other end of the table and putting a second clip into his pistol.

The man nodded. They rolled in opposite directions until they had clear lines of fire, the majordomo on his belly aiming knee high. He emptied his clip. He heard a scream, then a thud. He rolled back behind the table. He was starting to understand the layout now, sense the flow of battle, but he still didn't understand why. What did the mercenaries have to gain?

The majordomo loaded his third clip. Only one more after this. He nodded to the man with him behind the table, who was reloading his Heckler & Koch UMP submachine gun.

"*Ayn hi alakharin?*" Where are the others?

The man shrugged. The smoke was thick, adding to the darkness of the night. A torn shutter hung on one hinge. The majordomo thought of retreating and regrouping, but there were only three mercs and Farhan's foolish friends. He had twelve highly trained men. Or at least he had twelve when the assault started.

"Satchel charges!" he ordered in Arabic, signaling toward the back, where the gunfire was heavy. "I will cover you."

He could see the man's eyes inside the gas mask widen, then glance at the small pistol, an ineffectual weapon for this purpose. He seemed to be making up his mind. Refusal would end his career, if the majordomo could identify him later. And if they survived.

The man looked at the majordomo and shook his head no. The smoke curled around them, purple in the darkness. The majordomo could feel the anger burning inside him.

"I'll go," the majordomo said, grabbing the satchel charge out of the man's equipment pack.

The man nodded his agreement. He rose slowly to a crouching position, his smoke mask clinging to his face. He rested his H&K submachine gun on the top edge of the table, lined up his shot, nodded that he was ready, then jolted backward as blood exploded out the back of his head.

The majordomo stared at the body as it caught on the edge of the table, then tipped and slipped to the floor. He hadn't heard the shot, only the echo. A dozen echoes. A hundred.

The table was cracking, splintering to pieces. A dozen high-powered guns were firing. The mercenaries were advancing, and he knew he had no chance of fighting his way out of whatever this trap had become.

Green laser dots danced across his chest. He dropped the satchel charge and his pistol, and came out with his hands on his head. This wasn't over. There was no way, that he could see, for the mercenary to escape Sinjar with the prince, his friends, and a pregnant woman. One way or another, he would take Farhan dead or alive.

Dead is better, he thought. Dead is final. Dead is quiet.

He felt the rifle in the back of his head.

"Down!" an American voice said, and the majordomo slowly lay facedown on the floor. "Where are the mercs?"

The majordomo didn't know what that meant.

"Where are the Americans?"

"With you," the majordomo tried to say, but a boot was on the back of his skull, pressing his mouth into the ground.

Something hit the floor next to him. It was tobacco spit. "Where's the fugitive?"

A boot bore down on his head. He felt his hands being flex-cuffed behind him. Someone grabbed his arms, turning him over. He looked up at a huge man in body armor with enough heavy artillery to blast through a building. His face was painted in night camouflage.

"Identify," the man said.

"I work for—" he hesitated, wondering if his next words would doom him or save his life, then plunged ahead "—Saudi intelligence. General Abdulaziz."

The man stared down at him. He looked sideways at a second man in body armor, then spat again, inches from his ear.

"*You're* Abdulaziz's majordomo?" he said with disgust.

The majordomo nodded. "Who are you?"

The American kicked him in the ribs, and pain shot up his right flank. "You shot one of our guy's knees out," he growled. "Do you know how fucking dangerous it is to get your knee shot out in a place like this?"

"You killed my men," the majordomo objected.

"Getting a medevac out here is going to be a son of a bitch," the man said, spitting again, "and God knows if the company will pay for it, probably not, when they hear about this cluster-fuck."

"We're on the same side," the majordomo said, as the realization swept over him.

The boot came off his neck, reluctantly. The majordomo sat up and indicated his cuffs. The American stared at him, then cut him loose. The majordomo shrugged his way out of the flex-cuffs, then straightened his white suit jacket. He wiped something from the lapel and realized it was blood. He had dirt in his mouth from the floor. The smoke was clearing, and he could see five or six mercenaries in body armor with heavy weapons kicking corpses to roll them over. His men's corpses.

"*Muntahiki*," the majordomo muttered under his breath with disgust, using his pocket square to wipe filth from his lips.

"Jase," another merc yelled from across the room. It was an African; he was pointing at the floor. A corner of a carpet was flipped over. There was a trap door.

The leader walked out of the smoke. "The slick bastard," he said.

The mercenaries put their fingers on the triggers of their assault rifles and aimed toward the door. The African nodded, then flipped it open.

"Fuck," the leader yelled, when he saw the C-4 wired to the underside.

"Bloody hell," Wildman said, as he watched the other merc hit team and the Saudi in the white suit sprinting out the back of the house together. He had watched the mercs sneak up and blow a hole in the back wall, rushing in through the smoke. Brave. He had listened to the firefight, knowing the mercs were cutting the Saudis down. He could have killed them all, if he'd wanted to. He could have blown them all to bloody hell.

Instead, he'd waited for everyone to get out, then hit the detonator. The explosion was a burp. The house exhaled smoke, then settled. Wildman had shaped the charge to explode the tunnel and leave everything else standing. The people in this town had endured enough. They didn't need another building going down. And he didn't want their attention.

"Didn't expect that," I said, lowering my night-vision binoculars.

"Which part?" Boon asked. We were standing on the roof of a building two blocks away, near where the secret tunnel came out, with a perfect vantage point to the front of the building.

"All of it," I said, looking over my shoulder at Farhan. "Every damn thing."

CHAPTER 29

The majordomo slipped away from the mercs in the confusion of the explosion and slunk down the dark street. The assault had been a shock. Worse, it had been an embarrassment. He had lost his team. He had lost his cool and *begged* for his life. Like a woman. Now he was angry. At himself, but also at whoever had complicated things.

The mission was simple: find Farhan. It was his mission. He'd performed. So why were the American mercenaries here? Had Abdulaziz lost faith in him? Likely, he had to admit. Istanbul was a disaster, and this was no time for caution. The majordomo had done everything he could to secure Farhan, including hiring Locke's merc team, among others. Why wouldn't Prince Abdulaziz do the same?

One thing was clear. He had to kill the brat.

"Locke," he cursed under his breath. The scumbag had betrayed him. Failing to hand over the prince, as was their bargain, was a capital offense in the majordomo's book. The rigged house? Unforgivable. Locke must have assumed he'd be followed and planned to double-cross him. Was there no honor among hired guns? Was there no professional code? When he paid money for services, the majordomo expected obedience. Otherwise, people lost their heads.

Locke will lose his head, the majordomo swore.

He glanced back. The Apollo team was out of sight. They

hadn't worried about his leaving. Why should they? They were on the same side. Probably. It was hard to say for sure, since he was no longer sure how many sides there were.

He pulled out his sat phone. Untraceable, except by the man who had given it to him. He paused. Was that how the Apollo team had shown up in Sinjar?

"We have a problem," he said, when his call was answered. "The American double-crossed us. I need . . ."

He choked, unable to form the words. He felt a searing pain in his fingers, and he dropped to his knees, holding his hand. There was blood pouring down his arm. Half of his top two fingers had been cut off. The phone lay cracked on the ground beside him.

"Get up," a voice said.

For the second time in an hour, the majordomo looked up at an assailant. This time, a man in a robe and long beard was standing over him, a bandolier across his chest and a scimitar in his hand. The waning moon was behind him, backlighting him so that the majordomo couldn't see his face. But he knew that voice.

"Youssof," he said, clutching his bleeding hand.

"Stand up, Majordomo," the Wahhabi said. "Do they still call you that?"

The majordomo spat. "Are you planning to kill me?"

"Of course."

The majordomo went for the pistol in his suit pocket, even though he knew it was hopeless—he was missing his index and middle fingers. The Wahhabi kicked him in the face, then stomped on his arm. The pistol clattered away.

"Not like that, old teacher," the Wahhabi said.

The majordomo struggled wearily to his feet, gauging angles.

He grew up a street thug in Medina and had survived worse than this. The gun was a short dive away. He marked its location, in case he got turned around in the struggle.

"You were never a good student," he said, glancing in the direction of the mercenaries.

"They won't come," the Wahhabi said. "You won't scream for help. You will die with honor."

"I don't care about honor. And neither do you."

The Wahhabi laughed. "I am changed."

"You found religion," the majordomo chuckled. *Fool.*

"Even better, I found purpose. I no longer serve you and your kind. I am a prophet now."

"A prophet?" The majordomo laughed. "A prophet of what?"

The Wahhabi eyed the majordomo's Italian loafers, white suit, and red pocket square. It disgusted him. "You were my superior once," the Wahhabi said with disgust. "What are you now?"

The majordomo pictured the gun. He considered diving for it, but this wasn't the moment. And yet he couldn't sit by and be insulted by his former underling, a stupid man who had shown no proficiency in anything but cruelty.

"I hired you, *waghadd ghabi.* I am still your leader."

The Wahhabi paused. He shut his eyes.

Of course, this cretin wouldn't know, the majordomo thought. He had used cutouts and middlemen.

"I found you in the gutter. *I* gave you purpose, not this false piety." He gestured at the Wahhabi's pilgrim robes. "I am the man who hired you for this mission. I am paying you to kill Farhan."

"No," the Wahhabi said. "This mission did not come from you."

"Of course it came from me, working through middlemen."

"I no longer take orders from you, or any man. My orders

come from God." He tossed the majordomo his sword and drew his curved *jambiya* dagger. "Pick it up, old teacher. Unlike you, I kill with honor now."

"And if I don't?"

The Wahhabi didn't answer. The majordomo relented. He reached down and picked up the sword. The Wahhabi was no fool. He had thrown it away from the side with the pistol, but the distance was only two steps. The majordomo straightened, the plan fully formed in his head. He held the sword in front of him, as he had learned to long ago.

"Breaker of oaths," the Wahhabi intoned, "torturer of the faithful, one of us must die. We fight as equals. Let Allah decide justice."

The majordomo raised his sword, feinted and lunged, knowing that when the Wahhabi parried the blow, his momentum would carry him down to the left, where he could grab the pistol and raise it in one smooth motion, ending this foolishness.

But the Wahhabi didn't parry. He deftly sidestepped, grabbed the majordomo's sword hand, and twisted violently. The sword dropped and the man screamed; the Wahhabi thrust his shoulder into the majordomo's chest, knocking him off his feet.

"Have mercy!" The majordomo begged for the second time this night. "Please!"

"I will give you one gift," the Wahhabi said slowly, picking up the scimitar. "I will kill for you those you wanted dead."

"No," the majordomo started to say, but the Wahhabi sliced his old mentor's head from his neck. The two parts flew soundlessly apart and fell to the dirt. The Wahhabi picked up the head and noticed the phone, cracked on the ground. It was still working. Whoever the majordomo had been talking with, the call was still live.

"Al-kafir mmayit"—the infidel is dead—the Wahhabi said and threw the phone into the shadows. *"Saif al Haqq,"* he cooed to the sword, calling it the Sword of Truth. "You are Allah's judgment. I am slave to your will."

He turned. There was a little man ten meters away, watching. The Wahhabi walked past him without a word. Then he stopped and, severed head in hand, turned back. "Did you get it?" he asked.

The man closed the camera on his mobile phone. "Yes, *sayyid*," he said.

"All of it?"

"Yes, *sayyid*."

The Wahhabi smiled. "Good. I am Allah's sword and prophet. Let it be known."

"What happened?" I asked, as Wildman stowed his detonators. I could tell he wasn't in a hurry. He took out his canteen
and drank a long gulp of water. It was the middle of the night,
and it was chilly on the rooftop, but the zero percent humidity
of the northern Iraqi desert would still dry you out in half a
minute.

"Unexpected visitors," he said.

Wildman had rigged the whole building, not just Farhan's
escape tunnel. He had the option to blow up as much or as little
as he wanted. He had chosen a small explosion. I'd known the
man for three years; it wasn't his usual choice.

"So?"

He finished drinking. He looked around at the eight people on the roof: me, Boon, the prince's posse, the woman he'd
knocked up. We were a ragged crew.

"They were Apollo," he said.

Apollo Outcomes?! That hit me hard. Our vantage point had
given us a clear view of the front of the building and the trap we
set. We had seen the majordomo, with a dozen highly trained
men, rush in. We didn't have eyes on the other group, which
had entered from the back, but I knew they had done quick and
violent work. They had taken out a Saudi hit team in minutes.
They were professionals. But Apollo?

"You sure?"

Wildman nodded. "I went through the Ranch"—Apollo

Outcomes's private training facility and proving ground in Texas—"with two of them."

"They may have moved on."

"They didn't."

The way Wildman said it was final. He was certain. And I was going to have to accept it. My old company, Apollo Outcomes, and my old mentor, Brad Winters, were here.

Maybe the mission was a favor for a business associate. The prince's father? Winters had business associates everywhere; of course he had Saudi princes in his pocket. But that was a full Apollo Tier One team down there. That was a snatch-and-grab operation, with shoot-to-kill authorization. And apparently, the majordomo had no idea it was coming.

Did Winters know I was here?

The thought invoked a fight-or-flight response. I reached for the ground and sat down. I needed to think this through.

Keep calm, Locke, I thought.

I reviewed what I knew. Winters had sold out my Apollo team in Ukraine. Since then, Wildman, Boon, and I had hoofed it down to Erbil, where we could lay low until I figured out how to action Winters. We'd be truly safe only with Winters dead, but killing the CEO emeritus of the world's largest mercenary corporation was no easy day.

Maybe we got sloppy? My mind wandered to Kylah. My old Airborne buddy Bear. The oil executives. Did one of them know Brad Winters?

The majordomo. He was the linchpin. He was the man who offered me a million dollars to kidnap the Saudi princeling, whose father was the head of Saudi intelligence's black operations division. And an ISIS special forces killer. And a lover who had a change of heart and was starting a family with an

American-Persian woman in the middle of a war zone. Father
uses majordomo to retrieve son, but majordomo doesn't tell
Dad about the pregnant girlfriend. Majordomo is also in love
with his boss's daughter and Farhan's sister, Umma something
or other (I still had trouble with the local names), but is rejected
by the family due to his low birth—and especially by the very
prince he was hiring me to find.

Then there was Istanbul. Why was Farhan there? *How* was
he there? His father didn't sound like the kind of man to let in-
mates, even his son, take a weekend pass. Farhan must have been
sent there for a purpose, only to escape and return for Marhaz,
his pregnant wife. Father is outraged, sends his majordomo to
retrieve Farhan yet again. Majordomo hires us.

Now an Apollo team shows up, also looking for the prince.
Coincidence? Or did Winters know I was here? I had smashed
my satellite phone, destroyed my Apollo-registered tech, lived
off cash and barter on the fringes of the globalized world for
four grueling months. We had walked hundreds of kilometers,
hitched rides in the back of Turkish tobacco trucks, smuggled ourselves across multiple borders, and lived like paupers
in a lousy squat with no electricity and hardly any running
water.

No way Winters could have tracked us. We were off the grid.
The Apollo team could have been a nightmarish coincidence.

But why were they also after Farhan? How important was this
prince? And why?

"What is going on?" I whispered. I saw the prince turn, trying to avoid my sight. Wrong move. He knew more than he was
telling me.

"I need to know what is going on," I said, standing to face
him. "Now."

He glanced at his wife. "I told you my father was ruthless," he said.

"This isn't about bringing you back to be a good son," I said. "Those men didn't seem to mind if they killed you. Why?"

He didn't want to talk. I could tell. But he had information, and I didn't have time for games.

"You're asking me to risk my men for you," I said. "That involves honesty. And trust. So tell me what is going on, Prince Farhan, or tell it to those men down there."

He looked at his wife. She nodded, a hand on her belly in an instinctual protective position. The prince pulled a cheap chain from his black ISIS robe. At the end was a metal card. "I stole this from my father. In Istanbul."

"A credit card?"

"A KSV-21 enhanced crypto card."

"What is that?"

"A key."

"To what?"

"Arm a nuclear bomb."

I blinked. "Your father has a nuclear bomb?"

"Actually," he said, "he has fifteen nuclear bombs. Or he will very soon."

CHAPTER 31

"Gentlemen," Brad Winters said as he entered the ambassador's office. It had been less than a day since he was here last, and he was in a buoyant mood. He knew this call would come. *No need to gloat.*

Ambassador Ensher stood and shook his hand, looking resplendent in a three-piece suit. The room smelled of stale coffee. It was early morning, but these men had clearly been here much earlier.

"This is Emmanuel Garcia, my deputy chief of mission," Ensher said with his usual formality. "This is Col. Charlie Mullens, our military attaché. He's keeping us abreast of Fifth Fleet's search. And Forsythe Martin. You probably know what he does."

Winters did. Forsythe Martin was the CIA chief of station.

"A pleasure," Winters said. It was clear they had been working the loose-nukes angle most of the night. They were taking it seriously, and even better, they needed help. Otherwise, Ensher wouldn't have extended the invitation. It must have been grinding his worsted vest to have "the mercenary" back so soon.

Good, Winters thought. He had realized long ago that the person who can walk away from the negotiation table first has the power, and everything was a negotiation. Especially national security.

"Your country owes you a debt," Ensher said in a flat tone, as Winters took a seat.

I'll take it in Euros, Winters joked to himself.

"We've been checking your story," Martin, the spook chief, said. "The CIA believes it credible. We've always been concerned about Saudi Arabia's nuclear connection with Pakistan, but we didn't think they would be foolish enough to exercise this option."

"The Saudi government officially denies it, of course," Ensher said.

"Good God, you didn't mention it to the Saudis, did you?" Winters said, almost bolting out of his chair.

The room shifted uncomfortably. "They are our allies," Ensher said.

"Excuse me, sir, but I thought they were the ones we were trying to prevent from getting the nukes. If you hinted at our knowledge—"

"Don't get your knickers in a twist, son," Martin broke in. He was only six years older than Winters, but he seemed to be from a previous generation. His Brooks Brothers suit was ten years out of style. "We've got people on the inside. People we trust. It's en passant."

Martin gave him a steely look on the last phrase, a spook's term for "back channel," unofficial and off the books. *You're not dealing with amateurs here,* the look suggested. *These men are among America's best.* Winters found that mildly unsettling.

"A deal was transacted three days ago," Martin said. "But it wasn't sanctioned by the king. As far as we can tell, it wasn't sanctioned by anyone."

"Who else knows?" Winters asked. Ensher looked at Martin, preferring not to share such sensitive information with a creature like Brad Winters. Winters waited him out. They needed his help; this was part of the price.

"Right now, only the Five Eyes," Martin said. The Five Eyes were the intelligence alliance of the United States, the United

Kingdom, Australia, New Zealand, and Canada. "We're keeping it as tight as possible."

"Frankly," Ensher said, "there's only one party I'm worried about, and he's in this room."

"Don't worry," Winters said, taking the taunt as a compliment. "I understand the gravity of the situation. Even a rumor, substantiated by United States actions, could cause a nuclear panic in the Middle East. Israel and Iran would feel threatened. They might launch preemptive nuclear strikes."

"Not to mention the possibility of a Middle Eastern nuclear arms race," Garcia, the embassy's second in charge, said.

"It won't get that far," Winters replied. "Not if they find out Prince Farhan might have taken something nuclear into Iraq."

"Has he?" the marine colonel barked, clearly alarmed.

"I don't know."

Ensher started to respond, but Winters held up his hand. "I know, I know," he said. "No need to play out scenarios. No need to start rumors we can't control. I understand that perfectly, Ambassador. That's why I brought this situation to you, gentlemen, and to you alone." He looked around. Everyone was impressed. He'd sidelined Ensher already, even from his right-hand man. Time to get down to business. "So what do you need?"

"Abdulaziz," Martin said. "What do you know?"

Winters shook his head. "Just what I shared with the ambassador yesterday."

Ensher looked dubious. "You understand the gravity of your situation. Abdulaziz is your business partner, and this is not sitting well with USG." United States Government.

It was Winters's soft spot. Apollo Outcomes needed to keep its number one client—USG—happy, even as it serviced its lucrative Saudi clients. This arrangement rankled some in the

National Security Council, as Ensher was reminding him, but it was the way the contracting world worked.

"You would not even be aware of the situation, Henry," Winters said with a smile, "if I hadn't already betrayed the confidence of my client. I'm a businessman, sir, but I am first and foremost a patriot."

"Here, here," the marine colonel muttered. What was his name again? Mullens? Winters made a note to keep him close. He would make a good ally.

"I've already deployed a top Apollo team to action Farhan Abdulaziz," Winters said, looking at the colonel. "They're in theater right now, vicinity Mosul." No need to mention Sinjar, of course. It wouldn't help him, so what was the point?

"Excellent!" Martin exclaimed. The colonel nodded his approval.

"Do you have teams in Iraq?" Winters asked.

"That's classified," Ensher said, but Winters had seen the colonel nod.

"What about Abdulaziz?" Martin asked. "What are his plans?"

"He's kept them close to the vest"—Winters smirked at Ensher—"but I know his best man is there."

"Do you have his trust?"

Winters sighed. "Abdulaziz is paranoid, with good reason, obviously. When he's paranoid, he's dangerous, and unpredictable. I tried to talk with him about his son. He wouldn't bite." *He almost bit my head off, actually,* Winters thought.

The colonel squirmed.

"You're not putting our minds at ease," Martin said.

Well, they shouldn't be, Winters thought.

"So you've confirmed the nukes?"

Martin nodded. "Human intelligence sources confirm that a suspicious shipment left Gwadar, Pakistan, on a freighter about"—he checked his watch—"fifty-four hours ago. We don't have enough intel for target identification."

"Hence, Operation Urgent Vigilance," the colonel said abruptly. He was a military man. He despised nuance. "A top NSC priority. We're scrambling every asset from Bab el Mandeb to Hormuz. Planes. Ships. Satellites. Boots. If nuclear assets are moving"—military men loved the word *assets*—"and that's a big *if*, mind you, we will intercept them."

Martin didn't look convinced.

"What about Paris?" Winters probed. "What was stolen?"

Martin was about to speak but Ensher interrupted. "That's classified."

"But it was nuclear in nature?"

Ensher shook his head. "I told you, that's classified."

Garcia grimaced at his boss's rudeness. There was clearly an imbalance of trust at the table. *Divide and conquer,* Winters thought.

"I just want to know if we've conclusively PIDed"—positively identified—"the nuclear nature of the assets," Winters pushed, adopting the colonel's nomenclature.

"We believe we have," the colonel said, before Ensher could intervene.

"But not conclusively, no," Martin backtracked. "We're still working with hypotheticals."

"What about Prince Mishaal? Where is he now?"

Ensher looked at Garcia. "Al Ha'ir prison," Garcia said. "He's receiving, umm, spiritual instruction for his addictions. We're monitoring the situation."

"You have a man inside?"

"Nobody has a man inside al Ha'ir prison," Martin said.

Naïve, Winters thought. "Prince Khalid does. The Wahhabis run that institution. They control what goes on there."

Winters didn't know much about the furtive Khalid, other than he was one of the few men Abdulaziz feared in the Kingdom. Khalid was top brass inside the Ministry of Interior and commanded the Kingdom's notorious secret police, the Mabahith. There wasn't much in the Kingdom that Khalid didn't know about, or couldn't touch. And Winters hadn't found a way to touch him in return. The only thing more menacing than what he knew of Khalid's power was that there was so much about the man he didn't know. And Winters was in the business of knowing.

"Khalid is a dangerous man," Winters said. "You should keep eyes on him."

Ensher sighed. "Mr. Winters," he said, "we did not bring you here so that we could listen to your conspiracy theories about Prince Khalid. We have an assignment in mind. A favor."

Winters knew that must have hurt Ensher to say, but he nodded, as if it were nothing. He'd pushed the Saudi conspiracy angle as far as he could go. He turned to the colonel—the military man in the room—like a good student waiting for his assignment.

"We have a solid plan in play," the colonel said. "Nearly wall-to-wall surveillance on the ocean. The Gulf States are cooperating, although they are obviously not fully read into the situation. They think we're chasing a major arms dealer for Shia terrorists. Between our intelligence capabilities and partners, we have the entire region locked up. Everything, except one gaping hole."

"Let me guess," Winters said. "Yemen."

"Affirmative," said the colonel. "The country is a civil war wrapped in a lawless desert inside a black hole. We have assets in place. SOCOM. CIA. Partners. But conditions on the ground are deteriorating, and the coastline is simply too damn long. You, however, have been running counterinsurgency operations in Yemen for the past two years—"

"At Abdulaziz's request," Winters pointed out.

"We need those men and their skill sets for this mission," the colonel said, barely registering the interruption. "The black SOF units. You know the ones I mean. How many do you have, Mr. Winters?"

"That's classified," Winters said with a straight face.

Ensher scoffed. Winters knew he was thinking of Ukraine. There were some in USG who appreciated his efforts against Putin. Many more, like Ensher, did not.

"Where's the gap?" Winters asked the colonel.

"Hadhramaut region, especially the port at Al Mukalla."

"That's a lot of coastline."

"We know you have the assets to screen it."

"And you don't?" Winters said, with mock surprise.

"We have planes in the air, ships on the sea, satellites in space, but we don't have the"—the colonel paused—"political will to put more boots on the ground beyond our current SOF assets, and they're overstretched. The top brass worries that dead SEALs might raise questions. No one cares about dead contractors."

"No offense, Mr. Winters," Garcia added.

"None taken," Winters replied. "It's why I have a job."

"Understand, Mr. Winters," Ensher said, "we want you to watch the coast. *Not* intercept the nuclear weapons. We have a SEAL team on station for that."

"I understand. Screening operation only."

The colonel nodded. "So, do you think you could help out your country?"

The room fell silent, as everyone looked at him. Even Ensher, although the ambassador was looking down his nose. He was a stuffed suit. He'd spent his whole life in air-conditioned offices. What did he know?

"Abdulaziz won't like it," Winters said, looking down at the table. "I'd be taking assets away from him to cover the coastline for you."

"The U.S. government will compensate your losses," Garcia said.

Winters winced.

"Double your losses," Garcia corrected.

Winters held up a hand, as if the thought of payment wounded him. "I meant, he will be suspicious. He might change his plans."

"It's five days, Mr. Winters," Martin said. "He won't even notice."

"Five days," Garcia said, "for fifty million dollars. And another five-day contract, if and when needed, to follow."

Winters sucked in his breath, as if impressed by the number. "It's not about the money, gentlemen."

"But you'll take it," Ensher sniffed.

"Title 50 tasker under my existing IDIQ umbrella contract with the Agency, I assume?"

Martin nodded. "You'll have a Langley COTR on paper, but we run it out of this embassy, is that clear? Keep Washington out of it."

Winters sat motionless, enjoying the moment. He didn't even have to look at Ensher to know the man was sweating this deal already.

"As a private military company," the colonel said, "you don't need to observe our rules of engagement. You may board any ship, raid any facility, risk collateral damage, do whatever it takes. This is a license to kill, Mr. Winters," he said. "I expect you to use it."

"You have my word," Winters said. "Now all I need is the intel."

He went around the table shaking hands. He held the colonel's for a moment, making a show of noticing the ring on his finger, although he'd actually noticed it upon entering the room. "An Academy grad," he exclaimed. He held up his own hand. "I'm West Point, class of '80. Pride and Excellence!" It was that year's class motto.

"Annapolis, class of '81," the colonel beamed. "Second to None!"

Ensher caught him by the door as he was about to leave. "You don't fool me, Mr. Winters," he said. His breath smelled of stale pipes. "You're a snake."

"I'm a patriot, Henry," Winters purred. "Second to none."

Ensher looked like he tasted vomit in his mouth. "Don't touch those nuclear weapons."

"Don't worry," Winters purred. "You can trust Apollo. You have my word. Just feed me intel, and my assets will do the rest. I promise."

CHAPTER 32

The recently renamed *Eleutheria*'s fax whirred on the bridge and spit out a weather report as soon as the radio operator turned it on. The navigator read it, then handed it to the captain, then turned the fax off again. Fax machines were hard to track and easily forgotten, but it could be done.

"Fair weather?" the captain asked, taking the paper.

"Fair weather."

"Good. Last time we sailed these waters, there were seventeen-foot waves."

"That's the Arabian Sea for you."

Captain Goncalves walked across the bridge, examining the report. There was more here than the weather, but only he could read the code. His contacts had changed the exchange location. Again. Whoever they were, this commission was careful. Good thing, since he'd spotted aircraft more than once this morning, and the captain knew they weren't flying training missions this far out.

He lit his pipe. Dolphins frolicked in the bow wake as the ship cut nine knots due south, along the sixty-two-degree longitude line, out beyond the reach of the regular cutters that policed the ocean's freeways, and well beyond the coastal patrol boats. His longitude. The smuggler's route. The sea spray wet the deck and the prow sliced the waves, a few hands working the endless tasks of repairs and keeping the rusty scupper shipshape.

The captain smoked as he watched the men work, then

looked upward. He couldn't see anything above him but scattered clouds—even the seagulls had given up and flown back to shore—but he knew they were up there: satellites, passenger planes, drones, naval jets, weather balloons released weeks ago in Madagascar or Mumbai, still drifting on the upper currents, tracking. Always tracking.

But not tracking me, he thought, crumpling up the fax and tossing it overboard.

He would give the men half an hour, then order the new coordinates, as coded into the weather report.

"I'm picking up radio chatter, probably a fax, but no Navtex or AIS signals. Sending you the location. Confirm."

The U.S. Navy P-8 Poseidon, a flying surveillance platform, was thirty-five thousand feet in the air. It could track a small boat hundreds of miles away, eavesdrop on any kind of electronic communication, read billboards from cruising altitude, and more. But this Boeing 737 could also kill. It could launch sonobuoys, depth charges, SLAM-ER cruise missiles, torpedoes, and Harpoon antiship missiles. The P-8 redefined Flying Fortress, and it was looking for just such an anomaly: a fax being received by a boat that, according to AIS info, wasn't there.

The supervisor looked at the blip sent to his screen. It was within their search area, and profiled like a smuggler. "Confirmed. Magnify."

With a few keystrokes, blue ocean became a ship, as the camera zoomed in.

"We have a group-three freighter, aft pilothouse."

Meets our target description, the supervisor thought. "Ship name?"

The operator zoomed in further, so he could see the letters on the ship's stern. "I read *E, L, E, U, T, H, E, R, I, A. Eleutheria.*"

"Flag?"

The operator checked, swiveling the camera.

"Malaysia."

A second passed as the plane's computer looked up the ship against a classified database stateside. The Office of Naval Intelligence, located outside Washington, DC, collected information on nearly everything that floated at any given time. The *Eleutheria*'s last known port was in Singapore, according to the computer, but that was six months ago. It must have been running black ever since. That was illegal, but far too common. It was possible it had been in Gwadar, but doubtful. Ships like this usually stopped in even more dubious ports of call.

"A negative. Not our target," the supervisor said.

"Why do you say that?"

"This ship is carrying contraband for sure, but its heading and position indicates it's coming from the Far East, having rounded the tip of India."

"But it matches our target profile," the operator said.

"So does every fourth freighter in the Indian Ocean. We can't call in SEAL Team 6 every time we see a ship of this class."

The operator stared at the screen, not fully convinced.

"Besides, would you transport nukes in that rusty scupper?"

The operator shook his head.

"It's not our ship. Log it and move on," the supervisor said. *It's a smuggler,* he thought. *Just not our smuggler.* At least now it was in the navy's database.

CHAPTER 33

Brad Winters knew it was trouble the moment he entered Abdulaziz's office. The man was trying too hard to look calm. The two guards on the door were too alert, aware this wasn't a typical meeting. Winters pulled on his suit lapel to straighten it and brushed lint from his sleeve. He took a seat. He had considered the angles in the car ride over. He had been considering them since the moment Farhan disappeared in Istanbul. Talk wasn't cheap. Talk made deals. It ran the world. Today, he sensed, talk would have to save his life. Fine. He was ready. This is what he did better than anyone in the world.

"Farhan has escaped," Abdulaziz said, coming straight to the point.

"Maybe."

"So you know. You don't deny it. You had men in Sinjar. They participated in a firefight against my men."

"The fog of war."

The prince pounded his fist on his desk. "I told you to stay out of Iraq."

"I told you I didn't like that idea."

"I didn't hire you to think," Abdulaziz said.

"Then you shouldn't have hired me at all," Winters replied calmly. His honesty had the prince off balance; now he had to push him the right amount to tip him over.

"No, Mr. Winters, I shouldn't have. But mistakes can be

corrected. No loose ends, as you always say. Above all else, this operation stays confidential."

Winters knew the guards were in position to grab him, but he also knew Abdulaziz wouldn't shoot him here, on his million-dollar rug. He had black torture cells for that.

"I agree. Those responsible for the debacle should die," Winters said. The prince stared, wrong-footed again. "But it was not my men who made the mistake."

"They killed my team."

"But Farhan wasn't there. You understand that, right? Your son was not in the building when the assault took place." Abdulaziz clearly didn't know, so Winters pressed on. "He had help. It was a ruse, allowing your son to escape through a secret exit in the floor. Your men had already let him escape, before they met their unfortunate demise."

"They could have caught him. He couldn't have gone far."

"Agreed. Farhan is still in Sinjar. My men will apprehend him, and kill whoever is helping him."

"Your men shouldn't be in Sinjar," Abdulaziz thundered, bashing his fist on his desk again. "I said I would take responsibility for my son."

"This isn't about your son."

Abdulaziz started to object, but Winters cut him off.

"This is about nuclear weapons, Prince Abdulaziz. It's not about managing your personal affairs. You want to keep your family together. You want to hide the fact that both your sons are a disgrace. You want to keep your high treason a secret. But the Americans know. They told me of their suspicions not one hour ago."

Pause. Let him chew. Hit him again. "I don't doubt your intentions, Prince. I know you and the Sudairi clan would never use a nuclear device. It is a deterrent against the Shia, a guarantee to keep the Kingdom safe. But what about the other side? What would Prince Khalid do, if he had the power? What would ISIS do, if your son gave them the ability to kill a hundred thousand people fifteen times over?"

Abdulaziz didn't say anything.

"A hundred years ago, terrorists initiated World War I with a single assassination in Sarajevo. ISIS will do the same, except they will assassinate a whole city. Fifteen bombs, fifteen cities, fifteen mushroom clouds."

Abdulaziz was seething.

"You care about your son, Prince, to the detriment of your judgment." Winters leaned in. "I fear him."

"I'll shoot you in the face for this," Abdulaziz growled angrily. "I'll strangle your children."

"Maybe. But I cannot sit aside while you let Farhan walk to the ISIS Caliphate with the key to a nuclear arsenal. I'm not going to wait while your son gives ISIS the power to destroy us all."

"Farhan is changed."

"Is that why he fled your men in Istanbul?"

"Do you think I'm a fool? I trusted him to exchange the $5 billion for the nuclear controller key. I trust his loyalty."

"Do you trust him enough to risk the world? Because that's the stakes."

"I know my son," Abdulaziz snarled.

But he glared at Winters, grinding his teeth. Winters could tell the man wanted to shoot him in the face, as promised. If they'd been in a torture cell, he might have done it. He was that angry. But a portion of that anger, Winters knew, was because he was right. It was foolish to trust Farhan with the world, and the prince knew it.

"This is not a game, Prince."

"I never thought it was."

"Then why did you send your boys to play it?"

Winters could tell from the expression on the prince's face that the man was beat. He had come in blaming his American advisor, but Winters had turned him with the truth. The problem was his sons. Now the father was blaming himself. It was the leverage Winters needed.

"Who else could I trust?"

"I advised you against it. So did your majordomo."

Abdulaziz looked away.

"I am doing this for my family," he said. Winters knew this was a lie. Abdulaziz did everything for himself. He wanted to live on through the success of Farhan and Farhan's sons and grandsons, so he had manipulated the boy and given him far too many chances. He believed that was love. "Would you not do everything for your sons?"

"It's time to cut the ties," Winters said. He had no sons. He didn't share Abdulaziz's weakness.

"It's the Iranians," the prince said, suddenly slamming his fist on his ornate gilt desk for the third time. "The Persians are behind this."

Brad Winters relaxed, although not that anyone noticed. The dangerous part was over. He'd saved his own ass. But there was still hard work to do. "We have been over this, Prince Abdulaziz," he said calmly. "It was not the Iranians. The original operation was too precise. The thieves knew where to hit Mishaal's convoy. They knew when he would arrive. They knew what he was carrying. It was an inside job."

"It was not Farhan," Abdulaziz said, halfway between resignation and anger.

"Then it was the work of someone else with inside information, and surely you are not suggesting the Iranians have someone inside the upper level of the General Intelligence Directorate."

"Of course not," Abdulaziz barked. A castrated dog is still dangerous, maybe even more so, especially in the moments after the snip. Winters made sure not to forget that.

"Maybe it was the Pakistanis," Abdulaziz suggested.

"It was not the Pakistanis. Why would they betray you? You framed it as an official back-channel request from the Saudi government. They have their money, and they have no incentive to renege. It was Farhan"—Abdulaziz growled, annoyed at Winters's persistence—"*or* it was the Wahhabis."

He let the suggestion hang in the air, hoping the choice between Farhan and the Wahhabi faction would pull the prince's mind in the right direction.

"You know this is true, my Prince. They are inside the Saudi government, even on the security council. Their numbers are growing in the royal family, even among those near the throne. You know the Wahhabi faction wants their own king on the throne and hates what you stand for. They have eyes and ears everywhere. I realize this was your operation. I know it wasn't sanctioned by your government. Believe me, I also take matters into my own hands, when the opportunity arises. Every good and important man does."

He paused. *We are the same, Prince, you and I.*

"But the Wahhabis would sense things in motion. Prince Khalid . . . your abhorrent rival . . . is a Wahhabi sympathizer. The Mabahith would be the first to hear rumblings. Who else but Khalid would attempt to intercept the nukes instead of exposing you? Only a savvy prince. A brilliant prince. You would do it that way yourself, if the Wahhabis were planning a similar move."

Winters paused again. Flattery will get you everywhere, especially with princes.

"Khalid," Abdulaziz hissed.

"The Paris convoy was hit by a secret faction within the Mabahith, operating illegally outside the Kingdom. They stole the nuclear weapons controller from Mishaal. Last night, they acquired Farhan's key."

Abdulaziz started to object.

"Surely they were the ones helping Farhan escape, my prince, which means Khalid's men also have your son."

Winters said it softly, as if he hated the obvious. He knew this was delicate. The prince might crack, or swerve in the wrong direction.

"Impossible," Abdulaziz said.

"Not if Khalid has infiltrated your inner circle."

"My inner circle is impenetrable."

"No circle is impenetrable."

Abdulaziz shook his head. "I pick my men when they are pups, and hand-feed them until they are wolves, loyal only to me."

"It is the only plausible explanation."

"My circle is tight."

"What about these guards?" Winters said.

The prince looked at them, hesitated. "My circle is tight," he repeated. "Even these guards have proven their loyalty to me time and again. I trust them because I've tested them. I test everyone, Mr. Winters. Except, of course . . . you."

"Finally," Winters said, with exaggerated exasperation, "you are beginning to think. Everyone is suspect. Everyone. Don't think I haven't wondered if you are playing a back door game."

Abdulaziz laughed harshly. Winters had knocked him off track again. "There is nothing in it for me," he said.

"True. But what about the majordomo?"

"He is a son to me," Abdulaziz snapped.

"He *wanted* to be a son to you. You turned him away."

Winters saw the recoil in the old man's eyes, the moment of doubt. He'd hit his mark. Never underestimate the importance of due diligence.

"No," Abdulaziz said. "No. He is loyal to me. He is my right hand."

Abdulaziz stopped.

"Have you spoken to him since last night?" Winters asked calmly. He had received a call from the Apollo team just after midnight. He knew what Campbell had seen, that the majordomo was dead, and he had made an educated guess on the rest: that Locke had outsmarted them all.

"Your majordomo is not a traitor," Winters said. "He is dead. Killed last night in Iraq."

Abdulaziz breathed deeply, and Winters saw his anger and despair. Despite turning away the marriage proposal, the old man had cared for his majordomo.

"Your men killed him," the prince muttered.

"No. It was another."

"Who?"

"I don't know. He left only one message. *Al-kafir mmayit.*"

"'The infidel is dead,'" Abdulaziz said.

"ISIS," Winters muttered.

"Or Khalid," the prince replied, and Winters's heart did a triumphant backflip. Abdulaziz had reached Winters's own conclusion, as planned. The prince would never doubt him now.

"Or the two of them, together," Winters added.

They sat in silence, letting that possibility percolate. The Saudi Wahhabis were Sunni fanatics who agreed with ISIS in principle, if not always in practice. They were the group's primary financial backers. Winters had never, in his most optimistic scenarios, thought such titanic screwups would accrue to his advantage quite like this.

"We have to call it off," Abdulaziz said suddenly. "If Khalid is involved, the Wahhabis are too close and the danger too great. We need to wait. Send the nukes back to Pakistan. Try again later."

"There is no later," Winters said. "The operation is in play. The Pakistanis won't trust you again. The ship is en route. All this work—"

"The work is meaningless. We have to protect the Kingdom."

"The Americans know, Prince Abdulaziz. The Americans know a deal has been made. They have informed people in your government. Worse, Khalid has stolen both nuclear controllers. He can hang you for the Pakistan deal."

"Then I must inform my government. Cut my losses."

"No, Prince, you must go forward. Victory is the only way to save your neck, and it is within your grasp. If everything goes right, I might even be able to save your son."

CHAPTER 34

We made it back to our hideout before sunrise and slept hard. The sound of the Yazidis making breakfast woke me up too soon. Children were playing and the adults were doing chores. It looked like village life, in an old garage, in a war zone. Wildman and the Kurds sat in our Humvees' turrets cleaning the "Ma Deuce" fifty-caliber machine guns, or fifty-cals, while I sat at the back of the garage, pondering. The presence of Apollo Outcomes caused cognitive dissonance in my head, but I had to ignore it. I needed to figure out our next move.

I considered the prince's story: a recovering jihadi, escaping a ruthless father, returns to the Caliphate to rescue his pregnant wife . . . while possessing a key that arms fifteen nuclear bombs.

I had to assume the nukes were real. Why else would an Apollo Tier One team and a Saudi black-ops unit be on his tail? Why else would the majordomo offer me a million dollars to find a disgraced son? It was never about Farhan; it was about the nukes. It was about possessing the power to redraw the Middle East map.

So what was I supposed to do?

I needed to figure out all the pieces, to make sure they fit together. It was math, all angles and degrees, and if my calculus was wrong, the impact could go far beyond my own death. The smart move was obvious: kill Farhan, burn the bodies, and buy back my life with the key. Or I could just leave them here without the key, to find their own way to whatever life was waiting for them.

But my heart wasn't in it. I didn't want to kill the prince, much less a pregnant woman, and leaving them behind wasn't much better. The prince's father, even if he was only half the tyrant everyone claimed, would never let them get away. Not after what Farhan had stolen from him.

And I couldn't forget the Apollo team. I kept trying to cut them from my calculations, but my thoughts always circled back to the same conclusion: *Brad Winters knows I'm here.* That realization was like swallowing a sandbag. All our efforts to dust our tracks after Ukraine didn't matter. I was never off the grid. Brad Winters knew where I was the entire time.

Then the realization hit, harder than the one on the roof: *Winters had hired me.*

Or he had told the majordomo to hire me, which amounted to the same thing.

Winters hadn't just been watching me. He had been playing me like a grand piano. He had been keeping an eye on me, waiting for me to become useful to him again.

And I was *useful to him,* I admitted. How else did that Apollo team locate Farhan in Sinjar so quickly? After all, I was the company's best man by far, and those yahoos at the house didn't have the subtlety to develop the kind of contacts necessary.

It had to be me. Was that pride? Hell yes. But I'd earned it.

And what did you use it for? I chastised myself.

Brad Winters was the mastermind, not me. He had been manipulating the situation all along. He manipulated every situation. It was what the man did.

And I'd never realized it. In the nine years I'd worked with him, I'd never fully grasped who he was. And in the four months he'd been following me since Ukraine—laughing at my pathetic efforts to disappear, no doubt—I'd never suspected he could still control me.

He had trapped me. Again. He had tried to kill me again, just like in Ukraine. He *would* have killed me if I hadn't been testing Farhan's story and his father's men. I thought of myself as a great mission tactician. A master in the field. But for the second time in four months, I had been outwitted by a . . . a businessman . . . and I had been lucky to survive.

"Oy!" Wildman yelled at one of the small kids. They were running around, playing terrorists and mercenaries. "If you're going to low-crawl, get your fockin' arse down. Do it right! And when you shoot, aim for center of mass, not the head." He made a gun with his hand and aimed at the child's chest. "Center of mass. Chest." He thumped his chest. "More likely to get a kill that way, mate. And fire in short, three-round bursts. Bang, bang, bang. Got it? Bang, bang, bang!"

The children looked excited, even though they spoke no English. They were just happy to have this big merc talking to them. *Ban, ban, ban,* they screamed, running after each other. I was surprised, after all they'd seen, they still wanted to play war games, but what else did they know?

"Can't teach kids anything these days," Wildman lamented, as he turned back to his work.

Unbelievable. We were sitting on a nuclear key, in the middle of ISIS hell, and Wildman couldn't have cared less.

Boon? Yeah, he cared. He'd badgered me for an hour, trying to figure out what we should do. Then he'd gone on walkabout.

"Don't forget these people," was the last thing he said.

I admit it: I was happy that these refugees weren't my biggest problem anymore. After four months, I was tired of bashing my brains on little things. It sucked to be nobody. What I decided now, since this nuclear key had fallen into my lap, could change the world. I could make a difference.

I'd missed that.

I closed my eyes and let my mind wander over Kylah's breasts when her shirt fell open, the faceless girl in the *sabaya* bus, the shootout, the cookies, Jimmy Miles calling me a fucking butterball piece of shit with a big stupid grin on his face, and Brad Winters pulling me aside in a boardroom somewhere back home, putting his arm around me and whispering, *You and me kid, you and me, together, we'll make it right.*

I felt like a fool for ever listening. I felt marooned on an asteroid, watching the sun grow smaller. My brain started humming the introduction to the second part of Stravinsky's queasy ballet *The Rite of Spring,* the music disorienting, creepy, even violent, celebrating the sacrifice of a virgin girl forced to dance to her death in a pagan ritual. The Parisians hissed it offstage at its premiere in 1913, causing a riot in the theater. They didn't realize that the primitive society was them. None of us ever did.

I could never be free, that was what my brain was telling me, not if Brad Winters cared enough to find me.

Once my utility was concluded, though, once Brad Winters had what he wanted, he would have us killed. No loose ends. None of us, not even me, could dance on their own forever.

Mercs don't panic; they get organized. They take things one step at a time. Right now I had an opportunity, because right now my old mentor needed me.

And he was coming. He had a hit team in Sinjar waiting for us to make a move, but that wasn't the extent of his reach. Apollo would be coming in numbers. The Saudis would be coming in numbers. They were surely on their way. We needed to get out of Sinjar as quickly as possible.

But where could we go? This was no longer a matter of escaping a war zone. Winters could track us anywhere. He had proven that.

We needed a plane, and we needed it fast. My list of favors had run dry, so I couldn't call any pilot friends. There was only one active airport in northern Iraq: Erbil. That was a dangerous road, and an expected one. If I were Winters, I'd watch my two escape routes: north to Turkey and east to Erbil. Everything else was war zone.

I took out my map, looking for another way out. My fingers traced routes as if they were printed in Braille. Different roads led to different dead ends: ISIS, the Syrian army, Shia militia, the lawless tribes of the interior, Winters, the Saudis.

We looked cornered, but my intuition was screaming there was a way. So I used a trick that had long helped me hear my subconscious voice: I closed my eyes and let the music flow. *The Ring of the Nibelungen* entered my head, faintly at first, then louder, until I recognized "Rhine Journey." Before there were hobbits and Smaug, there were Nibelungen and Fafner, chasing a magic ring to rule them all. "Rhine Journey" is ten minutes of musical transformation, from doubt to certainty. It starts as an unformed universe and ends with the cosmos complete in seven days. The music confirms creation with trumpets of optimism and crescendos of destiny. Go to God, it told me. Go to the Father. It is the only way.

It could work, I thought. It was crazy, dangerous, and stupid . . . which was why it could work.

The prince was asleep with Marhaz in his arms when I rejoined the team. I stared at the two of them, so young, so foolish. To my surprise, I was moved by their affection, but I wasn't surprised that I thought of Alie. She was Marhaz's age, early twenties, when I met her, and she was smart, erratic, and very, very bad for me. We'd proven that in Ukraine, if it hadn't been clear before. She was gone now, disappeared in Europe somewhere, but I knew I'd see her again. That's the way this works, right? There are people you can never get away from. And really, that's the only thing that keeps you going sometimes: the thought of seeing them again.

I was surprised to see Marhaz staring at me, trying to read my face. "We're going," she said. Farhan didn't move from his unconscious embrace. The baker was sleeping sitting up nearby, his AK-47 across his lap. He was supposed to be on guard duty.

"Tonight," I whispered, bending down beside her. "But it will be a fast run with limited space. We can't take your friends." She nodded. "Do you think Farhan will object?"

"He will go along," she whispered firmly, biting off the words, and I believed her.

"Will his friends?"

"They will do it for me," she said, and I realized who had been keeping them alive in this hellhole the last six months, while Farhan was in his father's prison.

"If they go north and are captured, will Farhan's father have them killed?"

She thought for a moment. "They can't be captured," she said.

I nodded and slipped away. Moments later, I found Wildman and Boon.

"Here's the plan," I said, unfolding the map. It took a few minutes to explain.

"Fook no," Wildman said immediately.

"That's insane," Boon said.

"Which is why it might work, right?"

Boon shrugged. He was looking at Marhaz, probably thinking about the baby. My plan was the only way. He hated it, but I knew he was going along.

I looked at Wildman. "You can walk away if you don't like it," I said. "They need your type here."

"I'm not bloody walking," he snapped back. "Not if that means staying in this desert. And besides, what would you knobs do without me?"

"What about the Kurds?" Boon asked me.

"What about them?"

"We can't expect them to follow us, not on this." He was right. I'd fallen into the typical American trap of thinking our allies, in this case the Kurds we'd been partnered with for the last few months, should just do what we said, even if it wasn't in their best interest.

"I'll talk to them," I told Boon. "Wildman, you set the demolitions."

Wildman smiled, his missing teeth cracking his black bear beard in the dim light of the warehouse. I looked down and saw his little friend staring at us, the one who had led us to the first meeting place yesterday morning.

"Take the kid," I said. "He knows this town."

Wildman didn't argue, just cuffed the kid and pointed toward the canteens. Apparently, my gruff explosives expert had made a friend. First time for everything.

One last task. The moment of no return.

I woke Farhan roughly, laughing as he sprang into a defensive position, his AK-47 in firing position. He must have been exhausted to fall asleep that deeply. He'd been on the road from Istanbul for three days.

"I need your phone," I said.

"What phone?"

I had frisked everyone for phones so that nobody could track us. It was a rookie move to carry a mobile phone on the run. If it was turned on, even for a second, it could give us away. But I suspected Farhan hadn't complied with my orders. So-called leaders never did.

"Don't be stupid," I said.

"Don't worry," he assured me, as he pulled a phone from his robes. "It's not mine. And it's untraceable. Yes, I'm sure. I'm no fool."

It was a satellite phone, but unlike any I'd seen before. Custom-made. I extended the small boom antenna and dialed a number. "Hey. It's me . . . I need a favor. I'm gonna be coming in hot." I looked at my watch. "ISIS. Maybe others . . . After midnight . . . Yes . . . Of course . . . Roger . . . wilco, out."

Farhan reached for his phone. "I'm keeping it. And I need something else from you, too."

"The key?"

I nodded. He understood my price. "The key."

He hesitated but Marhaz appeared behind him. She must have been listening. She guided her hand slowly over his. "We have to trust him, *habibi*."

He looked at her. Was that what love looked like?

He handed over the nuclear key.

"Don't worry," I said. "I'll get you out of here, or you'll die trying."

He grunted. I don't think he heard the joke.

"What would he have done, had he not met you?" I asked Marhaz, after we'd both watched the prince walk away.

She was silent, but only for a moment. "Gone home and rule his little kingdom in Saudi Arabia," she said.

CHAPTER 35

The Sikorsky MH-60R Seahawk helicopter settled in to cruise five hundred feet above the waves.

"Knight Rider Six Five, this is Icepack. Say 'Status,' over?" *Icepack* was the call sign for the air surveillance controllers in the Combat Information Center aboard the USS *Lexington*, a Ticonderoga-class cruiser and the helo's mothership.

"Long run complete, Icepack," the pilot replied into his headset. "Ten miles due south of Masirah, point five, inbound mother, overhead plus forty-five, two-plus zero-zero. Five souls."

The Knight Rider had just picked up the ship's new chaplain in Fujairah, a major airhead and refueling port in the United Arab Emirates. Its strategic location outside the Straits of Hormuz allowed U.S. ships in the area a chance to top off before heading into or out of the Arabian Gulf. But Fujairah was no shore station; coming that close to land was too dangerous, as the USS *Cole* learned in Yemen in 2000, when terrorists blew a hole in the destroyer's hull while it was at pier. Now the U.S. Navy refueled at sea. Underway replenishment, or UNREP, is a ballet of tankers and supply ships refilling warships on the high seas. Fujairah was a primary stage.

"Is that Masirah Island?" the chaplain asked through the headset, the rising sun lighting up its beaches. They had just flown over Oman, and this island was the last dry land between them and their ship. The chaplain had the enthusiasm of a tourist.

"Affirmative," the crew chief said. "Our last bailout point."

"Say again, fuel state?" Icepack said.

"Two-plus zero-zero. Full bag." Standard aviator lingo for "two hours."

Radio silence. The pilot sensed a change of mission coming.

"Thank you, Mr. . . . ah, Mr. . . ." said the chaplain, as he fumbled with his headset. He was fresh from the States, fresh from seminary, fresh to the navy.

"Dice," the pilot said.

"Dice?"

"Call me Dice. Call sign 'Dice.'"

"Okay, Mr. Dice."

"Just Dice."

"Okay . . . Dice. I wanted to thank you for . . ."

"Not now, zip lip. Standing by for tasking from Icepack."

"Oh, right. I understand." He clearly didn't.

"Chief," Dice said to the crew chief. "Please explain things to the Chaps."

"Father," the crew chief said. "Shut up."

"Knight Rider, this is Icepack. FRAGO to VID. Small group-three freighter with an aft pilothouse. Sending coordinates."

"Copy, Icepack," Dice replied, and changed course.

"What is it?" the chaplain asked, unable to stop himself.

"FRAGO."

"What's that?"

"Fragmentary order. A new mission."

"So we're not going to the *Lexington*?"

"Not yet. They want us to check out a freighter first."

"Is that safe?"

Dice turned off the chaplain's headset. *Fuckin' newbies,* he thought. He had a freighter to find before he could go home, and the chaplain's prattle was giving him a headache.

Open ocean and gray haze. For forty minutes, that was all they saw, which pretty much sums up every day when flying Navy Air.

"Dice, I think we got something," the copilot said. A blip showed on the fringe of their radar screen.

"That must be it. Let's go."

Fifteen minutes later they could see the freighter. Dice switched to maritime channel 19, the universal channel for bridge-to-bridge communication.

"Cargo ship in vicinity Socotra Island," he called down to the ship, "this is U.S. Navy helicopter Six Five, half a mile off your port beam. Request description of your cargo manifest and destination port."

Silence.

The helo closed to about four hundred yards from the freighter's bridge so they would know they were the one being hailed. Dice repeated the call.

"Captain, captain!" the radio operator called, stumbling to the bridge. "A U.S. Navy helicopter is hailing us. They're off our port bow."

Captain Goncalves grabbed binoculars and peered out the left windows. In the distance he could see the chopper, gray on gray.

Not good, he thought.

"Cargo ship in vicinity Socotra Island," the chopper pilot repeated.

"Captain, what do you want to do?"

Goncalves just stared through the binoculars.

"Captain." It was the first mate this time, just arriving at the bridge. "If we don't answer, they'll come back with two choppers of marines."

Goncalves turned suddenly, seized the helmsman by the collar and dragged him to the bridge radio. "You're Filipino, yes?"

"Y-y-yes, captain," the man answered nervously.

"Then answer in Filipino."

"In Tagalog?"

Goncalves grabbed a three-ring binder from the navigator's desk and beat the man.

"Stop! Please, stop!" the man pleaded.

"Did I not just give you an order?!"

The man whimpered to the radio.

"Speak, damn it," the captain said.

"What should I say?"

The captain hit him across the face with the binder. The man started speaking ragged Tagalog.

"I am bihag sa barko ito. Tulungan mo ako!"

"What the hell is that?" the copilot asked.

"I am bihag sa barko ito. Tulungan mo ako!"

"It's a foreign language," Dice said. "Sounds like Spanish."

"Amateurs."

"Or smugglers. Let's take a closer look," Dice said, as he nosed the Seahawk toward the ship.

"They're coming toward us!" the helmsman shouted.

"What the fuck did you tell them?" Goncalves demanded.

"N-n-nothing! I swear it!" said the Filipino, but it didn't save him from the binder.

"Get some hands on deck! Look busy," the captain said. "Do . . . routine things."

Dice maneuvered carefully around the freighter, hovering fifty feet above sea level.

"Icepack, this is Knight Rider. I've located the cargo ship. Name is the *Eleutheria*, Malaysian flag. They are not answering in English."

"Roger, Knight Rider. What do you see?"

"Wait one."

This was Dice's third tour in the Gulf, and he'd seen more than his share of smugglers. Once, he'd seen a tugboat dragging a submersed shipping container of cigarettes. He circled the freighter, looking at the machinery, tackle, other things that a normal cargo ship would use. They looked like they had been recently operated. Of course, the ship was in such disrepair that it was hard to tell. Men on the bridge were waving.

"Knight Rider, we ran it. It's already been bagged and tagged. Not our target. Return to Mother."

"Roger, Icepack. Returning to ship."

"They're flying away," the first mate said, waving at the helicopter.

Assholes, Goncalves thought, also waving.

"That's the last we'll see of them," the mate said.

"No. There will be more."

CHAPTER 36

Brad Winters stared at himself in a garish gilt mirror that took up half the wall as he waited in the antechamber for Abdulaziz to allow him admittance. His hair was cut short but impeccably groomed, with a sharp part and an old-fashioned rise in the front, like a small wave curling toward a beach. A Princeton, they used to call this haircut, on the old illustrated 1950s haircut charts.

White boy cut, his barber had called it with a laugh, back in the inner-city Baltimore neighborhood where Winters grew up. The man was used to African-American hair; he could never get the Princeton right.

Winters had it just right now, though, even if it had been five days since his last trim. He had gone gray over the last few years, but he was lucky: the hair was stone white and distinguished, with just a bit of color at the temples. He made his face as blank as possible and stared into his own eyes, but he couldn't find anything hidden there. Good. If he couldn't find his true self in his face, then neither could anyone else.

Clooney-esque, he thought, tipping his chin a quarter inch to the right and allowing himself a mirthless smile.

"Mr. Winters," the prince's male secretary said, opening the door.

He went inside, the computer tucked under his arm. He had brought the largest flat-screen he could find, for effect.

"What do you have for me now, Mr. Winters?" Abdulaziz

sighed. Winters could see the strain under his eyes. The man hadn't been sleeping. *Just wait, my prince. It gets worse.*

"I'll let the video do the talking," he said, even though the video had been recorded, possibly accidentally, without sound.

He set up the computer and found the bookmarked site, while the prince sighed impatiently. He was in his late sixties and pampered; he had no use for computers. But his eyes widened when he saw the majordomo in the alley with his phone in his hand, and the gaunt figure stepping into the frame behind him. He didn't flinch when the man cut his majordomo's fingers off with a ludicrous sword, nor did he flinch when his head came off with one blow. He had seen these kinds of things before. He lived by them. But Winters knew the death had unnerved him.

"Where did you get this?" Abdulaziz demanded.

"We monitor the fanatic websites. It's a valuable part of our job. The video appeared this afternoon, shortly after the noon prayers."

"Is it real?"

Winters nodded. "Yes. And there are seven others with earlier time stamps, all the same assailant, all beheadings."

The prince stared at the screen, although the image had gone black. He wasn't thinking about the majordomo. He was thinking about his son, out there somewhere, with this fanatic nearby.

"Who is he?"

"I don't know his true name, but he has a nickname by which he is known."

The prince looked up as Winters paused for effect. "Yes?" he said.

"The Wahhabi," Winters said solemnly, knowing the name would hit Abdulaziz hard. The man was a Saudi. The man was a Sunni religious fanatic. The man would lead the prince's mind exactly where Winters wanted it to go: to a palace conspiracy, to the rival faction, to Prince Khalid.

"Anything else?" the prince asked, pointedly looking away. Winters could almost feel his mind churning. Abdulaziz was paranoid, unstable, and surrounded by enemies. He was not a man to be pushed too far.

"Not right now, my prince."

"Then please go. And take this blasted machine."

One less loose end, Winters thought with a small smile, as he tucked the blasted machine under this arm. *One more push.*

That push was happening forty kilometers away, in al Ha'ir prison. Even as Brad Winters was slipping into the backseat of his chauffeured car, contemplating how to find Prince Farhan, or at least how to keep him from escaping Sinjar, Mishaal was on his knees, begging his faceless attendant for his cure.

"I am nothing," the prince was saying. "I am unclean. I am"—*anything you want me to be, if it means one more shot—*"yours."

"Now you see the truth," the attendant said, as he pulled the hypodermic needle from his robes, and plunged it into the base of Mishaal's skull.

The prince felt the relief sweeping over him, like desert rain, like the Nile flooding its banks in the spring and covering the dry fields with the basic nutrients of life, the dead plants, the rotten timbers, the broken-down shit. He felt his cells open to receive, crying out, and then collapse on themselves. He found himself crying, his face to his prayer rug, his lips intoning silently the glory of the father.

Six minutes later, he was dead.

CHAPTER 37

We sat quietly in the Humvees, waiting for 0445. Boon was in the lead vehicle with Wildman manning the turret. I was in the commander's seat of the trail vehicle, with our Kurdish driver and turret gunner. Marhaz sat behind me and Farhan across from her. He looked like the ISIS killer he was trained to be, yet his eyes doted on Marhaz. It was a Romeo and Juliet action story.

The younger Kurd fighters had voted to come with us, a sign of respect. Warriors don't let brothers down, even if it started as a brotherhood of convenience. The older Kurd stayed with the refugees, hoping to guide them to freedom. It was my decision to mix the team between the two vehicles. It was going to get violent out there, and this was our best operational arrangement.

"One minute," I said over the headset.

It was almost five, just before morning prayers and at the beginning of dawn twilight. This sliver of time afforded us sufficient darkness for stealth, yet enough light should a fire-fight erupt.

Farhan was whispering to Marhaz in Arabic, stroking her belly with one hand and holding a Kalashnikov in the other. But Marhaz didn't need reassurance. She knew she might die in the next fifteen minutes, but she'd lived that way for months. It would have been hell for an unmarried pregnant woman in ISIS territory. A true living hell. If she'd been stopped and questioned, she would have been shot, defenestrated, or stoned to death. I don't know where she'd been hiding, but she was tough. She and her prince made a good match.

"Thirty seconds," I said.

We donned our night-vision goggles, switched on the infrared headlights, and powered up the engines. Two Yazidi children swung open the garage doors. We would go first, sprinting south toward the desert, attracting ISIS's attention. A few minutes later, the refugees would sneak out heading north, past the mountain and, eventually, hopefully, to Turkey.

The last thirty seconds seemed the longest. My mind wandered to the middle movement of Bruckner's ninth symphony. The orchestra creeps along, ready to pounce. Waiting. Waiting. We would have to be Bruckner's symphony, quietly holding back then exploding in a fortissimo of firepower. No wrong notes. Not this time.

"Go!" I said.

"*Allahu akbar!*" Wildman screamed. "Yahweh, Jesus, and Mary!"

We rocketed out of the garage like the Bruckner symphony, the Hummers' turbo diesels screaming. It was six blocks to the main road, another three blocks to the Mosul road, and then into the Jazira.

"Detonate," I said over the headset.

The first explosion rocked the Humvee. It felt like a building collapsing or an ammo dump going up. Or both. Wildman and the kid had done their job well.

"Shit," I yelled, as a man darted across the street. We clipped him, his body disappearing as we hurdled around a corner. I had no idea if he was ISIS or just some poor guy trying to sneak a smoke.

The second and third explosions felt even bigger. Rocks pelted the Humvee's skin, someone started firing, and my gunner collapsed.

"Are you okay?" I shouted over my shoulder.

No response. Lifeless. I unbuckled and crawled from the front seat to the turret, swinging the fifty-caliber gun forward. Boon's Humvee was five meters in front.

"Slow down!" I shouted to my driver. If Boon was hit, we would rear-end him, incapacitating both vehicles, but the driver didn't hear me. Twenty seconds in, and we were already down a man and barely maintaining control.

In the distance I heard the fourth explosion, and then at least three more. I heard gunfire, wild and undisciplined. ISIS wasn't sure where the attack was coming from. I could picture the grin on Wildman's face as he pulled each detonator, creating his own personal symphony.

We cut through Yazidi mass graves, fresh from ISIS's recent ethnic cleansing, and careened onto the main road, the Humvee lifting up on two wheels as we cornered.

I saw the ISIS flag, black against the gray night. Two technicals were blocking the road, with dirt embankments on both sides. There was no going around them. We were barreling down the highway in blackout drive, and that gave us an advantage of vital seconds. Even better, they were facing out, away from the city.

I turned the fifty-cal to face them as the night exploded. It wasn't another C-4 charge. It was Wildman, in the front Humvee, launching an RPG. I pressed the thumb trigger of the fifty, and the Humvee rocked with the jackhammer of the heavy weapon. Tracers zipped in front of me, riddling the technicals. Three militants fell to the ground.

"Ramming speed!" Boon cried over the radio. The lead Hummer plowed through the road block, knocking the rear ends of both ISIS pickups backward.

"Fuck yeah!" I heard Wildman scream. He tossed a grenade into a technical's flatbed as he passed, and I followed with another grenade. Both vehicles blew up, leaving the scene a smoking wreck. The only thing untouched was the ISIS flag, flapping black in the desert wind. It wasn't worth the bullets.

Wildman was singing "It's a Long Way to Tipperary" at the top of his lungs, a joyously inappropriate drinking song.

"We made it," Marhaz sighed.

"Not yet," I said, swinging the fifty to cover our rear.

Behind us, I could see tracers streaming toward us. An RPG flew above our heads and impacted the desert fifty meters in front of us. I ducked as we burst through the dirt plume. Sand and stone cracked loudly against the windshield, which was traveling at almost 120 kilometers per hour, and bit against my skin.

ISIS headlights in pursuit, about five hundred meters to our rear.

"Seven pursuit vehicles," I said over the radio, counting headlights.

"Eight," Wildman corrected, somehow holding binoculars to his face as we hurtled across the rough terrain.

The lead vehicle was an MRAP, a massive U.S. Army armored scout truck. Even the fifty-cal was going to have trouble chewing that up.

"Where did they get a damn MRAP?" Wildman yelled. With the headset, it was like we were riding side by side.

"Must have captured it when they took Mosul," I said, cursing the cowardly Iraqi army.

Muzzle flashes from the MRAP.

"Contact! Taking fire," I said.

"Where?" It was Boon.

"Five o'clock. Heavy weapons."

"Zigzagging," Boon said, as his Humvee began to lurch left and right. Our driver followed, and I was almost thrown from the turret. Random zigzagging would slow us down, but a fifty-cal round from the MRAP could take out a tire, finishing us.

We needed more time. I scanned the horizon with my bin-oculars for a wadi or similar terrain feature to shake off our pursuers. Nothing. Then a glisten in the sky.

"Reapers," I yelled, pointing to the CIA drones.

"They're skipping," Murphy said over the headset. "Two Hum-vees, heading south in blackout drive." The drone's camera zoomed in on the speeding vehicles.

Jase Campbell nodded to his driver, who started the engine. Large explosions were rocking the center of Sinjar. ISIS was scurrying like ants. He was focused on the monitor in the Viper. A powerful forward-looking infrared scope, or FLIR, was mounted on the top of the vehicle.

This is it, he thought, as the Humvees neared the checkpoint on the edge of Sinjar. *The mercs are making their move.* A few seconds later, a vicious barrage lit his viewfinder a rainbow of color.

"Holy crap, they just smoked that ISIS position," Bunker, his lookout, yelled. "Burn in hell, assholes."

"That's them," Campbell said, grabbing the twin joysticks. "I've got control of the drone."

"Bet you a case of Red Bull it's a diversion," Murphy ven-tured. "Why would they be headed back to Mosul?"

"Bet's on. That's them. Move out!"

Jase Campbell kept his eyes on the drone's screen as the Vipers sprang forward, honeycomb wheels kicking up dirt. None of the men at the checkpoint were moving; the mercs had been ruth-lessly effective. He panned left. To the naked eye, the Humvees were difficult to see when running blackout drive in the middle of the night, but the FLIR's thermal imaging made their engine blocks appear white on the screen. He locked on.

"Vehicles in pursuit," Bunker said over the radio. Campbell

panned the drone's FLIR right and saw the engine blocks of the ISIS vehicles, all eight of them.

"Lock and load," he growled, the anaconda tattoo rippling around his neck. "We've got competition."

"Rules of engagement?" Bunker inquired.

"Weapons free. Take out their turrets and shred the tires with the Gatling guns. That ought to clip their wings."

The Vipers tore through the desert toward the highway four klicks from where they had been hiding out, watching as many exits as they could. Two minutes later, they passed the obliterated ISIS checkpoint. Dead militants lay scattered on the ground. A wounded man held up a bloody hand as the three Vipers tore through, the last one swerving to run him over. All the other ISIS vehicles in this area had taken off in pursuit of glory. Nobody had bothered with the dead or wounded. Campbell hoped the flies ate their dicks and laid eggs in their eyeballs.

"Fan out. Run them down," Campbell said to Duke, his driver, as the thermal image of the trucks blinked on the horizon. The desert was an optical illusion, especially in the dark; it was difficult to gauge distance. "We need another two hundred meters to be in range."

He watched the kilometers click by, knowing his men were priming the antitank missiles. Locking on and hitting moving targets from two klicks out was possible, but the odds were poor.

"Almost in range."

"Fire when ready."

The CIA drones were banking. An RPG flew above our heads, fired from the ISIS column. More muzzle flashes.

"Faster!" Boon said over the radio.

The enemy of my enemy is my friend. I stooped down into the Humvee, searching the bouncing cabin. Ammo boxes, satchel charges, a C-4 teddy bear made by Wildman, flares. I grabbed the flare gun and popped up the turret. I aimed in front of the drones and pulled the trigger. Reload. Fire again. Two red star clusters shot into the sky.

Both drones swung toward us.

"What are you doing?!" Wildman asked.

"Getting their attention."

"Mission accomplished," he said, deadpan, as the drones banked toward us.

The first drone assumed an attack profile, perpendicular to the convoy. Seconds later, four Hellfire missiles streaked from the Reaper. Three ISIS technicals vanished in clouds of dirt, metal, and fire. The MRAP took a hit center of mass, blowing in the cabin and hurling the vehicle on its side. A technical plowed into the wreckage and flipped end over end. Five down, three to go.

"Just like you planned it, mate," Wildman yelled, as the Reaper veered away.

"It's coming back," Farhan yelled, eyes alert. He had maneuvered to the front seat for better visibility.

"Negative," I said. "They only carry four missiles."

"How did you know they would use them on ISIS and not us?"

"The MRAP. They target the biggest stuff first."

"What about the second Reaper?" Marhaz asked.

"One problem at a time," I said.

"Three vehicles on our six," Boon said, pointing out our next problem. The technicals were lighter than the Hummers, and catching up. It would be a fair fight, not my favorite odds.

The first Reaper assumed an attack profile again, this time toward us, since we were the largest targets left. Two bombs dropped from its wings.

"Hard right! Hard right!" I shouted, ducking into the cabin. The Humvees fishtailed right, moving out of the bomb's trajectory.

A flash, then a massive concussion as the five-hundred-pound bomb blew a crater in the desert, lifting our up-armored Humvee off the ground. *Missed*, I thought, as we slammed back down, dirt crackling off the windshield, and kept driving.

"I thought you said it only had four missiles," Marhaz yelled.

"It does. Those were laser-guided smart bombs. Fortunately, they aren't that effective against moving targets. If it had been Hellfire missiles, we'd be dead."

The second Reaper assumed an attack profile.

"They're maneuvering," Bunker yelled. A second later, they saw the two star clusters in the sky. The Reapers banked toward the star clusters and locked onto the ISIS convoy.

"Clever," Campbell muttered, as he saw the Hellfires wipe out the MRAP and half the technicals.

"ALCON, we got two MQ-9 Reapers on station," Murphy said over the command channel.

"I need those Hummers alive," Campbell said. "Do not kill them. Repeat, do not kill the Humvees."

The three Vipers assumed a wedge formation, with Campbell's vehicle on point. They were closing fast on the remaining ISIS vehicles.

"Reaper making another pass, targeting Humvees. Hummers conducting evasive maneuvers."

"Those boys at Langley better not hit my target," Campbell

said. When he was in Iraq with JSOC, three of his kill missions were scrubbed because of the Agency. Turned out his target worked for the CIA scumbags. He wasn't about to see them ruin another day.

"Bombs away," Murphy said.

"Sonsabitches!" Campbell yelled.

Two smart bombs streaked toward the Humvees, which were now skidding hard right. The impact splashed dirt a hundred meters wide and high, barely missing the rear vehicle.

"Both bombs went wide. Targets still on the move."

Thank you, Lord Jesus, Campbell thought.

"Second Reaper assuming attack profile."

"Stingers, quick reaction drill. Move! Move! Move!" Campbell ordered. All three Vipers' top hatches opened and men emerged, each holding a Stinger missile on his shoulder while screwing the battery coolant unit into the grip stock and leveling the surface-to-air missile at the CIA drones.

"Got tone," one of the Stinger gunners said.

"Take the shot," Campbell said, the anaconda tattoo on his neck throbbing with anticipation.

Foooossh.

"Away." As the missile left the tube, its main rocket kicked in, propelling it toward the sky.

"It's locked onto the first Reaper."

"Goddammit!" Campbell shouted, pounding his fist into the dashboard.

The missile spiraled toward the drone, which blew up in a puff of black smoke. "Reaper down."

"Second Reaper on attack run."

"I want that second Reaper knocked out the sky!"

"Got tone. Firing."

Foooossh.

"Second Reaper firing on Humvees. Four Hellfires away."

Missiles streaked through the sky. The Stinger missed its mark, flying high and then tracking away at the rising sun. The four Hellfires impacted. The rear ISIS technical exploded in a fireball, and the other vehicles vanished in a cloud of dirt.

"GODDAMMIT!" Campbell yelled.

"Humvees down," Bunker confirmed.

"Reaper turning on us," Murphy said.

Fuck a duck, Campbell thought.

CHAPTER 38

The Wahhabi watched the battle from a rise several kilometers away. He stood exposed, letting the spirit of jihad pass through him, his robes whipping behind him in the wind. He watched the tracers tear into their target, blowing metal and bone outward in all directions. The checkpoint was martyred. His brothers gave chase but were intercepted by the American drones. The infidels lacked the courage to face them, murdering from the sky.

Flashes of gunfire between the Humvees and mujahideen, bombs falling, their explosions echoing across the desert. By Allah's will, the Humvees emerged from the plumes of smoke. Then three combat vehicles, unlike any he had seen before, emerged from the bluffs outside Sinjar and gave chase. They fired on the drones, who fired on the rest. Smoke trails danced across the black sky, flashes of light, then distant explosions. It was beautiful.

"*Allahu Akbar,*" the Wahhabi muttered as he dropped his head and opened his palms to the sky, overcome by the majesty of creation.

"*Allahu Akbar,*" his driver said, bowing and muttering in prayer.

The Wahhabi turned and seemed to notice the little man for the first time, even though he had been at his side since he arrived at Sinjar, the first of many followers.

He had been like that little man once, as a child. He had been like those men in the desert, an instrument for destruction, killing without conscience. Now he was Allah's instrument. Trained as an assassin by the *kafir* Saudi government, he had abandoned that wicked life and even his name. Now he would redeem his past sins by cleansing the Caliphate of infidels, specifically those like the mercenaries, who were worthy of his skill.

The Wahhabi cupped his hands in prayer, and whispered a *dua* for the dead.

Whoever asks Allah to be killed in His cause sincerely from his heart, Allah shall give him the reward of martyrdom.

And whoever survives, Allah shall give him fame . . . and power . . . and maybe riches, if Allah is wise.

"*Daena nadhhab,*" he barked. Let's go.

CHAPTER 39

"Look for a deep wadi," I ordered, as the second Reaper banked toward us on an attack run. The desert around us was rocky and flat, like Mars, but there had to be a wadi somewhere. If only we had those Apollo three-dimensional topo maps now.

Muzzle flashes as the ISIS technicals hit the Humvee, but nothing exploded.

"Contact! Six o'clock," I said, walking the fifty-cal's tracers into the lead technical. The shooting stopped and the gunner's body fell overboard. The man in the navigator's seat skillfully slid out the door window and took up the gunner's position. Firing resumed. Bullets zinged around my head.

My fifty-cal jammed.

Shit. I worked the bolt lever to recycle the round. "Can't we go any faster?"

"Wadi, eleven o'clock, half a klick," Boon said.

"Get us there. Warp speed."

The Reaper was closing, about to fire.

We swerved left, but I couldn't see a wadi, just desert. The zinging was increasing. Four jet trails from the Reaper, heading right for us.

"Reaper firing!"

"Buckle up!" Boon yelled.

Then we were airborne, a sickening feeling in the pit of my stomach. Humvees should never be airborne. We hit like a ton of concrete, ten feet below the ground, earth on both sides of us, as the Hellfires swished overhead and exploded with a vicious roar. I heard Marhaz scream from the impact, both hands on her pregnant belly, but we were in a tight wadi, traveling fifty mph, and there was no time to check on her as our left-side mirror was sheared off. We were scraping the wall at speed.

Two ISIS vehicles also made the leap into the wadi, closing fast. The tiny ravine offered us some protection from the Reaper, but not completely. It circled above us, stalking its prey.

I glanced around the Humvee cabin. Marhaz was staring at the ceiling and clutching her seat and belly.

"Take this," Farhan said, handing me four blocks of C-4 and a C-4 squirrel taped together with a short fuze.

A satchel charge.

I grabbed the explosive and popped up the turret. The nose of the lead Toyota was less than ten meters behind us, snaking around the turns. He fired on me, and I ducked.

"Fire in the hole!" I shouted, pulling the fuze and holding the satchel charge. *One thousand, two thousand, three thousand,* I counted as the Humvee cut left and right, following the contours of the dry river bed.

Four thousand, five thousand. If I threw it too soon, the ISIS vehicles would drive right over the charge before it blew. If I held it too long . . .

"Now!" Farhan yelled.

Six thousand. "Fire in the hole!" I shouted, starting to toss the satchel charge, but the Hummer hit a rut and the charge bounced out of my hand.

Seven thousand. Oh shit. Eight thousand. The satchel charge was stuck in the camo net strapped to our tailgate.

Nine thousand. I lunged forward to push the satchel charge off with the tip of my SCAR rifle, swaying with the vehicle as it swerved around the oxbows. I heard the bullets impact around me, puncturing the spare tire strapped to our rear.

Ten thousand. It was gonna blow.

Buddha calm, Tom, I thought, closing my eyes and nudging the C-4 with my rifle barrel. We hit another bump hard, sending the charge and me flying. Time slowed as I grabbed a cargo strap and saw the satchel tumble to the wadi floor.

Thank you, Ogun, I thought.

I felt the explosion before I heard it. The concussive wave lifted the technical off its wheels with a deafening boom. It lifted me, too, and I slammed into our fifty-caliber's deflective guard, the only thing that saved me from being catapulted a hundred meters into the desert.

Pain in my head. Ears. Side. The vehicle moved beneath me and I slunk down the turret hatch, falling headfirst into the cabin. Warm blood streamed over my face, in my eyes, through my hair. A hand was shaking my shoulder. The ringing in my ears drowned out all noise.

"Are you all right? Are you all right?"

We were slowing down now, but I wasn't all right. I couldn't breathe. I wanted to vomit. Battle focus.

"Enemy down," I heard Boon say over the radio. He seemed a million miles away, but I knew that was the ringing in my head. My driver smiled. The blast must have wiped out the ISIS lead vehicle and buried the other one in the wadi's walls like that World War I trench in Verdun, France. An artillery shell hit near the trench, and the concussion buried the men alive. All that remained were the top inches of their rifles, in a line, a fitting fuck-you to a terrible war.

"Sitrep?" I gasped over the radio.

"We are free and clear," Boon said.

"Charlie Mike," I said. Continue mission.

"Wildman?" I said. "You still there?"

"Roger dodger!" He was now singing some Beatles song. "I am the Walrus."

"We lost our gunner. Boon, anyone injured?"

"Negative, lead vehicle," Boon said.

Marhaz was grimacing, one hand on her belly and the other on the Humvee's roof as the vehicle lurched side to side with the riverbed. Farhan reached behind and put a hand on her thigh, trying to reassure her.

"Boon, slow down," I said. "And get us out of this wadi."

I had a phone call to make. Probably the most important call of my life.

CHAPTER 40

"They've gone Elvis," Murphy said, spitting a wad of tobacco juice into the wadi. "They've flat-out disappeared."

Campbell sat on the hood of his Viper, fuming. He thought the Reaper had destroyed the mercs, but all his men found were the carcasses of the ISIS technicals, no Humvees. They must have disappeared down this dry riverbed, meaning they were either very lucky or very smart. He didn't care for either, but he was leaning toward smart.

"Who is this guy anyway? He's not like any arms dealer I've chased before," Bunker said, flinging a stone into the wadi.

"This mission is officially a soup sandwich," Black Jack said.

Campbell agreed, but couldn't admit it in front of his men. Sinjar was a debacle, and now this. Inexcusable, especially since Mr. Winters had handpicked him for this important mission because Jase Campbell was a man who got shit done. That was the reputation he had built over fifteen years in the service, and he wasn't about to forfeit it now.

"Sure as shit means the Agency will be on us now," Black Jack said, as the wreckage of the second drone smoked in the distance.

"Those CIA weenies couldn't find their own asses if both hands were holding their cheeks," Murphy laughed. "Took 'em a decade to find Osama bin Laden."

Campbell didn't answer. The anaconda tattoo on his neck was pulsing. After a while, his silence began to unnerve his men, but Campbell wasn't budging. Only he knew the true extent of this mission. This wasn't just another manhunt. It was personal. It was Apollo cleaning up one of its own, before anyone else found out. An operative gone rogue, deceiving two other Tier One operatives into his delusion. They were all traitors now, as far as Campbell was concerned, and deserved their fate.

"Bring them in alive," Winters had told him. "I need to debrief them. I don't know what they've been doing out there, son, and ignorance is dangerous to us all."

Campbell had heard the rumors floating around the Ranch, AO's five-thousand-acre training base in Texas. He didn't believe them. Hell, no one believed them. That a Tier One team leader went rogue, abandoning his mission in Ukraine, then sacrificed his team to cover his escape. And that he had done unspeakable things to the dead. *We're professional soldiers,* Campbell thought, *we don't do that. It's not the warrior's way.*

Back at the Ranch, they had joked about a rogue merc going "Kurtz," like Brando in *Apocalypse Now.* He had laughed then, thinking how fun it would be to be Willard, going off to kill the madman.

But Jase Campbell wasn't laughing now. That was a former American army officer, not just a mercenary, and that level of disloyalty was inexcusable. There was nothing more disgraceful than a U.S. soldier who turned savage. It was like wiping your ass with the American flag and everything it stood for. And Jase Campbell didn't have any tolerance for that kind of shit. *I guess that's what you get,* he thought, *when you take the flag out of military ops.*

CHAPTER 41

Lewis stared at her mapboard of the Middle East in a back corner of the intel shop's "SCIF," or secure office. She had carved out this small nook despite the fact that she was a contractor, the lowest of the low in the intel world. The cubicles around her buzzed with keystrokes, as analysts worked the classified databases shared among the sixteen different agencies of the U.S. intelligence community.

Computers are mindless. Human logic is more powerful than computational speed.

She held a minority opinion on this. The range fans of all the possible places the freighter could be right now blanketed the ocean from Pakistan to the Persian Gulf. Her division chief said the U.S. and allies had locked down every port from the straits of Bab el Mandeb to Hormuz, but everyone knew this wasn't enough. Not even close. A clever captain could drop off small cargo almost anywhere, or rendezvous with another ship at sea.

I need to think like a sailor, Lewis thought. She picked up her legal pad and walked down several rows of cubicles until she found Chief Petty Officer Rick Hernandez, the lone enlisted man in the SCIF. She learned in the army to trust the common sense of NCOs, something often lost among senior officers.

"Ricky, have a minute?"

"Sure, Lewis. What's up?"

"Find anything interesting?"

"Not yet. I'm charting all the new islands off Yemen's coast in case they're hiding there."

"New islands?"

"Yeah, from volcanoes. I'm looking at recent satellite imagery and comparing it to pictures taken a few years ago. There's quite a few around Zubair Archipelago."

"I need your help," she said. "I'm an army girl, and need to think like a sailor. These guys are at sea for weeks on end. What do they do day to day?"

"It's pretty monotonous," Ricky said. "Daily chores, TV, chores, card games, chores, sleep, Internet, and more chores."

"Wouldn't the smuggler captain turn off the ship's Internet, like the AIS?"

"Of course, but sailors are clever, especially the bored ones."

"How would they access the Internet?"

"Using a satellite phone like Thuraya or Inmarsat. They're cheap these days and easy to smuggle aboard."

"Wouldn't our SIGINT guys catch them if they tried to make a call or text?"

"Not necessarily. It's a small signal in a big ocean full of millions of signals."

She bounced her pen off her chin.

"Did you read the CIA's INTSUM from Gwadar?" he asked. INTSUMs are intelligence summaries. "They just came in."

"No, not yet."

"Four freighters matching our description left Gwadar yesterday," he said. "A fifth was also spotted, according to a source, but not registered as leaving the port."

"Interesting. What was its name?"

"HUMINT sources say *Dona Iluire*. We're looking for it, but it vanished. Its name has probably changed, and the shipping lanes are full of group-three freighters with aft pilothouses. We're trying to verify every single freighter, but there are too many. I'll forward the reporting to you."

"Thanks, Ricky."

She made her way back to her computer, and logged on with her CAC card and password. Like all intel analysts, she had two computers: one for classified material and the other for everything else. Analysts rarely had their unclassified terminals on, but she knew better. The intelligence community fetishized secrets, ignoring open sources like the Internet to their peril.

She Googled *Dona Iluire*. Then she created a fake Twitter account and searched for all tweets that mentioned *Dona Iluire*. Nothing much.

"Lewis!" Colonel Brooks bellowed across the room, walking over to her. "Have you checked the reporting from DIA yet?" Translation: he wanted to know if she had scrolled through the endless intel reports from her parent organization, the Defense Intelligence Agency, in Washington, DC.

"Working on it," she lied. It would be a dead end, but he wouldn't believe her. If DIA had anything, they would have already flagged it.

"Work faster," he said, walking away.

She nodded, then ignored him as she launched a Web Scraper, a proprietary software tool that could search thousands of social media accounts in milliseconds. She typed in "free," "woman," "ship," and "navy," and translated it into Arabic, Urdu, Farsi, Somali, Mandarin, Greek, Tagalog, and other languages.

"What's that?" Brooks asked. He had circled back to look over her shoulder.

"Running a lead," she said, quickly pulling up the DIA reporting.

"Taxpayers don't invest billions in the intelligence community for you to check Facebook," he said, loud enough for the entire SCIF to hear. "You're the DIA liaison officer. Liaise!"

Prick, she thought, turning back to the Web Scraper results as he went off to terrorize another cubicle. Seventy-two million hits. She began quickly scrolling, scanning a hundred hits in a minute. Several minutes later, she paused on a tweet from a sailor aboard the *Eleutheria,* "freedom" in Greek. Her intuition flashed. Intuition wasn't something you learned in school or coded into a computer. If she thought about it, she could have rationalized her intuition. Smugglers like their freedom, a cocky captain might change the name from *Dona Iluire* to *Eleutheria,* and only a cocky captain would take on a cargo of nukes. But ultimately it was a hunch.

Lewis opened the sailor's Twitter account. It was written in Tagalog, the Philippine language, which the computer translated automatically. Most of it was complaining. They had no shore leave in Pakistan, even though they were in Gwadar for a week. The only thing they took on was a dozen small crates of machinery.

She continued to scroll. The captain beat him because he refused to speak Tagalog over the radio to the U.S. Navy. Finally, he grabbed the radio and said, "The captain can eat shit." The skipper was satisfied, not understanding the language, and so was the sailor, who took the opportunity to gloat.

She scrolled down further, finding a dusk photograph of two sailors giving each other a high five on a ship. She zoomed in. It was a small cargo ship with an aft pilothouse, and a real piece of shit, too. The time and date was yesterday.

The ship matched the *Dona Iluire*'s profile, but where on the planet was it? She tapped her pen on her chin, then zoomed in on the constellations above the sailors' heads. Opening a star-watching website, she plugged in the time and date of the photo. Then she punched in the estimated longitude and latitude of the mystery freighter at that time. The website displayed the night sky, and she compared it to the photo. The sky was hazy and the picture not so sharp, but she could definitely make out consistencies of the brighter stars and faint constellations. They were not identical but close enough.

Could this be our freighter? she thought.

CHAPTER 42

The ISIS fighters jumped into their four technicals and tore out through the barbed wire perimeter of their temporary base. They had been tasked with watching the main highway south from Mosul a few hundred klicks north, but watching the main highway was boring, and the two vehicles jackrabbiting into the desert were easy prey. Bandits out of the Jazira, probably, come to scavenge and steal. They didn't even call in the sighting. Killing them would take ten minutes, at most; their commanding officer, who never bothered coming this far from his headquarters, and who was Lebanese and didn't know his way around this part of Iraq anyway, would never even know they had abandoned post.

The two vehicles disappeared suddenly, a few hundred meters in front of them. *There must be a low dip in the flat desert there,* the ISIS leader thought. It didn't help that the moon had been waning for the past week, so the Jazira wasn't as brightly lit as it had been only a few days ago.

"*'Asrae,*" he yelled, smacking his driver in the head for emphasis. "*'Asrae.*" Faster.

They lipped the low spot and saw the two vehicles, or more precisely their dust clouds, because it was dusty even in slight depressions, where sand collected. The commanding officer covered his mouth with his head scarf, but he wasn't worried. If they were this close to the dust cloud, the bandits couldn't be far.

They never knew what hit them, but it was small arms fire, perilously close. It cracked across the desert and then fell silent, the fire discipline a wonder. By the time the technicals rolled to a stop, the desert had fallen silent again. The survivors didn't even have time to fire back. They were executed with single shots, even the two gunners in the back technical who tried to surrender.

"Impressive," a handsome young man said, turning to the older man beside him.

Colonel Hosseini took his binos from his eyes. His men were cleaning up the mess; he had seen it before.

"We are twelve," he said, "but the Iranian Quds are always more than their number. How many do you have, Qais Khazali?"

"Two hundred," Khazali said. "They are already north of Tikrit. They will be here before morning."

"Good. We'll need them," the colonel said. He had never met a commanding officer who traveled with his advanced scouts before. Even General Suleimani, legendary for his presence at the front, traveled with his main force. No trained military man would do more. But of course, militia leaders weren't trained. They recruited on the strength of their reputation, and commanded respect by being brave. Khazali, he knew, had fought with Muqtada al-Sadr during the American War. He had broken away and founded the League of the Righteous because he thought al-Sadr too soft. Under his leadership, the Righteous had grown into one of the most feared Shia paramilitaries in Iraq. Now that the Americans were vanquished, the militia even had a seat in parliament.

Most men would be sitting in that seat, the colonel thought, but instead Khazali was fighting with his men in the field. No wonder he was so respected, despised, and feared.

I awoke with the sun in my eyes. My watch said 1143, more than five hours since we'd left Sinjar. We'd been traveling overland through the Jazira and were making a final piss stop. The horizon was flat and brown in every direction, as if we were marooned on another planet. There might be the occasional Bedouin or Shammari, the bandit tribe of the Jazira, but otherwise no one ever came into this unforgiving desert. We were safely alone.

Boon attended to Marhaz. The hard pounding of off-road travel wasn't good for a pregnant woman. Earlier, Boon had rigged a makeshift hammock for her in the back of the Humvee, but it could absorb only so much of the rough travel. Fortunately there was no blood, and the baby was restless, or so Marhaz thought. Boon couldn't feel her moving, but that wasn't unusual. Farhan looked distraught. Many men can be trained to assassinate, but most still fall apart over the birth of their child.

"Where are we?" I asked Boon.

He handed me the binoculars. "South of Baiji," he said, and I could smell it. Baiji was an oil town.

We had traveled 120 kilometers through the desert, avoiding human settlements. The Jazira was hard-packed desert with chunks of rock, not the flowing dunes of the Sahara, but it was still a slow and bouncy route. Marhaz, resting in her makeshift hammock, must have been nauseous, at least. Most of us were.

Girl's got grit, I thought.

"That's our objective," Boon said, pointing toward the east. Camp Speicher lay on the horizon, in all its containerized-housing-unit, Hesco-barrier, chain-link-fenced glory. The place was no "camp" but a mammoth former American military base, thirty-six square kilometers large. Now it straddled the front line between ISIS, Iraqi, and Iranian forces, plus your random bandit tribes bunkering oil from the nearby refineries. It was a deeply unsafe place, but for us, it was cover.

"Plan?" I asked Boon, thankful that he had taken charge while I caught a quick nap. A week ago, I wouldn't have expected it, but since he'd stolen Kylah from me . . . Okay, since I'd found out he'd won Kylah's approval, I'd begun to realize Boon had the quiet authority of a natural leader.

He spread out the laminated map on the Humvee's hood. "Here's Speicher," he said, pointing to a huge square with a felt-tip marker. "According to the Kurds, ISIS holds the center, near the runways. The southeast is held by Shia militia. They've been fighting since July. We need to get to the northeast corner, but ISIS patrols the perimeter, except the southern border. We run into a patrol, we're dead."

"Agreed," I said. "Once we're spotted, more will come."

Boon frowned at the map. "The south is less guarded than the north, but we'd have to cut through miles of base. No telling what's in there. Even the Kurds don't know for sure. Could be tens, hundreds, thousands of militants."

"I don't like it. No go."

"That leaves the northeast corner," Boon said.

"The main entrance?" Wildman said, hovering nearby. That was always his favorite tactic: frontal assault.

"Not quite," I said. "There's a few entrances, here, here, and here." I pointed to the map. "Take the first available."

"We won't make it," Boon said.

He was right. The highway ran along that section of the base. It would be impossible to sneak up there. We'd be spotted for sure.

"We creep as close as we can get to the northern edge," I said, "then take the hardball and make a dash."

Wildman nodded. Boon looked unconvinced. So was I. It was the least worst option.

"Mount up," I said. Wildman took up the fifty-cal in his vehicle. I took ours.

"Radio check, over," I said through my headset.

"Lima Charlie," replied Wildman, Boon, and my driver in succession.

"This is starting to be like *Mad Max*," Boon grumbled, as we powered up the diesels.

"Iraq's a postapocalyptic world," I said. That was half true; ISIS was trying to destroy the other half.

We sped through the desert toward the massive base. I looked ahead and saw a berm topped with a barbed wire fence stretching far into the desert. *Speicher.* "Shots fired!" Boon said. Wildman began shooting his fifty-cal, and I followed the tracers. Six ISIS technicals were coming at us from our one o'clock.

"Fan out," I said, and my driver swerved next to Boon. Now two Humvees were facing the ISIS patrol. I unloaded the fifty-cal, and so did Wildman, but we were bouncing so much in the desert we couldn't target effectively, and neither could they.

"Hardtop!" Boon yelled. The Humvee bounced hard as we hit the paved road, and tires squealed as an old Toyota Corolla was forced off the edge. Inside, a mother, father, and three young girls stared at us as we passed.

I waited until the ISIS vehicles were in closer range before I unleashed.

Thunk, thunk, thunk, thunk, thunk, thunk, thunk. The fifty sounded like a jackhammer. I fired again. *Thunk, thunk, thunk, thunk.*

Bits of metal flew off the nearest ISIS technical, but it didn't slow. The Hummer jerked as a tractor trailer truck approached us head-on, blowing its horn. We swerved off-road, ruining my shot, but ten seconds later the ISIS pursuers had passed it and I unloaded again. Wildman did the same from his Humvee, battering the road, and together we forced our pursuers to fall back.

"Faster," I yelled, pounding the Humvee's roof above the driver's head. Speicher's perimeter fence whizzed by our right, the Humvees redlining at seventy mph.

Wild ISIS fire raked past us into oncoming traffic. A car's windshield imploded in machine-gun rounds and the sedan spun out of control, our Humvees narrowly dodging it. The g-force threw me against the rim of the turret.

"Two klicks out," Boon said, as a second car's engine block took direct hits and black smoke billowed from under its hood. A third car steered off the road, but I saw its chassis catch on a rock, ripping its suspension apart at speed.

"The first entrance is coming up on our right," I yelled over the slipstream and the hammering of my fifty-cal.

"Roger," Boon replied over the headset.

"Do *not* take it. Copy?"

"Copy."

"Look for a breach in the wall, two hundred meters *past* the entrance."

The chain-link fence turned to a concrete wall, as the tank ditch disappeared. We sped past the front gate as my fifty-cal started clicking, out of ammo. Faded American and Iraqi flags were painted on the wall, with "Welcome to Camp Speicher" written underneath. Two bewildered Iraqi soldiers stood to watch us pass, then were gunned down by the ISIS technicals.

"Do you see the hole?"

"Roger, I see it."

"Punch through."

Our vehicles fishtailed off the road, and the six ISIS pickups followed. Ahead of us was a three-meter gap in the concrete wall.

"We are not going to fit!" yelled my driver.

"We will fit!" I yelled back, bracing myself.

Boon's Hummer smashed into the gap, sending up a plume of concrete dust. I ducked as we charged into the cloud, chunks of concrete bouncing off our bulletproof windshield. The hole was a meter wider.

"Hold your fire!" I yelled as we emerged on the other side and the technical, flying a black ISIS flag, leapt through the hole. "Wildman, hold your fire! Boon, get us out of here!"

"Yes sir," he yelled, as the ground behind us erupted in automatic gunfire and RPGs tore through the ISIS vehicles as they came through the breach. The technical with the black flag exploded, a direct hit from an antitank rocket. The following vehicle's tires were shredded by bullets, followed by its cab. An RPG hit the third technical, flipping it and exploding. The next vehicle swerved to avoid it. A fifty-cal sniper round blew a hole through the windshield and out the back, killing the driver. Machine-gun fire perforated the Toyota a second later. The fifth technical was raked by precision gunfire: driver's head, tires, engine block, gunners. I saw a militant leap from his vehicle, sprinting for cover, but a sniper put him down. The last technical turned sharply to escape, but it was far too late; a crew-served machine gun tore it to bits.

Silence.

The ambush was over as quickly as it had begun. Only smoke, the sound of flames, and the smell of gunpowder remained.

"Pull over, Boon," I said.

He did. We were on the edge of the kill zone, but nothing was moving. No survivors. I looked at the buildings around us, but they were empty, as silent as the rest of the world. Then silhouettes emerged from the landscape. Snipers on the roofs, machine-gun teams in windows, RPG gunners around corners. Twenty in all, weapons pointing at us, a big burly son of a bitch with a shaved head walking point.

"You told me you'd be coming in hot," Bear said, "but goddamn!"

CHAPTER 44

Two Navy SEAL helicopters skimmed the waves, approaching the freighter from its stern. The lead helo broke right and hovered just off the ship's starboard side, its door gun aimed at the bridge. The other helo hovered above the stern, six SEALs fast-roped to the deck. The choppers switched places and another six SEALs hit the deck. Within seconds they were inside the ship.

"Down! Get down! On your knees!" the SEALs shouted as they stalked the decks, catching crewmembers by surprise. "Hands where I can see them."

Men kneeled, hands up. A crewman did not move fast enough and the SEAL slammed his rifle butt into his head, knocking him unconscious. The first SEAL stepped over him as a second flex-cuffed his wrist to a pipe.

"The rest of you, move to the wardroom. NOW!"

The crewmembers shuffled down the passageway, a SEAL at their backs. The remainder of the team continued, Mk 18 carbines' muzzles pointing the way.

Within minutes of landing, they came to the ship's bridge.

"Locked hatch. Shotgun!"

A SEAL came forward, carrying a Mossberg 500 shotgun.

"Fire in the hole!" The shotgun blew out the door's lock and the SEALs flooded onto the bridge.

"Get down! Down now!" the SEALs shouted, but the crew shouted back in a foreign language.

The SEALs raised their carbines. "On your knees! Face on the floor!" But the crew refused.

One man reached behind a console, and a SEAL put a round through his right leg. The man fell. The crew attacked. One seized a fire extinguisher and smashed it into the back of a SEAL's helmeted head, sending the SEAL to the floor. Another pulled a knife and lunged at the closest SEAL, but the SEAL caught the flash of steel in his side vision, pivoted sideways, and swatted the knife out of the assailant's hand. Simultaneously, he kicked the man in the groin, lifting him off his feet. In seconds, the bridge crew was writhing on the deck, clasping body parts as the SEALs stood over them and took control of the ship.

"Bridge secure," the SEAL leader panted through his headset, then turned to the bridge crew. "Where's the captain?"

The crew remained silent.

"Where's the captain!" the SEAL shouted, grabbing the most frightened crewmember by the shirt and throwing him against an instrument console. The man blubbered and pointed to an old man slumped against the wall. He wore nothing to distinguish himself as the captain: no uniform, skipper's hat, not even binoculars around his neck. He could have been the ship's steward.

The SEAL approached him. "Are you the captain?"

The old man looked away, ignoring him.

"Why did you not answer our radio hails?"

Silence.

"What was your last port of call? What is your destination?"

The old man ignored him.

"Where is the ship's manifest?"

The old man finally looked at the SEAL and shrugged, as if he did not speak English. English is the lingua franca of the international merchant marine.

"Bunch of fucking pirates," the SEAL leader said, flex-cuffing the old man to the bridge.

"Tear this place apart," the leader commanded. "Get me some intel." The SEALs began ripping the bridge apart.

"Engine room secure," the SEAL radio squawked. "We finished our search. Negative on the hold. No nuclear contraband here. No isotope readings."

"What's in the hold?" the team leader asked.

"Cigarettes and sheep pelts. Tons of them. Smells like road kill."

"Hidden compartments?"

"Negative. We tapped the bulkheads. Nothing. The ship is clean. Repeat, the *Ranga* is not our ship."

Another false lead, the SEAL leader thought, as he leaned against the freighter's radar console and took off his helmet, exhausted. This was the fifth ship they had searched in two days, and their fifth miss. *Our mystery freighter is still out there,* he thought. *Somewhere.*

"Copy all," the SEAL team leader said. "Abort mission. Team Alpha, prepare for evac." He left the captain flex-cuffed to the bridge.

"Eureka!" Lewis shouted. "I know where our ship is!"

The conference room fell silent, as did the people watching via secure satellite feed. Seconds ago, everyone was arguing about possible trajectories of the mystery freighter. Time was running short.

"I know where our ship is," she repeated.

"What do you mean, you know where our ship is?" Colonel Brooks said, contempt in his voice. From his point of view, she was the least valuable person in the room. In his twenty-five years of service, he didn't have much use for inexperience, females, or contractors. She was all three.

"Do tell," a voice broke in from one of the satellite conference rooms. It was the admiral coordinating the search.

"I believe our ship changed its name to the *Eleutheria*. Last estimated position was here." She took the laser pointer from Brooks's hand and highlighted a patch of sea south of Oman. "By this time, they could be here." The laser dot circled a wider swath of ocean off Yemen, big but searchable.

"How do you know this?" the colonel barked.

"I read the stars."

The colonel was about to say something, when the admiral interrupted. "We can't afford to let any leads go. Ms. . . ."

"Lewis. Just call me Lewis."

"Lewis, we've had two hundred of our best analysts puzzling over this since yesterday and getting nowhere. What makes you so confident?"

She explained how she found the disgruntled sailor's Twitter account, and his entries about the *Eleutheria*, Gwadar, the suspicious cargo, and the U.S. Navy incident, which she confirmed in the logs. What convinced her was the photograph, and how the constellations, date, time, and location were all consistent with their mystery freighter.

"Good job," the admiral said. "Colonel Brooks, you got a live one there." She gave a slight smirk to Brooks, knowing it would boil him. It did.

"Ops, what assets do we have in that vicinity?"

"Uh," came a voice from another satellite conference room, "not much, sir. We deployed everything farther north by northeast. We can FRAGO them, but they won't make it in time."

"Who else is out there?"

"CTF-151," another voice said. Combined Task Force 151

was a multinational naval task force with the mission to hunt down pirates off Somalia, just across the Gulf of Aden from Yemen. "They're within range, and have enough ships to cover the area."

The room fell silent as the admiral considered it. Retasking a CTF was no easy thing. It was a diplomatic challenge as much as a military one, and would require the White House, State Department, and others. Not only would it be a bureaucratic mess, but it increased chances of a media leak, especially if some of the countries in the multinational force didn't quite share America's priorities.

Gawd, the admiral thought. It would be the biggest news story of the year. Yet to not engage CTF-151 would risk the nukes falling into the hands of terrorists. He could never allow that to happen on his watch.

"Request a FRAGO mission for CTF-151 immediately, and do not wait for approval from higher. Send it directly to them, with the coordinates of the search box. Tell them it's terrorists related, but say nothing about the nuclear weapons."

"Yes sir," said Brooks.

"And get me a line to the White House. I expect there will be questions."

CHAPTER 45

Bear's compound inside Speicher was a fortress of steel shipping containers stacked three high. It was reached by a narrow alley with heaped tires on each side, and the gate was a deuce-and-a-half military truck with an iron wall ratcheted to its outfacing side. In the center was a two-story building and a small warehouse used as a garage. All in all, it was a comfy little hole, and I told Bear that as soon as we arrived.

"We could bunk up in Baiji with the oil works," he said, "but I like to fuck with ISIS. They know not to mess with us here. You look like shit, by the way."

"Go have sex with yourself," I said, jumping down from the Humvee.

"Speaking of which, I have a surprise for you."

He pointed toward the warehouse, which was clearly the living quarters. "I hope it's a cold beer," I said.

"Even better," Bear said with a sadistic smile, as Kylah came walking out of the darkness on the other side of the door. She sparkled in the midday light, her red hair radiant. Did I mention she knew how to walk? Kylah knew how to walk.

"Dr. Locke," she said, putting the sexy into it, as Bear looked on with a grin. She grabbed my cheek, patted it, then walked past me to Boon. They were already kissing, Kylah clearly putting on a show for the lads, by the time I turned around.

"Holy shit," Bear laughed.

"She chose the right man," I said, and I meant it.

"Oy! Get a room, you birds!" Wildman yelled. "Nobody wants to see your rumpy pumpy."

"Sorry about that," Bear said, still laughing as we walked toward the warehouse. "I was in Erbil when you called, and I just assumed you'd want to see her."

"Oh, I do," I said. "Wildman is the best piece of ass I've seen since I left."

"I don't know. What about the pregnant girl?"

I had forgotten about Marhaz. When I looked back, Farhan was helping her down from the Humvee. She had her hand on her belly and a queasy look on her face.

"Oh shite," Kylah said, pulling away from Boon. "You didn't tell me you had an eight-month-pregnant woman as cargo."

She rushed over to help Marhaz out of the vehicle. The Humvee's door was narrow, and Farhan was in the way. It was a terrible maternity wagon.

"How do you feel?" Kylah asked Marhaz, who nodded, then winced in pain.

"Strong," she said, without her past conviction.

Kylah took her pulse. "A bit fast," she said. "I need to check your blood pressure. When was the last time the baby moved?"

"Hours," Marhaz said. It looked like the only word she could muster.

"Careful now, *habibti*," Farhan said, as he helped her along.

"You need to lie down," Kylah said, leading them toward the warehouse. "Have you been drinking water?"

Marhaz shook her head no.

"I thought you were a doctor," Kylah said to Boon as they passed him, but he didn't respond. Did I mention that Kylah knew how to walk? And load an AK-47? And hopefully deliver a baby.

"Your surprise is better than mine," Bear said, as he watched them disappear. He took out a cigar. It was a cheap one. Smoking a cigar at the end of a mission was an Army tradition since the days when the corps was winning the Wild West, but some guys never got the details right.

"No thanks," I said, when he offered. I went to my ruck and took out my portable humidor. I only had two quality cigars left, and I felt a pang of regret as I took out the Cohiba Siglo IV. I didn't have any idea where or when I'd get another as good, as I offered my last to Bear.

"I usually only smoke after the mission's done," I said, biting off one end and starting to toast the other end so I'd get an even burn, "but for you, Bear . . ."

I didn't need to say any more. This wasn't the life either of us really wanted, that much was clear.

"I miss the boys, Locke," Bear said, already puffing away while I continued working the end of mine with the lighter. "I miss the professionalism. Half the guys I hire out here are American vets who couldn't adjust back home. Good guys, but damaged goods. Short tempers. Too happy about the killing. Some wake up at night, screaming, still hearing the gunfire."

I breathed deep. There's nothing like the first hit off a quality cigar. "Heroes nonetheless," I said. "It's not their fault our country pissed away their lives."

"Touché," Bear said.

I knew what he was thinking about. He was thinking about the list: the dead friends we'd shared since our time in the army. Was he, like me, thinking about Jimmy Miles, or did he have someone special he'd lost? Or was it the length of the list that got to him, the fact that, if Bear was anything like me, he still wasn't sure what the sacrifices of those good men were for?

"I hope you're not going too far with the pregnant girl," Bear said.

"Only the landing strip."

"Here?" He took the cigar from his lips. "I don't like the sound of that."

I smoked before answering. "I hear the runway here is big enough to land the space shuttle," I said.

"You're flying a plane in here?" Bear replied, the cigar smoking in his fingers as he strangled it.

I nodded.

"When?"

"This morning."

Bear shook his head. "That's a bad idea, brother."

"I thought you said this was your base."

"This is my base," he said, pointing around him. "You got two hundred ISIS out there, at least, holed up in a hangar by the runway. You got fifty Shia a few kilometers to the south."

"And I've got, what, thirty of the best damn men in Iraq with me here," I said. "And $25,000 to spend."

Bear smoked, looking out at his fortress of shipping containers. "Sorry, brother, it ain't gonna be enough. These men don't even know you. Why would they risk their lives for you?"

I have to tell him about the nuclear key, I thought.

But before I could say the words, an explosion knocked me to the ground and gunfire burst around me. I looked up, dirt in my face, in my eyes, in my mouth. The gunfire was Bear's guards on top of the steel container wall, firing out at an enemy on the other side. Below them, smoke was billowing inward from a rocket attack or mortar attack.

There must be a breach in the wall if the smoke is coming inward, I thought, as a figure appeared out of the smoke. *He's short,* I thought, but then I realized why. He was a boy, no more than eight or ten, running as fast as he could. He took a shot in the arm, but he didn't stop. Instead, he reached to the side of his bulletproof vest . . . except it wasn't a bulletproof vest.

"Suicide bomber," I yelled, as the child pulled a cord and obliterated himself. Seconds later, his head returned to earth, bouncing on the hard-packed sand.

CHAPTER 46

"Get the fuckers!" Bear screamed. He was already in his turret, firing the 40 mm Mk 19 chain-link grenade launcher into the breach point. He must have moved while I was staring at the suicide boy. I guess he'd seen it before, but that was my first time, and you never forget your first time for something like that.

I flipped my SCAR's safety to auto and unloaded half a magazine at the nearest technical, blowing out its tires. It slammed sideways into the container wall, and I switched to semi.

Pop, pop, pop. Three head shots.

"Yaaaaaaaah!!" Wildman yelled, firing his fifty-cal as their Humvee zoomed past me, destroying a technical in the breach, effectively plugging it.

"Fox Two One, Fox Two One, over," I shouted into my radio, calling for my driver. No answer.

An explosion, behind me, from the central building.

"RPG, ten o'clock," someone shouted. "Behind the bladders."

Bear's mercs laid down suppressive fire, riddling the two-thousand-liter bladders that had held their water supply. Water gushing out, turning sand to mud. Someone tossed a grenade onto the ISIS position. The RPG team tried to run, but slipped in the sludge. The grenade detonated, splashing water and ISIS in a fifteen-meter radius.

It was clear the surprise attack wasn't going to succeed. The mercs were putting up a ferocious fight, cornered but more skilled than their attackers. The wreckage of two burning technicals blocked the breach point, making it difficult for more vehicles to enter the base. But there was a hell of a lot of ISIS firepower already inside the wire, and I didn't want this battle of attrition.

Bear must have been thinking the same thing, because I heard him yelling, "Forward. Snuff the fuckers! Push them out," as I turned toward the warehouse where Kylah, Farhan, and Marhaz had taken cover from the morning heat.

It was on fire. Smoke obscured the rear quarter of the building. *Marhaz,* I thought, surprising myself.

I sprinted across the dirt track into the burning building. I could feel the bullets around me. Three ISIS followed me inside.

"Down!" I heard, and dove. Three shots zinged overhead and three bodies dropped behind me. I looked up to see Farhan lowering his Kalashnikov.

"Are you all right?" he asked. I got to my feet and followed him down the hall.

"Kylah!" I shouted. "Marhaz!"

"Here," Kylah yelled. "We're here."

I ran down the hall and turned into the last room. Marhaz was huddled on the floor while Kylah stood against the wall beside a window, AK-47 in her hands. She gestured outside; a stopped ISIS technical.

Kylah nodded to me. "On three," she said.

I took up a firing stance and flipped my safety to semiautomatic. "One, two—"

Kylah smashed the window with her rifle butt and emptied her magazine on full auto, peppering the truck. I took my time. *Pop, pop, pop,* a round for the gunner, two for the driver. The man in the passenger seat slid out and went behind some crates.

Kylah showed me a grenade.

"Was that in your med kit?" I asked.

She gave a shrewd look and pulled the pin. "Cover!"

Farhan dropped to cover Marhaz with his body. The technical exploded, and the shock wave blew out the remains of the window. The opening was drawing smoke into the room around us, so I turned and gave my do-rag to Marhaz.

"We're going," I said, as Kylah climbed out first, then Farhan, who helped his pregnant wife over the sill while Kylah covered them.

"Boon, this is Locke. Still there?" I said over the radio.

"Roger, buddy."

Thank God, I thought.

"I need a pickup ASAP. Four pax, east side of main building."

"I got you," he said, as I slid out the window before the smoke choked me. Bullets hit the window frame, too close.

"Where's it coming from?" Kylah asked, her body shielding Marhaz.

I saw him twenty meters away, behind more crates in a supply area, and I knew I wasn't going to get around on him fast enough, but the crates blew apart as Boon's Humvee passed the corner of the building, Wildman standing through the roof, firing the fifty-cal.

Our second Humvee arrived two seconds later, one of the Kurds at the wheel.

"Inside," I yelled at Marhaz and Farhan.

"Kylah," Boon yelled, but she shook her head.

"I'm staying with the baby," she said, as she tore open the passenger door and tried to physically push the pregnant woman inside.

Around the corner, I could hear a truck engine accelerating, and then an explosion.

"Let's go! Let's go!" I yelled, picking Marhaz up.

"Farhan in the other vehicle!"

"No," the prince yelled.

"There's not enough room," I said.

"*Habibi!*" Marhaz yelled, stuck in the door. She was covered in sweat. "Go. Do what he says."

Instead, Farhan climbed into the front, taking my seat. Wildman opened up with his fifty-cal to cover us.

Thunk, thunk, thunk, thunk, thunk, came the reply, as bullets walked up the back of the Humvee.

"We're going out," I yelled to Boon, as I climbed over the prince and took up the turret.

My driver took off so fast I lost my footing, but I managed to fall inside. Rounds plunked off the sides of the vehicle. Part of the building collapsed, hit by automatic grenade launchers.

"Through the breach," I yelled to Boon on the radio.

Bear's mercs had pushed forward in my absence. There were still ISIS inside the compound, but the mercs had gotten to their Humvees and were rounding up for an advance. The first vehicle passed us, Bear grinning like a bastard, and we swept in behind him, second in line.

I knew we were going to hit resistance when we broke through the smoky container wall into the clear, and we did. The ISIS forces outside the wall opened up full auto and blocked our way. Bear's vehicle swung hard right, driving along the container wall. We followed.

And then Bear's vehicle exploded, as a massive vehicle rammed it into the container wall, nearly toppling the top container.

"Holy shit," I yelled, as my driver skidded past the wreckage and spun halfway back toward where we had come from.

ISIS had captured a U.S. Army cargo "Hemmet," a cross between a Humvee and an 18-wheeler, and converted it into a mobile gun fortress: six fifty-cals, two 40 mm grenade launchers, and a squad of RPGs, surrounded by steel plates welded to its sides. The vehicle rolled on eight wheels, each the size of a man, and had a dozer blade affixed to its front. As it backed away from Bear's crushed Humvee—*no survivors,* I thought sadly, *no way*—I could see twin black ISIS flags flying just behind the cab, and Koranic verse scrawled in Arabic along the sides. When it turned toward us, I saw English words written across the bulletproof windshield: *Martyr Maker.*

One of its fifty-cals turned toward us, as the Martyr Maker started to plow forward. Then all six of its fifties and automatic grenade launchers swung in our direction.

"Get us out of here," I yelled to my driver. "Go, go, go, go, go."

CHAPTER 47

The Shia militia's eight technicals crossed the second runway and fanned out as they approached the hangars. The lieutenant could feel the excitement, even as he wished he had more vehicles to show Khazali and the Righteous. They had never ventured this far into the military base or come this close to ISIS's headquarters. He wanted to yell something to his men, to inspire them, but he didn't know what.

"*'Iilaa al'amam!*" he yelled, as his technical surged toward the front. Forward! It was a dumb thing to yell, he knew, since they were already moving forward, but it was the first thing that came to his head.

"*Allahu Akbar!*" he yelled, and that seemed more correct to him, especially since they were within range of the enemy's fifty-cals, but the enemy wasn't firing.

They are afraid, he thought. *They know the Righteous are here. Maybe they have run.* He tasted victory. Funny, he thought it would taste like cinnamon, but it burned his nostrils, like acetylene.

Boooom. The Toyota next to him was blown fifteen meters in the air.

Hidden bombs, he thought, as his driver eased back on the accelerator. Like al Qaeda, ISIS liked to bury artillery shells in the earth. *It shall not save them.*

Six hundred meters. Five hundred meters. The eight vehicles formed a single front, facing the enemy. Four hundred meters.

The hangar's door was partially open. Three hundred meters. One of his men started firing and everyone followed, as a barrage of lead hit the cavernous building. Bits of the hangar flew apart. Two hundred meters. Two ISIS pickups parked inside fell to pieces in a blizzard of bullets. One hundred meters.

The line decelerated as they entered the hangar. They drove two laps around the football-field-size area. No one was there.

"*La yutlaq alnnar ealayk albulida'*," a voice yelled. Don't shoot, morons. The lieutenant's heart leapt. The enemy was surrendering, although it was odd that a beaten foe had called them morons.

His heart sank when he saw Khazali, leader of the League of the Righteous, drive out through the hangar door. He was standing in the back of the pickup behind twin ZPU-2 antiaircraft guns that could put 150 rounds of 14.5 millimeter lead into a target eight klicks away. Next to him, squeezed into a corner of the truck bed, was a twelve-year-old boy. During a fight, he would help reload the ammo boxes.

Khazali jumped out of the bed of the technical. Beside him, an older man in an Iranian Quds uniform stepped out of another technical. Their men had formed a professional perimeter, the lieutenant couldn't help noticing with admiration, even as it caused concern.

Khazali and the Quds commander walked to an area with cots and blankets. Khazali picked one up and smelled it. A copy of the Koran was open, as if for prayer. On a makeshift table were a partially filled AK-47 magazine and pile of rounds, the task abandoned.

"What happened here?" someone behind the lieutenant asked.

Khazali didn't hear. He bent over a small cooking stove and kettle. The stove was still on, the kettle's water yet to boil. Next to it was a pot with tea at the ready and nine cups. Whoever was here left in a hurry, and did not even bother with a rear guard.

"Lieutenant," Khazali said.

"Yes sir," the young man said. He hadn't left his technical.

"You told me this was ISIS's headquarters."

"Yes, *sayyid*," the young man stammered.

Khazali scowled. "Then what do you think happened here?"

The lieutenant groped for the best possible answer. "They ran. From us. No, no. From you."

"You are a coward and an imbecile," Khazali said, loud enough for everyone to here. "You have failed your mission. You have failed your people. You are relieved of command."

The young man winced. The militants stood silently, watching him, as he stepped out of the technical, wondering what he was supposed to do now.

An explosion sounded in the distance, like an exclamation point at the end of his final embarrassment. He wanted to go home, but not to the home he had: broken, burned, most of the people he had loved dead or fled. He wanted to go back to who he used to be, but the explosions kept coming, followed by gunfire.

He looked up. The Quds commander had turned north, toward the battle. Khazali had turned to listen as well, but when he turned back to address his men, he didn't seek the older man's advice or consent.

"*Allahu Akbar*," he said calmly. "Allah is merciful. The battle is heading our way. All of you," he said, including the lieutenant's men in his glance, "ride with me."

CHAPTER 48

"Right. Go right," I said, as my driver fishtailed around another corner. The good news was that we had escaped Bear's fortress. The bad news was so had the Martyr Maker. The beast was much faster than I expected with all those extra tons of steel.

Tracers streamed over my head. *How to lose it?*

"There! There! Two o'clock," I shouted. To our left was an abandoned barracks complex. The Americans had brought premade containerized housing units, or CHUs, that were walled-in fortresses. A twenty-foot-high concrete wall surrounded the complex, and inside was a maze of Hesco barriers: stacked seven-by-seven-foot cubes filled with dirt and rocks and held together by heavy-duty fabric and wire mesh. They served as blast protection around what seemed like an endless yard of trailer-like living quarters. CHU villages were meant to be the last stand, if the base was ever overrun.

Perfect, I thought.

"Focking 'ell," Wildman said over the headset. "Locke's led us into a Choo village."

"Bad place to get cornered," Boon added.

"Then don't get cornered," I said. CHU villages were dense mazes, with narrow alleys. It was our best chance at losing the Martyr Maker.

Thunk, thunk, thunk, thunk, thunk—the fifty-cals cut into a CHU beside us, as if reminding me of the danger.

"Keep making turns," I yelled to the driver, knowing our

advantage was cornering. The forty-foot-long Martyr Maker lumbered around the tight blocks of the CHU village. Of course, it could just crush one of these CHUs like an empty beer can, but at least that slowed it down. Maybe.

"They've got reinforcements," Boon said, and I noticed the two ISIS technicals trailing the behemoth.

"Split up and lose them. Meet me on the other side."

We took two turns, then straightened out on what appeared to be a main road. We passed a defunct Burger King and a Green Beans Coffee before an ISIS technical appeared behind us, firing toward our tires. My Kurdish driver took the next corner (I noticed a blue U.S. mailbox as we went past) but he had turned too late and we drifted into a Hesco barrier before bouncing off and accelerating. The technical took advantage of our mistake and unloaded. Bullets pounded our left side, cracking the side windows in spiderweb patterns.

"How's she doing?" I yelled to Kylah.

"Better than expected," Kylah yelled, urging Marhaz to breathe.

I needed to get Marhaz to safety, but that was going to have to wait. I fired the fifty-cal, but within seconds it was jammed. Smoke. Sand. Too-rough terrain. I ducked behind the turret's front deflector, flipped open the cover, sprayed lube on the chain-links, slammed the cover closed, and cycled a round.

Thunk, thunk, thunk, thunk, thunk—the trailing ISIS technical laid into us as I cleared the jam.

Boon's vehicle appeared behind it and zigzagged to avoid our cross fire. But the fanatics were boxed in and they knew it. Wildman swept their tires with his fifty and the pickup flipped sideways into the Hesco barriers, Boon cornering around it.

"Another one bites the dust!" Wildman sang over the radio.

The Martyr Maker appeared two corners ahead, already shooting.

"Scatter!"

Boon went left; we went right.

"Use the angles," Boon said. "That monster can't corner."

"There's still at least one more technical in here with us," Wildman said.

"Look for the exits," I said. Cornering or not, if we went down the wrong alley, we could easily get stuck in our own trap.

Fooosh. An RPG smoke trail whizzed across our hood.

Instinctively, I stooped into the Humvee's cabin for cover. Bullets plinked off our armored exterior. Through the door window, I could see the Martyr Maker. It was waiting for us. Boon cut across us from a side alley; Wildman unloading into the Martyr Maker from no more than fifteen meters, but all it did was crack the Hemmet's bulletproof windshield.

"Hard left," I yelled, a different direction from everyone else. Within a block, no other vehicles were in sight. But I knew they were in here, and I could hear the main battle raging between ISIS and Bear's mercs not too far away. At one point, I saw the taillights of the ISIS technical, but it vanished around a corner. At another point, we passed a concrete building standing incongruously above the one-story CHUs. It had a faded painting of Saddam Hussein on the side of it, smiling and drinking tea.

"They're on our ass," Boon said over the radio. "I can't shake him."

I started to ask where he was, but then I heard Wildman's fifty firing.

"Straight ahead, then sharp left," I told the driver, as we sped up a parallel alley. We skidded around the corner and came out, quite by accident, between the Hemmet and the technical.

Thunk, thunk, thunk, thunk, thunk, thunk, thunk. I let loose on the Hemmet to get its attention before we disappeared down another Hesco row.

It worked. Both the Hemmet and technical were chasing us. We turned south and raced down an alley, outpacing the Martyr Maker. The Toyota was trying to pass it, but the alley was narrow, and the massive Hemmet took up the entire width, blocking the pickup truck. I fired a quarter of a belt, but the Hemmet's steel plating was too thick. The fifty-cal rounds bounced off, leaving divots. Even the wheels were covered.

On top, the gunners brought their fifty-cals and grenade launchers around to fire on us. With our windows cracked and armor cracking, I doubted we'd survive another barrage.

"Heads down," I yelled into the backseat, as I lined my cal on the lead gunner. I started low, hitting the windshield, but managed to walk my bullets into his head before he could get off his shot.

"Keep going straight," I yelled to the driver. We seemed to be in a long chute, with Hescos on both sides. "No turns."

"But there's a dead end ahead," Kylah screamed.

Farhan was yelling in Arabic, too.

"Make him keep it straight," I yelled down to her, as a second gunner on the Martyr Maker struggled with the automatic grenade launcher. "And floor it."

"You better be right," Kylah yelled, and I felt the driver speeding up as we passed the last turn.

"I am," I yelled, as the fifty-cal started kicking in my hand, my bullets bouncing off the deflector shield in front of the automatic grenade launcher. The Martyr Maker was right on top of us now, its dozer blade meters from our bumper. They were so close the gunners couldn't even get the angle on the shot. I pulled my Beretta and shot him in the face.

"Hold on," Kylah yelled, and then I was swinging out to the side, holding on to the fifty-cal, as the driver skidded perpendicular a few meters before the dead end, bounced off the wall, and accelerated down an alley no wider than our Humvee. The Martyr Maker plowed into the dead end, running through Hescos and concrete walls until it was off its first four wheels and hung ten feet deep in rubble. The technical skidded sideways, smashing into it at speed and exploding. The last thing I saw as we disappeared down the alley was a gunner recoiling backward then slamming into his launcher, knocking it upward and shooting a grenade straight into the sky.

"Hemmet down," I called to Boon. "Hemmet down. Technical down. Returning to the fight."

"Right behind you," Boon said, as Wildman cut over him with, "Another one bites the dust."

"How did you know about that alley?" Kylah asked, as I pulled myself back down into the front seat.

"I didn't," I said, without looking back at her. *Badass,* I thought.

We took a few wrong turns in the CHU labyrinth, but before long I could see the main fight beyond the housing area ahead. I banged the roof above the driver's head and he slowed down. There was a small courtyard, hidden from the fight.

"What're you doing?" Kylah asked, as the driver pulled to a stop.

"Letting you out," I said.

She started to object, but I cut her off. "I'm not taking a pregnant woman into that firefight. And I'm not staying out. I have friends in there." But the only friends I had left in there, I realized, were the Kurds who had risked their lives beside me for the last two months. Boon, Wildman, and I could have stayed out altogether. But what kind of person would I be then?

"You can't keep me out," Kylah said, as she offloaded Marhaz onto a dusty concrete step.

"She needs a doctor," I said. I nodded toward Farhan, who was amassing a small arsenal of weapons from our Humvee and breaking into Wildman's C-4 stash. I almost felt sorry for any ISIS that might stumble into him.

Kylah smirked. I wanted to kiss her. But I knew she didn't want that.

"Good luck out there, cowboy," she said.

I climbed back into the turret and motioned the Kurd forward. He hit the accelerator, and we tore out of the CHU village at sixty mph. Speed was our cover. It wasn't until we cleared the last CHU and were flying into the open that I realized at least a dozen technicals—no, more like two dozen, or even ten dozen—were speeding toward us from the left. To my right, another several dozen technicals heading straight for us, their gunners howling with rage. They were enveloping us in a pincer move.

"Oh fuck," I yelled, as the bullets slammed around the Humvee. "Abandon ship!"

CHAPTER 49

"Whoa! Whoa! Whoa!" Boon said.

"It's the entire ISIS army," my driver said, panicking. Thirty technicals raced toward us, while another twenty were chasing. We would be crushed.

"Get out of their way," I said, but there was no escape. Seconds later the horde swallowed us. Technicals side-swiped each other, gunners mowed down other gunners. Vehicles blew apart and tumbled end over end. No one seemed to notice us.

"They're shooting each other!" Wildman exclaimed.

"Whiskey tango foxtrot?!" I said. What the fuck?

"Brace!" my driver yelled, lurching the Humvee to avoid an out-of-control technical. "Civil war. Sunni ISIS versus Shia militia."

"Battle Royale Speicher! Yee-haaaaw!" Wildman said. I really wished he'd shut up, but this was Wildman's ecstasy.

A side window blew out, one bullet too many. Another bullet ricocheted inside the cab, my driver screamed.

Once the ISIS and Shia lines passed through each other, they turned about to face each other again. Vehicles collided, shattering into a million parts. Bodies flew through the air, run over before they hit the ground. A man with an ax leapt from one technical to another, cleaving a gunner in the skull before he was torn in half by another technical's fifty-cal.

"What the fuck, over?" Boon said.

"Just get us out of here," I said. *Anywhere but here,* I thought.

The first thing they teach you in the infantry is: if you're being ambushed, get off the X.

Then I saw the battling horde turn toward the CHU village.

Kylah, I thought. There would be no escape for them.

"About-face," I said. "Back to the CHUs! We need to get to Marhaz and Farhan before the battle does." The driver spun the Humvee in a J-turn and sped toward the barracks complex.

I was shooting technicals in our path with the fifty-cal, clearing a path. Those we could not hit, we destroyed. Boon was right behind us. Dust kicked up by the battle obscured vision, and we had three near misses with speeding technicals. But we could hear the heavy weapons firing, see the muzzle flashes through the dust cloud, and feel the blast shock waves rock our two-and-a-half-ton vehicles. The noise was deafening, even at fifty mph.

Kaboom. A technical in front of us blew into the air sideways, then landed and rolled another hundred meters. We fishtailed around it, nearly clipping it.

"IED!" I shouted—improvised explosive device. We were racing across a minefield.

Another technical blew ten meters high.

"It's raining Toyotas!" Wildman said.

Yet the technicals didn't slow. That's the problem with fanatics; they will continue to fight no matter how futile.

Enjoy hell then, I thought.

The Humvee erupted beneath my boots, flinging me through space. My body bounced off a Hesco barrier, then the dirt. There was pain in every cell. Behind me was the burning hulk of our Humvee, destroyed by an IED. My driver's body crumbled against the inside windshield. I could move my limbs. Things ached, but nothing was broken.

I'm exposed, I realized. Jihadists of all stripes were entering the CHU village. Some were in vehicles, some on foot like me.

In a firefight, you focus fast. The world gets small, as you search out immediate danger. Amateurs flip to full auto, empty the clip, and usually miss. The barrel superheats and bullets go wide. Better to be disciplined on semiauto. Acquire target, inhale, sight picture, exhale, squeeze. Shooting is like violent Buddhist meditation. No time to focus? Then a three-round burst center of mass. *Pop. Pop. Pop.* Target falls. Move on.

The best among us never fired full auto. For us it was one shot, one kill.

I brought my SCAR to firing position, finding them one by one. The air reeked, the temperature was scorching, and the smoke was so thick it was stinging my eyes. I moved quickly through the maze, dodging battling technicals, to where I had dropped off Kylah.

"Boon, Wildman," I said over my headset. "Anyone, come in." Static.

I heard popping, saw an ISIS fighter drawing down on me from a tight angle, and knew I wasn't safe. I ran to a wrecked Humvee, smoking and shot to hell, but still offering good cover. I scooted around to the rear, staying low, and broke off the vehicle's side mirror. Angling it, I could see around the corner.

Five meters away. Two ISIS, one firing, one looking for me. I slung my SCAR behind me and grabbed my Beretta pistols. I spun around the bumper and put them both down, firing both pistols at once, then crouch-ran to them as quickly as I could. The first was dead. The second was fumbling, trying to get a grenade from his bandolier with a bloody hand. I killed him with a headshot.

One more block, I thought, as I moved. Another technical exploded, the gunner coming off his perch in slow motion and slamming to the ground as if he'd already shattered all his bones.

Then I saw her. "Kylah!"

"Locke!" Kylah shouted back. "We're trapped!"

She was ten meters away on the edge of the action, firing on ISIS with her AK-47. Behind her was the CHU where Marhaz presumably hid. Farhan was in the middle of the courtyard, bloody and holding a knife. Five jihadists lay dead around him.

"Farhan!" I yelled, but he didn't hear me over the din of the battle. He returned to Marhaz, carrying only his blade.

A technical nearly ran me over, as I rolled out of its path. By the time I got upright, a figure walked toward me, like a ghost coming out of a wall: a tall man in a dirty white robe and a long beard, striding casually through the gunfire and smoke. He had no gun, as far as I could tell, but a long scimitar was strapped to his back. He looked so completely at ease, not looking to either side, that I hesitated for a second, and in that time he slipped up on Kylah and chopped into the wooden handguard of her AK-47 with his sword, wrenching it from her hands and knocking her to the ground.

"Kylah!" I screamed, but the man barely slowed. He didn't care about Kylah. He had his eyes on Marhaz. I leveled my SCAR at the center of his back, two kill shots, *pop, pop,* easy as that, but before I could fire I felt burning in my shoulder, then a sharp pain, and I turned to face an ISIS attacker closing so fast I could see the filth in his teeth. He leapt on me and knocked me down, grasping for my throat as I fumbled for my knife.

CHAPTER 50

The Wahhabi strode toward his target, oblivious to the shooting around him. *Allah sawf tuaffir*, he thought. Allah will provide. The letting go of fear and worry—the confidence it provided—it wasn't easy, but it was what had brought him this far. There was no need to question the universe now. The small man followed him, filming him with his iPad and ducking at every explosion.

Coward, the Wahhabi thought, as he glided through the fire-fight. He saw the red-haired female before him, and he relished the opportunity to show her his power. She was half turned when he cut into her AK-47—*The steel Allah has blessed is strong!*—and kicked her to the ground. It was unnecessary and fulfilling not to look at her again. She was a woman. She was nothing.

"No man can stop me!" the Wahhabi shouted, eyeing his prey, a man and a woman and—yes, a baby. It was obvious what had happened here, and why they needed to be cleansed.

"Prince Farhan Abdulaziz," he intoned loudly so that it would rise above the battle sounds.

He drew his scimitar with care, like someone taking the last step on a long journey. "You are judged a *kafir*, unbeliever, un-clean and apostate in the eyes of Allah. You are sentenced to die!"

He locked eyes with the young man and raised the scimitar above his head, but Farhan attacked with the zeal of an ISIS Emni, knocking the Wahhabi into the wall. The man ducked as Farhan went for the death blow, leaving a small crater in the CHU's wall. The Wahhabi swung the sword at the prince, but the prince was too fast. Crouching, Farhan made fast jabs at the Wahhabi's inner thighs, seeking the femoral artery. The Wahhabi hopped backward and counterattacked, but the narrow space hindered the long scimitar. He reversed the grip, so the scimitar was facing downward, and thrust.

The prince screamed, but something next to him was screaming louder. It was the pregnant girl, the Wahhabi saw too late. She had risen somehow, despite her condition. She had gone animal, attacking him with her claws, trying to gouge his eyes. He staggered to regain his balance and then grabbed her around the throat, lifting her up. She tore at his arm, drawing blood, but he only looked at it and laughed.

"*Wasawf yakhudhuk swa' alan*," he said, wrapping his hands around her throat. She gasped. He felt his power, and he reveled in it. "I will take you both now," he said again in Arabic, marveling at the ecstasy of strangling a life. It was even better than the sword. "No man can kill me!" he said. "I am the sword of Allah. I am the prophet. No man can—"

He felt the pain shoot up his back and turned, dropping the lives in his hand. He saw the woman standing there, the one with the red hair, and he swung his sword in a wide arc. He felt it bite into her chest, felt its power, and saw the knife drop from her hand. He raised his sword again, to administer justice. He said, "No man can kill me—"

But he never finished. He fell to the ground, a metal pole thrust through his back, its sharp point pinning him to the CHU.

"I am no man, fucker," Marhaz said.

I stabbed the man's side, to make sure he was dead. He fell on me like a weight, and I pushed him off, his body slippery from blood. I was covered in it, we both were, and I wasn't sure how much was mine.

A technical rounded the corner, then accelerated to run me down. I tried to stand, but I fell, slipping on guts. The world was fuzzy, and my balance poor. I crawled backward, away from the charging pickup truck. The ground shook, then the Martyr Maker burst through a CHU and rammed the charging technical, scattering man and machine into a million parts.

The gunner in the back of the next technical turned. He had twin antiaircraft guns, ZPU-2s, if I wasn't mistaken. *It might be enough,* I thought, but the men on top of the Martyr Maker unloaded on the technical, blowing off the head of the gunner's assistant beside him and allowing the Hemmet time to knock the vehicle aside and crush a technical coming up quickly to assist.

The Martyr Maker paused, its huge front wheels spinning. It backed up to free itself from the crushed truck, paused again, then turned toward me and began to advance. I knew it wasn't coming for me. I was too small. It was headed for the center of Bear's remaining mercenaries, to change the flow of the battle, but I was directly in its path.

I thought of trying to roll out of the way, but I had no strength. I thought of tossing a satchel charge over its walls as it passed, but I had no satchel. I thought of the way people put skulls inside wheels in movies, and then the wheels grind to a halt, until the skulls explode from the pressure. I thought of Mozart's Fifth Violin Concerto, the first major piece of music I ever learned to play like a master.

The missiles struck. I couldn't tell the type. They zoomed over my head, from behind me and moving fast, and then they exploded into the Martyr Maker.

The concussion blew me sideways. I lay there, ears ringing

and my face in the bloody dirt, and summoned the strength to look up. The Martyr Maker was dead. I could tell the battle had broken and that the surviving ISIS militants, seeing their behemoth felled, were fleeing back to their barracks complex.

I thought of the stranger with the sword, and I looked toward Marhaz. I saw them: Kylah, Farhan, Marhaz, the madman. They were all on the ground, not moving.

I had to get to them. I started to stand, but slipped. I was halfway to my knees again when I felt the barrel in the back of my head and the click of the hammerlock.

"Don't fucking think about it, traitor," someone said. "Don't even move."

CHAPTER 51

I sat, drained and bloody, the pistol pushing my head toward the ground, as the battle sounds ebbed away. I stared down at my hands, wondering what was happening to Boon and Wildman, the Kurds, Kylah, Marhaz and Farhan.

"Stay still, bitch," the man behind me hissed, when I tried to raise my head. He wasn't fighting. He seemed to be waiting for the fighting to end, which was happening quickly, by the sound of the diminishing gunfire. It wasn't hard to figure out who he was. He was an American. A merc. He must have been from the Apollo team in Sinjar.

"What we have here," the man said, "is a Mexican standoff."

He put his hand around my neck and pulled me to a sitting position. In front, facing me, was a force of Muslim fighters with their assault rifles drawn. I saw three men in Quds uniforms, two in attack position, and one quietly staring, and realized they must be Shia militia. Facing them, the remaining ISIS force of a dozen men, weapons up, glancing over their shoulders like they wanted to run. To their left, Wildman and a remainder of the mercenaries, along with a remnant of the Iraqi army that must have joined the battle, were standing with rifles pointed in all directions. I figured my captor had a team behind him, probably ten Tier One warriors, if they'd all survived.

Shia, Quds, mercs, ISIS, Americans, Kurds, and Iraqi Army irregulars, all staring at each other across a jihadi-scarred battle-field. It wasn't a Mexican standoff, exactly. It was an Iraqi one.

And me, right in the middle.

"They came for me," I yelled into the silence. "The others fight with me. We have no fight with you."

"We have fight with you," the Shia leader said in English. It was the tall man from the technical, the one whose small gunner's head had been forcibly destroyed.

"And we have issues with you," my captor snarled. Beside him, someone spit tobacco into the dirt. They were both right, of course. The Americans and the Iran-backed Shia had been killing each other, off and on, for the past decade. This mutual hatred was inevitable, and justified. But if someone started shooting, the chances were good we were all going to die.

I looked to the right, at the body of Farhan, the man who had brought us to this impasse. I saw Boon huddled over Kylah, working his med kit. He was moving quickly but precisely. I could see his tension.

"*Salam!*" I said. Peace. "There is no reason for us to die. We came here to fight a common enemy. They are beaten and on the run. They are fleeing to their brothers now."

Nobody spoke. The Shia leader was staring with anger above me, at my captor, who I assumed was staring back the same way.

"Put down your weapons," I yelled to Wildman and the remains of Bear's mercs. "Show them this battle is over."

Nobody moved. Then a man behind Wildman stepped forward and put his AK-47 on the ground. It was one of the Kurds, the one who had convinced the rest to fight here with us, when they could have gone back to Erbil. I thought others would follow, especially the Kurds, but nobody did.

Failure, I thought, but then the Quds leader spoke. "We will give you four hours," he said, "while we pursue and destroy the remnants of this ISIS force. When we return, everyone must be gone. This place is ours. We will kill anyone who remains."

"Fuck you," the man behind me snarled, but I cut him off, even though I was his prisoner.

"Accepted," I said, and immediately the Quds commander turned to the assembled Shia and spoke to them in Arabic. The ISIS soldiers looked at each other, then laid down their weapons. Thank God there were no martyrs among them.

"You mongrel whore," my captor said, forcing my face back to the ground with the point of his gun. It didn't matter now. The deed was done. I turned as he ground my face into the dirt, so that with one eye I could see Boon, bent over Kylah, moving up and down as he worked on her.

"I'm calling Rodriguez," my captor said to his second, as the sound of the last Shia technical faded away. It was just us mercenaries now.

"Don't bother," I said through a faceful of dirt. I didn't know who Rodriguez was, but I knew what kind of man he was: middle manager, mission manager. I'd answered to one myself, not so long ago.

"Who asked you, traitor?"

"Winters. Your boss," I muttered, through a mouthful of mud.

My captor pulled me up, but only an inch. "What's that?"

"Winters. Brad Winters. He's coming."

The man didn't answer. He hadn't been expecting that.

"Rodriguez. He told you I'd be here," I continued. "That's how you found me, after we lost you in the desert." I was guessing, but I knew I was right. My captor's silence confirmed it.

"I told him," I said.

"You told Rodriguez?"

"I told Winters. Last night. I said to meet me here."

"You're bullshitting."

"Then call him," I said. "I have his private number, in my sat phone." It was the prince's sat phone, but no need to get picky. "I called him on it eight hours ago."

I didn't need to say anything more. Let the man call Winters; let Winters sort this out. I could tell, from the way he was acting, this team leader liked to keep things simple. That was why Winters hired men like him: to complete missions. I'd hired men like him myself. They were useful. But the last thing you wanted a man like that doing was thinking too much.

Thinking was my mission-critical skill, not his.

CHAPTER 52

The printer spit out another page, and the chief petty officer snatched it. He squinted to read the papers in the dim light of the frigate's intelligence center, a few compartments down from the Command Information Center.

Shit, he thought. It made no sense. Since CTF-151 had been retasked from hunting pirates around Somalia to chasing a mystery ship off Yemen, the faxes grew increasingly frantic. But this fax was something else altogether.

He was the ship's intelligence noncommissioned officer, and he had never seen a more classified document. Its level of secrecy used code words he had never heard of, and it came right from the top. "Anything the matter?" asked the junior sailor next to him.

"No," the chief lied. He sealed the message in an envelope and stamped it TOP SECRET: CAPTAIN'S EYES ONLY.

Be calm, he thought, as he stood up to leave.

"Going to the head," he told the others as he exited the hatch. He scampered along the passageway of the Oliver Hazard Perry–class frigate, squeezing by a sailor mopping and muttering to himself as he approached the bridge.

"Is the captain here?"

"Negative," replied the officer of the deck. "Try the wardroom."

The chief trundled back down the passageway, past the mad mopper, down the ladderwell, and finally to the officer's wardroom. The admiral was sitting with a few of his top commanders.

The chief knocked on the bulkhead. "Sir, permission to interrupt."

"Come in, Chief," the admiral said in a genial tone.

"Sir, this just came in," the chief said, holding out the envelope.

"You could have called for me."

"No sir. You will understand once you read it."

Admiral Balloch took the envelope and nodded to the other officers, who cleared out. He opened and removed the orders, head bobbing as he read. He didn't say anything.

"Do you wish to respond, sir?"

The admiral shook his head, stood up, and stretched. *Orders are orders,* Balloch thought. "Do we have the freighter's last known position and heading?"

"Yes sir. We've plotted an intercept course and should be there in a few hours."

"Plot a new course for the coordinates in this envelope. Tell no one where the coordinates come from, admiral's orders."

"Yes sir."

"And Chief, no one but us knows what's in this envelope. Is that clear?"

"Yes sir."

It was good luck they were in my quadrant, the admiral thought. Staring out at a gray and angry sea, he hoped that, maybe, the weather would bring him good luck, too.

CHAPTER 53

It took an hour and a half for Winters to arrive. I don't know what happened in that time, because I was hooded and driven to an abandoned hangar immediately after the Shia left. I guess Campbell—I overheard the name—didn't like the gist of the phone call, because he was even grumpier than before, pulling my arm and smacking me in the head whenever he had an excuse, and twice as hard when he had no excuse at all.

The only excitement was when they found a Shia militant hiding in the back office where they wanted to stash me. There was yelling, the threatening kind, but only for a few seconds.

"I am not gunned," the man said in terrible English. "I have no more my command. I want to go home." He sounded tired and broken.

"Go to hell," Campbell replied, as a shot echoed through the hangar.

After that, they kept me flex-cuffed to a pipe in an office adorned with pink plastic flowers and the scent of rosewater. I assumed the AO team worked to clear the runway of debris and enemy, because I was alone after that. I was asleep when I heard the whine of the Gulfstream V's jets as it taxied into the hangar. I imagined the Apollo mercs in their extraordinary vehicles racing alongside as escort. I was jealous of those vehicles. If I'd had them, I could have taken out the Martyr Maker and saved Bear, my Kurdish driver, and a bunch of other good men.

At least Farhan and Marhaz were alive. They'd told me that

much, even if they refused to let me talk to Boon. I assumed Boon and Wildman were flex-cuffed in another room.

"Uncuff him," Winters said the moment he walked into the room.

"Sir?" Campbell started.

"You've taken his guns and knives. You've given me his satellite phone. What can he do to me?"

"You'd be surprised, sir."

"You'd be surprised, son, by what *I* can do."

I kept still as the flex-cuffs were cut off, resisting the urge to rub my wrist back to life as I rose from a leaning position for the first time in ninety minutes. My back was killing me. I hated getting old.

"Water," I said.

Campbell threw a canteen in my face. He had a buzz cut and a snake tattoo crawling around his collar. I'd seen his kind before.

"He's going to question every order you give him from now on," I said, after he'd left and Winters and I were alone.

"No he's not," Winters said confidently. He was wearing a blue Brioni suit, the best money could buy, but slightly rumpled at the sleeves. His white shirt was open at the collar, no tie. This was his business casual. "But he'll never give up wanting to kill you."

I shrugged. Campbell didn't bother me, although he probably should have. Men like him were dangerous, even if you were on their fighting side.

"I was surprised to get your call," Winters said.

"You thought I'd fight."

"I thought you'd run. Most people would have."

"You would have caught me."

"True. Most people figure that out too late."

Fine, Brad, let's talk this through, if that's what you want. And yes, I used your first name. I don't kowtow to you anymore. At least not in my own head.

"You betrayed me in Ukraine," I said.

"We've been over this."

"No, we haven't."

Winters sighed, like I was wasting his time. Fine with me. I knew he wanted to be at Camp Speicher even less than I did. I was comfortable in this environment; he wasn't.

"If you had died in Ukraine, Thomas, you wouldn't be the man I thought you were." He looked me in the eye for dramatic effect, but I didn't squirm under his gaze. Not anymore. "But you weren't killed, and you are the man I imagined."

"My friend died there," I said. "A man I trusted like a brother."

"Men die, Thomas. You should know this better than most. It's what you do."

He didn't understand. He didn't have anyone in his life that mattered to him like Jimmy Miles had to me. He probably didn't even have someone like Boon.

"Why did you track me?"

He laughed. "You know the answer to that, Thomas." But I didn't, and Winters realized it. If he was disappointed, he didn't show it. "Sometimes, we are the last to know ourselves," he said.

Since when was this snake a philosopher?

He leaned back. "I could have killed you, of course," he said, "but what's the point? I could have let you go. Cut you loose to fend for yourself." He glanced at me for a reaction, but I kept a stone face. "I could have brought you back into the fold," he said, and I resisted the urge to tell him to fuck himself. "But it never would have worked out. We both know that."

It's true. I would have killed him.

"So I waited you out," Winters continued. "You needed to cool down. I let you bring yourself back, when you were ready. That's what you did, Thomas. You came back."

"I didn't have a choice."

"Of course you did."

"I did it for my men. They didn't need to die for me."

Winters looked away. "The excuses we make," he muttered with a smile. It was supposed to be fatherly and wise, I suppose, but he was leaking oil, letting his real personality get in the way. He must have been under a great deal of stress.

"When I was in my thirties," he said slowly, looking around the faded pink and purple office—the favorite colors of the Iraqi army, no wonder they failed—"I left the military to work on Wall Street. I thought they would show me true power, not just firepower. I thought they were Masters of the Universe. But they were limited people. They only cared about money. The making of it, sure, but also the counting, the hoarding, the comparing of piles. I spent six months there, adrift and unfulfilled. In many ways, it was the best six months of my life, because it showed me who I was and what I wanted." He turned to me with that oily stare, and again I resisted the urge to curse him. "The most important step to power, Thomas, is to know ourselves. To accept who we are."

I am not who you think I am. "You don't know me."

"I didn't expect you to call. But when you did, Thomas, I knew you. Nobody I have worked with in my life would have thought strategically enough to make that call—or had the balls, to be honest—except you." He was smiling like a shark now. "And me."

"I called to save the princess and her baby."

"You called because of the key. Admit it. You felt alive, when you found out what was at stake. You felt a sense of purpose again, knowing you could change the world. You felt power. It sharpens the mind, Thomas. It enhances the senses. You can taste it: the sense of destiny. You are part of the world, but you are standing above it, beyond it. You matter. That's true power, Thomas. That's why you called."

He was wrong. I called because it was the only way out. I called because I didn't want anyone else to die. I called because every life is precious. Didn't I?

"Know thyself, Thomas. Accept it."

I could see it then. I knew why he had been following me, waiting for me to come back, like the prodigal son. Brad Winters, it turned out, did have someone like Jimmy Miles in his life. That someone was me.

But I hated Brad Winters. Didn't I?

"You have the money?"

He put a briefcase on the table. One million dollars, the price agreed to with the majordomo—Winters's traitor, of course—in Erbil. I didn't need to count it, or even look inside. I knew it would all be there.

"You have the key?" Winters asked.

"Of course not."

"Good. That would be foolish."

I paused. Did I really want to hand the key to a nuclear arsenal over to Brad Winters? Was my life worth it?

"What's the matter, Thomas?"

"I don't think a private military company should go nuclear."

"Nor do I. But it's safer than the Middle East going nuclear. The weapons will be secure with us. It's a CIA contract. You can see for yourself, if you come with me."

Yes, I thought, *let's do it that way.*

"When can I recover the key, Thomas?"

"When my men are free, and Farhan and Marhaz are safe."

Winters nodded. "There is no need for us to disagree, Thomas. Not when we can work together."

"I need to see my men."

"If you must," he said. He looked at his watch. It was a Patek Phillippe, probably worth a hundred grand. It was new since I had seen him last. "Two minutes," he said. "Even I have to stay on my flight plan, or at least close enough to avoid suspicion."

The Gulfstream V jet was in the middle of the hangar, already turned around to face the runway. The surviving mercs were outside, packing their vehicles, all except Campbell's men, who were standing inside staring at me with open disgust. *FIDO*, I thought. *Fuck It. Drive On.*

The three remaining Kurds took our working Humvee. They would ride with the mercs' convoy back to Erbil. Speicher, Bear, the contract . . . it was all over.

I needed Boon, and I saw him near the back, next to a technical that an hour ago had been ISIS. Now it was serving us, flying a red flag with a crudely drawn dagger in the middle, Wildman's handiwork, no doubt. Boon was loading a wrapped body into the truck bed with delicate care, and I didn't have to ask who it was.

"Are you going to bury her in Erbil?"

"I don't know," Boon said. He was as down as I'd ever seen him, but the sadness made him hard. "I don't know who else she has."

Nobody was the answer, and it could have been said for any of us. It was what I said about Jimmy Miles, when I'd burned his body to ash.

So instead of offering bullshit comfort, I handed Boon the briefcase of money. "Distribute it to the men any way you see fit."

He looked inside. He couldn't have cared less that he was holding a fortune. He pulled out a bundle of cash and handed it to me. I heard cursing from Campbell's men; one of them was literally spitting mad. They were holding him back.

"It was good getting to know you these last few days," I said. I meant it.

"It was good knowing you these last few years," he replied. He meant that, too. Boon was a better person, in his soul, than me. But I was trying.

"You don't have to run," I said. "It's over."

He started to say something, then stopped. "Only for Kylah," he said finally.

I gave Wildman a mock salute, open palm, British style. He laughed. "Fock yourself," he said.

I walked back to the plane. Farhan and Marhaz were disappearing up the stairs to the cabin, unsteady but determined. Brad Winters was to the side, standing with Campbell. He was holding an iPad. Both stared at the screen.

I disappeared into the cabin and sat across from the couple. Nobody said anything. Brad Winters came onboard and took the seat across from me. He was laughing and watching something on the iPad. "Amazing," he whispered, winding me up. "Amazing."

I couldn't resist. "What is it?" I said.

He put the iPad on the little table between us and started the video. It showed the madman, from the back, walking through the battle untouched. It showed him pushing Kylah down and standing over Farhan. He said something, but it was inaudible. He raised his sword above his head and brought it down in a violent arc. But the video ended there, in a fireball, a massive explosion that shook the screen, and then snapped to darkness.

"They found it on the battlefield, next to a dead man," Winters said.

I just stared at the black screen, too worn out to say anything. Why would someone risk their life to film something like that? What was the point?

"The Lord works in mysterious ways," Winters said. "But he works, Thomas. He works."

CHAPTER 54

The knocking on the door grew louder.

"Admiral Balloch, wake up! Wake up, sir."

The admiral rolled over in his bunk and checked the time: 0012, just after midnight. He had slept less than three hours in the past twenty-four. "What is it?"

"The ship. We found her."

Finally, he thought.

"Excellent. Get a helo in the air and plot a course to intercept. Make the closest point of approach four thousand yards. That should give us plenty of standoff room in case they have RPGs."

"Already done, sir."

"What's our ETA?"

"Forty minutes in current conditions."

The storm hadn't abated. The admiral could feel it raging beneath him. "Meet me in the CIC," he said.

"Yes sir."

Balloch cleaned up, slipped on his duty uniform, and ate a stale samosa. It was never a good idea to go into action on an empty stomach. He walked to the Combat Information Center, swaying as the ship rolled in the high sea.

"Admiral on deck!" a sailor shouted, and the CIC crew snapped to attention.

"At ease. Status update. And someone, please fetch me a tea."

The CIC buzzed with people under low light. Large color

screens showed the positions of the fleet and the mystery freighter.

"Sir, we have confirmed it's the *Eleutheria*," the Executive Officer, or XO, said, pointing to a blip on the chart on a large screen. "She's six miles off our starboard bow, making seven knots, heading north-northwest in sea state five. We have a helo on station, and the *Eleutheria* is refusing our hails."

The admiral stared at the monitor with their helicopter's live video feed. The helo was circling the ship in the gusting rain, the old ship struggling against the heavy weather. Except for the gale, all looked normal with the ship.

"Any signs of distress?"

"None sir," the XO said.

"Is their transmitter broken?"

"Unknown, sir."

"Are the assault teams on station?"

"We have two RHIB boats with VBSS teams ready to launch. Just give the word."

The admiral sipped his tea. "Hail them again," he said.

The helicopter buzzed the *Eleutheria*, spotlight locked on her decks as she heaved in the squall. The bridge crew was fearful but didn't dare speak. The last man who challenged the captain was in sick bay with three stiches in his lip and half his wages withheld. All sailors knew the only law that mattered at sea was the captain's. Mutiny was possible, but Captain Goncalves kept the one key to the ship's armory around his neck, and punishment for attempting mutiny was death.

"*Eleutheria*," the radio blared over channel 13, the bridge-to-bridge frequency. "This is frigate hull number F270, four thousand feet off your port beam. Switch to channel fifteen, over."

"Ignore them!" Goncalves growled, holding on to a handrail as the ship rolled in ten-foot waves. For the past thirty minutes, the multinational naval task force ship had been trying to contact them. The radio operator looked down at the floor, thinking what every man onboard the *Eleutheria* was thinking: what has the captain done?

"Goddammit, eyes front!" the captain ordered. "Ignore them."

The captain is insane. He will get us all killed.

Yet no man had the courage to instigate a mutiny. Finally, the first mate spoke up. "Captain . . . perhaps it will go easier if we answer them."

Goncalves remained a statue. Wind beat the rain into the bridge's windows.

"They committed an entire task force to find us," the first mate said.

"What are you suggesting?"

The mate shuffled his feet nervously. "I've been smuggling for twenty-five years and I've never seen a navy task force being reassigned to chase down a lone freighter. It makes no sense." He paused to choose his words carefully. "What did we pick up in Pakistan?"

Goncalves turned to face him. The mate instantly knew he had gone too far.

"That is none of your concern," the captain said.

"*Eleutheria* . . ." the radio message again.

"No one touch that radio!" the captain bellowed, facing the bridge crew. "No one questions me! I am the captain of this vessel. Any man who takes issue with my command is free to leave my ship and swim to shore. Is that understood?"

Silence, save the whipping rain.

"Good. Then we have an understanding," the captain said.

The mate saw the chain around the captain's neck. He could take control of this vessel with that key.

"Captain," the mate said. "We understand. Isn't that right, men?"

They grunted, without enthusiasm.

Good, the mate thought. *They will probably rally to my side.*

"Then do as I say or there will be a flogging, so help me God."

The mate had been measuring Goncalves for years. He knew he could take him down. The captain was half his build and twice his age.

"I'll rig a noose from the yardarm and do it the old way," Goncalves thundered.

If he could tackle him from behind, surprising him, it would be over in less than a minute. When the bridge crew saw him win decisively, they would rally. He could snatch the key to the armory and take control of the ship, with just a loyal few.

It will be more than a few, the mate thought.

"How far are we?" the admiral asked.

"Ten minutes," the XO said. "The VBSS teams are asking for permission to deploy, the RHIBs ready to launch."

The admiral sipped his tea again, rolling with the storm surge. The freighter was on several monitors now. It had not changed course or responded to their radio communications.

"Get closer," the admiral said.

"Sir, this is highly irregular," the XO said. "Our orders are clear."

"My order is clear, Commander," the admiral said. "We get closer, and we wait."

CHAPTER 55

Amr Diab, the Justin Timberlake of the Arab world, was blaring over the radio.

I want you to feel my happiness, be at my place and feel the happiness to live with your loved one, not someone else.

This night, baby, is the night of our lives, this night is the night of my life!

The music was giving Abdulaziz a headache. *Allah protect me,* he thought, turning off the Land Cruiser's radio. It was bad enough that his teenage daughters liked Justin Timberlake, but now Arab culture was imitating the irritating rat. Pop culture was America's true weapon.

That, and casual cruelty, the prince thought.

He was speeding along at a hundred kilometers an hour, surrounded by the flat and empty Saudi Arabian desert. There wasn't another soul in any direction, all the way to the horizon. He rolled down the window and breathed deeply, his white robe and red-checkered head scarf flapping in the wind. He loved the desert because it was unforgiving.

Sitting next to him was Princeling Abdulaziz, or "Zeez" for short. Among all his companions, Zeez was a favorite. They understood one another, despite their many differences.

"Zeez, how are you feeling today?"

The bird said nothing in return. It sat motionless on the custom-built bird bar Abdulaziz had installed between the Land Cruiser's front leather seats, despite the strong wind through the open window. Abdulaziz smiled at the dignity. Zeez was a saker falcon, a species favored by Saudi royals for generations and known for its speed and power. The falcon could spot prey kilometers away and fly at over a hundred kilometers per hour, nearly doubling that when diving on prey. Watching it obliterate its quarry brought inner light to Abdulaziz. He had bought the falcon illegally in Dubai for a mere $10,000; the bird would have been worth it to the prince at ten times the price.

"Zeez, you are the light of my eyes. You are magnificent," Abdulaziz cooed, stroking the bird's feathered breast. The hawk jerked its head left then right. It could see nothing with its hood on, but it let out a screech of anticipation.

"There, there, Zeez, have patience," Abdulaziz said.

The back of the Land Rover was stacked high with rectangular bird cages holding pigeons, each named after one of Abdulaziz's enemies: Ahmad, Abdullah, Nassar, El Amin, Muhammad, Mohammad, Nejem, Tawfeek, Mahmoud Ali, and Khalid.

Khalid, he thought. The man's very existence was an offense.

Brad Winters had reported Farhan's death in a firefight in Iraq less than two hours ago. If not for the video, Abdulaziz might not have believed him. Winters wasn't a trustworthy man; at this level, nobody was. He had recognized the Wahhabi from the video, though, the same man who had killed the major-domo. True, he didn't see the killing blow, but the prince was happy for that. He had watched a hundred men die, a few by his own hand, but he didn't want to see his last son murdered. It was like watching everything he had spent his life building collapse.

No, it wasn't like that. It was deeper. It was true, grinding pain. He would never see his son again, he would have no heir, and the only thing he would have to bury, according to Winters, was a few fingers and teeth.

The Land Cruiser glided to a stop. "Are you ready, my precious?" the prince asked the falcon, as he stepped out and took a big breath of sweet desert air.

Out here, nothing mattered. No e-mails, conference calls, annoying subordinates, moronic superiors, crises, or stress. Out here, nothing could touch him: no heartbreak or betrayal. Winters would fix things. The prince knew that. The nuke was gone, and the evidence would never point back to him, the General Intelligence Directorate, or the Western-leaning side of the royal family he served.

But Winters could never fix what truly mattered, and Abdulaziz was just beginning to feel the pain of that.

The hawk screeched again, wondering at the delay and sensing the feast to come. The eternal struggle: animal versus animal, man versus time. In a country flush with money and opulence, falconry was a bulwark against the tide. Hawking offered communion with the prince's Bedouin heritage, and the long line of tough desert nomads who had made him.

"Yes, yes, my moon," he said, as Zeez fidgeted on his glove. The hawk was beautiful in the desert light. Its chest was white, with streaks of brown. The top feathers were brown, with white highlights, a camouflage worthy of the Louvre.

"Let us get your first quarry," Abdulaziz said, pulling a pigeon from one of the cages. "You shall be named . . . Khalid, the first to perish."

He threw the pigeon overhand, like a baseball. The bird fluttered and squawked, flying upward. Lovingly, he stroked the saker's breast then removed its hood, and its head rapidly dipped up and down as it scanned the horizon. It locked onto the ascending pigeon and started flapping, its talons still tied to Abdulaziz's glove.

"Show Khalid his fate," he said as he let the hawk go. It shot straight up like a rocket, soaring well above the pigeon. It locked on to its target, then dove with claws outstretched. But Khalid showed moxie and dodged at the last second. The hawk banked hard. The saker had the speed of a jet with the agility of a helicopter. The pigeon was wily, though, and plummeted toward the ground. Zeez followed. Both accelerated to full speed, straight toward the desert floor. The pigeon flattened out, rear tail feathers flared to control its extreme velocity. Zeez extended his talons for the kill. Khalid saw the shadow from above, and jerked left, but Zeez anticipated the ruse this time, and hit the pigeon like a missile. Pigeon down.

"Tear him, Zeez," Abdulaziz said, letting go of his binoculars. The violence was brutal yet beautiful, but it offered only partial relief. He climbed into the Land Cruiser and sped to the saker, so that he could watch it disembowel its prey. White and gray feathers blew into the desert wind as the hawk's beak tore into the body. Abdulaziz stood and admired.

Ten more pigeons, all named Khalid, met the same fate. Zeez stopped eating after the fourth bird, choosing instead to kill and eviscerate. That was what made Zeez a special bird, why he was worth $10,000, and why he had earned the Abdulaziz family name. This raptor was intelligent enough to cherish the pleasures of victory.

The phone rang. He answered it. "Yes."

He listened without expression, occasionally nodding.

"Good," he said at last.

The plan was in motion. It would not take long. Winters and men like him could plan and scheme. They were useful. They would set the evidence right, if anyone looked. But that wasn't

Abdulaziz's preferred method. You didn't give a man like Prince Khalid room to maneuver. They were too dangerous for that. You ended it, then sorted out the details later.

He grabbed the last pigeon, a very special, ugly bird. "Fly, Khalid," he yelled as he hurled the pigeon as hard as he could.

The raptor was on it before it had a chance to unfurl its wings, diving from above and hurling the helpless pigeon to the ground. The bird was gutted before it hit the sand.

CHAPTER 56

It had been thirty minutes. Admiral Balloch was pushing the situation to the point of breaking, and he knew it. He couldn't wait any longer. "Clear the deck!" the admiral ordered.

The Combat Information Center crew stiffened, turning to face the ambitious career officer who had been in charge of this ship for the last three years. The CIC was never deserted, especially during a potential action.

"Clear out," the admiral yelled, iron in his voice. "Now!"

The crew fumbled over each other getting out the small hatch.

"You stay," the admiral said to the XO. "And you too, Chief."

The chief froze by the bulkhead. The XO stood at attention, bracing himself for the worst. Perhaps he had displeased the admiral and was about to be relieved of his post. Or perhaps he had inadvertently compromised the mission. The fact that the chief remained to witness his imminent ass chewing only deepened his humiliation.

The hatch of the Combat Information Center sealed shut, leaving the three of them alone.

"Commander," the admiral said calmly, and the XO winced, waiting for his punishment. It was always worse when senior officers were calm. "Recall the helo."

What?! "Sir?"

"I ordered you to recall the helo. And stand down the marines."

The XO's face twisted. On one hand, he was relieved not to be sacked. On the other, what the admiral had ordered was treasonous. A court-martial offense.

"Sir," the XO said. "Our orders are clear. We are to intercept and search this cargo ship. Why would you recall the helo and stand down the marines? How will we search it?"

"We already have."

"Sir?"

"Commander, you will mark in your log—as will the chief, as will I—that the *Eleutheria* has been searched and nothing was found."

"What?"

"The *Eleutheria* is clean," Balloch said calmly.

"A-Admiral," the man stammered, "you're asking me to falsify a log entry on a priority mission. I can't do that." The XO felt light-headed. He realized he was breathing heavily. He had never questioned his commanding officer before. "With respect, sir, why are you ordering this?"

"I have my orders, too," the admiral said.

Captain Goncalves turned to face the oncoming frigate. The navy ship's mass was a foreboding black silhouette against the night sky. It should never have come this close in such high seas, and especially not for so long. One rogue wave, and it could smash their hull and kill them all.

Now is the time, the mate thought, preparing to tackle the captain from behind. *Now is the time to end this madness. Before the soldiers board and send us all to the brig.*

"Captain, they are six hundred yards and closing," someone said.

The mate glanced around the pilothouse, looking for some sort of club, but saw nothing of use. He would have to use his bare hands.

"Five hundred yards." The frigate loomed out their port

windows. The more experienced crew recognized its profile as an American warship, and their knees buckled.

If the mate pulled off his mutiny, he would have to deal with the Americans once they boarded. No one wanted to deal with Americans.

"Four hundred yards. Captain, should we do something?"

"No. You have your orders."

The man is insane, the mate thought, as he slid behind the captain. The frigate was on course to come across their bow.

"Three hundred yards," the crewman said, voice shaky.

The mate clenched his fists. *Courage,* he thought, as he counted down. *Three, Two . . .*

"Captain, they are changing course!" the helmsman yelled.

The mate looked up. He saw the American warship veering out of their way.

"The Americans are turning!" another crewman shouted.

The helicopter's spotlight turned off.

"Holy shit!" the men shouted in a dozen different languages. "Hurraa! *Zito! Ohana! Keallam!*

Impossible, the mate thought, as Goncalves walked up the bridge windows, watching the frigate disappear into the storm. It seemed to take a very long time.

The mate was disgusted. Why did the warship let them go? How did the captain know? The crew would love the captain now. They would talk about this for years. The man with the iron balls. With one decision, the old man had become untouchable, and the mate's chance of taking over the ship had become spit in the wind.

"Old friend," the captain said, turning to his first mate. "You are not the man you thought you were, are you?"

The first mate looked down.

"Well, neither am I."

CHAPTER 57

"Tea?"

"No, thank you," I said, gesturing away the young man. Winters sat across from me, impeccably groomed and dressed in Jermyn Street's finest bespoke cloth. So was I. The tailor had finished with the suit an hour ago, and we'd come straight here. Even my new Berluti leather shoes were so au courant they hadn't yet come into fashion. I can't lie. It felt good, especially after four months of living in the dirt.

I'd had a good dinner after the private jet landed, six fingers of Woodford Reserve in a "sky bar" at a five-star London hotel, and, most important, a good night's sleep on five-hundred-thread-count sheets and three pillows. I'd had a good shit, shower, and shave, in that order, making me feel like a new man. No one would have guessed I had been fighting a battle in the Jazira desert almost exactly twenty-four hours before. I suppose that was the point.

"Try the tea," Winters said. "It is quite good, and we may be here awhile."

The small antechamber was richly appointed with upholstered chairs, a Qom rug from ancient Iran, oil paintings, an eighteenth-century chandelier, and a marble fireplace. It was perfectly quiet save the *tick tock* of a grandfather clock somewhere downstairs.

"The scones are dry to my taste," Winters added, offering me the plate.

"No thanks."

The music from *The Sorcerer's Apprentice* stuck in my brain, a running theme since I'd boarded the Gulfstream back at Camp Speicher. It was Dukas's orchestral fantasy, based on Goethe's poem, about a student wizard who tries to imitate his master and nearly dies from his arrogance. Faced with endless chores like fetching water, the young apprentice enchants a broom to do the work for him. It works, until the apprentice realizes he never fully learned how to un-enchant the broom. Even Mickey Mouse knew the feeling. And yet few, I kept reminding myself, could avoid the pitfalls.

Nine gongs of the grandfather clock. Nine o'clock. Outside, London plodded along in a morning rush hour rain, the damp and rheumy opposite of the dry desert heat. Eventually, the large pocket doors slid open.

"Mr. Winters," an Indian gentleman said. He looked healthy, happy, and put together by a valet.

"Kabir," Winters said, rising to shake hands. He didn't introduce me, and Kabir didn't ask. He barely looked my way. It was only after I'd followed on Winters's heel that I realized the young man serving tea had followed on mine.

The private office looked extracted from a Pall Mall social club circa 1850. Lit portraits hung from crown molding along red silk damask walls and oak paneling. Floor-to-ceiling windows with polished brass fixtures and frothy curtains overlooked an English garden. A four-tier crystal chandelier hung from a twelve-foot coffered ceiling, and wall-to-wall Persian carpets obscured the parquet floor. Decanters lined a credenza near a Venetian marble fireplace. At the far end of the room sat an enormous carved desk that could have been plucked from the lord chancellor's personal office.

We took the leather chairs across from it, as Kabir seated himself behind the desk.

"Tea?" he asked, as the young man slid to the silver set on the credenza. He poured carefully and stirred in a cube of sugar. He was late twenties, dressed in Savile Row with ostentatious pinstripes. It struck me that he wasn't a manservant, as I had assumed, but Kabir's protégé. He took a seat in the back, eyeing me silently as he passed.

"Prince Khalid has been arrested," Winters said. "Prince Abdulaziz has accused him of trying to buy a nuclear weapon in a palace coup attempt."

"What is Khalid saying?"

"Nothing. He is in Abdulaziz's black cells. If he meets an unfortunate accident, there will be trouble, but many will understand. A man is not fully in control when his two sons and heirs have been recently murdered, especially a man like Abdulaziz. The evidence, when it comes to the nuclear deal, will point to Khalid."

Kabir nodded. "And Farhan's death?"

"Unfortunate. He was a troubled boy, but not the first prince to join the extremists. It is the death of the other son, Mishaal, who perished mysteriously in a Mabahith prison, that will hang Khalid . . . although a hanging will most likely be unnecessary."

It occurred to me these men were casually discussing the framing of an innocent man, while drinking tea, no less. In some other state, it sounded as if this Khalid was powerful. In his home, at least, he must have been loved. In this office, he was merely a convenient prop.

"And the . . . key?" Kabir asked.

"I have it," Winters said.

"In your possession?"

"No, but I will have it soon."

I fought the urge to speak up. I expected him to reference me, or simply to look in my direction, but neither man seemed aware I was in the room. It was clear that, like Kabir's protégé in the back, my job was to listen and learn. So many brooms to control. So much sweeping.

"That was a clusterfuck," Kabir said suddenly, dropping the uptight British tone. I didn't know if that was for Winters or for me, but it was startling. "I don't expect to ever be put in that position again."

"All's well that ends well," Winters said.

"No, it's not. Shoddy practices make shoddy partners."

Winters hesitated. He looked contrite, but I could see the act. "You're right, of course, Kabir. It was a clusterfuck, as you so accurately put it. But the crisis was averted, Abdulaziz has been managed, and the Saudis won't go looking for nukes again in our lifetime, not after this . . . clusterfuck. Bagging that madman Khalid, and pushing our chosen faction closer to the throne: that was a stroke of genius."

"And luck."

"They go together, of course."

Kabir laughed. He couldn't keep his anger. He was too relieved. In fact, for British aristocracy, he was positively giddy. The knot around his neck must have been quite tight before Brad Winters cut him free. "Mr. Winters," he said, "you are certainly confident. I will give you that."

"I'm an American," Winters replied. "Confidence is our greatest quality."

CHAPTER 58

Balloch took a long drag on his cigarette, then exhaled calmly as he studied the envelope the intel NCO gave him.

I hate these conversations, he thought. Twenty-seven years in the Pakistani navy didn't make such talks easier. When Islamabad assigned him command of this multilateral task force, CTF-151, he had mixed feelings. On paper he commanded a fleet of twenty-six ships, drawn from a dozen countries, but in reality the only thing he controlled was this Pakistani frigate. International politics dictated the rest.

Yet a command is a command, he thought as he stubbed out his cigarette. Like many multinational forces, the admiralship rotated among the participating countries. This year, it fell to Pakistan, and he was the next available Pakistani admiral. Not the command he hoped for, but the command he got.

The time had come. "Enter," he said.

The XO walked in with his head down, like a sullen child, then stood at attention. It looked like the XO hadn't slept since they received the mission to hunt down the *Eleutheria*. The admiral wasn't surprised.

"You're a good officer, Commander Jalbani. A good officer follows orders, even if he doesn't understand them."

"I am not so sure, Admiral."

The admiral motioned to the table between them, which took up a large portion of his private quarters. "A crisis of confidence, then? Don't worry. We all have them." The younger man didn't answer. "Join me in a cup of tea."

The man sat. He was a good officer, a loyal follower of protocol. He would go far, if he could make it past this first test. "No thank you on the tea, sir," he said. "I just want an explanation."

"I don't owe you that."

"No sir. But I need it."

Admiral Balloch poured his tea. "Orders are orders, Commander Jalbani," he said as he stirred his cup. "I must follow them just like you. We are Pakistani taking orders from Washington, DC, as happens in international task forces. The Americans said to board the smuggler ship *Eleutheria*."

The commander nodded agreement.

"But our secret orders," Admiral Balloch pulled out the envelope from his uniform's inner pocket, "in this envelope, are from *Islamabad*. They countermand the American orders. They say to let the ship pass. Now, which orders do you think have priority?"

"But why the contradictory orders?" Jalbani asked.

"For twenty-seven years," Admiral Balloch said, "I have served my country proudly as a Pakistani naval officer. When this ship became part of CTF-151, I didn't abandon that loyalty. We are one of thirteen nations in this task force. We work with them for the greater good. But our allegiance remains to our country. Always. That is why these multinational forces fail."

"But why the contradictory orders?" Jalbani said again.

"Politics," the admiral said. "That's all men like us need to know."

The admiral could sense the man was ill at ease. He needed Commander Jalbani's full commitment; they would both be recalled and punished if any of this was ever spoken of again. "What's on your mind, Commander? Speak freely."

Jalbani hesitated. "I don't like lying to our fellow naval officers in the task force. I respect them. They respect me. They are good allies and personal friends. This"—he knocked on the ship's bulkhead—"is American made, a decommissioned U.S. Navy Oliver Hazard Perry–class frigate. This"—he gestured vaguely toward the Pakistani order—"is not why I joined the navy. It is unprofessional and immoral. We are not . . . spies."

Balloch sighed. The man was upset. *He is young,* the admiral reminded himself.

"Just because Pakistan bought this frigate from the Americans," he said slowly, "does not make us their slaves. We steer by our stars. They steer by theirs. Don't think the Americans would do differently, if the situation was reversed."

Jalbani hesitated. "I don't know, sir."

Yes, you do. You know the Americans work for themselves, first and foremost.

"Don't forget that doubt," the admiral said. "Don't forget that nothing is clear in this command but one thing: we follow the orders of our superior officers. If you are going to wear stars one day, that knowledge will serve you well."

The commander was still not convinced, and the admiral could see it. He didn't have time for such insubordination. "We have done a difficult thing. We will be rewarded. Don't let a poor attitude undermine the good we have done, for ourselves and for our country. High command would not have issued this secret order unless it was important."

Jalbani looked like a beat boxer, clinging to the ropes. The admiral softened, realizing how hard this was for him. The real world was always a shock to the young.

"Your morality is a virtue," the admiral said. "I am pleased you came to me with these concerns. You are a man of solid timber, Commander Jalbani. But I expect you to follow my orders. I won't explain myself to you again."

The XO nodded, then turned and left.

Lewis dumped the last of her personal items into a burn bag. They didn't even give her a box to clear out her cubicle.

"You got a bum deal," Hernandez said.

"Brooks is a dick," she said.

"Affirmative."

"I was so sure the *Eleutheria* was our ship. I still am. All the data points to it. It just doesn't make sense."

Hernandez let out a sigh. "But it wasn't our ship."

"I failed," Lewis said, unaccustomed to the feeling. The admiral expended considerable political capital in Washington to reassign CTF-151 to their search mission, over the official protests of Pakistan. Then he ordered the task force to intercept the *Eleutheria*, on her hunch. When the ship was cleared, it proved too much for American-Pakistani relations, and the National Security Council decided to cut CTF-151 loose rather than risk a diplomatic incident. It didn't look good for the admiral; it looked worse for her.

"Shit rolls downhill," she said. "Brooks was just waiting for me to slip up, then he could fire me."

"Fate of the contractor."

She slumped into her chair, feet up on her desk, as she stared at the ceiling. Her exhaustion was palpable.

"What are you going to do now?" Hernandez asked.

"Go home. Have a glass of chardonnay. Break out a dance movie."

CHAPTER 59

"The thirty-year Château de Montifaud XO," Winters said. "Two, please."

"Very good, sir."

The waiter disappeared through a doorway hidden in the golden walls. Bookcases of bound leather spines surrounded us, with a Greek-themed relief lining the twenty-foot ceiling and a palatial Persian carpet covering the floor. The private library could have been the set for a Jane Austen movie, or it could have been Mr. Darcy's actual house. Most important, this library was rentable to members. Brad Winters and I were dining alone.

"It's good to be back at the Travellers Club," Winters said, running a cigar under his nose. The club had a strict no-smoking policy, but that too was rentable.

"Indeed," I said, still slicing my rare filet mignon, although it was so red it barely needed the knife. I was still working on my glass of 2006 Les Forts de Latour, a Bordeaux red, but I couldn't begrudge Winters the premature digestifs. He had pushed his steak away five minutes ago, barely touched. And the thirty-year Château de Montifaud cognac was impeccable.

From the outside, the Travellers Club looked like all of London's most prestigious social clubs: unassuming. There were never any signs or other markings on these venerated two-hundred-year-old institutions. There was only a nineteenth-century building with an address: usually St James's Square or Pall Mall. In this case, 106 Pall Mall, a five-minute walk to

Buckingham Palace. Inside, as the library attested, the club was a time capsule of Victorian splendor.

"I'm sure you have questions about the meeting today, Tom," Winters said, rolling a cigar in the flame of a wooden match. It was a Cuban. Nicaraguans were better, but Winters had never truly known cigars.

Finally, the invitation. I chewed slowly, laid my knife and fork carefully across my plate, and touched my lips with my cloth napkin. God, I was a million miles from the Tip Top and its rowdy crowd. I couldn't help but wonder if Wildman was having a drink there for lunch right now.

"Who is Kabir?" I asked, starting at the beginning.

Winters laughed. "That's Sir Basrami-Heatherington to you, Dr. Locke, a descendant of a long line of British-Indian bankers dating back to the British East India Company in the 1700s. Now a senior banker, although senior to what even I am unsure. One of the most powerful men in England, and possibly the world."

"He who controls the purse strings," I said.

"Oh, that bank controls much more than purse strings," Winters said casually, still rolling his cigar. "He trades in power, not money. It's not even technically a bank."

The waiter returned with our digestifs. He looked at my plate, but I signaled that I was still working. It was the best meal I'd had in six months. I wasn't going to waste a bite.

"Leave us, please," Winters said, as he relit his cigar with a six-inch wooden match and puffed smoke toward the gilded ceiling. "We will ring you if we need assistance." A small silver bell lay beside his snifter.

"Now," Winters said, turning to me with his cigar, "to us."

He raised his cognac. I raised my wine.

"You put together the nuclear deal. Why?"

"Because it was inevitable. It was the wisest move for the Saudis, or more specifically for an ambitious prince with the right connections. I saw that Abdulaziz was going to reach that conclusion himself, and soon, so I gave him a push."

"How?"

"We infiltrated his organization, had a trusted aide whisper the idea in his ear. I have been close to Abdulaziz for years, his most trusted outside contact. Once he made the decision, he would ask for my help. We knew he would need outside assistance structuring the finances, help on the delivery, and—most of all—utmost secrecy, since he was concealing this from his own government. That is one of the primary services I sell: plausible deniability."

"How much did it cost?"

"In this case, one billion dollars. Ten percent of the deal price."

I swallowed hard on the number, but Winters ignored it. He was puffing hard on his cigar to get the ember started. Eventually, he shook out another match.

"How did you slip that much through the international monitors?"

"Kabir can manipulate SWIFT." The Society for Worldwide Interbank Financial Telecommunication, or SWIFT, is the brain stem of international banking. It's the conduit big banks use to wire money to each other.

"SWIFT is airtight. Impossible to hack or manipulate."

"Nothing is impossible to hack or manipulate. We've done it. Besides, money is fungible. There are far more precious things."

"Like nuclear weapons?"

"Precisely."

"But the deal went sideways. The Paris convoy was hit, and the nuclear weapons controller stolen. Only Khalid knows where it's hid, and I assume he's dead now."

"You're right about Khalid being dead. Not much else."

He waited for me to pick through the clues. If Paris wasn't the mysterious Khalid, then who else had the knowledge and the skill for such a high profile . . .

"You," I whispered. "You stole the briefcase in Paris."

Winters grinned. "Yes, an Apollo team ambushed the Paris convoy. I have the briefcase."

"And you framed Khalid for it, and I assume had Mishaal murdered."

"Just to dust my tracks."

"But the Istanbul hit didn't go as planned."

"No. Farhan escaped before we could snatch him and his assets."

"So you hired me to find him."

"Among others. But yes, I saw the chance to kill two birds, as they say: get the key and get you back in the game."

I hated Brad Winters right then. For the smooth ease with which he made the pieces fit together. For the assumptions he was making about me. I hated him even more because they seemed true. I had been slumming it in Iraq, and for what? Saving one life while a hundred more are killed. Trying to get in bed with a bartender. Hoarding a warehouse full of cheap rugs. My efforts were pitiful.

But worst of all, I hated Winters because he reminded me of myself.

"So now you have the briefcase that activates the nuclear weapons, and the key card that activates the briefcase. But you don't have the weapons."

Winters held up a satellite phone. It was the one I had taken off Farhan in Sinjar. He had confiscated it from me at Camp Speicher. "In a few hours, the captain of the freighter will text this phone the exact location and time of the dropoff. Apollo teams are prepositioned, awaiting my orders."

Now that I thought about it, the phone hadn't been confiscated. Everything else I owned had, but Winters had pointedly asked me to give it to him. He was already thinking of this moment. He wanted me to realize that I was the one who had given him the vital missing piece. How little I had always understood. How easy it had always been to manipulate me, even now.

"Why do you need nuclear weapons?"

"Thomas," he said, shaking his head like he was so disappointed. He took a puff on his cigar, for dramatic effect. Brad Winters lived for the dramatic effect.

Well, that and the power to control the world.

"Go to the window," he said.

I stood up and walked to the windows. They overlooked Waterloo Gardens, catty-corner to the Duke of York Column. It was a leafy sanctuary available only to members of Pall Mall's social clubs.

"What do you see?"

I scanned carefully, trying to puzzle out what he was after. It had stopped raining, but only just, so hardly anyone was out. Two gentlemen smoking cigars with tumblers in hand under a canopy, a servant carrying drinks, an elderly couple leaning on each other as they walked.

Farhan and Marhaz.

They sat on a bench beneath an ancient oak tree, Farhan with a trimmed beard, Marhaz with her nine-month belly protruding beyond her shirt.

"Let me share with you some wisdom," Winters said, taking a drag on his cigar. "Loyalty is key, but sentiment is not loyalty. Sentiment kills."

I stared at Farhan and Marhaz. He touched her belly.

"There can be no loose ends."

Winters was right, of course. If his father found out Prince Farhan was alive, even ten years from now, the whole careful plan would collapse. But if he never discovered the deception . . .

That was when I realized, too late, that the merciful thing would have been to run, to leave the young couple in Sinjar to their own fate. I was death. I was the crushing power of the state. The final test of my loyalty, of my acceptance back into Winters's family, would be killing Farhan, Marhaz, and their baby girl. But even if I didn't do it, someone else would.

"Kill the sentimentality, Thomas," Winters hissed. "Kill the weakness."

I stabbed him. I picked up the steak knife and jammed it through his hand, cracking through his bones until the blade lodged in the leather upholstery and wood underneath. Before he could scream, I punched his larynx with a spear hand. His other hand reflexively went to his throat for protection, clearing my way to his torso. I dropped to one knee, pounding his solar plexus with a palm heel strike. He crumbled forward, making an exhalation-gasping sound. As he fell, I maneuvered behind him, wrapping my right arm around his throat in a vise grip and locking it in with my left arm, Marine style, and choked him out. His body flailed then went limp. I released him, unconscious, back into his overstuffed chair.

I relieved him of the satellite phone, his watch, and his cash. I straightened his tie and leaned his head against the chair's upholstered wingback, as if he was asleep. I pulled an antique book off the shelf and laid it across his belly, as if he were reading it. I looked at the title: *The Golden Woof: A Story of Two Girls' Lives.* Kinky. Carefully, I placed his left hand on the cover and tucked the right under the pages, hiding his injury.

"Sir, is everything satisfactory?" the servant asked, as I pushed through the golden door into the hallway.

"Let the gentleman rest," I said. "He has had a stressful day. I am going to make a phone call outside." I showed him the sat phone for effect. "Please don't disturb him until I return."

"Very well, sir," said the footman, and he disappeared.

I saw Farhan and Marhaz as soon as I exited the club's basement entrance to the garden. They were holding hands on a wooden bench, recessed in the shadows. Farhan's beard made him stand out in the damp lushness of Waterloo Gardens, and the elderly English couple were eyeing him suspiciously.

"Come with me," I said to them, barely slowing down. I saw Farhan start to speak, but Marhaz rose slowly to her feet, her hands on her belly, stopping his objections.

We walked swiftly across the garden to the far exit, as I contemplated my next move. I hailed a cab as soon as we hit the street, pushing Marhaz and Farhan in before me.

"The Harley Street Clinic," I told the cabby.

"Aye sir."

I stared out the window, watching the gardens recede. Farhan and Marhaz must have been in shock, because we had gone three blocks before they asked what I was doing.

"We're going to the best private hospital in London," I said. "You're going to tell them you are having complications with your pregnancy. You are going to stay there—both of you— while they do tests. You understand that, Farhan? You are not to leave the hospital room. Not even for a sandwich."

"Why?"

"Even if they say the tests are fine, Marhaz, and advise you to go home, you stay. Do you understand? You stay until you have the baby."

"Winters?" Farhan asked. He knew a snake when he met one. Smart man.

I nodded. Then I smiled. "I stabbed the bastard through the hand."

Farhan laughed.

"Anything else?" Marhaz interrupted. She was a doer. I liked that about her.

"Yes," I said, turning to Farhan. "Call your father. Tell him what's happened. All of it."

"No—" Farhan said immediately, but Marhaz was there again, a hand on his elbow.

"Do we have to?" she asked.

I nodded. "He'll forgive you," I said, and I meant it, or at least hoped it, because I didn't know Prince Abdulaziz. "He'll be happy to have you back, because when you tell him what happened, he'll have someone else to hate."

We were coming to a busy intersection, with buildings along both sides of the road. Pedestrians flooded into the street, a dozen anonymous people hurrying God knows where, and God alone cares.

"What about you?" Marhaz asked.

"I'm walking," I said, opening the taxi door and stepping out into the traffic. I didn't look back. I just walked. There were cameras on every corner, security monitors on every inch of sidewalk, but I wasn't worried. Winters would never report me to the police. And by the time he had spun up Apollo Outcomes to find me, I'd be gone. I wasn't sure where, actually. I didn't have a plan. But I felt better than I'd felt in six weeks, six months, maybe even six years. The divine sounds of Fauré's *Requiem* filled my soul. The piece was a death mass that ended in a musical ascension, the sinner rising into heaven and God's merciful grace.

CHAPTER 60

Winters's bandaged right hand opened the warehouse door of the garage near the World Trade Center Apartments in Erbil. It was full of rugs, brass lanterns, and other junk.

"Ain't that a sorry sight," said the AO team leader.

"Get in there and find me that key," Winters ordered. The five-man team started kicking things over, ransacking the loot house.

God damn you, Locke, Winters thought.

The team overturned rugs and kicked open chests. They were a Tier Two team, a far cry from Campbell's men. Normally they would be defending oil refineries in the Emirates, but they were the best Winters could muster on short notice. Campbell's team had left Iraq shortly after Winters took Locke.

Six stories up, in an adjacent half-built building, Boon had Winters's head in the crosshairs of his Dragunov sniper rifle. It was a clear 450-meter shot. He knew Winters would come back for the key, and he wanted to finish this. Not just for Kylah, but for the world. He was a mercenary. He didn't need permission from headquarters to do the right thing.

He flipped the safety to off and steadied his breathing for the shot.

"Find anything yet?" Winters asked.

"Negative."

"Keep looking."

"No need," an accented voice said. The men dropped what they were doing, red laser dots dancing across their chests. They raised their hands in surrender.

"Abdulaziz," Winters said flatly. A Saudi black-ops team stood behind the prince. There was no escape.

"Did you really think you were going to steal from me, Mr. Winters? From me!" Abdulaziz struck Winters hard across the face. Blood trickled from the corner of his mouth.

Winters spat blood. "I am working for you, my prince. I am here on your behalf."

"My son called me."

Winters didn't flinch, although it was a devastating blow. Locke. That damn Locke. He was good. "Impossible," he said smoothly. "I saw him dead."

"I recognize my own son's voice, Mr. Winters. All fathers do." It was pointed. Abdulaziz looked down on men, like Winters, with no heirs. "He knew things only my son would know."

"Then it was a recording. It was made before—"

"He told me you would say that. He also said you would have this," the prince said, pointing to the wound on Winters's hand. "You didn't have that two days ago."

For once, Winters was at a loss for words.

"He had a daughter, my former friend. Philomena. In a London hospital. He and his . . . wife flew there, I understand, on a private jet."

Winters thought about running, but four laser sights danced across his torso. He wouldn't make it two steps. He held out his wrists, and one of the black-ops operators flex-cuffed him.

"The first smart thing you have done since we met," Abdulaziz said. "Take them away."

The black-ops team marched Winters and his security detail out of the storage bunker.

"What now?" Winters said, as they shoved him into the back of a minivan.

Abdulaziz grinned. "I traded my son for this information. My son will call me every year to assure me he is alive, but otherwise we will have no contact. This is a grave sacrifice. I'm glad you aren't going to make this harder on any of us."

A hood went over Winters's head. Blackness. And for the first time in his life, doubt.

Boon watched the ambush. He saw them corner the Apollo team, and the shock on Winters's face. He could have killed Winters anyway, but he thought better of it. The Saudis knew what to do.

He stood up as the vehicles pulled away and yanked a chain out from around his neck. It was the key. He dropped it on the concrete floor, crushed it under his boot, then kicked the pieces into the wind.

CHAPTER 61

The *Eleutheria* bobbed off an uninhabited stretch of Yemen's coastline. Captain Goncalves smoked his pipe while checking his watch. He had made this location fifty-five minutes ago. He had not gotten a return call. His instructions were clear: wait one hour for a response, and one hour only.

"Quite a night," the mate said. In the calm of day, it was hard to believe he had come so close to murder and mutiny. It would be his secret to the grave.

"Aye."

"I was certain that frigate would board us."

"Aye."

The mate paused to see if the captain would fill the void with explanation. Only silence.

"Why do you think the frigate pulled away at the last minute?"

More silence.

"How did you know?"

The captain continued to smoke his pipe, staring at the shoreline. Frustrated, the mate lit a cigarette and thought: *Was the captain lucky or smart?* He preferred lucky. Smart would make him too dangerous.

"Our hour's up," the captain finally said. "Something has gone wrong."

"Can't trust anyone these days."

"Weigh anchor."

"Aye-aye, Captain," the first mate said, yelling out the order so the crew could hear. "Weigh anchor!"

"Heading?"

"South by southwest," the captain said. "To our next port of call."

"Make for Mogadishu!" the first mate bellowed.

"Prepare for the worst. We will be traveling through pirate waters. But I'll be holding on to this," he said, clutching the key to the armory with a wise grin.

The contraband was his now, Goncalves thought. That was the law of the sea. He would sell it eventually, whatever it was. But he wasn't in a hurry. It was a clear night and an ebbing tide, and Capt. Emanuel Goncalves felt as he always felt when the sea breeze was finally pushing him away from the shore and all its problems and back to where he belonged.

He felt free.

EPILOGUE

I shrugged off the bone-deep chill of the Welsh winter and entered the pub. I noticed the eyes of several men following me. One even cleared his throat to attract my attention, but I ignored them.

"Finally came in out of the cold," the bartender said with a smile. He was big and shaved bald, with a formidable beard and several tribal-looking tattoos on his arms. "Yeah, I seen you out there, watching."

"Woodford Reserve," I said.

"Never 'eard of it."

I scanned the Scotches on the back bar. "Oban, neat," I said. "And a Bell's for my friend."

"Bloody 'ell," Wildman said, eyeing my jungle green camouflage jacket, threadbare slacks, and the dockworker black-knit cap I'd taken to wearing everywhere, even before the weather turned cold. Even the thrift stores had cameras these days. But not this kind of bar.

"I see you had your eye on something specific," the bartender said, sliding us our drinks. "But this one ain't worth it, I can tell you from experience."

"Fock you, Bruce," Wildman snapped. "He's a mate."

Wildman pounded his shot, while I sipped my Oban. It was a smooth Scotch, light with some smoke, perfect for this type of weather.

"How'd you find me?" Wildman asked.

"I figured you'd come home to see your mum eventually," I said. "You always were a momma's boy."

He snorted. "Too true."

"I remembered you got in a fight outside this bar a half decade back, and eventually I put the pieces together." Took me long enough, but I was a dumb-ass, and selfish, too. I'd started to know myself, though, and that had to be a good thing, right?

"You still like the work?" I asked Wildman.

"It's all right," Wildman said. "But you heard Apollo went belly-up, I assume. Got a new name, Executive Actions, new bosses, but it's bollixed."

They hadn't gone belly-up. They'd changed the name, ousted a few directors loyal to Winters to try to shed the disaster with Abdulaziz, but it was the same company. They were probably blackballing Wildman because of his part in the Saudi affair, but no sense telling him that. It was better that way. At least they weren't coming after him.

"You in touch with Boon?"

Wildman nodded and signaled for another shot from the leering bartender. "I know where to find him," he said. "Why? You got an idea?"

I sipped my single malt. I could see men in the background, many built like Wildman and the bartender, checking us out. I didn't like it, too public, but I had to trust them not to talk to the wrong people, or hopefully anyone at all. Gay bars were good for secrecy, though. Outside these walls, there was no incentive to talk.

"I've got a job," I said. "My own operation this time, nobody to answer to."

"It dangerous?"

"Oh yeah."

"Borderline criminal, outside normal channels?"

"Of course."

"So black my own mum would be ashamed to know about it?"

"I don't know your mum, but it's a safe assumption."

He drank. "I assume there's no money in it."

"A bottle of whiskey or two at best."

"Sounds perfect," Wildman said, with a smile so big his missing teeth showed. "When do we start?"

Two hundred fifty kilometers and a world away, Sir Kabir Basrami-Heatherington was in his office late, writing at his antique desk. The desk had once belonged to Sir Francis Walsingham, spymaster to Queen Elizabeth I, who had risen from obscurity in the 1500s to become the shadow sovereign of England, entrusted by the queen to guide foreign, domestic, and religious policy, and to manage her most sensitive affairs. Walsingham was the man who kept order in a disorderly kingdom, and later in life he had formed a secret consortium, the House of Walsingham, to preserve that order. Sir Basrami-Heatherington was not only dedicated to the man's ideas, he was also a member of the consortium, and he trusted in the old spymaster's ways, both large and small. He never sent an e-mail, for instance. His offices didn't have computers. If orders had to be written, he preferred the security of pen, paper, and trusted courier.

The further we advance, he thought, *the more we go backward toward the truth.*

Behind him, a fire was lit, a Scotch was poured, and a large monitor showed silent news coverage of the Saudi coronation. The banker spun around in his antique chair to watch the new king and, more important, his son.

"We have big plans for you," Kabir muttered to the new king's son.

The new king was already old and ill. The young prince was in his early thirties, an infant by Saudi royal standards, ambitious and malleable. Kabir would convince him to break up Saudi Aramco, the massive state-owned oil company, even if it took the rest of his career. That was a snap of the fingers in the time line of the House of Walsingham, but it was long enough to change the Kingdom and thus the world.

The news camera panned across the doting audience. Kabir didn't notice Prince Abdulaziz standing on the periphery, in the shadows. Even if he had, he wouldn't have recognized his old business partner. The two had never met. That was Brad Winters's job, and he botched it, royally.

Kabir pressed a button, and the monitor retracted behind the bookcases. The fire crackled. His protégé entered the office, as if by telepathic command.

"Yes sir," the young man said.

"Courier these letters to Paris, Rome, Frankfurt, and Istanbul. Immediately."

"Very good, sir." The young man retrieved the envelopes and walked out the pocket doors. Outside, he passed two burly men in suits and earpieces, each holding a Heckler & Koch MP5SD submachine gun with built-in silencer.

He walked down the hallway, passing two more sentries, then downstairs. Another armed man stood near the antique grandfather clock. The young banker-in-training nodded at him, but the guard remained as stone.

Two framed notices were posted in the staff room, where only guard-mercenaries like that man would see them. The first bore the headline APPREHEND IMMEDIATELY and showed two photographs of Brad Winters.

The second had the headline WARNING in red block letters. Beneath were two pictures of Tom Locke, a physical description, and the instructions KILL ON SIGHT.

ACKNOWLEDGMENTS

I'd like to acknowledge my friends in the Middle East and Washington, DC, who helped clarify some of the details and geopolitics. My profound thanks to David Highfill and the William Morrow team.